I0549964

Sera, a strong-willed karate instructor, is living the ordinary life as a human when all hell breaks out. Apocalypse. A ravenous substance emerges through the ground and threatens the human race. Sera, a magical being, has always hidden who she was, living a normal life as an ordinary woman. But in a matter of minutes, she loses everyone she loves and is forced to leave her suburbia home, following the mental callings of her psychic sister, Sybil.

Sera, Sybil, and Sam were not just siblings but a trio born special with different abilities. Sera, being the oldest and furthest away, remembered her mother's dying words as she traveled from North Carolina to Florida. "You alone will be the one who can stop it. I don't know when this will happen or how, but I do know that you're the one who saves us all."

At the time, Sera didn't know what her mother meant, but now, she pushes on in search of the only family she has left to save the world.

The unauthorized reproduction or distribution of this copyrighted work is illegal. Criminal copyright infringement, including infringement without monetary gain, is investigated by the FBI and is punishable by up to 5 years in federal prison and a fine of $250,000.

This book is a work of fiction. Names, characters, places, and incidents either are products of the author's imagination or are used fictitiously. Any resemblance to actual events or locales or persons, living or dead, is entirely coincidental.

The Emergence Sera
Copyright © 2024 Jennifer D Torseth
ISBN: 978-1-4874-3508-0
Cover art by Martine Jardin

All rights reserved. Except for use in any review, the reproduction or utilization of this work in whole or in part in any form by any electronic, mechanical or other means, now known or hereafter invented, is forbidden without the written permission of the publisher.

Published by eXtasy Books Inc

Look for us online at:
www.eXtasybooks.com

THE EMERGENCE SERA

BY

JENNIFER D TORSETH

DEDICATION

To my family, who always believed in me no matter what.

CHAPTER ONE: THE EMERGENCE

Sera

"Eric?"
"In here."

Sera closed the front door of their little bungalow, locking it behind her. She dropped her keys in the bowl by the front door and entered her bedroom.

"Hey."

Eric nodded and licked his middle finger before flipping the page of his book. He looked up, meeting Sera's gaze with a playful smirk.

"What?"

"Nothing. You look sexy when you're grumpy."

"I'm not grumpy."

Eric's creased brows peeked over his book as he lowered it. "Really, girl. I know when my wifey is grumpy and has something on her mind."

Sera dropped on the bed beside her husband, looking down at her hands. "It's nothing."

Eric leaned forward, gently lifting Sera's chin, and pressed his lips against hers. He slowly pulled back, and Sera opened her eyes. She met his gaze and felt a heaviness in her heart.

She looked away, and Eric whispered, "It's okay to miss her, you know? She was your mom, and in her own way, she loved you."

Sera turned, meeting his gaze. "It's been three months, and I still can't stop thinking about—"

1

Sera —

Sera looked towards the window, facing the road, and cocked her head to the side. *Sybil? Is that you —*

"Hey, are you okay?" Eric touched Sera's cheek.

She turned back to him and forced a smile, nodding. "Yeah, I'm just . . . I'm tired."

Sera stood up and stared at the window as she walked over to her vanity.

Eric didn't know that Sera was . . . different. She'd never told him. It was forbidden. Her mother had adamantly said *If you marry an ordinary, then you can never tell him the truth. He would never understand, and it can put you and your family in danger.* So Sera never did.

Sybil and Sera, along with the rest of her family, could communicate mentally, but since Sera's mother died, there had only been silence.

Sera stared at her reflection, hoping to hear her sister's voice again. She rubbed her face, squeezing her eyes shut. *I guess I'm just imagining things.*

Sera wearily undressed, removed her street clothes, and grabbed her uniform hanging from her mirror. It was a karate uniform, or as her husband called it, a *Gi*. She slipped her arms in first, then pants, and as she wrapped the black belt around her waist, a deep sense of dread settled in her stomach. Her head swam with dizziness, and the room began spinning. She slowly turned, looking back at her husband and then towards the window again.

What the hell is going on? Sybil, are you okay? Goosepimples rose, trickling up her forearms and shivering down her spine. She reached back to stroke the hairs on the back of her neck.

Sera.

Sybil? I feel it. What's wrong? Are you okay? Answer me!

Sera stared at her reflection, expecting to see her sister looking back at her. She squeezed her eyes shut and breathed deeply. *Sybil, please answer me. Please?* A lump formed in

Sera's throat as she tried to reach out to her sister but only heard silence. She pulled her long, straight, fiery hair into a ponytail and turned to Eric. "It's almost three, so we need to get going before the kids start showing up for practice."

Sera, run. Run. Run. Run!

Just as Sera heard her sister's voice, a blood-curdling scream howled in the front yard of her house. She spun around and stared at the window. Her stomach dropped, and fear raced through her veins. Trembling, she slowly walked toward the window and felt a quiver under her feet. She looked down, and before she could take another step, she was knocked back, landing hard on her rump. The ground began to quake, rocking the floor back and forth as if something was trying to push through.

"Eric!" Sera screamed, but her house's groan swallowed her words. The walls started shaking, and the structure of her home crumbled as pieces of debris crashed down around them.

Sera rolled onto her knees and jumped when she felt Eric's hands cup her waist. She looked back, meeting his ghostly stare.

"What's—"

A blast against the front of the house shuttered the walls. The structure growled, and the frame collapsed, melting into the ground. Dirt and rubble polluted the air, filling the room with a haze. Sunlight peeked through the fog, and screams from her neighborhood echoed down the street.

Eric pushed the rubble off Sera and himself, pulling her to her feet. They walked to where the wall used to stand and froze, staring out at pure chaos. People were hysterically running along the sidewalk, screaming. Wrecked cars and demolished houses polluted the sky with clouds of thick black smoke.

A wave of sickness pinged Sera's gut, alerting her that evil was lurking. She knew if they stepped out of their home, it would be a death sentence. She tugged Eric's hand back and shook her head. "Eric, no, wait. Please. Let's just stay in here and wait it out. We don't know what's out there."

Eric shook his head and tried to pull her further outside. "No, the house is about to fully collapse, and we need to know what's happening."

"Eric. Please, wait—"

A malicious growl roared, like a creature awakening from a dark place. Sera cupped her hands over her mouth, holding her breath. A hissing sound followed, and the ground began to tremor beneath them. The house groaned again, and a crack spidered across the remainder of the roof. Eric pulled Sera out of their bungalow, and they collided with the ground as the house caved in. A mountain of dirt whirled up into a giant dust cloud, filling the air. Coughing, Sera stood up to catch her breath. Dust slowly settled down, and a woman appeared through the mist just a few feet from where they stood. She was crouched down over something in the road. As the tremors eased, Sera saw a cloud of thick black smoke hovering over the road near where the woman was sitting. Another long-drawn-out hiss expelled next to the woman, and then an eerie silence fell over everything.

Sera met Eric's gaze briefly before they walked hand in hand towards the street. As they approached the woman, Sera's breath caught. A long, narrow hole filled with a black sludge-like substance was now where her street used to reside. The ooze stretched out for what looked like miles, further than her eyes could see, flowing from north to south. As she walked up to the hole, the smell of rotten flesh and decay tainted the air. Sera's body reacted, sending her on high alert. Her eyes dilated, and she scanned the hole and realized she was staring down at a river. *A river of death.*

Eric let go of Sera's hand and walked towards the woman. Sera reached out for him, shaking her head. "Eric, no.

4

Don't." But he waved her hand away.

"Please, Eric, wait. Just—"

Eric ignored Sera's pleas and continued toward the woman. As he drew closer, Sera felt the woman's malicious intentions, alerting her that she was dangerous.

"Eric!" Sera begged, but he continued towards her.

"Miss?" Eric said, raising his hand and reaching for the woman. "Are you okay? I, um—"

The woman stood up and turned around, revealing that her face was covered with the black sludge from the hole she was crouched next to. It stretched from the right side of her face, going down her body to her right arm. Her right eye was missing, and the right side of her mouth appeared to have been ripped open, exposing the flesh around her jaw. She stood up warily and took a step towards Eric.

"Help me. Please. I can hear them." The woman patted her ears, taking another step towards Eric. "Whispers . . . whispers . . . whispers—"

"Eric, don't!" Sera snapped. He looked back and shook his head. Sera mouthed the words *please*, but he turned back to the woman.

"What happened to you?" Eric said, taking another step towards the woman. "Do you know what's—"

Before he could finish his sentence, the woman reached out and snatched Eric's arm with her right hand. Eric tried to pull away, but she clamped down on him with her ooze-covered hand, not moving.

"Let go!" he pleaded, grabbing her right arm.

Black sludge oozed from her limbs and traveled up his arm. Eric's body began to tremble as the sludge started to flow over the rest of his body. He looked back at Sera, and his eyes were glazed over with a blank stare.

Sera knew at that moment that it was too late. The ooze soaked into his skin, mauling his flesh and invading his orifices.

The woman turned, walking towards the river, and before Sera could react, she stepped into the hole, pulling Eric in with her. The sludge opened, and their bodies fell in without a splash. The woman's body sank down into the river of death, and an ominous hiss escaped from a bubble as she disappeared.

"No!" Sera screamed as she lunged forward, reaching for Eric.

Eric's body sank down slowly into the sludge and stopped, leaving his head and arm free from the ooze. His fingers twitched as if he were trying to grasp something, and his voice called out in a monotonous tone.

"Sera . . . Sera . . . Sera . . ."

His left eye looked back and forth systematically, not making contact with anything. Sera reached out for him, but he was too deep in the river. Jumping up, she ran around the yard, looking behind her for anything she could pull him out with, and spotted a broken tree limb.

Sera lowered the limb and waved it back and forth in front of his face. "Eric, Eric, grab it. I'll pull you out."

Eric continued to cry out her name, but his vision didn't focus on anything. He let the limb pass him by, wiggling his fingers.

"Eric, please! Grab the stick! Please, Eric. Please! I'll help you out!" She gritted her teeth with the last words. Her heart sank, and she felt acid rise into the back of her throat.

"Eric!" She screamed his name, pleading. She ran up and pushed the limb into his hand, but he let the wood pass him by again.

Devastated, Sera threw the stick, breaking it into pieces against her demolished house.

Eric, I can't do this without you. Eric, please come back to me.

Sera melted to the ground, sobbing, and watched as her husband's body floated away, trapped in his eternal prison.

He was gone, and there wasn't anything she could do to help him.

Gone. He's gone.

A cool breeze blew against her dampened face as she inhaled deeply. She peered into the new evil that had taken up residence and saw dozens of people floating away to die. Shock numbed her, and she didn't know if she could stand back up. *He's gone. He's gone.* The heartbreaking words rang in her mind. *Gone.* In a matter of minutes, she'd lost everything. Her husband. Her home. Her life. *Gone.* And now her insides were hollow. Ripped opened and left bare. *He's gone.* Sera pulled her legs up, cradling them with her arms, and dropped her head. *Gone. He's gone.*

Sera.

Sera slightly lifted her head and answered. *Sybil?*

Get up.

I don't think I can. Trembling, Sera's hand quivered as she wiped a runaway tear. *He's gone. He's —*

Sera! Get up! Now. Now. Now! Look! The river!

Sera jumped from her sister's screams and looked over to see a giant wave of sludge rising from inside the river, reaching for her like a giant hand. She quickly pushed back with her feet, scooting away from the terror. The ooze stopped a few feet outside the river and slowly started to return to its hole, as if watching Sera get away.

Panting, Sera stared at the ooze as it returned to its hole of death. *Sybil? What —*

Find me, Sera. Come home.

Chapter Two: Three Months Earlier

Sera

Sera opened the door to the hospital room and was welcomed by a monotonous ring of dings and bells from the medical equipment hooked up to her mother. She glanced down at the name card next to the door, which read *Cheryl Daniels*.

She stood over her and inhaled deeply before pulling up a chair and sitting down. Then she placed her hand over her mom's and patted them.

"Mom, it's Sera. I'm here."

"Sammy? Sammy? Is that you?"

Sera's lip quivered. *Even after all this time, she still favors him over me.* She looked away and wiped away a runaway tear, exhaling a deep breath.

"Mom, it's me, Sera." She squeezed her mom's hand and felt her squeeze back.

"Mom, I—"

"Sera? Is that you, honey?"

"Yes, I'm here now."

The door opened, and a tall, beautiful woman entered the room, back first. Her hair was auburn-brown with a long, thick braid flowing down her back. Long silvery streaks of gray peaked out of the tufts over the tops of her ears. She turned and looked down at Sera with emerald eyes that almost glowed when she met her gaze. She bumped into the table and nearly tripped over a cord as she maneuvered her full hands of medications, gauze, and medical items.

"Oh, I'm so sorry. I didn't see you come in. My name's Anya, and I'm Cheryl's nurse today. It's time for her two o'clock medications. I just need to set all of this down, give her two pills, and then I can get out of your way."

Sera stood up and stepped back so the woman could do her work. The woman towered over Sera's five-foot-two body by at least a foot. Her striking greens radiated against her rosy skin as she gazed down at her. The woman was familiar. Sera could feel a connection with her but couldn't pinpoint where or when. A moment passed briefly between them as they gazed into each other's eyes before Anya turned to go back to caring for her mother.

Sera knew Anya felt it, too, and cocked her head to the side. "Do I know you?"

"No. I don't know. Are you ... are you from around here?"

"Well, I used to be. I'm Cheryl's oldest daughter, Sera."

"Oh, my gosh. That was unexpected. I didn't know ... she only mentioned her son, Sammy, before, so I didn't ..." Anya's cheeks reddened, and she quickly turned back to Cheryl.

"Miss Cheryl, I have a couple of pills for you and some water to wash them down with."

"Can I have a cold Coca-Cola instead?"

"Miss Cheryl, you know I can't do that. Doctor's orders. Here's your pills."

Sera's mom nodded and took the pills with furrowed brows. She gulped down the last of the water and nodded.

"Thank you." Anya smiled down at her, lowering her voice slightly. "You can use the pain medicine if you need it. You don't have to wait. Just push the button. Okay?"

Cheryl nodded and said, "In a little bit. I want to talk to my daughter for a while." She reached up and clapped her hands over Anya's right hand. Her eyes changed from black to a deep wooded brown as she spoke, gazing into Anya's face. "Have you heard from him? My Sammy?"

"No, not yet. I left a message with his hockey league manager. He should get back to us soon. I'll let you know the minute he calls." Anya nodded and slowly pulled away from Cheryl's hands.

Sera felt her mom's power fluctuate. She briefly met her mother's gaze and shook her head slightly. Then her mother looked back up at Anya and smiled seductively.

"Very well. Thank you, honey." Sera's mother nodded at Anya, and her eyes slowly dulled back to her original color.

Anya looked back at Sera, nodding before letting herself out of the room.

Sera walked over to her mom and stared down at her. Cheryl was adjusting her sheet to cover her hands, and then she folded a magazine on her table as if she were trying not to make eye contact with Sera. Sera knew what her mom was up to without having to ask.

Sera's mother and her siblings were all gifted with special abilities inherited from their mother. Cheryl, a Lycan, had magical gifts passed down from her ancestors. Her mother never explained all her gifts, but she had many talents she used daily to get what she wanted.

Sera was a warrior who wielded agility, speed, and great strength. She could also heal quickly like a Lycan. She had manifested her gifts when she was twelve years old when her cycle began to flow, and ever since then, she and her mother couldn't be more than strangers to each other. Once Sera's gift came about, her mother was disappointed and bitter that she hadn't shifted into a Lycan like her. As far as Sera was concerned, she would've rather not gotten anything at all from her mother if that meant she could have the relationship they'd had before everything changed.

Sera was the oldest of three children. Her younger sister, Sybil, wielded the gift of sight. She could see into the future, sometimes unwillingly, and when she touched people, she could see their deepest, darkest secrets. Sybil and Sera had a connection that no one else did. Like Sera, Sybil was shunned from her mother's love and ached to regain it.

Then there was Sammy, the youngest of the three and the only male. He was the apple of Cheryl's eyes. On his fourteenth birthday, he inherited the gift from their mother and morphed into a Lycan. Everything seemed to fall into place once he morphed into what their mother so greatly desired. Sera and Sybil drifted apart from their mother and grew close to their father, who was ordinary and tried to live a normal life.

"Mom, are you going to look at me?"

"Why? You're just going to fuss at me, and I don't care. I do what I have to."

"Really, Mom? That poor girl doesn't need your voodoo hoodoo in her head right now. She's just trying to do her job and take care of you." Sera shifted her weight, putting her hand on her hip. "I'm honestly surprised Sam isn't here already. He's your favorite, after all."

Cheryl's eyes shot up, and she glared at her. She gripped her hands into tight balls, and a hint of her fangs slipped out from under her top lip. "You know that's not true. After all this time. Seven years. You don't call. Text. Write a damn letter. Anything at all. Let me know if you're okay. That you're still alive."

"You knew I was alive." Sera cocked her head to the side. Whether she wanted to admit it or not, they all had a connection, and no matter where they were, they could seek each other out if need be.

"Well. You know what I mean."

"Mom, I'm here now. I'm —"

"Mom!"

Sybil burst through the door and went straight for Cheryl to hug her. Her long golden tendrils flowed down her five-foot-two back and touched the tip of her round buttock.

"Oh, honey. You came. I'm so glad to have both my girls here."

Sybil turned, and her crystal blues brightened. She ran over and nearly knocked Sera back with a hug. Standing side by side, Sera and Sybil looked almost identical. Sera's father used to tell people they were twins to get a reaction out of them when, in all honesty, they were two years different in age.

"Sera! When did you get into town? You have to come to stay with me! It's so good to see you! I've got so much —"

"So, ladies, I'm very tired. I just wanted to see if either of you had heard from your brother. He, um . . . he isn't returning my calls, and I'm worried something might be wrong. Can either of you please get in touch with him? I really need to talk to him. It's been too long."

Sybil and Sera gazed at Cheryl and then at each other. Sera knew what Sybil was thinking, and it was odd that their mother hadn't spoken to their brother in a long time.

Long time. The words lingered between them, bouncing back and forth in their minds. *Long time. Why has it been a long time, sis?*

I don't know, Sera.

I don't know either.

Sera looked over at their mother and shook her head. She wanted to know the answer, even if it poked the bull or, in this case, the wolf.

"Mom? Why haven't you talked to Sammy in a while?"

"Well, it's complicated . . . I don't know. You need to ask him yourself."

Cheryl looked over at the nurse's station and huffed

loudly.

"I need to speak with you."

"Okay, Mom. What's up?" Sybil answered.

"No, I need to speak with your sister. Alone." Cheryl panted and inhaled a deep breath before speaking again. "I don't have much time, and I need to . . ." She swallowed hard and inhaled another deep breath.

Sera nodded at Sybil, and she turned to the door.

"Oh, okay, then. I'll wait for you out front, Sera. Okay?"

"Yeah, I'll be down in a minute."

They nodded at each other, and then the door clicked closed.

"So, what's up, Mom?"

"I'm . . . I'm dying, and I—"

"You're not dying. Don't say that—"

"Don't interrupt me, girl! You're just as bad as your father."

Sera's eyes glared at her mother, and heat rushed into her cheeks. Shaking her head, she inhaled deeply and spoke so quietly that it was almost a whisper. "Don't talk about Dad like that."

"Like what? He did. He always interrupted—"

The fire burned in Sera's belly. Before she knew what she was doing, the words spewed from her lips like lava. "At least he was a good father!"

"What's that supposed to mean?"

Sera inhaled deep breaths, calming the anger rising in her chest. She balled up her fists and exhaled slowly, breathing out. She had to pull herself away from the anger and try to move forward with the conversation.

"What do you have to say, Mom?"

The machine attached to her mother began to beep quickly, and her mother's body vibrated under the sheet. She turned her head to the side and gripped the bars that hugged her bed.

13

"Mom? Mom!"

Anya pushed the door open and stood over her. "Cheryl, just relax and breathe through it. Deep breath in . . . and let it out. Deep breath in . . . and out." Anya was motioning as she breathed deeply with her mother's frigid body. Cheryl was gripping the bar as her body seized uncontrollably against the frame of the bed. Sera stared at her, frozen and helpless.

Cheryl's stiffened body slowly began to relax, and she eased into her bed's mattress. Anya looked back at Sera with glowing eyes, and it dawned on her—*she's special.* She used her abilities to help her mother get through her ailment. Anya nodded and looked back at Cheryl.

Sera gazed through moist eyes and knew she shouldn't have been so cruel, but the childhood spent with a loveless mother pinged her chest when she mentioned her dad.

Anya smiled down at Cheryl and petted her hair back from her forehead. Then she turned and pressed a few buttons on the monitors. She lifted a little button, sitting next to her mom's hand. "Are you ready for this yet?"

Cheryl slowly moved her head back and forth on her pillow.

"Okay, I'm right outside if you need me." The door clicked behind Anya, and Cheryl's gaze reverted to Sera.

Sera stepped forward and reached for her mom's hand. "Mom, I—"

"Just listen to me now, Sera. I don't have much time."

"Mom, I—"

"Something's going to happen. Something that will change everything. And . . ." She panted, trying to catch her breath. "You alone will be the one who can stop it. I don't know when this will happen or how, but I do know that you're the one who saves us. You save everyone."

"Wait. What? Mom, I . . . I don't understand."

Her head dropped to the side, and she panted heavy gasps

of air. Her voice grew horse, and she reached out with trembling fingers for her water. Sera grabbed her cup and held the straw so she could take a drink. Her mother gulped two long drinks and opened her lips, licking her mouth.

"You need to find your brother. He needs you. Together, you and he will fight and win. You need him as much as he needs you. Do you understand?"

Sera shook her head and opened her mouth to speak but didn't know what to say. Her mother's gaze met hers, and she lifted her hand, touching her cheek.

"I'm sorry I wasn't there for you. I—"

Sera's mom began coughing uncontrollably and spat red all over the front of her gown. Sera jumped up and opened the door.

"Anya!"

Anya ran in and held a tissue to her mouth, dabbing her blood-painted lips. She looked back at Sera with sorrow in her eyes. She knew as much as Sera did. Her mother was right— the end was near.

Anya pushed the button for her mother, and Cheryl closed her eyes, breathing heavily. Sera followed Anya out and shook her hand. "Thank you for everything you do for my mom. She, um—"

"Parents are . . ." Anya's eyes drifted off for a moment before she finally met Sera's gaze again. "If you need anything, just let me know. I'm always here. I work too much." She shrugged her shoulders and forced a half grin. She handed Sera a piece of paper with a number jotted on it and returned to her mother's room.

Sera followed the corridor until she reached the elevator and pressed the arrow pointing down. The door opened, and there he was. *Sam.*

CHAPTER THREE: SAMMY'S HOME

Sera

"Sam." Sera's voice cracked when she spoke his name.

"Sera."

He wrapped his large, muscular arms around Sera and pulled her into his chest. He towered over her, reaching at least six-foot-four, like their dad. He released her and stood next to her, staring.

"It's been too long."

"Yes." Sera's heart pounded in her chest. She didn't know what to say to him. She didn't know how to act or who he was anymore. Her mom had just unloaded on her, and she didn't even know what her mother was talking about. She was still in shock from the whole conversation. She wondered if she should tell Sammy what their mother said or just wait.

As she gazed up at her younger brother, she realized he looked terrible. He had dark circles under his eyes, and his face was a tint of gray. His body was very muscular, but he appeared thinner than she remembered him being. His black hair had grown a bit longer than normal, and he had a long, scruffy, unkempt beard.

"Sam, are you okay?"

He looked away and forced a grin. "Oh, yeah. I'm good. And you?"

She knew he was lying. *Why would he lie? He knows that, of all people, I would know he wasn't okay. What's he hiding?*

"How's hockey? I guess you're on a break right now. I saw

that your team made it to the playoffs this year."

He ran his fingers through his hair and looked around. His eyes returned to Sera, and he said, "Yeah, we almost won this year. So are you on your way out?"

"Yeah, um, Mom's sleeping right now. Hey, do you want to get a coffee or something? I'll buy."

He looked back at the nurse's station for a long moment and then at Sera.

"Sure. Yeah, if she's sleeping, then I'll just come back in a little bit."

The elevator door opened, and Sybil sat on a bench near the entrance door. She looked up, and her face brightened immediately. "Sammy! I didn't see you walk in!" She ran over and wrapped her arms around their brother. Slowly, she pulled back with furrowed brows. "Sammy? What's wrong? You're . . . you're very sick."

Sam pulled away from her and ran his fingers through his hair again. His eyes were ebony with a glisten of moisture. "I'm fine, Sybil."

"Sam, you can't lie to me. You can fool Sera, but I touched you, I know—"

"You don't know anything. Shut your mouth!"

"What is it?" Sera asked.

"It's nothing, Sera. Are we going to go have coffee or what?"

"Yeah. Yeah, let's go."

Sera met Sybil's eyes, and a message passed between them. *He's sick, Sera. Very sick. He's on medical leave with hockey right now because he's so sick.*

Sam looked over at Sybil and gritted his teeth. "Damnit, Sybil!"

"I'm sorry, brother, but we're just worried about you. What's going on?"

"Let's just get to the car. Okay?"

"Okay." Sera met Sybil's eyes and nodded.

"Why don't we go have lunch instead? I'm starving, Sam."

Sam nodded and turned to glare out the window of Sybil's Ford Lightning.

The restaurant smelled of burgers grilling when they opened the door. The waitress led them to a large round booth with pictures of rockstars and guitars decorating the walls. She handed them all a menu and three glasses of water on napkins.

After they ordered, Sera and Sybil glared at Sam, waiting for him to explain what was going on.

He looked up and exhaled loudly. "What! Do we have to do this? Now?"

"We're just worried about you, brother. What's going on? Why are you so sick? You're a young guy, Sam. You just had a birthday and turned twenty-one. There's no reason in the world why you should be sick. Like, I don't—" Sybil rambled on.

"Okay. Okay. Just stop." He looked around him and then leaned forward. "I, um... I ..." He inhaled a deep breath and exhaled before speaking again. "I dropped on the ice just before the season was over, and they took me to the hospital. The doctors ran a lot of tests and couldn't find anything. They said ..." He rubbed his eyes and looked around the room as if trying to escape what he was going to say. He turned to look at Sybil and blew out a long breath before continuing. "They said—"

"How you guys doing? Do you all need anything else? Maybe some ketchup?"

"Oh, no, thank you. We're good," Sera answered.

"Okay then. Just let me know if you do."

Sera nodded and looked over at Sam.

Sam shook his head, and his face hardened. "The doctors said they don't know what's wrong with me. That everything's coming back fine. That maybe I . . . maybe I need a psych eval."

"What?" Sera snapped.

People around them looked up from their food and stared in their direction. Sera shook her head and mouthed *Sorry*.

Sam shrugged his shoulders and shook his head slightly. He looked up, and his eyes were glowing a wooden brown, like their mothers. His lip began to quiver, and a glossy glaze filled his lids. "I don't know what to do. I'm not well. I can't sleep. I can't eat. My body aches with tremendous pain, and the doctors think I'm crazy. I . . . uh . . . I just don't know." Sam wiped his eyes aggressively and sniffed deeply. "And the sad part is that everything in my life has always been easy. I wanted to play hockey, and boom, I went pro. I fell in love with a beautiful woman, and boom, we were engaged to be married." Sam turned away just as his lips began to quiver again.

Sera and Sybil met each other's gazes. *We were engaged.* Sybil slightly shrugged to Sera.

"And now it's . . . it's all falling apart. I'm falling apart. If I'm not playing hockey and getting married to Liz, then I don't . . ." He shook his head, and a single tear rolled down his cheek. He wiped it away and pushed his plate away so he could put his elbows on the table. He rubbed his eyes and ran his fingers through his mane again before meeting Sera and Sybil's eyes.

Sybil scooted around the table and cupped her arm around his shoulders. "It's going to be okay, Sam. Really. Things always work themselves out. Playing hockey just wasn't meant to be. You know?"

He brushed away more tears and dropped his hands into his lap, gazing down at them.

Sera stared at them and heard her mother's words ringing in her ears. She wanted to tell them what she'd said but didn't know what it meant. *Am I supposed to help Sam now? Is that what she was saying? Mom said, "Together, we will fight. Fight what?"*

"Sera, are you okay?" Sybil said, staring at her.

Sera looked up and nodded. "Yeah, I was just thinking about Mom."

"Mom? Why? Did she say something?" Sybil asked.

"She . . ." Sera hesitated and calmed her emotions. She knew Sybil would know something was up if she didn't keep cool. "No, she said she was tired, and I needed to come back later to chat."

"Okay, but you got this look on your face. It was weird."

Sera forced a smile. "Yeah, sorry. It's just a lot to take in. Mom being sick." Sera motioned to Sam and said, "And Sammy's sick. And now, all of a sudden, Mom's going to die. Did she tell any of you she was sick, or was it just me?"

"No, she called me and said she needed to see me. That she was in the hospital because she wasn't feeling well. Sam, did she say anything to you?" Sybil asked.

"No, I visited her right before the playoffs, and she—"

He stopped in mid-sentence, gazing behind Sera with a haunted stare. He slowly spoke as if he was watching the past repeat itself. "She said she wasn't feeling well when I visited. She . . ." Sam paused and shook his head slightly as he said, "I passed out on the ice, and after I got out of the hospital, I went to her. She kept calling me and calling me. And it wasn't by phone either." He lowered his voice to almost a whisper. "When I saw her, she was gray and had dark circles under her eyes." His fingers brushed against his face briefly as if he was trying to feel the gray tint that took up residence over his skin.

"She . . . she said she needed to see me because she hadn't been feeling well, and she wanted to make sure that I was okay. She grabbed me and held me in a tight hug for a long time." Sam met Sera's eyes. "Now I realize what she was doing. She kept me from feeling it, but now I . . . I know what she did. She was—"

He looked at Sybil, and a single tear rolled down his cheek. Sybil reached out, touched her brother's arm, and closed her eyes. Trembling, she opened her eyes, and a ghostly white peered through her irises. Blinking, Sybil stared at Sam and then met Sera's gaze. Her lids fluttered as her eyes transformed back into crystal blues. She exhaled slowly as she broke her connection with Sam.

"Mom was healing you, Sam. She . . . she knew you were sick and was trying to help you. Now she's the one who's sick. She's dying. She did it for you. And there's something else . . . I can't . . . I can't see it." Sybil raised her fingers as if grasping something from the space in front of her.

Sybil turned to look at Sera, staring at her.

"What?" Sera whispered. "What is it?"

Sybil shook her head slightly, looked down at her drink, and sipped from her straw. Sera felt her sister trying to read her, so she put up a wall as best as she could. She didn't want her sister to see what happened between her mother and her today. She wasn't ready to talk about it.

Sera's mother's face came to mind again. *It doesn't make sense. Why did Mom say what she said? What was she trying to tell me?*

CHAPTER FOUR: THE BEGINNING

John

"Hey, good morning."

John felt arms wrap around him as he prepared his instant coffee. Sunlight peeked through his little kitchen window blinds, sharing just enough light for him to see what he was doing.

Shit, I thought she left last night. What's she still doing here?

"I didn't feel you get up. Why didn't you wake me?"

Great, now she thinks we're an item. John wiggled himself out of his overnight guest's arms and pulled away to grab his dry coffee creamer from the cabinet next to the refrigerator. She walked over, fingered the hair over his ear, and leaned in to kiss him. John jerked back and shot her a look over his shoulder.

"Wow, someone's not a morning person."

Now I have to be nice. John turned to face the girl and forced a smile. "Look, honey, I'm going to be late. I have to get going."

She batted her cute blues at him and attempted to wrap her arms around his muscular abs when he blocked her and grabbed her wrists. He cocked his head to the side and slowly shook. *Should I go in late and bend her over right here? No, I'd better not because she really will think we're together.* John shuddered and inhaled deeply.

"Look, you're . . . nice, and we had fun last night, but that was it. Last night was . . . you know . . . it. Do you understand?"

Her sweet blues faded as a frown creased her forehead. She took a step back, ripping her hands from John's grasp, and stomped back to the bedroom. The door slammed behind her, rattling the walls of the little apartment.

Shit, now I'm the asshole.

John finished making his coffee and packed his lunch of chips and a cold turkey sandwich. He grabbed a soda for later and threw it all in his little lunch bag. He was heading for the bedroom when his door flew open. She stopped in front of him and gazed into his eyes.

She was a beautiful sophomore at the College of Florida Keys he'd seen wandering around the library, looking for a book on *Chemistry Two*. John had taken off his readers, walked over to her, and helped her pull a hard back down from the top shelf. After a sub sandwich and beer, the rest was history.

Maybe I should apologize. She's cute when angry, and this is my last year before I go off to Princeton. John broke the stare and looked over her head, not making eye contact. "Do you need a ride or anything?"

"Nope!" She stomped past John, opened the front door, and whipped around to face him as she stood in the doorway. "Oh, and John?"

"Yeah."

"Go fuck yourself!"

He saluted her, and she flipped him the bird as she slammed the door behind her.

"Okay, well, I'll see you around," John whispered to himself. *Maybe I should have fucked her first. Oh, well.* John shrugged his shoulders and disappeared into his bedroom.

The wind wheezed a high-pitched squeal as John opened his apartment door. He was on the second floor, and as soon as he closed his door, the neighbor across the way opened his.

"Morning."

"Morning, Jim."

When John turned the corner and walked along the sidewalk, the air was tainted by the peculiar smell of something burning. He reached into his pocket and pulled out his key fob when the ground vibrated under his feet.

"What the f —"

A monstrous growl echoed, grumbling underneath the pavement. *Earthquake?* John thought to himself as he continued towards his car. *Fucking, global warming.* The minute he turned the corner and stepped foot onto the parking lot asphalt, an explosion lifted him and catapulted his body through the air. John dropped hard on his back, knocking the wind out of him. His lungs heaved as he looked up and saw black steam blowing around his *Honda Civic.* A hissing sound taunted him, and then another rumble quivered the cement. The metal of his car howled, and the ground opened up, dropping his car into the unknown. The rest of the parking lot began to crumble along the parking spaces, dropping the cars into a newly opened dark hole. A pungent smell of rotten flesh and decay wafted up with the smoke, polluting the air.

John picked himself up, and a shrill scream echoed behind him. He spun around and saw the girl he'd brought home the night before sitting on top of the roof of a black car. It was sinking down into what looked like a river of black sludge.

"John!" Her scream echoed in the parking lot.

John ran over to the edge of the hole and reached out his hand. "Grab it!"

She stretched her digits out, and just as her fingertips touched his, the car shifted, plummeting down into the dark liquid. Her muffled screams went silent, and she disappeared into the unknown.

John's body wavered back and forth on the edge of the rock as he almost fell in with the car. He regained his balance and dropped to his knees, panting. Shivering, he stared into the black liquid as it fizzled and bubbled. He stumbled upright and spun around, staring at the empty parking lot. All the cars parked just minutes prior sank into an elongated black hole filled with a sludge-like substance.

John raised his hands, rubbing the sides of his temple. "What the fuck? What the fuck is going—" He spun around and didn't know what to do, so he sprinted towards his apartment.

As soon as he turned the corner, he saw his neighbor standing next to the newly created hole in the ground. The woman turned around and met John's gaze. Her eyes were glazed over with a haunted stare. Shaking her head, she opened her mouth to speak when a black wave of sludge raised above her head and slapped down over her body. She crumpled in its grip and was pulled into the ooze effortlessly.

John's mouth dropped open, and he couldn't breathe. His chest heaved as he gasped for a breath of air. He stared in disbelief and slowly backed away from where the woman was when a scream sounded behind him. A little boy was reaching his arms out, running towards the hole in the earth. John stood there and stared at him. His body was frozen. He couldn't move. He couldn't speak.

The woman's body slowly sank down into the sludge, disappearing into the unknown. As the boy approached the hole, another wave of sludge slowly rose into the air, waiting for his arrival.

It's like it knows. It watches and waits for its victim.

No. No. No. John forced his legs to move, and in one sweep, he grabbed the boy and ran up the stairs to his apartment. The little boy screamed in John's ear, deafening him as he skipped up each step. He sat the boy down and said, "Shh, buddy. You have to stop screaming now."

The boy stared at John with glazed-over eyes. Tears streamed down his face as he slowly closed his mouth.

John dove into his pocket, looking for his keys. *Empty. No.*

No. No. He looked down the stairs and turned to the apartment behind him. He trudged over and knocked. "Jim. Please, man. It's . . . it's John. Your neighbor across the hall." John waited a minute and raised his fist to knock on the door again when the deadbolt clicked. The door slowly opened with a chain stretched across Jim's face.

"Jim. It's—"

"Yeah, I heard you. What do you want?"

Jim's gaze moved down, and his vision landed on the boy. John looked down at the boy and shrugged his shoulders slightly. "Please, man. I lost my keys and found this little boy and his mom . . ." John looked down at the boy and shook his head. "We have nowhere else to go."

Jim slammed the door, and the door opened again after a minute.

CHAPTER FIVE: PRESENT DAY

Sera

Sera raised her hand, shielding her brow as she gazed at the sun settling in the west. She reached into her pocket and pulled out her compass. Her fingers ran over the old brass that had a dull inscription engraved.

Go have an Adventure . . .
Love, Dad

Sera's dad had given her the compass on her eighteenth birthday, and it was one of the last things he said to her before he died the following year.

Turning it over, she checked the clip on the backside and saw the folded picture was still secured in its grasp.

Nodding, she flipped the compass back over and followed the direction going south. She knew she would eventually find her way back home to Florida, where her family, Sammy and Sybil, were. Sybil had spoken to her, warning her that the sludge was coming, but that was the last thing she said to her.

The newscasters on television called it an *apocalypse*, naming the new entity in the ground as *Sludge River of Death*. Shortly after that, the world went silent.

Sera called out to her sister daily, but as usual, she never responded, so Sera continued traveling south in hopes of finding her. No matter the distance or situation, Sera was always able to send or receive messages from her family. She knew that Sybil and Sam were alive. She could feel them, but the fact that Sybil wasn't answering her sent a numbing chill down her spine. She knew deep down that something was wrong. Something had happened.

Sera pushed the compass down into her pocket and dropped her backpack from her shoulder. She scanned the area once more, then reached into her bag and pulled out a thermos and a bag of nuts. She threw a couple of handfuls into her mouth and washed them down with her water. Panting, she wiped her mouth and unwrapped her red bandana from around her neck. The water trickled down her arms as she dampened the rag and wiped her sweat-covered brow. Her black cap fell onto the ground, and she leaned over, pouring a little water over her short hair. She ran her fingers through her freshly cut locks as cool water ran down her scalp, drizzling into her eyes. She remembered how Eric used to look at her when her hair was long, flowing down her back—his smile—his eyes glistening in the sunlight.

Eric. A vision of his hand reaching out and his voice chanting her name over and over again rang through her mind. She squeezed her eyes shut for a moment before securing her bag over her shoulder. As she stared ahead, she noticed the trees thrashing and leaves swirling over the foliage-covered path.

Exhaling, Sera continued forward until the trees parted, revealing a shopping center in the distance. An aging white sign with a tinge of rust around the corners and a picture of the ocean struck a memory.

Sybil's smiling face laughed as she walked out of her house. Sera could see the ocean waves behind Sybil crashing into each other as they rolled onto the beach.

Smiling, she remembered the moment like it was yesterday. A sharp ping struck Sera's chest as her smile faded.

The back of the shopping center had overgrown grass, with clumps of foliage wildly bordering the walkway up the alley. Exhaling, she looked both ways and jogged to the building's wall. She turned to walk along the stone when a shrill scream hollered. The sound was close, and Sera exhaled loudly.

Shit.

She ran along the back of the stores, staying close to the building. The ominous path looked bare, but she knew looks could be deceiving. She fingered the bowie knife secured to her hip and slowly inched along. Then, as she got closer to the alley dividing the buildings, the ground rumbled beneath her, followed by another set of screams. Sera picked up the pace and looked around, scanning the area.

Sera peeked down the alleyway and ran along the wall, keeping herself tucked in the shadows. Just as she made it to the end of the street, a dark laugh echoed from the front of the shopping center. Then a series of screams followed, crying for help.

As if the sludge river wasn't enough for Sera to worry about, another enemy had emerged when the apocalypse happened—*Scavs*. Scavengers were the people left behind who roamed the streets, taking and doing what they wanted when they wanted.

Sera slowly peeked out from the alley and looked both ways down the street. Shopping centers lined the road, going down both sides. She stepped out and walked along the sidewalk, peering into each shop for salvageable items. All the stores were broken into with knocked-over shelves and trashed floors. Glass crunched under Sera's shoes as she stopped in front of a boarded window with the words sprayed in blood-red paint—*The End of the World Is Here.*

Exhaling, Sera trailed along the sidewalk when she heard the hissing from the street. The cement crackled, opening the ground, and a growl roared as the sludge began to emerge. She picked up her speed and stopped at the end of the shops to see another alleyway, returning her to the back of the stores. Panting, she peered behind her when a loud banging noise startled her. A door was flapping open and closed, hitting a railing of some stairs. It appeared to be a loft room located above one of the shops.

She gazed up at the sun, estimating the time she had before the sun went down. The sun was already headed west for the evening, and from the looks of it, she only had a few good hours before dark. She quickly checked around her and ran for the foot of the stairs. The ground began to tremble under her feet, so she grabbed the railing and sprinted up, two steps at a time.

The stairs wobbled, rocking her body back and forth until she reached the top. She peered through the old stairs and saw steam seeping through the ground. The river was driving towards her, forming a new path under the stairs. The road slowly opened, and a deep howl grumbled as the ooze dissolved the ground and pushed through the surface. The road slowly crumbled, falling into the earth and revealing the river of death's new path. Sera knew that it was following her. The vibrations her body made as she walked alerted the entity where she was.

It's always following me.

The door slammed against the stair railing, rattling the steps. Sera slowly turned back to the door and stood before the dark opening. Wincing, she shuddered as the door slammed again, vibrating the metal under her feet. She put her hand out and caught the door in mid-swing, holding it still. She propped her shoulder against it and pulled out the little flashlight attached to her belt. The beam from the light cut through a layer of dust across the darkroom. The room appeared to have been abandoned for a long time. Moldy trash and old food wrappers were scattered on the floor. Sera slowly crept through the doorway and walked into a tiny living room. A turned-over chair and a loveseat faced a small television attached to the wall, and a pile of dirty clothes was on the floor.

Sera continued forward and walked straight into the

kitchen. The refrigerator door was ajar, and bowls of moldy food lay on the floor in front of it. All the cabinets were hanging open and bare as if about to collide with the floor.

She returned to the front door, stuck her head out, and looked through the stairs. The sludge river had fully emerged under the steps, making its way along the side of the building. Sera turned back around and went to the right into the hallway. The bedroom door was closed at the end of the hall. She followed the beam along the walls to the floor and stopped at the door. The wooden floor rippled a loud creak as she stepped closer to the bedroom door. Stopping, she held her breath and waited. After a moment, she took another step, and a soft thud from the bedroom stopped her in her tracks. She slowly reached for her bowie knife, pulling it out of her belt. Shifting her weight, she bit her lip and watched the door. She looked behind her and took another slow step.

Swallowing, she licked her lips. "Hello? Come out."

Stepping forward slowly, she grabbed the doorknob, turned, and pushed the door open to see sunlight flowing through a crack in the window's curtain. Holding her breath, she watched for movement, but the room appeared empty. Exhaling, Sera took a step forward when the bedroom door creaked as it moved, opening more.

She stopped and stepped backward, adjusting the knife in her hand. Her fingers shivered as she took another step back and said, "Come out and show yourself."

The bedroom door moved slightly again, bumping into the wall. Sera jumped back and pressed her body against the wall just as a dozen mice rounded the corner of the bed towards her. She kicked her feet as they ran over her boots, passing her in the hallway. Panting, she dropped her hands to her knees. She sat up and dropped her head against the wall, looking up.

She looked back and forth between rooms and exhaled loudly. "Shit."

The room had an enormous bed and some bedroom furniture. The drawers were all pulled out and emptied onto the floor. The bathroom door was opened, and broken glass from the mirror was scattered across the floor. Sera shined her light on the bathroom sink and turned on the knob. *Nothing.* She went over to the tub and did the same. *Nothing.* She turned around and checked the toilet for water. It was full. She took the backplate off and checked the tank for water. It was full and looked clean. Sera reached into her bag, pulled out a plastic cup, and dipped it into the water. She sniffed it and sipped a small drink. *Clean.* She grabbed a two-liter bottle out of her bag, unscrewed the lid, put the bottle into the back of the toilet, and filled it with water. Then she took out her thermos and did the same.

Sera walked back to the front door and checked outside before pulling it shut and locking it. The room filled with darkness as soon as the door closed. A small beam of light trickled out of the curtains of a small window between the kitchen and family room. Sera peeked out, looking both ways. She stared for a moment, and just as she was going to walk away, she noticed a group of people walking the street a few blocks away. *That's who was screaming.* A mob was walking with a few armed men behind them. Shaking her head, she quickly shut the curtain, leaving only a little crack of light to see with. *Scavs.*

The small loveseat was big enough for her tiny body to rest on. She walked over, unsnapped her wool blanket from her backpack, and draped it over the cushions. She pulled out her nuts, ate a few handfuls, and looked around the room. Shadows hovered over pictures on the wall of the family who used to live there. Sera's heart fluttered as she gazed along the photos. Memories flashed of her and Eric's wedding pictures littering the walls of their home. She squeezed her eyes shut and exhaled deeply before gulping water. Eric's face came to her mind. His hand reached out for her as he sank into the sludge.

Stop it. Stop it.

Shaking her head, she dropped to the floor and stretched her limbs and back. Once she finished, she forced herself to return to the couch and pulled the blanket over her. She stared at the ceiling until sleep finally came.

Chapter Six: Scavs

Sera

"*S*era"
*S*era opened her eyes to feel warm water flowing underneath her sleeping body. A salty breeze blew against her, pushing her into the angry waves of the sea.

"Sera." Sera recognized that voice. It was Sybil.

"Sybil! Sybil, I hear you. I hear you! Where are you?"

The violent sound of waves and strong winds echoed over the beach, deafening Sera. She stood up and spun around, looking for her sister.

"Sybil!" Sera's voice screamed, but her words were swallowed by the sea.

A sailboat appeared just past the shoreline. Sera stopped and stared, cocking her head to the side. The sea thrashed, throwing waves high up into the air and dropping down around the boat, but it seemed unaffected by the sea's behavior. A bright white light peeked from the cabin's window and continued to move up on the deck. Sera watched, squinting as the light slowly dimmed, revealing a woman. The woman's body turned towards her and stared at Sera. A deep feeling of sorrow filled Sera's heart, burning her insides with pain and despair. Sera's lips began to quiver as she hugged her arms around herself. A single tear strolled down her cheeks, mourning for the woman.

Sera inhaled a deep breath and started walking out into the angry waves. The sea pummeled against her legs, pushing her back, but she kept walking. The woman turned her head slightly, meeting Sera's gaze.

"Sybil, is that you?" Sera stopped and waved her arms over her head. The woman turned, and the bright white light beamed in her direction, blinding Sera. She covered her eyes with her forearm, shielding them from the blazing glow. Blinking, she slowly lowered her forearm and saw the light had dimmed, and the woman was standing just a few feet away in the water.

"Oh, Sybil. I —"

Sybil's body jumped in front of Sera, and before she knew what was happening, she cupped her hands over her forearms. Sybil's fingers squeezed Sera, crushing her arms. A surge of fire struck her, sending sharp pains through her body. A scream bellowed from Sera as the images flashed through her mind. The pictures of people and places sped through her, causing Sera's body to seize violently. Sybil's fingers let go of Sera's arms, and her body collapsed into the sand, convulsing. The last picture to flash in Sera's mind was a house.

Sera opened her eyes and looked up at Sybil standing over her. Sybil's lips didn't move, but she heard her whispers. Find the house.

Sera shot up in the darkness. Panting, her hands fumbling under the blanket, she searched for her flashlight. She knocked the light off her chest, and the sound of it rolling away rumbled across the floor. "Shit."

She draped her body on the ground, running her fingers across the carpet until her hand bumped into the light. The beam flashed in front of her, lighting up the dark room. She followed the light to the front door to see it was still closed and locked. Then she followed it down the hallway to the bedroom door, still ajar. Whistling sang from outside, drawing her over to the window. She peeked out the curtain and saw dark shadows filling the bare streets. The glass flexed and moaned as the wind pushed against it, begging to come in.

Sera rubbed her face and turned to go back to sleep. The couch welcomed her as she pulled her blanket up to her chin. She flipped off the light and closed her eyes.

Daylight poured in through the crack of the curtains, bringing in another day. She rubbed her eyes and stood up, strolling down the hall to relieve herself in the bathroom. A flash of *The house* flooded her mind the minute she stood back up. The remnants of her dream, of Sybil, just everything, all came back at once. She closed her eyes and tried to focus on what Sybil was trying to tell her, but the only thing she could fully recall was the image of *The house.*

The house was a large white two-story Cape Cod-style home with white shutters. A long porch wrapped around the front of it with white rocking chairs and tables to sit on in the afternoon.

The house. Where the hell is the house? How am I supposed to know if I'm going the right way, Sybil? Sybil, are you there? Are you waiting for me there? Sybil, please answer me. Sybil?

Sera opened her eyes and walked back into the living room. She knew that she must be getting closer to her siblings. Sybil was connecting with her now. She'd never had a nightmare with her sister in it before, but she knew it had to be a message — a premonition — telling her where she needed to go next — *The house.*

Exhaling, she rolled up her blanket and snapped it into the side of her backpack. Morning sunlight warmed her face as she walked over and looked out the door before exiting. Two men were walking down the road holding guns and searching inside the shops along the sidewalk. Sera eased the door shut and waited several minutes before looking out again.

The wind blew hard against the door as she slowly pushed it open and closed it behind her. A creak rattled as the hinges cried from lack of mobility. Sera peeked out, slowly looking down into the street first. Then her gaze followed the river's path, and she saw it was still flowing steadily underneath her staircase. She descended the stairs and searched for a vacant spot to drop her bag. She checked around her and threw her bag over. She knew she needed to move quickly in case the *Scavs* were close.

Sera jumped over the staircase, did a drop roll, and landed on her feet. She stood up, walked over to her bag, and leaned over to pick it up. As she stood back up, she met the gaze of a slender man standing about twenty feet in front of her. But she remembered he had a partner, so she glanced behind her to see his accomplice. A slight grin curled her lips as she knew she could easily outrun these two *Scavs*.

The man in front of her was as thin as an evergreen. He was holding an old pistol that looked like it had rust covering the barrel. He had both hands on the gun, one on the butt and the other along the barrel. Sera knew from past experiences that the man obviously had no knowledge of using a weapon or had any intentions of firing at her. The safety was still turned on, and he was holding the gun as if he'd never shot a firearm in his life. Sera glanced back again, and his partner was in the same shape. A little shorter, holding an old revolver that looked like it came out of a movie scene from the sixties. He held the base of the gun with one hand, shivering in old work boots, as he stared back into her eyes.

Sera knew what needed to be done. Play dumb and act fast.

"Easy, girl, easy. We don't want to hurt you. We just want to help you." The slender man grinned as he winked at Sera.

Sera's eyes widened as she loosened her stance and held her hands up. "Don't hurt me, please." *Two can play this game, stupid.*

A loud rumble in the earth vibrated their feet, and a burst of steam bellowed from the river under the staircase. It was mere feet away from where they all stood, and Sera knew if she waited long enough, the river would catch up with them and reach for its next victim.

As soon as the slender man began stumbling forward, Sera bolted. Her feet pounded down one after another, pumping her legs to move. Heavy breathing grew closer to her back, so she zig-zagged to throw off her pursuers. She turned around to check, and both men were still on her tail, so she ran towards an abandoned car. Dropping her bag, she ran up onto the roof and held up her fists. Both men stopped, dropped their hands to their knees, and panted.

"Leave me alone, assholes."

The men looked at each other, smiling. One nodded, walked over to Sera's bag, and reached to grab it.

"Hey! I wouldn't if I were you!"

He looked up, aimed his gun, and smiled at her. "Come stop me."

Very well, then, asshole. Sera knew the men didn't know what they were getting themselves into. She ran down the car, leaped off the hood, and kicked the slender evergreen in the face first. The guy's body flew and landed hard on his back, knocking the wind out of him. Gasping, he rolled over onto his side and spewed acid onto the concrete. Sera landed on her feet and raised her fists. She faced the second guy and waited for him to make his move.

Come on, stupid.

Nodding, a grin curled as she motioned with her finger for him to approach her. He came in fast, stomping towards her, and swung at her face. The wind whooshed across her cheek as she leaned back and dodged the hit. As his body was turned, she dropped to her knees and stabbed his gut. Then she pulled out her knife and stabbed it in his leg. Sera could see the slender guy rising from the concrete from the corner of her eye. She pulled out her knife, sprinted over to him, and sliced his throat open. The man clawed at his neck, gargling and spewing as blood flooded the front of his shirt.

The ground began to rumble underneath Sera, lifting her body up and dropping her back down abruptly. Boiling steam blew behind her, burning the back of her legs. She tried to run away, but the ground trembled violently again, throwing her forward onto her knees. She pushed herself up and turned around to see steam spewing from the cement as the river was emerging down a new path. Walking backward, Sera watched the sludge reach out with its long ooze-formed limb and grab the slender man from the concrete. Mesmerized, she gazed down into the river and watched as his body was absorbed into the dark goo of death. The river reached out for a second time, extending its long arm of sludge and grabbing the injured man, pulling him in. His screams echoed, but Sera just stood there, staring.

"Help me. Please, help me!"

The man scraped the concrete with his bleeding nubs, trying to escape, but it was too late. The sludge dragged him in slowly, absorbing his flesh immediately into its sea. His body sank into the sludge-like sand, stopping right before his head went under.

"It burns! Ahh! It burns!" The man's screams echoed.

Hypnotized by the river's ravenous nature, Sera felt her eyes gloss over as she peered down into the ooze of death. Her body jolted as glimpses of Eric's face popped into her mind. *Eric.* The sludge arm slowly reached out for a third time, roaming up toward her side in search of her. She stepped backward and turned away to grab her bag. She threw her bag over her shoulder and glared at the sludge reaching for her.

"Fuck you, sludge."

CHAPTER SEVEN: THE SCIENTIST

John

"Wake up, buddy." John ruffled Brandon's hair back out of his face. John pulled back the covers and rubbed his back, gazing down at his paper-thin arms clutching his bony knees. "I know, buddy, but we have to get up."

"Why?"

John opened his mouth to respond, but he knew he was right. Why? The words lingered in his head. *What's the point of moving on when we're stuck in this little apartment with no food or way of it all being over?*

John stared at the bedroom door and then looked back down at Brandon. An image of something struck him. A flash of a device and a beautiful woman with fiery red hair he'd never seen before strolled through his mind like a movie projector. He squeezed his eyes shut, but the image blinked in his mind again. *What the hell is going on?* His brow creased, and he opened his eyes to meet Brandon's gaze.

"Are you okay?"

John nodded quickly and said, "Because I'm going to find a way to kill the sludge." *Why the hell did I say that? What's wrong with me? I don't know what's going on.* But as soon as John spoke the words, he did know. He felt a deep knowing in his gut that told him he would build a device to kill the sludge and save the world. Even though John hadn't built the machine yet, he knew what the image was. As he stared down at Brandon, his confidence built, and he knew that was what he was supposed to do.

"You?" Brandon's voice squeaked as he looked up at John. "How? Do you know how to kill it?"

"Not yet, but I will." *I will. That's what I do. That's what I've always done. I find the answer.*

Brandon sat up, and a slight twinkle brightened his eyes. "Can you find my mom, too?"

Shaking his head, John didn't want to voice the answer to the little boy. His innocence was heartwarming and heart-breaking at the same time. John was never a liar or even good at sugarcoating things because he wasn't taught to do so. When he was little, he'd asked his parents questions, and they were always very honest and upfront about everything, so he did the same with Brandon.

"No, buddy, your mom died when the sludge took her body into its river. She'll never come back. I'm sorry."

Brandon nodded and said, "I know. I just . . . I miss her. Is there any food left?"

"Yes, half of a pop tart in the kitchen. I saved it for you."

Brandon forced a smile and walked out of the room. John dropped back on the twin bed, rubbing his hands over his eyes and cheeks.

"Shit." *Why the hell did I say all of that? Where did that damn image come from? What the fuck —*

"Hey. Did you mean what you said?" Jim's body was leaning against the bedroom doorframe.

John met Jim's gaze and nodded. He didn't want to tell Jim that he had a vision. He didn't know what was happening yet, but he knew living like this, hiding, and barely surviving wouldn't last forever. "Yes. I'll begin my research as soon as possible."

"How do you even know what to look for? I wouldn't even know where to start."

"Well, do you have some paper?"

"Yeah."

"I'll start with that. The basics. Scientific process. I'll write down everything I know about the sludge. All the facts. Then I'll research. Gather data. I'll analyze the data and lastly draw a conclusion on what and how to kill the sludge."

Jim chuckled and shook his head. "Wait, John. Are you . . . are you a scientist?"

John inhaled a deep breath and frowned. "I was going to be, but an apocalypse delayed my plans." John forced a grin and followed Jim into the kitchen.

CHAPTER EIGHT: THE BEINGS

Sera

You let him go.

Stop. Stop. Stop! Sera closed her eyes and chanted in her head. Keep moving. Keep moving.

The guilt was growing, eating at her insides as she continued on. She mindlessly kept moving forward. Searching for Sybil. Searching for the house that Sybil had directed her to. She didn't know what else to do. If she stopped and just gave up, she knew she would die. Die. Just like him.

In the back of her mind, she heard her mother's words. "Something's going to happen. You're the one who saves us. You save everyone."

What the hell does that mean, Mom? The sludge? I can't stop this. No one can. No one can.

Tears welled up in Sera's eyes, and her heart began to pound against her chest. Pain pinged on the top of her head as everything started to jumble up. She couldn't take it anymore. She squeezed her eyes shut and screamed inside her mind. Stop! A single tear rolled down her cheek as she opened her eyes. Everything went quiet, and she looked up to see abandoned shopping centers drawing near. She aggressively swiped the moisture from her cheeks and continued forward.

Sera stopped in front of a row of broken windows that were boarded up and spray-painted with the same words as every other town.

KEEP OUT! IT'S THE END OF THE WORLD! SAVE

YOURSELF!

A loud thud burst behind her, and then a rattling sound traveled down the street. She whipped around and watched as a soda can rolled through the town. A cool breeze blew her fiery hair, causing her to push back her overgrown bangs. She looked up to see a sign that read *Welcome to the Florida Keys*, with a woman standing in a bikini holding a surfboard.

Home. The words lingered in her heart as she stared up at the picture.

An image surfaced of her sister, brother, dad, and mom standing in front of their house. Her car was packed to leave for college, and her mom walked over first to hug her goodbye. Each sibling followed suit, and lastly, her dad squeezed her the longest. He whispered in her ear, "I put something in your glove box. Go have an adventure, kiddo." He coughed as if clearing his throat, but Sera knew he was tearing up. She inhaled deeply and tried to savor the mixture of Old Spice and Irish Spring.

"I'm really going to miss you, Sera. Take care of yourself, and if you need me, just call. I mean it."

"I know, Dad. I love you."

Exhaling, Sera blinked, pushing away her memories, and looked at the shop beside her. Something on the floor caught her eye. A grumble quivered in her abdomen, and she patted her stomach as she felt the hunger pains growing stronger and stronger.

Food. I need to eat.

She checked around her one more time before stepping through the broken window. Her sneakers crunched down onto shattered glass, echoing through the store. She proceeded down every aisle and waded through piles of plastic bags and food wrappers. Exhaling, she walked back to the front of the store and stopped when she heard voices approaching. A group of people were walking down the middle

44

of the road, tied to one another with a long rope. Two heavily armed men led the group, pulling the rope, and two more men followed closely behind. She slowly walked backward and squatted down behind the aisle.

"One, two, three, four, five, six, seven, eight, nine," Sera whispered.

At the end of the line was a woman following the group with a little girl who looked to be about ten years old. Sera took a step forward to get a better look when a cloud of black smoke hissed behind the crowd. A curdling scream from one of the women sounded, sending the group into chaos. The people in the back of the line pulled and started to trample the people in the front. The earth opened behind the people, quaking its victims into its dark hole. Gunfire rattled through the group, and half the victims running dropped, covering their heads. Steam flushed on their heels, and the rope tied to the people became their doom, pulling them into the river of death.

The men with firearms ran, dragging a woman behind them. She thrashed her arms and legs, screaming, "Run, baby, run!"

The man turned around and hit the woman across the face with his rifle, knocking her to the ground. "Shut up!"

The woman lay on the ground sobbing and protectively cupped her arms over her head.

"Get up. Woman! Get up!" He stomped his black boot against her body. Shivering, Sera turned away and closed her eyes.

A loud thump sounded, and something hit the ground in the back of the store. Sera cupped her hand over her bowie knife and scanned the room. The store appeared empty, but she sensed she wasn't alone and knew she needed to get out of there. She turned back to look outside and saw the woman the man was hitting lying in a pool of blood. The men holding

45

guns galloped into the store next to hers, banging around and knocking over shelves. Sera walked over to the south side of the store and crawled through a broken window.

She started jogging and followed the sidewalk along the stores. When the sidewalk ended, she stopped, looked down the alley between the stores, and saw an apartment building. The apartments were built of brown and tan bricks going up four stories with little balconies overlooking the street. Sera knew she either had to go down the alley behind the building, or she could try to go into the apartments to find somewhere to hide.

Panting, Sera was staring down the alley when a gush of steam hissed behind her, taunting her. Her heart pounded in her ears as she looked back. She turned towards the apartments and took a step when a hand pulled at her forearm. She flew around, holding her bowie knife erect, and looked down to see a little girl. She was filthy and covered in black dirt. The girl looked up at Sera, staring blankly. Sera lowered her knife, staring back at the little girl like a doe in headlights.

I never know what to say to kids. Eric always knew how to talk to people. Sera knew her days as a karate instructor had never actually taught her how to socialize. Eric was the outgoing, friendly one, and people were naturally drawn to him.

His smiling face popped into her mind, and she shuddered. *You could have saved him.* Shaking her head, she squeezed her eyes shut and inhaled deeply. *Stop it. Stop it. Stop it.*

She opened her eyes and glanced around her to see if anyone else was with the girl, but she was alone.

"Are . . . are you okay?"

The sounds of shattering glass and something large cracking as it hit the floor reverberated towards them. Sera looked back down at the little girl and gazed into her eyes. The girl cocked her head to the side, meeting her stare in silence. Then the girl cocked her head the other way as if she were sizing Sera up. The little girl lifted her arm, aiming to grab Sera. Sera jolted back, and a deep sense of evil from the little girl sent chills down her spine.

No. No, she's one of them.

Shaking her head, she slowly took another step back and spun around, running towards the apartments. She spotted a porch with an open fence. She pushed through, locking it behind her. Sera's fingers trembled as she slowly pressed her face against the wooden slats, peering through.

Shit. Where the hell did she go?

Sera looked behind her to see a sliding glass door standing open with a heavy curtain whirling in the wind. Slowly, she walked over to peek in and saw that the room was empty. She stepped into the apartment, and a loud crash rattled against the gate. Sera spun around, and the fence began to shake violently. She slowly walked out of the apartment, and as soon as her foot touched the ground, glowing red eyes peered through the wood slats, gazing into Sera's heart.

"Hey! Hey, girl. Where do you think you're going?" A man shouted from afar.

Sera slowly walked backward, heading back into the apartment, and hid behind the glass door. Footsteps stomped up to the fence, and the little girl's body slammed against the gate. A shrill scream echoed as the wood slats vibrated, and a loud thud hit the ground. Sera slowly stepped out from hiding, looked through the fence, and saw the little girl dragging the man by the arm to the sludge river. The little girl stopped for a brief moment and, without hesitation, stepped into the river of death, dragging the man in behind her. Sera's mouth dropped as she was at a loss for words. The little girl looked as if she were going home.

Shit. Shit. Shit.

Sera knew she had to get out of there fast before the little girl made her the next victim. Shaking her head, she quickly walked through the apartment and found the front door.

The hallway was dark with garbage flooding the floor.

Blood was smeared over the railing, and a pungent stench of feces filled the air. She turned and went to the right in search of an emergency exit. The hallway was a long, carpeted floor that wound around to the other side of the apartments.

Sera slowed her steps once she realized there was no exit door. Turning around, she jogged towards the front of the building to the door. She pressed her face against the glass, looking out. The glass was tempered, so Sera couldn't make out what was happening outside without opening the door. Sera reached for the knob, turning it.

"Oh, come on!" Sera gritted her teeth. *Locked.*

Sera's gut clenched when she spun around and searched for a way out. A trickle of moisture grazed her brow, and she took off again, jogging back the way she had come from.

Exit. Exit. Exit. Where the fuck is the Exit!

Even though Sera was a warrior and could fight off Scavs, she knew she didn't stand a chance against the evil emerging from the sludge river.

Exit. Exit. Exit.

Sera headed back down the hall, passing an elevator, to a door beside it, reading *STAIRS*. She guided the door gently closed behind her, clicked on her flashlight, and followed a short hallway that led to another door at the base of the stairs that read, *EMPLOYEES ONLY*. She stood in front of the door and put her ear to it before turning the knob. Something gently touched her leg as she opened it. A tiny peep chirped from Sera as she jumped back, holding her bowie knife erect. An old mop head was draped across her boot.

Exhaling loudly, she grabbed her chest, panting. "Shit."

It was a closet full of mops, brooms, and a couple of mopping buckets with wheels.

She closed the door and started climbing the stairs until she reached the top. Another sign reading *EMPLOYEES ONLY* was on the door.

"How many damn employee's rooms are there?" Sera's

voice echoed in the darkness.

Sera turned the knob quietly, opening it, and saw another set of stairs going down. Exhaling, she followed the stairs to the bottom and found another door that read *EMERGENCY EXIT* with a long black bar across it. She pushed the door open and was blinded by a glistening ray of sunshine. The smell of green grass and autumn leaves whooshed in with the wind. She braced the heavy door with her arm and peeked both ways before exiting.

CHAPTER NINE: SUPPLIES

John

As soon as the apartment door clicked closed, John felt this deep sense of dread wash over him. Something felt off. The usual thick, pungent smell lingered, tainting the wind from the new tenant that had moved into the parking lot's concrete. But that wasn't it. John felt a shift or a sick sense that something else was wrong. He slowly walked down the steps and popped his head out before turning the corner. The street seemed empty besides the new resident, so he headed towards the apartments on the far side of the complex in search of food.

As soon as he turned the corner for the second time, he stepped out and saw something hovering over the sludge river. John darted back and peeked out again to see a man crawling out of the river. Sludge dripped down his flesh, seeping into his skin as he stepped onto the concrete. His skin slowly turned a light brown as the ooze absorbed into his body and left the skin bare.

Fuck. Fuck. Fuck!

John eased back behind the brick and waited for the individual to leave. After a few minutes, he peeked out, and he was gone. Cocking his head, he knew that it was too soon. There was no way the man could have disappeared that quickly without lingering somewhere nearby. He stepped out further and peered around the parking lot when something stopped him.

No. Stay.

"What—" John spun around, looking for the person talking, but soon realized he was alone.

Shh. Stay.

The person sounded feminine, as if a woman was speaking to him, but she was struggling to connect.

The hairs on the back of John's neck rose, and his fingers began to tremble. He spun around again and again, searching. "Where are you—"

Shh!

Wait! Are you . . . are you in my mind?

Yes. Now be quiet!

Oh shit! Oh shit! I can't believe this is happening. I'm finally losing my fucking mind. I knew this would happen. I would lose it after all this. That one fucking party! That one party where I let Joe give me that pill, and he said it was—

Shut up! No. I'm here, and I'm trying to help. Be. Quiet.

A calming feeling rushed through John's body, and he felt slightly more at ease when she spoke. He stepped backward, and for some reason, knew he could trust whoever was trying to help him.

Okay. Okay, I'm listening. He responded in his mind.

Now, look.

John peeked out and saw the man standing next to the sludge, peering out at the apartments. He was naked, and as John stared at him, he realized the ooze was seeping from parts of his body.

Oh fuck. This is just fucking great. People are climbing out of it now. Just fucking great!

John's breath caught in his throat as he stared at what was happening. He took a step closer to get a better look, and a bright light blinded him briefly. He turned away, shielding his gaze. He took a step forward and looked up, meeting the man's stare. The man cocked his head to the side and took off running towards John.

Shit. Shit. Shit.

John backed up and turned back towards Jim's apartment. *Go. Go. Go! The woman's voice echoed in his head.*

He ran up the stairs and knocked on the door. Jim opened it, and he went inside. Panting, he sat down on the chair and met Jim's eyes. "Dead people are . . . are coming out of the sludge, and they're . . ." John inhaled deep breaths before finishing his sentence.

"They're what? John?"

"The sludge . . ." John rubbed his eyes and pushed his hair out of his face before answering. "It's like the sludge has soldiers, and it sends them out. I don't know. This changes everything. Fuck!" John slammed his hands down on the table, shaking his head.

John stared at Jim, and they both turned to look at Brandon. The whites of Brandon's eyes bulged as he stared back.

"So what does this mean?" Jim said.

"It means . . . I don't know." John rubbed his eyes and met Jim's gaze. "It means it's more dangerous than we anticipated."

I need to find a way to study it. Research it without getting killed. It's the only way I'll find any answers.

John squeezed his eyes shut and tried to shut out the image of the person sprinting towards him. Shaking his head, he rubbed his eyes again before looking over at Jim. "I need to get into my apartment. I need supplies, and we need food. I know I have a little bit of dry food in the pantry. It's just not much because I never really ate at home."

Jim nodded.

Brandon walked over and sat down on the opposite chair. "What did the man look like?"

John shook his head and pushed his hair back again. "Well, it was a man just like you or me, but he was —" John stopped talking mid-sentence when something clicked in his mind. *I know the sludge is alive and flows in the river. It pulls people in and kills them, but it actually seemed as if it was like a . . . parasite. Parasites need a host to survive. It needs a host – to survive.*

"Like what?" Jim asked.

John shook his head and looked back at Brandon and Jim. "What?"

"You were saying something and just stopped."

"Oh, I'm sorry, I was just thinking. Um, yeah, I need to get back into my place."

John stepped into his little apartment, and a flash of the last day he was there sent chills down his spine. A lot had happened since he left this place, and it had only been a month.

A month. The girl. I can't even remember her name.

John rubbed his face and aggressively swiped his hair back. He shook his head, exhaling loudly. *I don't even remember her name, and now she's dead. She's dead.* The words rang in his head. His gut pinged as acid rolled up to his throat. *What kind of person does that?*

John walked further into the apartment and peered around his dark family room. Sunlight beamed through one of the curtains, shining down on a spot on the carpet. He walked over to the window and peered out. The river was hugging the side of the apartment building, making its way around it, fencing it in.

John's car and the place where the girl's car went into the abyss were now a part of the river.

Carrie? No. Michelle? No. Susan? Nope, that's not right. I'm a piece of shit for not even remembering that girl's name. But I didn't love her – I could've loved her. I could've made her happy.

John swiped his mane back aggressively, exhaling slowly.

What the fuck am I saying? We're in a damn apocalypse. There's no such thing as love anymore. I don't deserve to fall – fuck! Get it together!

John pulled the curtain together to block out the daylight completely and went into his bedroom. He grabbed a large bag out of the closet and started filling it. The microscope was on his desk, where he'd left it. A box of blank slides, Petri dishes, more notebooks, pens, gloves, beakers, a stirring rod, and a tape measure. He stood over his desk and stared down at everything.

This is everything. This is what I came for.

What else? John gazed around the room, looking for anything that would be of some use.

Flashlight!

He darted into the kitchen and pulled open the drawers, grabbing all the batteries. He put them in his bag along with two flashlights on top of the refrigerator. *Why didn't I buy better flashlights? Dad always said to get good flashlights – you never know when you'll need them.*

He turned around, gazing around the room again.

Shaking his head, John returned to his bedroom, changed, and grabbed another bag for extra clothes. He also found the little teddy bear his mom gave him when he was seven and pushed it into the bag. He opened the frame that held a picture of him and his parents and stared at it for a long moment before folding it and pushing it down into his bag. Then he headed back to the kitchen, opened the refrigerator, and was almost knocked back by the stench of rotten food. The lunch meat and leftover sub sandwich the girl had brought back from a restaurant had a lump of mold that reeked.

An image of the girl's smiling face flashed in John's mind. Squeezing his eyes shut, he shook his head. *Stop. She's gone.*

Gritting his teeth, he slammed the door and headed for the pantry. A package of *Ritz* crackers, half a jar of *Jiff* peanut butter, and a box of *Honey Buns* were sitting on a very empty shelf in his pantry. *Why didn't I ever buy any damn food? Fuck.*

He grabbed a recycle bag, threw it all in, and shoved a *Honey Bun* into his mouth, chewing slowly. Nodding, he looked around the room as he walked back over to the door. *This is it. Goodbye apartment.*

Jim opened the door, and John handed him the bags of food. Nodding, Jim led the way to the kitchen, and they ate peanut butter and crackers for dinner.

John kept thinking about parasites. *Parasites.* He grabbed a piece of paper and jotted down some notes.

Parasites Vs. Sludge
A protozoa parasite is a parasite that needs a host to survive.
The sludge latches onto the human body or absorbs into the human body, taking over the specimen and controlling it.
Meaning the sludge is similar to the protozoa parasite and needs a host to survive. In its process of survival, it acts as an omni parasite.
Omni means a parasite that completely takes over the host, overpowering the human body mentally and physically.

Nodding, he stared at the kitchen wall and was chewing on his pen when someone touched his shoulder. Jumping, he jolted to his feet and looked down to see Brandon wide-eyed.

"Hi."

"Sorry, buddy, I'm just—" John rubbed his face and swallowed the words. *Jumpy.* He ran his fingers through his hair and nodded. "What's up?"

"Did you get your scientist stuff?"

"Yeah, buddy, I got it all."

"Can I see some of it?"

"Of course, but let's finish eating first. Okay?"

"Okay." He nodded and took a bite of his peanut butter cracker sandwich.

Brandon had a smear of peanut butter across his cheek. John smiled at him and ruffled his hair back.

CHAPTER TEN: WALKING ALONE

Sera

Sera looked up to see bolts of electricity skating across the sky and a cluster of angry clouds racing overhead. Moisture drizzled and dampened her face as a gust of strong winds pushed against her. Her cap rolled down her back, and she caught it just before it hit the ground.

"Hey, lady . . . come here!" A woman's voice called from inside the forest.

Sera peered into the maze of trees and watched the branches sway violently back and forth in the gusts. She looked ahead and saw that she had only a few more feet to go to reach the road. She began jogging to escape whoever haunted her and heard a woman's voice call out again.

"Hey, lady. Hey!"

Sera turned around to see a woman standing at the forest's edge. The woman had clumps of hair on her head and ragged clothes draped over her thin frame. Startled, Sera tripped over her feet, landing on all fours. She sprang up and looked back to see the woman almost on top of her.

"Hey. I'm talking to you! Stop," the woman yelled, waving her arms around.

Sera bolted forward and reached the front of the building, running out into the road. Panting, she stopped and looked behind her to see the woman had disappeared.

The streets were bare, and a small indention in the road had steam rising above it. Sera quietly walked along the sidewalk in front of the stores, away from the river. Thunder crackled overhead, and a bright flash of light sketched across the gray clouds. Drops of rain sprinkled little wet spots on the road and sidewalk, and then it started to downpour. Stopping, Sera stepped through a broken window in the pharmacy store next to her. Medication bottles were scattered across the entrance, and shelves were torn down and ripped from the walls. The floors were covered in empty bags of food and soda cans. Sera kicked through the trash, exhaling loudly. She walked to the end of one aisle and turned to go down the next. A glimpse of someone standing near the sludge river peeked through the broken shelves.

Sera crept back to the front of the store and saw a woman reaching down into the sludge. Black ooze flowed up her arms like tentacles, stretching across her forearms and wrapping around her shoulders. The woman began to vibrate as the sludge wrapped around her and transformed into the skin of another person. The person's body slowly started to emerge out of the ooze, changing into another woman. As the second woman was pulled out of the ground, the remainder of the sludge was absorbed through her eyes, nose, and mouth. The woman's body slowly inflated, filling with liquid death as she walked out of the earth. Frozen in place, she felt her mouth drop open, and she stared, fixated on what was happening.

The woman stepping out of the sludge stopped and spun around, looking directly at Sera. Sera dropped to her knees, backing up behind shelves. Her heart pounded against her chest as she scanned the store, searching for a way out. The only visible way to get out was through the store's main door. Panting, she slowed her breathing and peeked out to see the two women had disappeared. Sera crawled away from the shelf, inching to the front of the store. She looked out the window and saw the women walking up the sidewalk.

Shit. Shit. Shit.

Gasping, Sera crawled backward, trying to scoot out of sight when the doorbell rang. Her heart pounded in her ears, drumming as she hid from the women. Holding her breath, she peered around the store. Raindrops bounced off the sidewalk and rumbled over the pharmacy's roof, filling the ghostly silence around her. An eerie feeling of being watched crept into Sera's heart. She slowly inched forward, gazing at the door.

It's only a few feet away. I can make it. I can make it.

Slowly, she slithered out of hiding and made a run for it. Her feet skidded across the old linoleum, squealing as she went through the open door. The bell twitched and slammed against the wall. She turned the corner and was outside on the sidewalk when she heard the noise bellowing behind her.

Gasping for air, Sera felt her heart fluttering in her chest as she pounded the ground. Rain pummeled against her face, and the sky flashed with streaks of light. Her pants sloshed through the water puddles, soaking her legs. She wisped past all the stores and was running out of town when she finally slowed to a jog and looked behind her. The road was bare, with a sheet of rain coming down. Her hands dropped to her legs as she panted. Once she caught her breath, she pulled out her compass. Nodding, she whispered, "South."

Sera pushed on, and after an hour, the rain finally started to slow down to a sprinkle, filling the air with a thick humidity. Sera's sister's face flashed in her mind. Her heart ached every time she spoke her name and didn't get a response. *Sybil? Sybil?* She hadn't heard anything else from her since her dream of the white house. *Sybil, I need you. I need your help. Please.* But Sera only heard silence.

Nodding, Sera continued to follow the empty two-way road that led out of town. She peered behind her to see a mirage floating off in the distance of the city she'd barely escaped.

As Sera pushed on, the forest that hugged the road

transitioned into a ghostly swamp with sad trees wading in the water. A glaring heron met her gaze and followed her body as she walked along the road. Her footsteps echoed, bouncing off the trees. She picked up the pace, peering at the orange and yellow sky to the west of the road.

The movement of something giant splashed into the water right next to where Sera was walking. Startled, she pulled out her bowie knife, her fingers quivering. Squeezing the hilt, she gazed upon the debris alongside the road. A few abandoned bikes and clumps of trash littered her walkway. She weaved in and out of the blockage and watched as the sun slowly settled down in the west, extinguishing the light.

Sera pulled her flashlight from her belt and flipped it on. She ran her beam along the street and ahead of her to see if anything was coming up, but the road was empty. The rain finally started to subside, and the eerie quiet of the night crept in. Millions of crystals filled the sky, replacing the rain clouds, and a deep sense of exhaustion hit Sera like a wall. Her feet dragged along the ground, catching the tip of her sneakers and tripping her forward. She waved her arms and shook her head. Sera's body shivered as a giant yawn creeped out.

Wake up, Sera. Wake up. She slapped herself in the face and shook her head.

Another ripple of water splashed off in the distance, jolting Sera to a halt. Her head spun back and forth as she tried to see around her, but the dark, ominous road looked empty, with no end in sight. She picked up the pace, jogging along the beam of light stretched before her.

A large shadow appeared a few hundred feet ahead. Sera stopped and slowly raised her beam, peering at the object. As she walked towards it, she realized it was a vehicle parked on the side of the road. An SUV. It was tilted, half on the road and half off. The wheel looked like the tire had blown out and unraveled from the wheel hub.

Cautiously, Sera walked up to the vehicle and spun around her, checking her surroundings. As she got closer, the light revealed that the back of the SUV was empty. She continued to the front and saw a person slumped over with their head against the steering wheel. Sera peered in the window and saw that the body was decaying.

"Shit." Sera looked around her again and exhaled loudly. She knew this was her only chance of getting any rest. Exhaling, she dropped her bag and tried the driver's door. *Locked.* She tried the back door behind the driver's side. *Locked.*

"Oh, come on."

She walked around to the other side and tried the other back door. *Unlocked.* "*Yes.*"

A loud crackle echoed as the door opened, and the pungent scent wafted out of the car. The ripe smell of rotting corpses flooded out of the doorway and slapped Sera in the face. Sera stepped back, almost toppling over into the swamp. She stomped away and hung her head down, gagging and holding in the acid that was trying to spew out. Slowly, she regained her composure and stumbled back over to the opened door. She inhaled deeply, climbed into the vehicle, and hit the automatic unlock button. A thud clicked on all the doors, and she dropped back out of the tainted SUV. She shined her beam up to the front of the suburban to see the dead person was still buckled in.

"Fuck. Fuck. Fuck." Sera gritted her teeth and swayed back and forth. "Okay, I can do this. I can do this. I got this. I got this."

Sera inhaled a deep breath, opened the front door, stepped onto the sidestep, shoved the person back against the seat, and unbuckled the belt. Sera's gaze met the person's eyes, and her body shivered. *A young girl.* The little girl stared with a hollow blue tint, sending chills down Sera's spine. She quickly dropped out of the car, gasping for air. Acid rose up into her throat, threatening to spew. She dropped her hands to her knees and inhaled deep breaths. Once she was breathing more easily, she looked up at the girl and noticed movement.

"What the —"

A rat's tail whipped across the person's chest and moved it back.

Sera walked up, shoving the corpse's body to move it. "Get out of here!"

The rat's head popped up, and it hopped down towards her. Sera kicked her legs up in the air and ran back away from the critter. The rat ran down the road and disappeared in the darkness. Sera whipped her arms back and forth, trying to swipe the goosebumps that had risen on her body.

"What the fuck! I hate fucking rats! Always, the motherfucking nasty pieces of shit, fucking rats!" Her voice echoed around her, bouncing off the swamp. Sera wrapped her hands around her mouth, panting. *Shit.*

Her heart pounded in her ears as she breathed deeply. Shaking her head, she walked back up to the SUV and looked up at the dead body.

I still have to get her out of there. Sera inhaled a deep breath, grabbed the corpse's arm, and pulled. She was heavy. A lot heavier than what she expected. The girl didn't look big, but sitting there and rotting away had made her a dead weight in the car. Sera tugged and pulled, tugged and pulled, trying to loosen the body from the front seat. The corpse finally started to move, and she hopped down onto the road and dragged the body with her. It dropped out with a loud thump, and then the smell intensified. Sera jerked back from the body and gagged as vomit threatened to expel again. Heaving, she spat several times in the grass, trying to push down the acid in her stomach.

Shaking her head, Sera stood up, wiped her mouth, and

nodded. *I can do this. I can do this. I can fucking do this.*

Sera gritted her teeth and braced her legs in the dirt, grabbing the girl with both hands. She heaved, pulling back with everything she had, and the girl's body finally started to move. She dragged her around the SUV and over to the hill leading to the swamp. The girl's body stopped at the top of the hill, and Sera gave her one last push, rolling her down the incline.

Panting, Sera dropped her hands to her knees and caught her breath. She walked to the back of the SUV, opening the hatch. She walked back up to the front door and hit the switch to lock all the doors. Then she grabbed her bag, threw it in the back of the SUV, and pulled out the rope from inside her bag. She crawled into the back, ran the rope through the latch, and fed it down through the locking latch of the door. She closed the door, pulled the rope taut, tied the end off, and pushed on the door to ensure it was secure. Exhaling, Sera pushed her bag up against one side of the trunk and used it as a pillow. She covered her legs and body with the blanket and closed her eyes.

CHAPTER ELEVEN: LET THEM IN

John

John paced back and forth as he brainstormed the infor-
mation he'd collected from the sludge. Everything he
thought he knew about the sludge rolled through his mind at
a hundred miles an hour. His paperwork, slides, flashlight,
and microscope were strewn on the little dining room table.
He rubbed his eyes and stared blankly down at the table.

The woman's voice rang in his head. *No. I'm here, and I'm
trying to help. Be. Quiet.*

Who is she? How did she —

Jim walked around the corner of his little apartment and
nodded.

John looked down at his watch, which read six-fifteen.
Damn, I guess I was up all night again. He rubbed his face and
stroked his mane before walking to the table. He straightened
the paperwork strewn across the table and slowly sat down
in the chair. Brandon walked into the room and stopped next
to him.

"Hi."

"Hey, buddy. Did you sleep well?"

He nodded and sat down in the chair next to John.

"Did you find anything yet?"

John shook his head and stared down at the paperwork.
Brandon nodded and walked into the kitchen. He returned
with the peanut butter and a butterknife. He held up the jar,
and John nodded. He scooped a lump of butter and licked it

off before handing John the knife.

"Eww," John said, sticking his tongue out.

Brandon shrugged and stared at John while he wiped off the knife with his fingers. John gazed down into the jar and realized it was almost empty, so he handed it back to Brandon.

"You didn't eat any."

"It's okay. I'm not really hungry." John looked down at the peanut butter clumped on his finger and put it in his mouth. Shaking his head, he leaned forward and cupped his hands around his face, yawning.

Jim walked into the room and sat down at the table. Brandon handed the jar to Jim, and he nodded. They both ate in silence, watching John stare down at his paperwork. John looked up and met Jim's gaze first and then Brandon.

"We're about to run out of food, aren't we?"

Jim nodded, and Brandon slowed his chewing and looked at the jar. He lifted the jar to both men, and they shook their heads.

"So I guess it's my turn to hunt for food?" Jim whispered.

No, it's time for you to move on. Travel to the ocean and find the white house. Find. The. White. House. The voice stunned John, and he jolted in his seat when her voice rang, demanding him to go.

He squeezed his eyes shut and shook his head. Then, an image of the same beautiful woman with red hair and crystal blue eyes flashed in his mind. She turned her gaze and briefly met his before disappearing like smoke drifting in the wind. His heart pinged when she met his eyes. He felt like she was looking into his soul.

Are you speaking to me? Are you calling for me to help you? I don't understand. Is that you —

John opened his eyes and heard Jim's voice. "John? John, are you okay?"

John looked up, shaking his head. "Sorry, I, um, I'm tired.

I need to rest for a little while, and then we should get going."

"Get going? What do you mean by get going?"

"I mean, we need to leave here and find a safer place to go. I think we should go to the ocean."

"The ocean?"

"Yes, the ocean."

"I don't want to leave here, John. It's safe here. We—"

"Jim! We can't sit here and wait to die. We're out of water. We're out of food. We've broken into most of these apartments already and cleaned them out. It's time. We have to move on, and I think we should go to the water. Something inside me. A gut feeling is telling me that we need to go to the water. If that's something you don't want to do, then I guess this will be goodbye. But as for me and Brandon, we're not going to wait around for those things to break in here, or worse, the scavengers to come and kill us." John rubbed his eyes and slapped his palms on the table before standing up.

John didn't know why this woman was speaking to him. He didn't know why he was even listening, but what he did know was that he wanted to find a way to kill the river of death and its soldiers.

John walked towards the bedroom and stopped, turning around in the doorway. He met Brandon's gaze and said, "Brandon, if you don't want to go with me, you don't have to. I just . . . I think that we can find what we're looking for if we go towards the water. It's up to you."

Brandon looked down at the table and stared at John's paperwork before looking back up at John. He nodded and said, "I want to stay with you, John."

Jim said, "Me, too."

John nodded and left the room.

"John."

John's eyes burst open, and he looked up. Black, angry clouds growled a deep, malicious scowl minutes before a bright white light flashed across the sky. A warm sensation drifted up his legs and pooled around the crown of his head. He shot up and peered into the ocean's monstrous waves as they crashed down upon each other, fighting for dominance. His head danced back and forth, searching for anyone or anything, but the beach was bare. He picked himself up and started jogging down one direction. It seemed as if his legs were moving, however, the ground was standing completely still.

"Hello!" His screams were drowned out by the whistling winds whooshing past him. His hair whirled on top of his head, and then his clothes flushed against his body, pushing his slender frame backward towards the dunes. He screamed again, but nothing sounded except the echoing in his mind. "Hello!"

John stopped and spun around again, searching. But there was nothing. The beach was empty, and the only sound he heard was the wind pressing against his body. He turned towards the dunes and was peering over the mounds of sand when he felt a tingling sensation on his forearm. He looked down and saw a hand cupped over his right wrist. He looked back, and a woman as white as snow was standing there with her long, fine white hair blowing in the wind. She slowly raised her head, and a hard jolt shot through him when he met her eyes. Her crystal blues faded, and a pearl white absorbed the color of her pupil, then filled the rest of the eye. She opened her mouth and said, "Sera."

He recognized her voice. It was her, the woman who'd been guiding him. She's not Sera. She's not who I'm looking for. She's guiding me to Sera and leading me to find a way to kill the sludge. *"But why? Why are you helping me?"*

"She needs you, and you need her. Together, you will find a way. You will find a way. You have to go to the ocean and find Sera. She's waiting there for you."

"I don't understand. Why her?"

The woman squeezed John's arm, and it felt like fire was burning him from the inside out. She jerked his arm down, and his eyes were forced closed. An image of a beautiful woman with bright red locks flowed in the wind as she slowly turned to face him. She was standing in front of a two-story white house with white shutters. Her crystal blues glistened in the darkness as the light around her began to dim. John reached his arm out, and she disappeared. Her body turned to dust, and she faded away.

"John. John. Wake up."

John opened his eyes to see Jim and Brandon standing over him. He shot up in bed and blinked his eyes to focus.

"What's wrong?"

"Nothing. You um . . . you were yelling something in your sleep," Jim said.

"What?"

"I don't know," Brandon said.

John shook his head and rubbed his eyes. He didn't know what was going on. He remembered his dream, but he still didn't really know what it meant.

"Your arm was twitching."

A sharp pain shot through John's arm, and he looked down to see a mark on his right wrist. It looked like something had squeezed around it and left a bruise.

"Are you—"

A hard bang against the front door made everyone jump. John hopped out of bed and ran to the front door. Voices echoed from behind the frame, and then another round of banging began to slam against the door.

John stepped up to the door and looked out the peephole, seeing three men standing on the other side, slamming against the frame.

"Shit. Shit. Shit." He looked back at Jim and Brandon and saw fear glaze over their eyes.

"What do we do?" Jim asked.

Wait. Wait for them. Let them take you.

What? Are you mad? No, they'll kill us! No!

It's the only way. I'll lead them to her and to the house. It. Is. The. Only. Way.

"John! What do we do?" Jim asked again.

John shook his head and squeezed his eyes shut. When he opened them, he looked straight at Brandon. "We have to let them take us. If we fight, they'll kill us. We have to surrender to them and go with them. It's the only way we'll survive."

"No," Brandon squeaked. A tear rolled down his cheeks, and he walked over to John and wrapped his arms around his long leg.

"I know, buddy, but we must surrender and fight when the time is right. Do you understand?"

Brandon nodded his head as he buried it into John's jeans.

"Have you lost your mind? They'll kill us."

"No, it's the only way. We have to outsmart them when the time is right."

Jim whirled around and rubbed his eyes, then shook his head.

I hope you're right, lady. So what do I do? Just open the door?
Yes, open the door. Now. I'll lead them to her.

"Are you ready?"

"You're going to open the door? Are you fucking crazy?"

"We have to, Jim. It's the only way."

"Shit!"

"Get behind me, Brandon."

Brandon scooted behind John, still squeezing his leg, and buried his face into the back of his leg.

"Hello! Hello. I'm going to open the door." John turned the deadbolt, and then the lock on the knob clicked. He opened the door, and a giant man with a firearm smiled down at him.

"Well, hello there."

John stepped forward and felt his feet catch air as he hit the ground. His eyes fluttered open and closed briefly before they were finally sealed shut.

Chapter Twelve: The House

Sera

"Sera."

Sera opened her eyes and saw she was standing on a beach in front of the ocean. Sybil was lying on the sand with her eyes closed. The ocean tide rolled in, splashing against Sybil's body. Sera walked to her sister and had just squatted down to touch her forearm when Sybil's eyes opened. Sybil shot up and grabbed Sera's arm. The image of the white two-story house with white shutters flashed in her mind. A tall, slender man with sandy-blond hair and golden whiskey eyes turned in her direction as if he saw her watching him.

Sera woke up to sweat running down her face. Blinking, she sat up and saw double. Slowly, she lay back down and squeezed her eyes shut. Sybil's face burned in her mind.

Sybil, where are you? Are you at the white house? I don't understand. Is Sammy there? Who was that guy? I don't know. Sybil? Sybil? Please answer me. Please.

Sera closed her eyes and opened her mind, calling out to her sister. *Sybil, please answer me now.* Sera's head throbbed as she yelled the words.

In her mind, she searched, walking towards her sister's house. She reached out for the doorknob, and something pushed her back. Her body flew, and she landed back into her body in the SUV. Sera's eyes flew open, and she felt a heaviness weighing over her chest. It felt like her spirit form was being forced back into her body.

Panting, she inhaled deep breaths and whispered her sister's name once more. "Sybil." But Sybil didn't answer.

She opened her eyes, gazing at the cargo cover, and saw sunlight peeking through its surface. Exhaling, she sat up and pushed the cover up just enough to look out the window. Morning light peeked over the horizon, reflecting a shimmer of blue from the water. A slight smile brightened Sera's face as she hurriedly packed her things. She peeked out one last time before pulling the slip knot to release the door. Salty seawater filled the cab as she scooted out and put her feet on the ground. Grinning, she threw her bag over her shoulder and checked around her.

The sun's rays smiled over the horizon, glistening off the swamp moss. Sera knew she was close now — close to where her life began.

Sybil, I'm coming. I'm home. I hope you can hear me. Sera spoke to them even if they didn't answer. A slight twinge rumpled in her stomach, and worry weighed on her heart. She knew that something was wrong. Sybil only reached out to her in dreams, and Sammy was silent. A lump formed in Sera's throat as she blinked back the memories of her siblings.

Sybil, Mom, Dad, and Sam had always lived in Florida. Sera, on the other hand, couldn't wait to move to North Carolina and go to college. She wanted to be as far away from her mother as possible, and now all she wanted to do was get back to where she'd grown up.

She cupped her hand over her brow, gazing at the sun, and nodded as if greeting an old friend. She pulled on her backpack strap and began jogging. An hour passed quickly, and the swamps gradually transformed into a sandy surface with mature palm trees swaying in the wind. Drips of sweat pooled in Sera's eyes, so she stopped and washed off her face with water from her jug. She turned up the water and gulped several drinks before returning it to her bag. She grabbed her compass and held it up. *South-east.*

Sybil lived right off the coast on the beach, so she knew she would eventually make it there. Squinting, she searched along the water mirage until a bright light twinkled toward her. The nearest town's cell tower reflected off the sun, blinking at Sera. Shielding her eyes, she cocked her head to the side and saw a familiar sign. *Jet Ski and Boat Rentals Come in Today!*

Sera turned off the main road, waded through the sand, and headed towards the sign. After about a mile, she approached the back of a large building. She kicked off the sandy residue and stepped up onto an old cement road. Large potholes drooped down, holding pools of water from last night's rain. Sera stopped and cautiously headed around the back of the store towards the front.

All the stores resembled every other town Sera had passed, with boarded-up windows that read *KEEP OUT* written in spray paint. She continued down the sidewalk and realized something was different about this town.

Where's the sludge river?

There was no sludge river flowing, and it was hauntingly quiet. The town appeared abandoned, but Sera knew it could just be an illusion to lure vulnerable people in. Surveying the area, she continued walking and glanced into the stores that weren't completely boarded up. As usual, the shelves were bare, and trash littered the floor. She cupped her hands over her growling abdomen as she peered around the ghost town.

A few shopping centers down, a city limits sign flapped in the wind as if it were waving goodbye. Checking around her, Sera walked past and quickly exited the dead town.

The ominous road leading out of town stretched for miles, and the only thing she could see was the glistening glow of golden hills. She stopped, stretching up on her tiptoes, and saw a hint of ocean blue hiding behind the dunes. She looked ahead and then back over at the water and turned. Sera trudged through the sand mounds, hooding her eyes from the sun. As she drew closer to the water, she watched the aqua-marine waves roll in magically, dancing along the golden sand. Smiling, she started jog-walking towards the beach when she heard barking—

"What the?" She stopped, looking around her. The beaches were abandoned and seemed untouched for quite some time. The sounds of waves smashing into the coast echoed along the shore, and squawking seagulls drifted through gusts of wind. Shaking her head, Sera started walking again. *I'm just hearing things*—

Another round of barking echoed off in the distance, and the rolling tide sprayed mist, muffling the yips that filled the wind.

Sera stopped, holding her breath. "I know I heard some-thing."

She peered along the shore, spun her head around, and searched for the culprit. Shaking her head, she took another step and was stopped again—

A long, drawn-out round of barking sounded just over the dunes. Only this time it was an aggressive bark, deepening as it rattled on. It was as if the dog was trying to get someone's attention. Sera's head spun back and forth, looking for the beast, but there were only sand dunes.

"Okay, where the hell is that dog coming from?"

Sera walked up onto a hill of sand and slid down the other side. She trudged through sandy grass and stopped when beach houses came into her view.

Sybil. Sybil, I'm close. I can feel it.

She slowly walked along the sandy grass, searching for her sister's home, when a gunshot fired—

CHAPTER THIRTEEN: THE WHITE HOUSE

John

"John. John, open your eyes."

John's eyes fluttered open, and he looked up at Brandon. He leaned into John's ear and said, "John, wake up. Please, don't be dead."

"I'm not dead, buddy. Just—"

A cough spewed from John's mouth as he rolled onto his side. Red stained the gray carpet and dripped from his hand, which covered his lips. He looked up to see a man standing over him with a rifle and two other men ripping the apartment apart.

"There's nothing here. Just an almost empty jar of peanut butter. Fuck!" The man threw the jar across the room and put his hands on his hips.

"What do you want to do, Bob?"

Bob peered around the room and landed his gaze on John. "Where's your food?"

John shook his head and coughed again, trying to mouth the words. "We don't have anything left. We're out."

Bob shook his head and turned to the door, staring at it.

"We'll just take them with us. We can figure something out."

"Bob, we have people outside. You want to take them all?"

"Did I stutter? Let's go!"

"Okay, you heard him. Get up!"

John pushed himself onto his feet with Brandon's help and

held his hand, following their captors out the door. John looked behind him just before exiting the apartment and saw his work still sitting on the table. He wanted to sprint back inside to grab it but knew if he did, it would most likely end in his own death.

The sunlight burned John's eyes as he stepped out from under the covering of the stairs to his apartment building. It had been a long time since he'd walked out into the open without caution for what lurked around every corner. The men walked over to a group of other men holding rifles, totaling the number to ten men and a few young boys.

Shit. Brandon met John's gaze with a glazed-over stare. "It'll be okay, buddy. I promise."

John followed the group of men for what seemed like hours upon hours. The people walking in front of them were struggling to keep up the pace. A glossy fear burned in a young girl's eyes when she looked back, meeting John's gaze. John knew that if he stood up to the armed men, it would be the last thing he would do, leaving Brandon to fend for himself, and he wouldn't follow through with his mission.

Mission. That's a funny word. Is that what I'm supposed to do? Go on a mission and save mankind? The question rang in his head.

John looked down at Brandon and saw him dragging his feet, barely keeping up. John reached his hand out, grabbing Brandon's to keep him upright.

At midday, the men led them through a familiar town, stopping to search for food among the abandoned stores. John sat down on the curb, Brandon next to him. Jim stood behind them and shuffled his weight back and forth between feet.

You're almost there now. White house. She'll be there. I. Will. Lead. Her. To. You.

Then what? We save the world together. How the fuck are we going to do that, lady? Maybe I'm finally losing it, and you're a figment of my imagination. Fuck! I seriously don't know what the fuck I'm doing.

John dropped his head into his palms and rubbed his eyes. His forehead burned as his fingers glided over his skin. He pulled his hands back and met Brandon's gaze again. Brandon pointed up at John's head—when he looked down, he saw fresh blood on his fingers. *That SOB must have whacked me good. I'm still fucking bleeding. Great.*

You're not going crazy. My name is . . .

What? What's your name?

Sybil. And. I. Am. Trying. To. Save. You. I'm. Trying. To. Save. My. Sister. Sera. I'm. Trying. To. Save. The. World.

Is the world really worth saving? Say I can save the world. I have to be able to get away from these assholes first. Me and Brandon. We have to find safety from them, and then we have to find a hiding place from those things coming out of the river. It's . . . it's a lot to . . . overcome.

"You can do it, John," Brandon said, clasping his hand over John's shoulder.

"What?" *How the hell did he know what I was talking about? Is this kid—*

"You can still do it, John. It's going to be okay."

No. He. Loves. You. You. Are. The. Only. Hope. That. He. Has.

John squeezed Brandon's hand and said, "Thanks, buddy." *I love him, too.* A lump formed in his throat as he spoke the words in his mind. He didn't even think before he reacted. He couldn't bear the thought of Brandon getting hurt. He swallowed, forcing down any emotions that might show on his face.

You. Are. His. Father. Now.

Great. I'm no father. My dad died . . . I just . . . I never really had a dad. He died when I was young, and my mom didn't remarry until I was in high school. Wait, why the hell am I explaining this to you? I don't know what I'm doing anymore. I sure hope that you're real and I'm not losing it.

John glanced over his shoulder and caught a glimpse of the men still destroying the store. Then he looked up at Jim hovering over him.

Okay. Okay. I'll try. So, the white house?

Yes.

"Get up! Let's go, people."

John grabbed Brandon's hand and followed the men until the town ended. Palm trees hung overhead and sand trickled over the road as they followed the sounds of the ocean's waves calling them. The smell of the sea air made Brandon smile as he grinned at the approaching ocean. The man leading them turned and headed towards the water. They trudged through the dunes and filled their shoes with white sandy clumps. The spray of the ocean greeted them, and they stopped just far enough away from the waves not to get their feet wet. John wanted to scoot as close to the water as possible, but the men kept an extra close eye on him to prevent him from lingering.

Lady. Are you still there? So, how are we even talking right now? Are you psychic or something?

Yes.

How is this supposed to work? Do we just meet? I tell her, "Hey, I was sent here so we can save the world together," and high-five her?

Silence fell, and John inhaled a deep breath. *Great.*

A faint sound of a dog barking triggered John's attention. He looked all along the house and then back to the water. *I must be hearing things. There couldn't be a —*

Another round of yipping sounded, and this time, the dog seemed to be trying to tell someone something. John gazed back at the water and then looked over at Brandon. Brandon squatted down and tried to finger the dampened sand with his little fingers.

"Have you ever been to the —"

A loud noise echoed, bringing John's gaze back to the men.

Then another followed, and he realized that it was gunshots being fired. The giant man, Bob, cackled as he held up his gun, celebrating the fact that he shot a man in front of his wife. A shrill scream sounded over the loud thrusts of the waves, and another gunshot rang. The woman fell beside her beloved, turning the water from the tide red.

"Get up! Let's move!" One of the men yelled.

John's gaze met the lifeless man's eyes as he followed the group. He reached down and covered Brandon's eyes, pulling him close. He looked up and saw a white house with white shutters becoming closer and closer. *White house.* The words echoed in his head. *She said white house. She said that she would be in the white house.*

CHAPTER FOURTEEN: THE DOG

Sera

*S*hit. *That was close! I need to get the hell out of here.* Sera peered around her, and just as she went to stand up, she saw it — the *dog.*

A long-haired, reddish-white golden retriever-type dog with a fluffy tail and floppy ears was rooting underneath a house down the beach.

Well, shit. There's the damn dog that was barking.

Exhaling, Sera lay on her belly and shook her head. *No, I need to keep going. That dog is not my problem. Nope. I can't help the dog. Just keep going, Sera. Just keep going.*

Shaking her head, Sera crawled towards the houses and stopped, dropping into the sand. She looked back at the dog and down at the sand. Guilt ate at her. *What if the dog is all alone? What if it didn't have anyone to take care of it? I'm alone. Alone.* The words rang through her head. *Alone.* She kicked her feet and slammed her fists down into the sand before getting back onto all fours. *Okay. Fine. Fine. Fine. I'll see if the dog's okay, and then that's it. I'll just check on the dog. But that's it.*

Sera quietly crawled towards the furry dog, hiding behind the tall grass. *I don't know what the hell I'm doing anymore. I'm talking to myself again. I think I'm losing my damn mind. And now, I'm going to help a damn barking —*

As Sera approached the dog, she stopped and realized the dog was eating a dead body.

"Aw, come on, pup. No. No, pup. Gross. Hey. Psst, come

here, pup," Sera whispered.

The dog ignored her and continued to eat.

"Really, just going to ignore me. Huh?"

She stayed on all fours, crawling past the dog towards the back door. Glancing at the house's frame, she realized it was a white two-story. A vision struck her heart, jolting her to stop. *It's a white house with white shutters. It's the house. Sybil? Sybil, are you there? I'm outside. I'm here. Please answer me. Please?*

The dog looked up and cocked its head to the side, watching Sera. She reached the back door, stopped, looked around, and listened at the door. Then she gently turned the knob and took a step inside. The dog darted past her, nearly knocking her down and slamming the door into the wall.

Shit.

Sera stopped, holding her breath, and listened. The room was dark and appeared to be the kitchen. She slowly entered the house and gently closed the door behind her. As she looked around, she noticed that all the cabinets were propped open and bare. She tried the faucet, but nothing came out. A loud, crunching sound under her foot sent her a step back. She pulled out her flashlight and saw broken glasses and plates covering the floor. *Shit, it's an alarm. Sybil? Sybil, are you here?*

She pulled her bowie knife out, walked through the kitchen, and entered the dining room. A long table with six chairs had a thick layer of dust covering its top. The dining room was opened to the front of the house, leading Sera to the front door. She stopped and looked through the peephole. Heavy winds from the ocean's waves wheezed against the frame as she stared into the deep blue. Behind her and in front of the door were the stairs that led up to the second floor. Across from the dining room was the family room. Sera peered into the room and saw a couch and chair sitting side by side with a tall lamp-table between them. She walked in and stopped in front of the curtain, peering out. The house was surrounded by mounds of sandy grass with some lawn chairs folded on the ground. Shaking her head, she had just turned to go back to the stairs when her foot kicked something on the floor. She looked down to see a little red truck rolling along the hardwood. She walked towards it and stopped just a foot away from picking it up.

It's clean. Sera squatted down and examined the car more closely. The toy appeared to be free of dust, and as she peered down at it, she realized that the couch had indentations across its cushion where someone had sat down.

Sera shot up onto her feet and spun around. *Shit. Sybil! Please! What the fuck is happening. Please, answer me!*

She slowly walked towards the front door and noticed a door down a short hall next to the stairs. The hallway was eerily dark as she slowly walked up to it. Quivering, she turned the knob until a loud click thumped in the wood. The smell of rotten death hit her as she opened the door. She raised her beam, cutting through the darkness, and saw the bed sitting against the wall attached to the door. She walked into the room and saw a decomposing body lying atop the blankets of the bed. The person's hands were folded across their stomach as if they just died in their sleep. She covered her nose and peered down at the corpse. Sera's shoulders slumped, and she exhaled slowly.

Sybil. Where are you? Are you even in this house? I don't understand. I thought you were . . . please, just answer me.

Sera walked back out of the room, closing the door behind her. She hurriedly walked away from the door, and as she turned to stand in front of the stairs, a loud thump sounded from the second floor.

Upstairs. Someone's upstairs. Is that why the dog ran into the house so quickly? Sybil?

Sera scanned around her and then looked back up to the second floor again. *Sybil?*

She gripped the banister and took a step up. A dark shadow flashed along the door of one of the rooms. *I know someone's up there. Sybil? Please?*

Clicking rattled along the floor, and it sounded like something jumped onto a bed. *The dog.*

Shaking her head, Sera inhaled deeply and walked up the stairs. As she trudged higher, her footsteps creaked louder and louder, alerting whoever was in the room that she was coming.

Sera stopped and exhaled loudly before speaking. "Hello. Hello."

The dog ran out of the room doorway, walked up to the banister, and woofed at her. The pup looked back at the door it had just exited, down at Sera, and barked again.

Nodding, Sera said, "Okay, furry pup, I'm coming."

The pup anxiously ran back into the room and paced back and forth from her to the room. Sera stopped right outside the door and inhaled a deep breath.

"Hello."

She waited a minute and then tried again.

"Hello. Is anyone there?"

Sera inhaled again and stepped into the room. The dog's feet clicked along the hardwood floor, and it hopped onto the bed again. As soon as Sera saw what the dog was trying to show her, she felt a jolt throttle her heart. She turned away as moisture filled her eyes. She looked back to see two little boys lying in bed together, holding each other. They both looked like they had died in their sleep, too. The dog put a paw out, touching one of the little boy's legs, looked over at Sera, and whimpered. Tears rolled down Sera's face as she approached the Furry pup. She knelt and started petting the dog's head.

"You're a good puppy. I'm sorry, pup, but they're gone," Sera said, choking out the last word.

A lump rose in her throat, burning her nose as more tears threatened to fall. Looking away, she exhaled a long breath and wiped her face with her forearm. The furry pup scooted against Sera and laid her head on her chest, then lifted her head and licked Sera's runaway tear. Sera nodded and panted deep breaths as her lip quivered.

"You can stay with me, pup," Sera said.

She buried her head into the pup's neck and wrapped her arms around her. The dog lifted her head and licked her on the cheek again.

"You're a good puppy," Sera whispered as she stroked her head.

"Ugh! Wait a minute, though! No more kisses. I know what you were eating."

Sera stood up, walked to the window, and peeked out the curtains. Monstrous blue waves were crashing over the beach. She looked down into the yard and saw men looking up at her. She stepped back out of the crack of the curtain.

"Oh, shit!"

Chapter Fifteen: Finding Sera

John

The group stopped right in front of the house, and John looked up and saw her. A woman with fiery red hair was standing in front of the window on the second floor. Her crystal blues glistened in the sunlight as she gazed at the sky. She shifted her weight and looked down. Her already fair skin turned a ghostly white just before she spun out of sight.

John's heart skipped a beat the minute her fluorescent eyes gazed down at him. He was drawn to her. As if she was the one he had always been looking for but . . . never found until now. Breath caught in his chest, and for a brief moment, he felt like he couldn't inhale air. She was . . . perfect. *It's . . . it's her. It's Sera.* He somehow just knew.

"Well. Well. Well. What a pretty little bird she is."

Oh, fuck. He saw her, too. No. No. No.

Sybil? Sybil? What do I do? The men. They saw her, too. What —

Wait for Sera. She. Will. Find. You.

Seriously, just wait. What the fuck. I can't help her. I'm a prisoner, and these men are going to find her and kill her. Not to mention again, we're fucking prisoners. And what about Brandon? I don't know what they'll do with us.

Wait. She. Will. Come. For. You. Patient.

Easy for you to say. Just wait. Be patient. Fuck!

"Come on. Come on. Let's go. Let's go."

John was pushed with the rest of the group into the house, where they huddled in a family room. The place was dark, with a little bit of light peeking through the curtains. John spotted something peeking out from under the couch. He picked it up and realized it was a little red car. He handed it to Brandon, who held the toy against his chest.

The men stomped upstairs, and after a few minutes, they were all headed back down to the family room.

"Bob wants to stay the night and put them in the basement." The man pointed at them.

Great. The basement.

One of the men opened the basement door and pushed John to lead the group down into the darkness. Once they were on the floor of the room, the men led the prisoners over to an old furnace, tying everyone up with a rope.

"Hey, don't tie her up. Let's take her back upstairs," one of the men said, his voice ringing in the darkness.

"No. No. Please, no. Please let me stay."

John looked up to see it was the girl from before. Tears were streaming down her face as she cried out. He lifted his arm as if he were going to do something but was pulled back by the tether that bound him to the furnace.

You. Can't. Help. Her.

I can't just stand here and let them —

You. Have. To. If. You. Want. To. Survive.

Is Sera . . . okay?

Yes. She. Will. Come. For. You. Soon.

John nodded.

Chapter Sixteen: Hiding

Sera

Sera put her back against the wall next to the window, trying to figure out what to do next. *They saw me!*

Her heart pounded in her chest as the air left her lungs. The walls felt like they were closing in. *Sybil? Sybil!* Sera called out to her sister again and again, but she only heard silence.

"Come here, furry pup, we have to get out of here."

The dog jumped down off the bed and then back up onto it.

"It's okay, Furry, come here."

She ran back over to the window and peeked out. The group of men from the beach was headed towards the beach house.

"Fuck! Fuck!" Sera spun around, ran over to the door, and stared at the front door. "I think we have time. We can make a run for it to the back door —"

The front door flew open, and Sera stepped back, gently closing the bedroom door.

"Hello!" A man's voice rang through the beach house.

Sera's heart pounded against her chest, and her breath caught as she tried to inhale. She stumbled forward, hitting the floor.

I'm trapped. I'm trapped. The words echoed through her mind.

Footsteps started running up the stairs, and the laughter of several men drew closer and closer.

I don't know what to do. I don't know what —

Closet. The words whispered in her mind.

Sybil, is that you? What the fuck! I've been calling, and —

Closet, Sera. Closet!

Okay, okay. I'm going.

Furry Pup started growling and jumped off the bed. The footsteps sounded right outside the door.

"No, Furry Pup, come!"

Furry backed away, followed Sera to the closet, and then jumped back onto the bed.

Frantically, Sera ran over to the closet door, opening it again.

Sybil, I don't understand. They're going to find me. There are too many of them. Please. I don't understand. The closet? Why? Please answer me! Please!

Crawl in. Deeper. Deeper. Wall. Wall. Wall. Wall!

Okay. Okay!

Sera threw the clothes over to one side of the closet and stepped inside. I don't understand, Sybil. I —

Wall. Wall. Wall. Wall. Wall. Sybil repeated it over and over again.

"I know you're up there, little bird. I'm coming for you," a man yelled right outside the door.

Sera pushed against the walls of the closet, looking for anything. Sybil's voice echoed in her mind. Her hands quivered as she ran her fingers along the walls, pushing and poking with her digits. Her nails drug along the wood, splintering her hands.

Sybil, I can't. I don't feel anything.

Sera straightened up, pushing herself into the corner of the closet.

They're coming. They're almost here.

Sera's heart felt like it was going to explode in her chest. She inhaled deep breaths, trying to calm her breathing, but her vision doubled. Panting, she used her elbows, leaned into the corner of the closet, and felt something touch her ankle. She looked down to see a piece of the wall pushing out against her foot.

What the f—

The closet wall was pushed inward at the top, which she shoved with her elbow. The bottom of the closet opened against her ankle.

It's a — door.

Go! Now! Go!

Sera opened the door enough to shove her bag in and leaped out of the closet.

"Come on, Pup! Come on, sweet dog. You have to leave them now."

Furry paced back and forth in front of the bed, looking back at Sera. She wrapped her arms around the dog's body and returned to the closet. She closed the closet door behind them, shoved Furry Pup through the hidden door first, and followed closely behind her.

As soon as Sera was on the other side of the door, the man's voice rang as the bedroom door slammed against the wall.

"Little bird, where are you?"

She turned around, putting her trembling fingers under the hidden door, and pulled until she couldn't move it back anymore without crushing her hand. She stood up and gently pushed the top of the door until she'd closed it all the way.

"Little bird, the lion is here, and I'm hungry!" The man's words drummed through the room on the other side of the door.

A grumble vibrated against Sera's leg as Furry pressed against her, growling.

"Little bird! We know you're in there! Come out now, and we won't hurt you." He laughed and said, "Too much!" The group of men started laughing.

Sera turned and slid down to the floor, putting her back against the door. She wrapped her arms around Furry and waited.

The closet door slammed against the wall, pushing the things inside against the hidden door. Sera braced herself and squeezed her arms around Furry Pup.

"What the hell, Bob! You said you saw a girl up here. I think you're seeing shit!"

"I saw a girl standing in the window. And there was a dog! That damn dog that barked for over an hour! Remember, you asked where the hell that dog was coming from!"

"There's no one here! Well, except two dead kids."

"Hey, I think Bob sees ghosts."

The group of men started laughing.

"Ooh, Bob. Ghost girls." One of the men started tormenting him.

"So, what next? We need to stop for the night, anyway. Why don't we just stay here for a while? We can put the prisoners in the basement. If the sludge comes, it can eat them first."

"Fine. This is my room, and I'm not sharing," Bob said.

"You can have the haunted room," another man replied.

Sera sat and listened as the talking finally went silent. Mumbles of bickering faded off into the distance.

CHAPTER SEVENTEEN: THE HIDDEN ROOMS

Sera

The silence was deafening as Sera gazed blindly around the pitch-dark room. A pungent smell of mildew and moldy wood curled her nose as she reached into her belt for the flashlight.

Sybil? Are you in here? Sybil? Sera called out her sister's name. She'd spoken to her moments before, but now it was silent again. Closing her eyes, Sera tried reaching out for her. She tried to feel something. Anything that would help her locate her sister. She stood up in her spirit form, but something shoved her back down into her body. A steel wall rose in her mind, and she was pinned down. *Sybil! Please, let me find you, sister!*

Exhaling, Sera breathed deeply. A soft breeze blew against the roof, vibrating the loose shingles. She flipped on her flashlight, shining the light in front of her. The beam ran along the walls, following an incline that led up to a blank wall. Then she streamed the light down and stopped on another blank wall. The room wasn't actually a room at all. It was a long hallway hidden in the walls of the side of the house.

Sera ran her gaze up along the ceiling and back down to the floor, noticing that the walls and floors were all made of wood. She trailed her fingers along the flooring underneath her and felt it had been sanded down and treated. *Interesting.*

This was definitely built. Someone put care into making this hidden area and treating the wood.

She followed her beam up the incline again and stopped, staring.

Sybil? There has to be a reason why you called me to come here. I just . . . I have to figure out why.

Sera slowly rose and walked up the incline to the adjoining wall.

"Come on, Furry."

Sera inhaled a deep breath, and her chest wheezed as she exhaled. "It's . . . it's hard to breathe up here."

The slope was a lot steeper than it looked. If she made one wrong move, she could quickly lose her balance and fall backward.

"There has to be something more than just a hallway up here. It doesn't look like a storage area."

She put the flashlight in her mouth and gently pushed on the wall at the top of the incline.

"There's got to be another room here somewhere, Furry. Why would someone go to all the trouble building this without a reason? I bet there's a hidden room somewhere along this hallway."

Sera ran her hands along the wall, randomly pushing against every part before dropping her arms to her sides. She looked up and down along the bottom.

Exhaling, she turned around and leaned against the wall, looking down the incline and into the hallway. Her body slowly sank into the wood, falling backward. She caught herself and turned around with her light shining. There it was—another hidden door. She flipped off her light, put her shoulder against the door, and pushed. It was a heavy, stout door, different from the thin hidden door in the closet. Grunting, Sera used her weight and pushed again. The door spewed open, and salty sand exploded into her face. Instinctively, she drew her arm up to protect her eyes and mouth. A cough slipped out, and she covered her mouth with her hand to muffle the sound. Furry put her paw on Sera's leg and scratched, whimpering.

"It's okay, Furry Pup. Shh."

Sera continued pushing the door open enough to peek around the doorway and into the room. A stream of light flowed through the room from a small window. It was made of thick stained glass with small indentions of an oval shape inside each wooden square. The late afternoon sunlight exposed the room's dark corners, illuminating a layer of dust covering stacked boxes against the wall and bikes lying on their sides.

"We're in the attic, Furry," Sera whispered.

Her mouth gaped open as she looked back at the hidden door. It didn't have any kind of knob to enter or exit with, just a carved-out wooden hole in the wall. She would never have discovered it if she hadn't been looking for it. She took a step forward, and the floor crackled under her foot, echoing a loud creak.

"Shit."

Sera stopped and stepped backward slowly. She knew someone could have heard that.

"Someone's up there," a man yelled.

Sera turned around and headed back to her hidden door. The floor rattled, a door dropped open, and stairs unfolded down to the floor. She quickly closed the door and ran her fingers along it, frantically searching for something to pull it closed the rest of the way. The inside of the door that connected with the frame had a tiny indention where a thick fibrous rope popped out from inside the door. Sera pulled on it gently and eased the door closed. Trembling, she sat back on her rump and listened.

Footsteps stomped up the attic steps, and creaking floorboards groaned as the men walked through the small room.

Boxes and items were thrown against her hidden door, causing her to jump back. She inhaled deeply and leaned against the side wall as the attic was being destroyed. Furry laid her head on Sera's lap as she stroked her neck.

"There's nothing here, Tommy," a guy yelled.

"I'm hungry. Let's go eat."

"Okay, come on."

"I really think the house is haunted. Did you see the dead old lady on the bottom floor? It looked like she'd been there for a while."

"Rick, are you coming?"

"Yeah, I'll be there in a minute," answered a voice next to Sera's door.

Sera stared at the door, holding her breath. After a few minutes, footsteps walked away from her position and back down the stairs. She exhaled, pulled out her flashlight, turned around, and headed back down the incline toward the hidden closet door. She shined the light across from it, searching down the wall. She pointed it behind her at the closet. "This wall has the closet." Then she pointed to the attic. "This wall has the attic hidden entry, so that must mean that there's another hidden room or door along this wall." Sera faced the wall across from the closet entry and ran her beam along the wall. She walked up to it and touched the wood, pushing in and trying to see if any of the walls were like the hidden door to the attic. She walked all the way down and then turned around and tried again.

"Hmm, I'm not finding anything, Furry."

Shaking her head, Sera went back across the panels, running her fingers along the wood.

"I've got to be missing something. I know there has to be something else here. I feel it."

Exhaling, she started over, carrying her light across as her fingers pressed into the wood again.

"Wait."

Stopping, Sera ran her beam back over the wall one more time and noticed a difference. "The wood . . . it doesn't go to the floor. There's a gap, Furry. I think I found something."

She stood in front of the wall and pushed. The wood moved inward, and a gust of wind blew out the door. Hot, musty saltwater air filled the room as Sera opened the door. She closed her eyes, covered her mouth with her arm, and entered the doorway. She held up her light and saw a hidden room.

"Wow, Furry."

She gazed along the four bare walls, taking in the hundred-square-foot room. It was a safe room, just like in the movies. A wooden bunk bed and an upright dresser sat against opposite walls. There was no window or any other way out of the room except for the door she'd just used. Dust slowly settled back down to the ground, like a cloud of mist, as Sera ran her beam across the walls and then along the ceiling.

"There's a little vent at the top where the ceiling meets the wall. I guess that's why there's airflow in here."

She walked over to the bottom bunk and ran her fingers over the sheets. They were a soft cotton texture with a hint of polyester. A plump white feather pillow rested at the top of both beds, and a heavy wool blanket folded at the feet. Sera walked over to the dresser and pulled it open to see a row of dried food bags. She fingered through the bags, and a dust cloud floated into the air. A sneeze escaped, and Sera cupped her nose to muffle the sound.

"Shit."

She walked over, pushed the door to the room closed, and walked back over to the dresser. Shutting the top drawer, she opened the second to find canned foods. She slid it closed and opened the third to find water bottles. Then she opened the bottom drawer to find weapons, knives, and a can opener. "I can't believe it, Furry. It's . . . it's so much food and supplies."

Sera turned around, returned to the bed, and sat on the bottom bunk. Metal ground together as she sat on the old spring mattress. She bounced a little, lying on her side, and sank into the pillow. It had been a long time since Sera had slept on a bed, let alone with a soft pillow and clean sheets. Furry jumped up and lay up against her body. She reached down, pushed her bag under the bed, and pulled the covers over her and Furry. Her eyes blinked close, and she let sleep come.

Chapter Eighteen: Trapped

Sera

Sera opened her eyes, and darkness surrounded her. She fingered the bedding underneath her for the flashlight, but it wasn't there. A sharp pain pierced her side, doubling her over. She knew she needed to use the restroom soon.

"Furry, where are you, pup?" She rolled over, kicking her feet out of the covers. A loud thud hit the floor, and the flashlight started rolling away. Exhaling, she slithered off the bed and reached her fingers out, searching for the light. Her heavy panting echoed off the walls of the quiet, tiny room, sending chills down her spine. She stubbed her finger into something hard and realized it was the dresser's leg. A cool breeze ruffled Sera's hair back and jolted her upright. Shaking her head, she held her breath and frantically searched for the light. She reached past the dresser and found it wedged between it and the wall. Trembling, she sat up and clicked it on. Her breath caught, and she froze when her beam landed on the door. *What the fuck! It's opened.*

A cool breeze blew in her face, pushing the door open slightly more. Sera slowly backed away, facing the door, and reached for her knife under the pillow. When the door pushed open, she stood up and inched closer to the opening. Furry's snoot poked in first, and she walked up to Sera and pawed her leg.

"Oh, Furry. You scared the shit out of me." Sera lowered the knife and patted her chest. Furry cocked her head back and forth with her tongue hanging out on one side. "How did you open the door?"

Sera walked over to the door, looking out both ways. A cool breeze pressed against her face, blowing salty residue over her lips.

Where the hell is the wind coming from? She looked up at the attic door and down at the closet door. *Closed.*

A loud gust of wind whooshed against the roof of the house, squealing as it begged to come in. Sera pushed the knife into the belt of her pants and headed for the attic. Another burst of wind blew against Sera's brow as she drew closer to the hidden entry. Furry pawed at Sera's calf and whimpered.

"What?"

Furry nudged Sera with her snoot and huffed.

"Shh, Furry. I know. I know. I need to go, too."

Sera pressed her face against the door, listening in. A sharp pain pinched in her side, and she doubled over. She looked down at Furry, exhaling deep breaths, and looked back up at the door.

She pushed against the door, slowly entering the attic. The room was dark, with a trickle of moonlight peeking in the window, and the exit to the second floor remained open. A man's voice halted Sera mid-step as she crawled towards the door.

"I'll go down and get the girl, and you—" The man's voice trailed off as the stairs to the house rattled under his feet.

Sera crawled over to the attic's opening and peeked into the hole, slightly hanging her head down. Candles were lit on the table next to the front door, and another small light flickered in the direction of the family room. Two men whipped past as she leaned over. She lurched back, dropping to the floor. Furry walked beside her and sniffed her ear before walking a few feet away and squatting down to pee.

After a few minutes, she scooted her body from the door and turned toward the window. Sera eased beside the window, peeking out. Men walking in pairs of two were holding rifles and guarding the house's perimeter.

Fuck! There are men everywhere.

Sera sat down on her rump, leaning against the wall. The moonlight peered into the window, showing enough light to look around the room. A sharp pain shot through her stomach, doubling her over again. The sensation of her business was about to explode if she didn't find something soon to relieve herself. Sera's head whipped back and forth, and she spotted several boxes and an old bucket sitting against the wall. She pulled out the bucket, ripped the lid off, and hovered just before her body unloaded.

Exhaling, she looked over to see Furry waiting in front of the hidden attic door.

Once she finished, Sera returned to the boxes near the wall and found some old jeans. She cleaned up the Furry's mess and sealed the bucket. Then she shoved it all into a corner and looked around the room. A few more boxes were labeled pictures, and two toddler bicycles were huddled in the opposite corner of where she put the poo bucket.

Shaking her head, Sera was heading back towards the hidden door when a blood-curdling scream jolted her to stop. She looked towards the attic door, waiting for someone downstairs to say something. Then another scream howled, and this time it was coming from right below her. A light flashed, beaming beneath her feet. A perfect circular peephole was drilled so that whoever built this house could see into the room.

"Please! Please no! Please, sir, no, no, no!"

Exhaling, Sera stared down at the hole and gasped. Breath caught in her throat as she tried to inhale. She knew in her heart what was taking place beneath her and didn't want to see the horrors being committed below. She looked over at the hidden door, squeezing her eyes closed, and started crawling towards it. Stopping in mid-crawl, Sera let her fingernails press into the wood of the floor, aching as her digits screamed in pain. Burning bubbled in her stomach, and she slowly turned and crawled back over to the crack in the floor. Hesitating, she stopped before looking down and shook her head. She exhaled, swiped away the dirt from the flooring, and looked in. A giant man was nude, standing over a young girl with an erection. She was tied to the bed frame, thrashing back and forth like a little rabbit caught in a trap. He hit her with the back of his hand and hovered over her naked body, laughing.

"No," she screamed. "Please, no!"

Sera shot up, shaking her head. She couldn't watch this. Not now. Not ever.

She closed the hidden door to her attic behind her and went back to her safe hideaway. The girl's screams echoed through the house. She shook her head and pushed the door shut. Shoving hard against the wood, she secured the door, and the young girl's screams were a distant noise.

Sera opened the top drawer and grabbed the cereal. She opened the bag, cupped a handful, and threw it in her mouth.

"Ugh, this tastes awful."

She held the flashlight and tried to see the expiration date, but everything was written in another language. As she chewed slowly, she opened the third drawer and popped a bottle of water open. She turned it upside down and chugged it, letting it flow down her neck and shirt.

Gunshots fired, and the flooring underneath Sera's feet shifted. She stumbled forward and stood before the door with her hands on the frame. The house shifted underneath her feet again, and another round of gunshots sounded beneath her. Screams followed, and a deep, monstrous growl echoed as the foundation crackled and groaned.

Furry pawed at Sera's leg and pressed her body against her. "I know, pup. We're going to be okay." Sera heard the words as she spoke, trying to convince herself that it wasn't as bad as it seemed. Her heart pounded in her chest as she braced herself against the door.

Sybil, are you there? Please answer me. I'm trapped.

Trapped. The words echoed in her head, over and over again. Sera dropped down, sliding her back against the door, and wrapped her arms around Furry. The house shuttered beneath her as she trembled against the floor. Minutes had passed, but it felt like hours. Sera continued to chant *Sybil,* but she only heard silence. The house's quivering walls slowly eased back down and settled into the earth as if nothing had ever happened. Sera turned and put an ear to the door. Furry's hot breath burned Sera's cheek as she leaned in, listening.

She turned to Furry and whispered, "Do you think it's safe, Pup?"

Furry licked her face and continued panting.

Sera stood up, slowly opening the door. She flipped the light on and shined it in front of her. A haze lingered in the hallway, reeking of death and smoke. The smell of the sludge had already tainted the house.

The attic door to the house was still ajar when she entered the room. A small glimmer of light flickered from the bottom floor. Sera crawled over to the opening, looked down, and saw the candle by the front door turned over with wax surrounding it. She backed up, crawled over to the window, and peeked out. The men who were there before guarding the side of the house were absent, but as she feared, a new visitor had taken up residence right next to the house's foundation. Sera's breath caught in her throat when she whispered the words.

"The river."

It was only a few hundred feet from the house, flowing at full force as if it had always been there. She gazed down into the rapids of death and was mesmerized by its sheer strength, how it could fully construct a new direction with its sludge, and close in around the house within a few minutes.

Sera looked back, and Furry was at the hidden door, cocking her head from side to side. Furry's gaze reverted to the floor just as a bright light shined through the newly discovered hole. Sera slowly crawled over to the spot and looked in to see the man from before fully dressed. He walked from the door to the bed and lay down, pulling the covers to his chin. The girl was no longer in bed with him or in the room. He leaned over and blew out the candle's light beside his bed.

Sera sat up, staring over at the window. She crawled back over and looked out again. The sludge river was stretched from one end of the house, going all the way to the other end. *Is the sludge boxing us in?*

Sera's heart fluttered in her chest as she scrambled over to the hole in the floor again and then back to the attic door. She bit her bottom lip and looked back at Furry.

Before anyone notices, I can sneak down and look out the family room window and be back here. I need to know if I can get out of here.

Sera crawled over to Furry and then looked back at the door.

If I close the hidden attic door, I won't be able to get back to Furry, and I can't leave her out here. She shook her head and rubbed her face. Shit. Maybe I shouldn't go. But we could be getting trapped in here. I don't know what to do. Damnit. Sybil! Sybil! Answer me! You're the one who led me here. What the hell am I supposed to do?

Exhaling, Sera rubbed her face, squeezing her eyes shut. *I'm just . . . yep, I'm going to do it.* She crawled back to the hidden room and pulled out the bottom drawer. She grabbed two knives and put them in each boot.

She looked down at Furry and squatted. "I'll be right back. I need to see how bad the situation is for us. I need to know if we're . . . trapped." Furry pawed at Sera's shoulder and licked her in the face. Nodding, Sera stood up and directed Furry to stay inside the room.

Snoring greeted Sera as she pushed open the door to the closet. She quickly entered the room and slipped out, closing the door behind her. The hallway was bare, with dark shadows clinging to the corners of the house. Sera slowly tip-toed along the second floor and down the stairs.

A faint light flashed, peeking through the family room curtains and drawing Sera's gaze over. Peering around her, she drifted over to the curtains and opened them just enough to see some men standing in front of the house. Flames from a large bonfire were peaking high in the sky, and two men were standing on either side of a wooden platform, turning meat on a spit.

Oh. Shit.

Sera's heart dropped into her stomach. She felt the acid bubbling up and threatening to spew. Squinting her eyes, she focused on what the men were turning on the spit and realized it was a person's body roasting in the moonlight. *A girl. It's . . . it's the girl.* Her skin was charred black, and her head, which was once full of blonde hair, was now bald and fizzing.

Two men walked into Sera's view, both holding rifles. She stepped back and watched as a woman stumbled in front of the men and tripped onto her knees.

"Get up!" One of the men said, poking the woman in the back.

The woman wobbled upright and walked towards the spit. A rumble underneath Sera's feet shuffled her balance and knocked her back from the window. She steadied herself, stepping back towards the window, and saw the woman running from the men, her body hunched over as she ran away as quickly as she could. One of the men raised his gun, and a loud gunshot rang. The woman stopped and shuddered as she fell forward on her stomach. The two men holding the rifles began pushing each other, and one of the men reared back and punched the other in the face. The man hit the ground—

A loud demonic scream echoed from afar, and the men froze. The woman whom they'd shot minutes before began rising up onto her feet. Her body slowly turned around, and she cocked her head to the side. She opened her mouth, and black sludge oozed out of her mouth and nose as the same sound the sludge river made bellowed from her lips. The men scattered around the fire and headed towards the front door.

"Shit!"

Sera sprinted up the stairs and slowly opened the door to the bedroom to see the man who had been sleeping minutes before had opened his eyes. "Well, hello there, little bird. I knew you would come back to play."

Fuck! Sera locked the door behind her and nodded. *Fuck it. He's a piece of shit, anyways.*

The man stood up, and his giant body towered over her little five-foot-two frame.

Well, shit. This is going to be a challenge.

His vast erection protruded from his loose-fitted pants, and he held out his arms as if she was going to go to him willingly. She looked down at his length and smiled. The man nodded, and she stared up at him innocently. He unzipped his pants and released his member, nodding. He grabbed his manhood and shook its girth towards her mouth. She smiled and stared at his groin, gripping his penis with one hand. She licked her lips, reached into her boot, and pulled out her knife. She looked up at the man, smiled, and cut off his penis. Blood squirted and sprayed Sera in the face and mouth. She grinned and lunged backward. The man wobbled back and forth as he reached down and cupped the empty space where his cock was. Blood flowed down his giant hands and pooled at his feet. He looked up at Sera, and an evil glare crossed his brow as he lunged for her. She skipped to the side and sliced the arm reaching out for her. The cut didn't slow him down, and he stomped towards her.

The door rattled, and a man's voice outside said, "Let me in! Please!"

A scream echoed from the house, and a loud crash rattled the door in its frame.

"Please — "

The man ran toward Sera, pushing her towards the windows. She dropped down, slicing into his shin, then jumped to her feet. Before he could react, she plunged her knife into the side of his throat. The man's body folded into itself, and he dropped onto his belly. Blood flowed from his neck, and a gargling noise spewed from his lips as he tried to speak.

Sera's feet slid across his blood, bringing her to her knees. She crawled away from the man and grabbed the blankets from the bed. She wiped her shoes and knees first, threw the blanket over the man, and ran to the closet door. She pushed through the hidden door and quickly closed it behind her.

She opened the door to the room and pushed Furry back as she closed it behind her, dropping to the floor in front of it. She sat against the door, and Furry crawled into her lap. Panting, she petted Furry's neck and said, "Well, Furry, we're fucked. We're definitely trapped."

CHAPTER NINETEEN: KEEP QUIET

Sera

"*Sera. Sera. Sera.*"
Sera opened her eyes, and she was standing at a door with chains on it. The chains dropped to the floor, crashing down and shattering like glass. She leaped backward and watched the door eerily open with a haunting squeak. She stepped into the room and looked down into the darkness.

A basement.

A cloud of mist blew from her chilled lips. Her teeth chattered, and goosebumps trickled down her arms as she stepped inside. One step down, and her body glided down the rest of the steps with ease. She touched her foot on the floor, and a light blasted ahead of her, shining on a man tied to a piece of machinery. He was very tall, with sandy-blond hair covering one whiskey-colored eye. He shifted his weight, and a little boy stepped out from behind him. He had brown ruffled hair with dark ebony eyes. The boy had wrapped his body around the man's leg, hiding.

Sybil? Where are you? I don't understand.

I'm not here, Sera. This is John, and you need to find him. Find. Him. Find. Him. Find. Him. Find. John. John. John.

John? Who's —

Yes. John.

But Sybil. Where are you? Where —

No! Find. Him.

Sera shot up in bed, gasping for air and blinking. The room was dark. She leaned over and searched for the flashlight. She found it under her pillow but realized Furry wasn't on the bed with her.

"Furry. Where are you, Furry?"

As she flipped the light on, Furry poked her nose at Sera's hand. She dropped her face into her palms and squeezed her eyes shut.

John. A vision of him and the little boy flashed in her mind.

I don't understand, Sybil. Why do I need to find him? Where are you? I want to find you. "I don't understand."

Furry pushed her paw against Sera's calf and chirped a tiny yip. "Okay, I know. I have to go, too. Hang on. I'm getting up."

Sera stood in front of the attic door and heard the floor creak as someone was walking around upstairs. She shifted her weight and waited for whoever was in there to leave.

A man's voice yelled behind the barrier. "Rick! What are you doing up there, man?"

"Nothing," he responded.

"Come on and help me get Bob out of there. We're going to give him to the sludge," the guy yelled.

"Okay, I'll be there in a minute."

Furry showed her teeth, and her chest rumbled a low growl. "Shh, girl. I know. We have to wait a little bit longer."

After a few minutes, the stairs creaked as someone was walking down them. Sera waited five more minutes before pushing open the hidden door. The attic door was still open, and people's heads walked by as she crawled closer to the hole, looking down into the house. She briefly peered down before standing up to do her business. Furry had already walked over to her spot and was relieving herself. As soon as she finished, a light beamed through the peephole in the floor.

She crawled over and looked in to see two men in the room, cleaning up all the blood staining the floor. A smirk crept up Sera's lips as she watched the men struggle to destroy the

105

evidence of the rapist's death.

The piece of shit deserved to die.

A loud ruckus downstairs jolted Sera to look at the attic door. A booming voice echoed down the second-floor hall and commanded the men's attention. Sera crawled over on her belly and laid down to watch the show.

"Hey, come here. Yeah, you! I want more men patrolling the house. It is going to be your job to go to the east side. Can you do that?"

A tall man pointed his finger at one of the younger men to come over. He walked to the front door, opened it, and pointed for the boy to go outside. The tall man shut the front door, turned around, and looked at the attic door. Sera's face dropped to the floor, panting.

"Too close." She exhaled and slid backward, away from the opening. She crawled over to the window and stood up, carefully looking out. The sunlight beamed into the yard, glistening off the sandy grass surrounding the house. A younger man walked out, greeting the previous men standing in the yard. The sludge river was bubbling and flowing steadily along its path as the men stood a hundred yards away, chatting with the new guard.

"There has to be a clear path leaving this house," Sera whispered as she looked outside. A guard looked up towards Sera, holding his hand up to shield the sun. She dodged the looker and hid beside the window. Exhaling, she quietly walked back to the hidden door. "Come on, Furry."

Sera pulled out cereal for her and Furry. After eating, she stretched out her limbs and did some exercises. The man from her dream haunted her mind. His whiskey eyes were staring back at her, glaring into her heart.

Who was he? Did I know him before everything happened? He seemed so . . . familiar.

Sera crawled back into bed and grabbed her compass,

pulling the picture from the clip. She opened it, and Eric's smiling face stared back at her. The image was of her and Eric lying in bed, holding each other and laughing. Squeezing her eyes shut, she tried to remember what they were laughing about, but it disappeared with the life she'd left behind after the sludge river emerged. A single tear rolled down her cheek, burning her nose. She swiped it away aggressively and folded the picture to put it back in the clip.

"I'm sorry, Eric. I wish you were here. I miss you so much."

Furry pushed against Sera's forearm and crawled into bed next to her. She pressed her cold nose against Sera's cheek and licked her damped face.

"Hey, old girl. I'm okay." Sera scratched behind her ears and closed her eyes.

Flashes of when Eric dropped into the river flooded Sera's mind. She twitched as the breath in her lungs froze. She forced a deep breath and squeezed her eyes shut as she exhaled. *No. No. No. I love you, Eric, and I'll never forget you, but I didn't leave you. You left me. You left . . . me.*

Chapter Twenty: Hidden Tunnel

Sera

"Sera! Wake up!"
Sera opened her eyes and peered through the darkness. A cool breeze pressed against her body, chilling her to her bones. A strong hand gripped her shoulder, pulling her back. She turned to see the man with sandy-blond hair gazing into her eyes. His whiskey stare brightened as a smile pinkened his cheeks.

A bright light flashed, causing her to whip back around to see she was on the beach. The man handed her a gun with a long tube on it. Sera reached for it, and once her fingers touched the device, her heart sank. A flash of the sludge beings running up behind them came into view. The man turned to fight the beings, but he was —

Sera opened her eyes and sat up in bed. A bright white light appeared before her, outlining a person's body. Sybil's body began to take shape, glistening in all white. She opened her eyes, and they shimmered a glowing pearl. She raised her arms, reaching for Sera's hands. As soon as she touched her, a vision shot through her mind like a lightning bolt. Burning pain shuddered through her, and she saw the man again.

He. Is. In. The. House. Go. Hurry. Before. It. Is. To. Late.
Sybil, I —
Now!

Sera shot up in bed, panting. The room was dark, and the blanket felt like a heavy weight over her body. A sharp pain blasted behind her eye, and a vision of the man, *John*, flashed in her mind. *John.* His name lingered over her lips. She didn't know why or how this man was so important, but she knew she needed to find him, and fast.

She stood in front of the attic door and listened. After a few minutes, she pushed it open and was greeted by the moonlight peeking through the window.

She said he's in this house. This house. It repeated over and over again in her head. *Sybil? Sybil.* She wanted her sister to talk to her so badly. *Answer me, please. Sybil. What is it about this guy?*

Shaking her head, she walked to the stairs and looked into an empty room. The room was eerily quiet, with a shadow flickering on the wall from a candle burning next to the front door.

Too quiet. She crawled over to the peephole and looked down to see that the room was empty. The door was open, and a single candle burned on the table next to the door.

"It could be a trap, Furry." *Something feels off.* She could feel the uneasiness of the house. She sat up and walked Furry back to the hidden room.

She squatted down and said, "I have to find someone. He needs my help. I'm going to go down through the attic. I don't want you to get hurt. I'll be right back. Okay?" Furry cocked her head from side to side and pawed in the air towards Sera as she pulled the door closed behind her.

She looked over at the closet's hidden door and nodded before heading back up to the attic.

A cool breeze greeted her as she stepped down onto the second floor of the house. A low hum echoed, and whistling squealed outside the front door. She slowly crept along the hallway and walked down the stairs. The house appeared to be empty, but she knew that looks could be deceiving.

What if everyone left? Sybil? Sera peered up towards the attic and remembered that she'd forgotten to check outside. *Did everyone leave? What happened? Sybil, please answer me.*

She stepped down onto the bottom floor, and a vibration under her foot sent her forward, almost knocking her off her feet. The ground trembled beneath her, and a distant growl echoed within the earth.

Oh, no.

Sera looked around and grounded herself before jogging towards the kitchen. The room was dark, with no candle to guide her. She pulled out her flashlight and slowly walked through the dining room and into the kitchen. A flash of lightning flickered through the kitchen window, and then a low rumble followed. Sera spun around the room and stopped in front of a door.

The door. The image of the door with the chains peaked in her mind. She walked up to it and felt the thickness of the chains held together by a heavy lock.

Oh, no. Sybil. Help. I don't have any way of removing the chains. Sybil?

"Hey, Rick. Where are you going, man?"

Sera spun around, not knowing where to go. *Fuck. Fuck. Fuck.*

The cupboard. Go. Inside.

Really, now you're going to answer me. You're such a bitch!

Sera opened the cupboard door. It was a flimsy door that folded towards her like an accordion. The tiny doorknob wiggled when she grabbed the handle and made a loud crackle as she pulled the door open. The space was tiny, with shelves covering the top half of the small space and some old boxes sitting on the floor. She walked inside and pulled the door shut behind her. Little slats covered the top half of the door, allowing Sera to look out into the kitchen. Holding her breath, she watched as two men entered the kitchen. The tall man whom she'd seen previously walked in first and stopped at the kitchen window, peering out. Then a second man entered and stood behind him with his finger pointed.

"Rick, are you even listening to me?"

"What? What? What?"

The tall man whipped around and stepped into the other man's space, causing him to step back.

"I can't leave meat lying around, so I just started feeding it the leftovers. When I went out there this morning, it had moved down all the way to the end of the house, and now I'm worried we'll get locked in."

Sera's breath hitched, and she twitched a little when the guy said, *locked in*. She watched as Rick's gaze moved along the walls of the kitchen and stopped on the cupboard she was hiding in.

"Okay, let's see where it is in the morning. Let me know if it moves down the backside. We'll have to move before it gets to that point."

"Okay, Rick, I'll let you know."

Shit. He's looking at the cupboard, Sybil.

Scoot. Back.

What?

Scoot. Back.

I don't—

Now!

Sera scooted back and felt air blowing up the back of her shirt. She turned to look behind her and saw that the wall didn't go down to the floor like the rest of the walls. It had a tiny gap that only someone who knew what to look for would notice.

Sera pressed against the wall, and it began to move inward. She looked back towards the cupboard door, and the tall man's body seemed to be moving closer and closer to the cupboard.

Hurry. Hurry. Hurry!

Okay! Okay!

Sera slithered under the door and gently pushed it down behind her. She stood upright and reached out to feel four walls surrounding her. The room was snug with the same stench of salty mildew that tainted the air in the hidden room upstairs. She flipped on the light and peered around at the walls, running the beam along the confinement. Slightly pushing against each wall, she realized they were the same and weren't budging. Sera squatted down and ran her beam along the flooring of the walls, and the only one with any differences was the wall she'd just pushed through.

I don't understand –

Look. Up.

Sera looked up, and the room appeared to be a tunnel. She ran her beam back down, looked over the walls again, and found indentions carved into the wood.

Stairs.

She looked up, and the dark tunnel led to what seemed to be another door. She flipped the light off, put it in her pocket, and climbed up. Her fingers started to tremble after only three steps up. The etched-out steps were narrow and had barely enough room for her to grip with the tips of her fingers and toes. Huffing, she climbed for what felt like thirty minutes before another wall stopped her.

Oh fuck.

Drops of sweat pooled in her eyes as she shifted her weight gently from two hands to one hand. A loud grunt echoed down the tunnel as she maneuvered and pulled out her flashlight, turning it on and holding it in her mouth.

Another fucking door. Come on!

A heavy wall sat over Sera's head. She shifted her weight again, put the flashlight back in her pocket, and inhaled deeply.

"I can do this. I can do this."

Sera put her forearm across the wall over her head, planted her toes into the grooves, and pushed with everything she had. The wall groaned and pushed in slightly, so she took another step up—her foot missed, and she dangled with one foot holding on. A small yelp escaped her lips as she hung from the ledge with quivering fingers.

Okay. Okay. Okay. Sera pulled her foot up and pushed again. This time, the door slowly started to move. Dusty air spewed from the opening and dropped over Sera's head. The door opened, and she climbed the rest of the way in, dropping onto her back, panting. After a few minutes, she heard a scraping noise near her. She sat up, looked around, and realized she was back in the hidden hallway where she'd started.

Sera stood up, closed the door gently, and walked over to her hidden room, letting Furry out.

"Well, pup, I found the basement door." Sera looked back towards the door and then down at Furry. "Maybe every hidden room or area is attached to this hallway somehow."

Furry looked up at her, cocking her head back and forth.

Chapter Twenty-One: The Basement

Sera

Sera pulled out the drawer with weapons and nodded. "There has to be something here that I can use to remove those chains." She thumbed through everything until she came across a hammer and a pry bar. "Maybe." She nodded and held it up, looking at the hammer first. "It might make too much noise, but it's worth a shot, Furry."

Furry cocked her head back and forth and pawed at Sera. "What?"

Furry walked over to her and pressed her body against Sera's legs. Sera reached down and scratched behind her ears. "I know. It'll be okay, pup. I have to go back down there." *I need to save John.* Sybil's words rang in her head. *John. I hope he's worth saving, Sybil.*

Sera walked back up to the attic door and listened. The attic seemed empty, so she pushed inside and saw a flash of lightning skate across the clouds through the window. Shadows trickled along the walls, and then a low grumble followed as Sera eased the door shut behind her. She crawled to the peephole first, looking in. It was the same as before, empty with a tiny bit of light from a single candle burning on a table. Then she walked over to the attic door, looking down. The room was ghostly still as a gust of wind pressed against the front door, whistling to come in. Sera scooted back and sat up. A slight tapping behind her startled her to look back. Raindrops trickled down the glass, and then a monstrous blast of lights flashed. A downpour of water flooded from the dark sky, followed by a deep growl. The house trembled, and an angry wisp of wind screamed, proclaiming the arrival of a treacherous storm.

Sera eased over to the window and looked out to see the ocean's waves crashing against each other violently. The grounds were abandoned, and the sludge was a camouflaged ominous hole hiding amongst the dirt surrounding the house.

Shit. *Where the hell is the sludge river? It looks like it disappeared into the ground.*

Sera leaned in and tried to get a better look when something moved. A face with gleaming red eyes met her gaze. She dropped to the floor, out of view.

Shit. Shit. Shit. What the fuck.

Panting, Sera slowly rose to her feet and peeked back out again. The person was walking along the side of the house towards the front door.

Hurry. Sera. Hurry.

Sybil?

Hurry. Go. Now.

Sera stepped onto the first floor, and a chilling whistle screeched outside the house. She stared at the single burning candle, inhaling a deep breath. The front door jiggled as if someone was trying to get inside.

Oh, shit. That thing is trying to get inside.

Sera jogged into the kitchen and stopped just before entering the room. A flash of lightning shot shadows across the walls, and another growl rumbled outside. She tip-toed over to the basement and kicked something hard against the door. Looking down, her mouth gaped open.

What the fuck. The chains were lying on the ground in front of the door. *Unlocked. Why? It's a — trap!* Sera's breath caught in her throat as she swung around with her fists erect.

Shadows trickled down the walls of the kitchen, surrounding her. Another thunderous growl rumbled, and Sera peered through the kitchen into the dining room. The rooms were empty.

I don't understand. Why's the door unlocked, Sybil?

Hurry. Go. Help. John. And. The. Boy.

Sybil? But, what if it's —

Now!

Sera's fingers trembled as she opened the door. A loud creak sounded as she entered the doorway of the stairs. Gritting her teeth, she'd just begun walking down the steps when a pungent smell of rotting flesh slapped her in the face. A cough threatened, and she cupped her mouth with her hands. Another beam of floating light flashed down the dark tunnel as she entered the unknown.

Sybil, are you down here too? Sybil? Please answer me.

A rustling sound from the basement floor stopped her midstep. Swallowing hard, she waited a few minutes and then spoke, "Hello. Hello, is anyone down here?"

"Yes. We're here. Yes," a man's voice responded.

It's him. It's John. Sera knew his voice somehow. A tingling sensation quivered, and goosebumps covered her arms and legs. *Why do I know him? I don't —*

Hurry. You. Don't. Have. Much. Time.

Sybil? Are you down here, too? Sybil?

Sera hurried down the stairs, and her beam highlighted his face as she approached the bottom floor. He looked up, and it was like her dream. His sandy-blond hair was draped over one of his whiskey eyes. The tingling that had begun when he spoke grew, vibrating an electrifying feeling all over her body. She felt an instant attraction to him. A connection that she'd never felt with anyone else. Not even *Eric*.

Sera's heart pounded against her chest, draining all of the air out of her lungs. Her eyes locked with his, and she couldn't move. She couldn't speak. She opened her mouth, and her lips were parched, grinding together like sandpaper. She swallowed, pushing down the lump forming in her throat. *Pull it together, Sera. Pull it together.* Exhaling, she mouthed the words, but her voice was hushed. She cleared her throat and swallowed deeply before trying to speak again.

"I'm . . . I'm here to help you." Her tongue twisted, and she was lost for words. *Shit, what's wrong with me.*

Sybil? Sybil?

As she got closer, Sera realized he and another man were tied to an old furnace. A little boy peered around John's leg and met Sera's gaze briefly before hiding back behind him. She quivered and met John's gaze again. He slightly nodded as if he knew her. His head cocked and he forced a grin, showing his teeth. A flash of the beings coming up behind John sent shivers down her spine. She squeezed her eyes shut and opened them to John, who held up his wrist with a heavy piece of rope attached. She nodded and pulled out her knife.

Sera felt his eyes on her, but she continued to saw. She wanted to look up but was afraid. She was afraid she would get lost in his eyes and be unable to pull herself together. *What the hell is wrong with me? Why am I feeling this way? Pull it together, Sera.*

John's ropes dropped to the floor, and she looked up, meeting his gaze. She searched his face and stopped on his mouth, lingering over his luscious lips. Her eyes darted up, meeting his, and she slightly shook her head. *No. No. No. I'm not doing this. No. I can't have these feelings for him. What's wrong with me? I don't even know him. He's just — some guy.*

Sera handed John the pocketknife and let him free the other man. She took a step back and broke eye contact to look around the room. She followed her beam, breathing deeply. She wanted to try to concentrate on anything other than how John made her feel.

Sera walked around the basement, looking for anything that might give her some answers about Sybil. She stopped in front of a wall, and the smell of the river intensified. She looked back at John, and he was still working. She stared at the wall and squatted down, inspecting the flooring.

Something seems off about this room. Sybil? Sybil, are you still there?

As she gazed around the room, it seemed smaller than it should, considering the size of the house.

Sera knew this house had many secrets, and this basement was a part of that. She could feel it. Shaking her head, she stood up and inhaled a deep breath. Exhaling slowly, she spun around and saw the two men and little boy staring at her.

Sybil, please tell me where you are. I want to help you. Are you in this house? Sybil didn't answer, and Sera knew that time was running out. They had to get out of there.

"Was there a woman down here with you?"

"Yes, there were many women down here. But, one by one, the men took them upstairs." John responded with a twinge of sarcasm in his voice.

Really, asshole, I just risked my life to come and help you. Squinting, Sera stared at him for a moment and then walked closer. "My sister, she, um . . . I'm looking for my sister. She looks like me but has long blonde hair and blue eyes. My dad used to say—" Sera closed her mouth and swallowed hard. "Never mind. Let's get going."

Sera spun around and looked behind her, gazing through the opened door. Another flash of twinkling lights ran down the walls of the staircase. She flipped off the flashlight and stopped in the doorway of the basement. Rain pounded against the roof of the house, pummeling against the windows. She led them through the kitchen and dining room and headed for the stairs. Just as her foot touched the steps, screams bellowed from outside of the front door.

"Shit, hurry. Hurry!" As soon as the words left Sera's lips, the front door flew open and slammed into the wall.

Sera skipped up the steps and threw open the bedroom door, pushing everyone in first before turning to close the door behind her. As she turned around, Rick stepped into the doorway and looked up at her, meeting her gaze. He had a man draped over his shoulder, bleeding profusely from his chest. A shrill scream echoed behind Rick, causing him to push his friend to the floor and grab the front door to shut it.

Sera closed the door, locking it, and turned to meet John's gaze.

"Where are we supposed to go? Did that man see you?" John's eyes were glaring down at Sera.

She shook her head and didn't want to answer him. Shoving past him, she stomped towards the closet door. "Come on. This way."

Who the hell does he think he is? I just saved his stupid ass! He doesn't even know me. The more she thought about it, the hotter she got. Her face burned with fury, and her temperature began to rise. *I wouldn't ever put myself in danger. He doesn't even know me. I won't put up with his bullshit.*

A person's voice screamed right outside the door, and then a loud crash rattled the bedroom walls. "They're coming! They're everywhere!" Sera's gaze turned to the bedroom door, and her hands quivered as she scrambled to open the hidden door.

Gunshots sounded, and then another blood-curdling scream sent chills down Sera's spine as she pulled open the hidden door. "Come on, it's this way."

"Wait. What the fuck are you doing? We can't all hide in there. They'll find us." John grabbed Sera's arm and pulled her back.

Sera jerked her shoulder back, throwing John across the room. She stood up and glared at him. "Don't touch me!"

John lay on his back, panting with glazed-over eyes. His brows rose, and his breathing quickened as he stared at her. The boy and the other man stood there frozen, staring back and forth between John and Sera. She exhaled a long breath and said, "This way is the only way. There's a hidden room beyond this closet wall. My sis—I found it accidentally when those men entered the house."

Sera watched John as he stood up and limped back over to the closet. She glared at his six-foot-one body and waited for him to say something else to her, but he kept his mouth shut. His whiskey eyes dulled as his face eased from anger into a stoic stare.

Sera nodded slightly and inhaled a deep breath. She wanted to apologize but didn't know how. She couldn't bring herself to mouth the words. She knew she could've hurt him, but deep down, she didn't want to.

John slowly lowered himself, not breaking eye contact as he gently brushed his shoulder against hers. A flash of heat traveled down her arm and pinged her sex. Her body trembled with built-up anger and frustration. A heaviness weighed down inside her that teeter-tottered between wanting to knock him out and wanting to throw him down and mount him.

Fuck! What the hell is wrong with me?

She squeezed her eyes shut and turned to the hidden door. "It's a hidden—"

The doorknob in the bedroom rattled, and it sounded like someone or something was trying to get in. She looked back at the door and briefly met John's gaze again before first waving the little boy in.

The boy shook his head, and Sera whispered, "It's okay. I promise. It'll be okay."

Nodding, she waved the man in next and then John. She dropped on her stomach, slithered under the door, secured it, and sat against it with her back. Heavy panting and shuffling of people's feet echoed in the dark hallway.

"Where the hell are we?" John spoke.

"Shh," Sera whispered. "We don't know what's on the

other side of this door. Just wait a minute."

She breathed deeply and waited several minutes, listening at the door. Once it seemed like it was safe enough, Sera answered. "This house . . . it has a lot of hidden rooms and hidden areas. I've only discovered a few, and they were all by coincidence. I, um . . . we need to get going. Come on."

She flipped on her light and led the men to her hidden room, letting Furry out. Furry was holding a dirty sock in her mouth as she walked up to Brandon.

"This is Furry. She's my dog. I found her when I found this house."

The boy put his hand out for Furry. She sniffed it, dropped the sock, and licked his palm.

"She's very sweet," Sera said, scratching behind Furry's ears.

The boy looked up at Sera and smiled. The men looked around the room with their mouths gaping open. Sera walked in and opened the dresser drawer with food and water. She grabbed the cereal and two waters and handed them to John. He met her gaze, and their eyes locked again briefly before she turned to sit on the bottom bunk.

I'm not going to let myself care about him. No matter how he looks at me. I can't lose someone else. I can't lose . . .

She opened a water and chugged half before giving the rest to Furry. John handed her the cereal bag, and she poured a handful out for her and Furry. The men all sat down on the floor and ate quietly. Sera peered around the room before looking at John and the boy. She didn't know what to say to them. Her sister had directed her to help John and the boy, but she never said why. She never said anything else.

Bouts of thunder rolled over the house's roof. Sera jumped and wrapped her arms around her legs, staring at the door. Rain pounded the roof, and echoes of thunder vibrated against the ground again. She looked over at John and watched him as he interacted with the little boy. He was patient and caring — a good father.

Sybil? I helped him. Now what? Where are you? Are you trapped in this house?

"Ma'am? Are you okay?"

Blinking, Sera's gaze reverted to the man talking. Nodding, she stood up and walked towards the door. "Yeah, I need to use the restroom. We have to go up to the attic to do that."

"The attic?" John asked.

"Yes, this house has many hidden doors. I don't know them all yet, but I think they all lead back to that hallway."

Sera opened the drawer with weapons and grabbed a knife for each man to hold. John nodded and put his in his pocket. She dug around, found a little pocketknife, and handed it to the little boy. He smiled up at her and grabbed John's hand.

As the attic door pushed open, Sera peeked inside. She turned around and put her finger up to her lips. The men followed her into the attic as the lights flickered and danced along the walls. She walked over to the corner and pulled out the bathroom bucket. Motioning for the men to turn around, she dropped her pants and quickly did her business. Furry circled several times and did her business, too. Sera finished up and tapped on John's shoulder to go next.

Sera eased over to the window and peeked down. The grounds were still abandoned. Rain trickled along the window glass, muddling the view of the ocean. Sera dropped down and crawled over to the peephole. The room was empty, with dark shadows filling the corners of the walls. Sera sat up and glanced at the bathroom bucket and the hidden door. The men were standing there watching her.

John walked over to her and squatted down. "What room is that?"

"It's the room we were just in with the hidden closet door."

"How did you —"

"It's a long story. Come on, let's get going." Sera wanted to talk to John and tell him about Sybil, but she knew he would look at her like she was crazy. Honestly, she felt like she was losing her mind. Before everything happened. Before, when her mom was on her deathbed, she said, *"You will save them all."*

Save them all. The words echoed in Sera's head. *What does it all mean? How am I going to stop the sludge? Save everyone. I'm starting to believe that Mom didn't know what the hell she was saying. I don't even know how to kill the sludge, let alone save everyone. And John. Who the hell is this guy? Is he supposed to help me? The dream I had of him —*

Sera swallowed hard. She didn't want to think of the words. Her heart ached for him, and she didn't even know him yet. *I can't lose another person I care about.*

Sybil? Please. Please, talk to me. But she didn't, so Sera put up the bucket and headed towards the hidden door.

Lights flashed, and they all shuddered as they walked through the hidden room door. Sera stood before the bunk bed and looked at the men. "The bottom bunk is mine, and I'm only sharing with Furry."

She sat on the bed and waited for the men to decide what they wanted to do. The boy crawled up the stairs, and John looked at the other man and pointed. "You can sleep up there with him."

The older man said, "No, go ahead."

"Really, it's okay," he said.

He reached up and patted the little boy on the head. "I'm right here if you need me."

Sera reached down, pulled her blanket over her shoulder, turned onto her side, and held Furry. John lay down next to her on the floor. She turned over, facing the other way. Sera wanted to look down at him and talk, but she didn't know what to say. She didn't know where to start. Instead, she closed her eyes and let sleep come.

CHAPTER TWENTY-TWO: SITTING DUCKS

Sera

Sera opened her eyes, staring up at the ceiling of the attic. The stench of burning flesh curled her nose, turning her stomach as steam blew from her chilled lips. Slowly, she sat up and turned to see a woman lying beside her. A ratted mess of blonde hair clung to her blood-stricken shirt. She leaned over and touched the person's arm. "Hey. Are you okay?"

The woman's body twitched, seizing as it slowly staggered upright.

"Hello," Sera whispered through chattering teeth. Goose pimples rose, covering her body as she watched the woman slowly rise to sit up next to her. A dark shadow concealed the woman's face, so Sera reached her hand out. "Hello. Are you . . . are you okay?"

A hot drop of liquid hit Sera's fingers, burning through her skin, and ran down her body like lava. Shaking her head violently, she tried to throw off the hot liquid. She looked up, and glowing red eyes bore into her, glaring into her soul. Pain radiated through her body, gnawing into her frozen limbs. The woman leaned forward, and as soon as the moonlight struck her face, Sera's heart split in two. It was her. It was Sybil. Sybil lunged forward, grabbing Sera's arm. Her eyes were bloodshot, with black sludge seeping from the cracks of her mouth. She put her hand on Sera's face and opened her mouth. Screams from the deadly monster rattled through her body. Sera opened her mouth, but it was too late. The sludge was taking over, and there was no coming back.

Sera's eyes flew open, and she felt the screams escape her lips. Arms wrapped around her, and she pressed her cheek against a warm chest. Her eyes burned as hot tears flowed down her face. She cupped her hands over her eyes and sobbed into someone's warm body. Her body vibrated with pain, and finally, the tears ended. She laid back on her bed with someone's arms still wrapped around her. Their torso pushed up against her rump, and she felt hot breath on her neck. She hugged her arms over theirs, lacing her fingers through theirs, closing her eyes, and letting the dreams come again.

Sera blinked, opening her eyes to a dark room. She tried to sit up but felt the weight of someone's arm over her abdomen. She gently lifted their arm, laid it behind her rump, and turned to look back. The room was dark, but she knew it had to be John. She stared at his silhouette in the darkness, listening to him breathe. As she closed her eyes, the image of him smiling at her flashed in her mind. She quietly slid onto the floor and searched her belt for the flashlight. The loop was empty, so she ran her fingers along the surface and came across it, standing upright. She grabbed it and pushed the button to turn it on. She shined the light over, staring at John. He was lying on his side with his sandy-blond hair covering his eyes. He had a short dark brown stubble across his chin, and his torso was exposed, showing rows of muscles with tufts of hair that led down to his manhood.

A twinge of excitement sent a shiver through her body and vibrated in her groin. She squeezed her eyes shut. *Stop. Stop. Stop!* And she searched for Furry. A loud grumble from under the bed and her nails scraping against the floor alerted her that Furry was dreaming. Sera looked up and met the little boy's eyes gazing down at her.

Sera twitched, holding her chest. "Shit." She panted and said, "Hi, you scared me." She motioned for the little boy to climb down from the top bunk. "Come here, little one." She put the flashlight in her mouth and held up her hands to help the boy down. "Are you hungry?"

The boy nodded, and Sera pulled out a drawer and grabbed cereal and two water bottles. She sat down and laid everything out in front of her. Furry crawled out from under the bed, stretching her limbs as she approached Sera. She flopped into Sera's lap and laid her head against her shoulder. The little boy sat across from her and watched her set up the food. Sera handed him a handful of cereal and some water. She fed Furry and gave her some water, too.

After gulping drinks of water, the boy exhaled loudly. "Where are we?"

"In a hidden room in the house's roof, I think."

"Is this your house?"

Sera shook her head and looked around the room. "No. I don't know whose house this is."

The boy nodded his head. "Why were you crying?"

Sera's chewing slowed as she looked over at the bed at John. "I had a bad dream. What's your name?"

"Brandon."

"My name is Sera. Is that your brother sleeping?"

"No, he was my neighbor," the boy whispered and looked over at John. "My mom got killed by the sludge, and he helped me."

"What about the man on the top bunk? Who's that?"

"Jim," the man said from the top bunk. He sat up, swinging his legs over, and crawled down. He had a salt and pepper mane that draped over his thin silver glasses. His height was average, but he slumped over and wobbled with bony knees as he sat beside Brandon.

"Sera." She nodded and held her hand out to shake. "How

did you all get here?" Sera asked.

"Well, we all lived in the same apartment building," Jim replied.

Sera looked at the bottom bunk, and John took a long breath as he stirred in the covers.

"We were all captured about a week ago. The men came to our door, and well . . . we opened it. Then" —he exhaled deeply—"we ended up here."

Sera nodded. Jim looked at her as if he wanted her story, but she remained quiet and looked down at her food.

"How did you get here?" Brandon asked.

"Well, um . . . it's a long story. I'm looking for my sister, who lives in one of these houses out here." Inhaling a deep breath, she exhaled slowly and continued. "I heard a dog barking and followed her into this house, and . . . well, the men came, and I got trapped here."

Furry pawed at Sera's leg and whimpered.

"Yeah, me, too, Furry." Sera looked over at the door and exhaled. "We need to go to the restroom. Do you need to go?" Sera asked.

Brandon and Jim nodded.

"Do you want to get him up? What's his name?" Sera asked Brandon. She didn't want to let on that she already knew.

"John," Brandon replied. *John.* The sound of John's name made Sera's heart quiver. She pressed her hand against her chest and nodded.

Brandon walked over and shook John. He sat up quickly, looking around in a daze. His hair was sticking up on one side and slicked down on the other, covering his eye. Sera snickered, walking to the door and opening it. She flashed the beam down the hall, showing that the doors were still intact. She walked up to the attic and listened for a long moment before pushing the door open.

A warm ray of sun greeted her as she crawled in. She

127

pulled out the bathroom bucket, looking back at the men. They all turned around quickly and gave her privacy while she finished doing her business. Once everyone finished up, Sera turned to walk to the window when John touched her shoulder. She stepped out of the view of the window and looked up, meeting his gaze.

"Have you found a way out of here yet?" John asked.

"Yes and no. I, um . . . I'm not sure if we can make it. And I have to find my sister. You said you don't remember seeing her in the basement with you?"

"No, I said I didn't know. There were a lot of different girls, and I honestly don't know if one of them was your sister."

"She looks just like me but has long blonde hair instead of red." His gaze raked over her body, and he lingered on her red hair before shaking his head.

Exhaling, Sera pointed. "Then I have to find a way to go to her house. It's right over there somewhere." Sera knew it was risky, but she had to find her . . . *find her*. The words hung in her chest. A lump formed in her throat, stealing the air from her lungs. She didn't know what to expect. The minute Sera crossed the barrier of the basement to retrieve John, Sybil had stopped talking to her, and she couldn't help but have this uncanny feeling that something was seriously wrong. She looked down, whispering to herself, "I have to find her."

Sera looked back at John, shook her head slightly, and said, "There's something else. I think one of the men saw me yesterday when they rushed into the house—"

"Fuck! I knew it! So it's just a matter of time before they come up here looking for us." John rubbed his eyes and aggressively swiped his hand through his hair.

"Really? It's not safe anywhere anymore."

"Yes, I'm aware, but we're trapped up here just like we were in the basement."

"I don't know if you've noticed, but many people and

things are trying to get up here to kill us right now. So you'll have to be a little more specific. And I didn't—"

Jim stepped in between Sera and John. "Arguing isn't going to help anyone. Keep your voices down."

"You know I didn't have to help you. I wouldn't have if it weren't for—" Sera stopped herself before revealing too much. She didn't know John and what he was capable of.

Huffing, John stood glaring down into Sera's eyes. Then he turned away with his hands on his hips, mumbling something under his breath.

Sera walked over to the window to peek outside. Two men were back at their stations, guarding the side of the house.

"We better get back to the room. I don't like to be up here during the day. I only go out at—" Sera took a step backward and ran into something. She whipped around to see John gazing down at her with intensity in his eyes. A sensation shot down to her loins, and she craved his touch. Her hands had a mind of their own and started to reach for his abdomen to pull him closer to her. She took a step away from him, and his sandy-blond hair trickled down over one of his eyes as his lips parted. He licked his mouth slightly and exhaled loudly. She stared at his lips and felt her body freeze.

Pull it together, Sera! He's an asshole. Stop. Stop. Stop.

Gritting her teeth, she growled as she pushed past him. "Watch out." Her insides were on fire. She ached for him. She wanted to feel his weight on top of her. She wanted to feel his length inside her. Squeezing her eyes shut, she pleaded. *Stop. Stop. Stop.*

Why? Why him? Why now when the world is falling apart? Why, Sybil? You bitch, answer me!

Anger rushed through her, burning her insides. She didn't want to be attracted to him, but she was. She didn't want to feel anything for him, but she did. She just wanted to find her sister. She just wanted everything to go back to normal. As it was. With *Eric.* Not him.

Shaking her head, she made a wide birth away from John and squatted down to crawl over to the peephole in the floor. Tears welled in her eyes, and she felt her bottom lip quiver when she forced a deep breath.

Stop it. Stop it. Stop. Stop. Stop. She dropped her face into her hands and rubbed her eyes until they stung. *I'm so tired of this, Sybil. Please answer me. Please.*

"Is she crying again?" Brandon whispered.

"No, buddy, she's—"

Sera peered down into the hole. The room was fully lit from the window, but the space was empty. She inhaled a deep breath and released before pushing herself to her feet. As soon as she was on her feet, she met John's gaze. It felt like he was staring into her heart. She wanted to look away, but she was frozen in his gaze. She felt him looking into her soul. She closed her eyes and turned away, walking towards the hidden door to return to the hidden room. When she opened the door, an image of the red eyes glaring up at her stopped her in mid-step.

"Wait." Sera stopped, turning to go back to the window to peek out. She looked back at John, and then she looked out the window. "The sludge river. It—"

"What?" John said, walking towards her.

"Never mind, let's just go back to the room."

John grabbed her hand and said, "Wait! What were you going to say?"

She looked down at her hand and then met John's gaze. He gripped her fingers gently as if he was being endearing. He quickly dropped her hand and reverted his eyes towards the window as if embarrassed for touching her. A slight twinge curled her lip, and she said, "Let's go back to the room, and we'll talk about it."

Once they were all seated back in the hidden room, Sera pulled Furry into her lap and ran her fingers through her fur. She peered around the room at everyone and stopped her gaze on John.

"I don't know how to say this, so I'm just going to say it. I have a theory."

"Okay, let's hear it." John's sarcasm had returned.

Dick. Sera exhaled loudly and continued, ignoring his twinge of pessimism. "John, have you noticed that when it rains, the sludge river goes down into the earth?"

"No, we stayed in the safety of our apartment at all times and didn't get out unless we had to."

"John, didn't you go out to find science stuff to kill the—"

"Brandon!"

Sera glared at John. *What?*

She turned to look at Brandon. "Wait, what?"

"John said that he's going to find a way to kill the sludge because it killed my mom. He said he couldn't bring my mom back, but he went to his apartment and got all the stuff to be a scientist."

"Brandon!"

Sera and John's eyes locked for several moments before Sera broke her gaze. She now realized why her sister had directed her to him. *He was the key. But how? Sybil, it would be really great if you would say something right now. Anything. Please.*

Sera rubbed her eyes and finished what she had to say. "When it rains, the sludge river burrows deep into the earth and sends out its people or what I call them—beings." She peered around the room and then met John's gaze. His furrowed brow softened, and he seemed intrigued by what Sera had to say. "When I went to go look for my sister . . . the night I found you . . . I looked out the window in the attic, and one of those things was staring up at me with blood-red eyes. The river behind the being was an empty black hole, and the beings were emerging to the surface, crawling out of it to attack this house."

Sera looked around the room again, searching for an easy

way to finish explaining her theory. She exhaled another long breath and continued. "I think the human skin acts as a barrier, protecting the sludge beings from the rain. I think the rain harms it. Water harms it. Why else would it recede deep into the earth and send out the beings to . . . hunt?"

She waited a minute and said, "I think the only safe place to travel once we leave here is along the ocean, on the beach. If we stay along the shoreline, maybe we can find a boat. I don't know . . . that's all I've got. That's my theory."

John shifted his legs and met Sera's gaze. He swiped the loose strands of hair draped over his eye and said, "Well, that's not much of anything. You basically said that you think water harms the river and beings, but the beings are still attacking everyone and killing them. So basically, you've got nothing."

"Seriously, since minute one, you've been a total dick to me, and all I'm trying to do is find my sister and get the hell out of here. I could've left you down there to rot, but she told me, I—"

"What? Who told you what?"

"Nothing! It's nothing."

Shaking her head, Sera peered around the room. Although she didn't want to look at John, her eyes were drawn to him. *Why does he have to be such a jerk? I've never even met him, and yet he's still so damn egotistical. If I hadn't saved his stupid ass, he would still be down there, rotting.*

He glared back at her and huffed long, heavy breaths. His mouth opened, and she knew he would say some other smart-ass remark. She braced herself, wishing she hadn't said anything at all.

"Sera, even though your theory is stupid, it's possible that you're right."

Sera's mouth dropped. She was ready to argue, and instead, she exhaled a deep breath and shook her head. *Well, shit. Okay, then.*

John nodded and looked at the hidden door as if calculating something. He met her gaze briefly and said, "We'll have to test your theory somehow. It might be the only way to escape here."

Another thing dawned on Sera. Nodding, she said, "When they walked you in, did you see the sludge river go completely around the house? I saw the river outside the attic window, but where else does it flow down? Is it closing in around all sides? Do you remember?"

"I don't know about all sides. The river wasn't flowing down the front yet."

Sera stood up and paced back and forth in front of the door. She chewed her thumbnail and stopped. "Shit. Okay, I need to go out and look to see exactly where the river is flowing. Then I can plan an escape." Sera looked down at John and said, "Once we find a way out of here, I can go over to Sybil's house, and—"

"Sybil?" John's voice choked as he spoke her name.

He knows her. Sera knew it the minute he said it. *Did she speak to him, too? Sybil? Sybil?*

"Did you see her? Do you know her?" Sera rushed, speaking the words as fast as her mouth could move.

"No." His lips pursed together, and he shook his head.

He's hiding something.

"I can't leave without her."

"Have you talked to her recently?" John asked the last part slowly, as if he had.

Sera held John's gaze and waited for him to say something else. She felt him holding back, and she knew that he knew something about her sister.

"No." She shook her head and sat back down with Furry. *He's lying to me. He's lying.*

Sybil? Sybil? A sinking feeling began to burn in the pit of her stomach. Sera was afraid of what everything meant. Deep down, she knew what it meant if her sister didn't answer her anymore. *Sybil, please answer me. Please.*

John's voice startled her when he spoke again. "How are we going to get outside without being seen?"

"We wait until right before dark. We should all lie down and try to get some rest."

John nodded and helped Brandon back up onto the top bunk. Jim followed, and Sera lay down on the bottom bunk.

Sera opened her eyes and looked down at John one last time before flipping off the flashlight.

"I hope you're right, Sera."

Sera nodded. "Me, too."

CHAPTER TWENTY-THREE: THE TUNNELS

John

W hen John opened his eyes, a bright light glistened under the hidden room door. He sat up from the cold, hard cement floor and peered through the darkness, trying to see if the light had awakened anyone else. The bunk bed creaked, and Sera's body shifted to the other side, looking away from the door. His gaze ran up the bed, and a soft huff of breath escaped Brandon's mouth.

John's eyes reverted to the door, and the light appeared to be moving along the crack between the floor and the bottom of the door. He slowly rose and walked to the door, listening before he opened it. As soon as the door began to open, the light flooded into the room, blinding him at first.

John. The woman's voice spoke his name. It sounded almost musical, like a piano playing a note, humming his name at a low key. John. She spoke again, sounding further away from the room now. He turned, leaving the room, and there she was. Sybil. He didn't know how he knew it was her, but he did.

He entered a dark room with all the curtains drawn. Sybil was lying in the center of a giant king-sized bed with her eyes closed. The bright white light began to fade, and it was just her, lying there, sleeping.

John walked up to the bed, reaching out his hand to shake her awake. He leaned in and was almost close enough to touch her when she opened her eyes. They were gleaming a pearl white and bulged from her face. She shot up in bed and grabbed John's arm. A burning *sensation shot from his arm and ran through the rest of his body. He began to quiver, and a sea of flashes filled his mind – a whirlwind of images of Sera and the things that were to come.*

Sybil's mouth opened, and her voice deepened, echoing as she spoke. "You're the one who saves her." Images burned through his mind, slicing into his flesh. He dropped to the floor, still attached to Sybil's grip. His body began to glow a pearl-white light, and when he thought that he couldn't take any more pain, she let go. His body fell through the air, tickling his stomach as he free-fell –

John opened his eyes and shot upright. The darkness of the room blinded his vision. Shivering, he rubbed his face and scrubbed his eyes — an image of Sybil gleaming on the bed burned in his mind.

"Sera, are you awake?"

A loud creak echoed through the room as she exhaled a deep breath. "Are you okay?"

"Yeah. Sorry, I'm just . . ." John rubbed his eyes until they hurt. "Can I use the flashlight? I need a drink."

Another creaked rattled, and Sera's hand bumped into John's arm. "Here."

John flipped on the light and walked over to the drawer. He grabbed water and gulped loudly, letting water drizzle down his chin. Gasping, he pulled the water back and handed it to Sera. She sat up and met his gaze briefly before taking a small drink. She poured the rest for Furry to drink and dropped onto the floor, stretching her limbs.

John stared down at her as he shifted from one foot to the other. His gaze reverted to the door and then back to her before he rubbed his eyes again.

"You're the one who saves her," Sybil's voice echoed in his mind.

I know I saw her. The dream. It felt so . . . real. What the hell does it all mean? I don't even know Sera and can't help feeling something for her. I've never felt this way about anyone. Ever. I don't . . .

I don't understand. I need to get it together. Get it together, John.

John exhaled a long breath and gazed down at Sera. She was bent at the waist, touching her toes. He looked up at the top bunk to check for Brandon, but he was still asleep. Jim's body twitched slightly, and then a loud breath exhaled from his lips.

John. John. Her voice echoed in his mind. Images of Sera and him making love flashed and a machine. *A machine? What the fuck?*

"I need to get everyone up and get going. It should be getting dark outside now."

John jolted and twisted to look at Sera. She was standing before him, gazing up into his eyes. Her fiery hair surrounded her face, curling under her sharp jaw and accentuating her ocean blues. She furrowed her brows and turned away from John, looking at the bunks.

She hates me. I don't blame her. All I've done is act like a jerk towards her. I don't want to care about her. It just . . . works. Nothing more. We need to find a way out of here, and then it's back to finding a way to kill the sludge. I'm professional. I don't have time to feel this way.

Brandon sat up in bed and stared down at John.

"Hey, buddy."

"Hi, John." He swung his thin leg over the railing and hung from the top bunk. John walked over and helped him down the rest of the way. Brandon sat down while John pulled out the drawer and gave Brandon cereal and water. As he ate, Jim crawled over and sat down.

"I'm going to go now. The sun should be going down," Sera said as she walked to the door. "Stay in here, and don't open the door for anything. I—"

"Hey, I'm going with you."

Sera stopped at the door and shook her head. "No."

"Yes."

She propped her hand on her hip and glared at John with

furrowed brows.

She looks so sexy when she does that. No, John. No. John squeezed his eyes shut. *Pull it together. Stop thinking about your dick.*

"No. I work alone."

"Well, not anymore. I'm going." *She's not going anywhere without me.* John walked over to the door and reached out to open it.

Sera put her hand on the door and held it shut. "No. Damnit, I—"

Jim stepped up and said, "Maybe you shouldn't go alone. Just in case something happens."

John gazed into her beautiful blues, and he felt his heart skip a beat. *What the hell is happening? Why the hell is this woman doing this shit to me? Fuck.*

Sera exhaled loudly and slowly backed away from the door. "I'm trained. Are you?"

She's challenging me. John's loins peaked, and a shiver traveled through the rest of his body. *Oh, this woman is going to be the death of me. Don't get an erection. Don't get an erection.* John breathed deeply and shook his head. "I can fight."

"Really? The old man said that you just let the men into your house. Why in the hell would you do that if you knew how to fight? And from the looks of it, your face says everything from an almost healed black eye."

"I had to let them in. It was the only way." John stopped himself. He couldn't reveal that he was nuts, talking to a woman whom he'd never actually met except for in his dreams.

"That makes no sense." Sera started to pull the door open to walk out, and John grabbed her wrist. "Wait for me. Please. I want . . . I want to go. Please." He gazed into her eyes, softening his grip, and slid his fingers along her hand before releasing his hold.

The anger in Sera's eyes eased, and she opened her mouth

to respond, but something stopped her, and she nodded.

Brandon wrapped his arms around John's leg and whimpered a small cry. He looked up and blinked a tear as it rolled down his cheek.

John squatted down, wiped the tears, and whispered in his ear, "It'll be okay. I'll be back before you know it."

Nodding, Jim walked over and grabbed Brandon's hand.

Sera squatted before Brandon and said, "Brandon, will you look after Furry while I'm gone? She'll be worried and needs you to take care of her."

Brandon nodded and wrapped one arm around Furry as he sat on the floor beside her. She licked his face and leaned against him as if hugging him. John looked down at Sera, meeting her stare. A slight smile curled her lips before she tightened her mouth shut.

Sera led the way out the door and down the hallway towards the hidden closet door. She passed it and went to the end of the hallway. Her beam landed on a part of the floor.

She pointed down, and John said, "There?"

Sera nodded and started to run her fingers along the flooring. Stopping, she gripped a part of the wood and started pulling. A gust of dusty air spewed through the hole, revealing a dark tunnel. John leaned over, peering down into the darkness.

"Down there?"

"Yes."

"Shit." A cool breeze blew from the darkness and sent chills down his spine. "Is it a good time to tell you that I'm scared of heights?" John chuckled as he shivered, looking down at the dark opening.

"Seriously? You're like seven feet tall."

"I'm six-foot-one, and that's not very tall."

"Whatever. So are you saying you can't do it now?"

"No, I'm just trying to lighten the mood. With everything

going on, I thought it might . . . yeah, never mind." *I'm scared of heights, but I won't tell her that.*

Sera shook her head and exhaled loudly. "There are little indentions in the wall that act as stairs. I'll lead the way down. Once we reach the bottom, I'll show you the door."

"Another hidden door?"

"Yeah, this house is full of them. I'm pretty sure I haven't found them all yet, either. Ready?"

John nodded and watched Sera sit down, putting the light in her mouth. The beam disappeared into the tunnel's darkness as she stepped down, step by step. She stopped just before her head disappeared and nodded to John. John nodded back and slowly sat down on the edge. He peered down into the hole, and it was deep. Very deep. The ending appeared nonexistent, hidden by the depths of darkness. Trembling, he slowly turned over to crawl down the side when a clanking against the tunnel walls alerted him to look down. Sera's right hand dropped, and she was dangling from the edge. A loud crunch echoed as the light hit the floor. The beam went out, and John could hear Sera's breath heaving in the darkness. He fingered the flooring and bumped into Sera's single hand, grasping to hang on. John held her hand and gripped her wrist with his other hand. Her body rocked back and forth as she swayed, searching for the stairs of the tunnel.

"I've got you," he whispered through gritted teeth. "I've got you."

She swayed back and forth and finally found her footing. Panting, she stepped up and dropped over John's body, between his legs. Sera's heart pounded against John's chest as he held his arms around her tiny waist. The heat of her lips panted against his ear, touching him cheek to cheek.

"Are you okay?" John whispered, touching his lips to Sera's cheek. His manhood twitched excitedly, and he bit his lip to control the urge to kiss her. Sera lay over him, squeezing her hands around his abdomen. She lifted her body and was face to face with John. Her breath kissed his bottom lip as she heaved to sit up. John guided her voluptuous hips over and sat her down next to him.

"Yeah . . . thank you. I'm . . . I'm sorry."

Sera slowly lowered her foot back into the tunnel and found the footing before lowering her other foot. John grabbed her shoulders and held her as she slowly entered darkness for the second time.

"I've got it."

Even though John couldn't see her, he knew she was grateful for his help.

Once she was safely down enough, John stepped into the hole. The engraved steps were small indentions in the wall, and he had to concentrate to keep himself steady. Sharp pains shot through his fingers, and he felt his body shiver as he crawled further and further into the darkness.

"You, okay?" Sera whispered.

"Yeah, I—"

A beam of light shined right below his feet. He stepped down, touching his foot onto the bottom of the floor, and stood next to Sera.

"I thought the light broke."

"Yeah, it burst open and the batteries fell out. I was able to put it back together."

"That's good."

"The kitchen's through there."

Nodding, John waited for her to open the door. It was similar to the closet door. It lifted up, and Sera's tiny body could slither under it quickly.

She poked her head in and said, "Wait here. I'm going to check everything out."

After a minute, she opened the door and said, "Okay. I think it's safe."

A small amount of sunlight was glimmering through the

kitchen window. Sera walked over, pushed the curtain to the side, and looked out.

"Dusk." She inhaled a deep breath and let it out slowly. "I don't see the sludge on this side." She looked back at John and smiled.

John's breath caught when she grinned up at him. Her eyes glistened briefly, and her face softened as she nodded. His heart was struck like a heavy drum when he realized she was the most beautiful woman he'd ever seen, and at that moment, he felt, deep down, that he had to protect her.

Sera looked back outside, and John walked up behind her, peering out. He leaned in as close as he possibly could, brushing against her shoulder with his chest. As he looked, John realized that Sera was right. This side of the house was clear. No guards. No sludge. Only a glimpse of the neighboring dwellings peered through the trees.

"Where's your sister's house located?"

Sera shook her head slowly. "I'm not sure. I know it's further down the beach, but I won't know until I see it. I, um . . . I haven't visited in a while."

"So you're from here?"

"Yeah, I grew up here. Are you ready?" Sera said, looking back at John again.

"Yeah, let's get this over with."

John pushed past Sera and nodded. *I should go first, so I can show her that I'm not a pussy.* He peered out the window, looking long and hard both ways before he turned the knob to the door. It was locked, so he slowly unlocked the deadbolt above the doorknob. The door clicked open, and a cool breeze greeted them, its scent a combination of saltwater and burning flesh. John's nose crinkled as he stepped into the sandy grass and peered around the house. He reached back for Sera's hand, but she was using the door frame to step down.

Sera pointed down the side of the house. "You go that way,

and I'll go the other. Stay close to the house along the walls, and turn back if you see any men. Also, count how many steps it takes you, so we know how far in the dark."

John nodded and said, "Yeah, I'm not an idiot."

"I was just . . . never mind."

I can't help but be an asshole. That's who I need to be. The ass-hole. It's just easier. I don't have feelings for her, and I'm the asshole. John gritted his teeth and grabbed Sera's hand as she turned around to walk around the house.

"Be careful, Sera."

She looked up at him, briefly meeting John's gaze, and nodded. He let her hand slide through his, then turned the other way.

The sand was an off-white, chalky thickness that hugged clumps of green grass. John's feet trudged through it, sinking deeper into the clumps with each step. He slowly approached the corner of the house, and a loud whistling screeched as the wind blew against it. He peered out and saw that the sludge had made a home running parallel with the house. John stepped around and kept his back to the wall. As he approached the middle of the house, voices echoed from an open window.

"We need to get out of here soon, Rick. We're out of food and ammo, and those things keep coming back!"

John walked up to the window and ducked below it to crawl under. He crossed to the other side of the window and peeked in. A very tall man and a younger man were standing in the room. The younger guy was waving his hand and started walking towards the window. John dropped down and hid.

"And something's wrong with this house. I didn't use to believe in ghosts, but something dark is here. Empty room doors are locked from the inside, and the basement was opened . . . the prisoners . . . that was down there, they just . . . disappeared."

John smirked and continued walking along the wall. He made it to the front of the house and slowly peeked out. His body quickly jolted back from pure terror. He couldn't believe his eyes. He cupped his hands over his mouth and tried to swallow through parched lips. He slowly looked again, and his mouth dropped.

A gust of wind picked up, hitting him with the smell first, and then a wall of heat from a fire blanketed his face. His stomach did flips, threatening to unload right there. He swallowed hard and stared at a headless woman's body strapped to a large piece of wood. Two men were on either side of the woman, turning it so the flames would cook the meat evenly. They'd removed her head, but the rest of her body was tied up like a stuck pig.

Gripping the corner of the house, he didn't know if he should run like hell or beat the shit out of those pieces of shit who were turning the spit. He slowly stepped back and started to go back the way he came when a shrill scream echoed nearby.

Shit. John froze and pressed his body against the house. *Shit. Shit. Shit.* He looked back and forth. He slowly moved along the siding, peeking out towards the front of the house again, and saw that the men had abandoned their post. Another scream bellowed, and this time, it was right behind him. He slowly turned and saw a woman. She was crawling out of the sludge with black ooze dripping from her naked skin.

Shit. Shit. Shit.

Shivering, John looked towards the front again and stepped out into the open. The woman's flesh crackled and began to ignite as John walked past her. He was headed for the front door—and another scream sounded. He peered around and spotted a different being standing right next to the front door.

Fuck! Frozen, he looked around him and spotted an old shed. He galloped towards it and hid behind it. *Fuck! How the fuck am I going to get out of this shit?*

John walked towards the other side of the shed, and there she was. *Sera.* She was peeking out from the opposite side of the house, and a man was following closely behind her, holding a pistol.

No. No. No. John waved his arms back and forth, but Sera didn't look towards him. The being near the front door had also noticed and was walking towards her. The man following behind her with the gun was almost at arm's length.

John dropped his gaze and searched the shed wall for anything to use against the being and man. He looked along the ground and spotted a large rock. Picking it up, John launched it at the man coming up on Sera as he bolted out from the safety of the shed. His gaze met the being as he jogged towards her. The being's mouth opened, and black sludge oozed down her mouth as she screeched another scream.

The rock hit the wall right in front of the man, and Sera spun around. John was almost to Sera when she reared back and punched the man in the cheek. Blood spewed from his mouth as he doubled over. John stopped, wide-eyed, and stared at Sera. She spun around and kicked the man in the stomach with her right leg. The man dropped to his knees and slumped over, holding his bloodied face. John grabbed Sera's hand, pulling her back the way she came.

"Come on!" The path was clear, so they jogged back down the side, and he stopped to peek around the corner. The back of the house was safe, so they ran to the back door and opened it slowly. As soon as the door closed behind them, they heard someone yelling in the front of the house.

"Rick! Rick!"

Sera opened the pantry door, and John waved her in first. Once her feet were under the hidden door, he followed. He could hear the kitchen door open and slam shut as he closed the hidden door behind him. John stood up slowly and pressed his body against Sera. The room was tight, and he knew he could step back away from her, but he wanted to feel her heart pounding against him. She flipped on the light, and John gazed down into her eyes. Both of their chests rose and fell in unison as their panting filled the room. John swallowed back his gasps and inhaled her musk. *She smells so good, like wildflowers blowing through a summer breeze.*

He closed his eyes and exhaled loudly before saying, "Are you okay?"

"Yes. Are you?"

"Yes."

"Where did you learn to . . . um, do that?"

Sera exhaled loudly and pushed John away from her. She wrapped her arms around her shoulders, squeezing herself. Her eyes closed, and she inhaled deeply before answering. "It's a long story. Let's get going. Okay?"

Nodding, John pointed up. "You go up first."

Sera stepped forward towards John, and the flooring underneath their feet creaked as she stepped up. She looked down at the floor, ducked down, and quietly rapped against the floor.

"The floor's hollow," she whispered. She looked up, meeting John's gaze. "I think there might be a way out through the basement. Can you go up the stairs so I can try to open the door?"

"No, you go up, and I'll try to pull the door up." *Seriously, woman, let me feel like a man doing something useful, especially since you whipped that guy's ass without even breaking a sweat.*

John waited for Sera to go up enough to give him room to find a door.

Sera pointed and said, "Look, the flooring is different there compared to the rest of the floor. Do you see it?"

"No."

"Just try to pull up from that corner."

John stepped closer to where she said, and there it was—a difference in the wood. He fingered along the gap between the door and the wall, pulling on it slightly. The wood moved and pulled up towards him. He stepped back as far away from the gap and folded the floor in half, leaving just enough room to stand up.

"What the—"

Sera stepped down, and her body pressed against John's again.

She peered down into the hole and then up at him. "Let's go back upstairs, and then we can return here later."

"Okay."

Sera started back up the stairs, and John knew it was now or never. He had to ask her about her sister. *Sybil.* The woman. The voice that guided him to her.

"Sera?" He stepped up behind Sera, easing the door down behind him.

"Yeah."

"Your sister."

"What about her? Did she, um. Have you ever . . ."

John didn't know what to say. He was lost for words. *Hey, funny thing. Your sister guided me in trying to find a way to kill the sludge. Oh, and by the way, she also told me to find you to save you.* He shook his head, squeezing his eyes shut. He couldn't do it. He couldn't bring himself to say it.

"Nothing, it's . . . Nothing."

Sera stopped at the top and pushed on the door. She struggled to open it, so John stepped up and helped her ease it open. Sera's light beamed down the dark hallway as they crawled out and lay on the floor, panting.

John eased the door shut, and they walked to the hidden room door, opening it. Furry greeted them first, and then Brandon. He wrapped his arms around John's long limb and smiled at Sera.

"Hi!"

"Hey, buddy."

John opened the drawer and pulled out water and a half-empty bag of cereal. The drawer of water and food was dwindling down quickly. He looked over at Sera, meeting her eyes. A worried glare creased her brows, and he realized she'd noticed the same.

John walked over to the bed and sat down on the bottom bunk. He took a swig of water and handed it to Sera. After she drank, John watched her look over at Jim and Brandon.

She turned to meet John's gaze. "As you know, my side was free of the river. Did you have any on yours?"

"Yes, the river was down my side. And when I passed one of the windows, two men were talking about how they were almost out of ammo and food."

"That's great." Sera smiled.

John wanted to smile at her but bit the inside of his lip.

"I think if we run, we can leave here. But it'll have to be in the dark—"

"It's not going to work," John snapped.

"Why?"

"Because we have a kid and an old man who can't run very fast." John looked over at Jim and said, "Sorry, Jim. No offense, man, but you can't really run." Then he looked back over at Sera. "And in the dark. Really? We won't be able to see them coming. I want to leave here as much as you, but we don't have any kind of security blanket when we get out of here."

Sera's face reddened around her cheeks, giving her fair skin a natural, rosy glow. She was getting angry, sending John's insides into a frenzy. His groin reacted and hardened immediately. John's chest rose as he gasped back heavy breathing.

"I think we can make it. We just have to make it to the next house, and then we can—"

"Sera, listen to yourself. We have to come up with a better

plan. This one isn't going to work. I know you want to help your sister, but there must be a safer way to get to her."

She huffed, and her cheek flexed as heavy breaths of air exhaled from her nose. She was fuming, and John knew if he kept poking at her plan, she was going to go off. He looked at the door and then back at Sera.

"We can try the hidden door that we found."

"Another hidden door?" Jim said.

"Yes, it leads down to the basement, or that's what we think," John said.

Nodding, Sera exhaled deeply and stared at John. Her brows eased, and her gleaming blues settled as she breathed deeply.

Jim looked at Sera. "I was hoping to stay here a little while longer. It's nice having a bed to sleep on."

Brandon nodded. "I like it here, John. Do we have to leave?"

Sera looked at Brandon and said, "We can't stay here. It's a matter of time before they find us. Either it's the men or the sludge."

"John, do we have to go?" Brandon asked.

John looked over at Sera and then back at Brandon. "Yes, buddy, we have to go."

Brandon looked down and chewed his food. Everyone ate in silence.

Chapter Twenty-Four: The Plan

Sera

After everyone finished eating, they went up to the attic to do their business.

"So, what's the plan?"

"We go down and find out where the hidden door leads, and then we can plan our escape. I also want to see how much food we have left."

John zipped his pants as he turned around, meeting Sera's gaze. His brows eased, and he exhaled slowly as he stepped towards her.

Her heart began pounding against her chest as he stared down at her. She turned away and headed to the attic door.

The men were whispering, but she caught some of what Jim said. "What if we can't find her? What if she's dead?"

A shock hit Sera hard in the chest. She knew it was possible, but hearing it out loud hurt. Her heart drummed in her ears, and moisture filled her eyes as she swallowed a lump forming in her throat. She tried to control her emotions, biting her lip. She stopped mid-step and stared at the door, answering just above a whisper. "Then I move on and never look back."

Sera pulled out the drawers and started counting the food.

"Well, we have a few cans of food left and two water bottles, which we'll probably finish today. When we get ready to leave, I'll load up my bag with everything. We should look in the attic for another bag to carry extra weapons, blankets, and pillows. I don't have a lot of room left in my backpack."

Sera opened her backpack and dumped everything out. She started to organize everything in piles as she sifted through the items. Clothes, shoes, socks, and blankets were pushed to one side first. A set of matches, a bag of Firestarter, and a few pieces of wood. She unraveled a bag, and flints dropped out, so she rolled it back up. Two thermoses swooshed with water when she shook them. A zip lock bag filled with maps, batteries, and two small flashlights. Her compass rolled on the floor in front of Brandon, and another zip lock bag was filled with spoons, forks, and dental floss. She placed everything in their piles and gazed over the massive assortment of things.

John nodded and met her gaze. She forced a slight smile and started putting everything back into her bag. Brandon picked up the compass and looked at it.

"That's a compass. It tells you which direction you're going," Sera said.

Brandon turned the compass over and pulled out the picture folded inside the clip on the back.

"Go have an adventure," Brandon said.

"My dad gave me that right before he . . ." She looked down at it, staring at the faded words. "I've had it for a long time."

Brandon opened the picture, gazed at it for a moment, and lifted his eyes to Sera. He handed it to John.

John looked down at it for a long time and held it out for Sera. "Sera."

Sera was busy putting everything back into her bag when she looked up to see his face smiling. *Eric.* She gently grabbed it and smiled down at it. Moisture swelled in her eyes as she stared. *You left him. You let him go.* Sera closed her eyes and squeezed. *No. No. No. He let me go. He let me go.* She chanted in her head.

Exhaling, she swallowed hard and opened her eyes. John's gaze was filled with sorrow. He slightly nodded and cracked a smile. Sera pressed her lips together, closing off her emotions, and folded the picture gently. She held her hand out for her compass, and Brandon handed it to her. Nodding, she looked down at her bag and shoved it inside.

Silence fell over the room after Sera finished organizing. She sat with her thoughts and knew she should try to get to know the strangers sitting in front of her, but she was afraid to open herself up. Everything had changed so much. Everyone she loved either died or disappeared when the sludge river emerged. She didn't know if she could take the risk and open her heart again.

She didn't know if she could be who Eric always told her she was. Eric was the social one, and she was the stoic loner who would rather keep to herself than socialize. Eric always told her she was a good person with a big heart. He would hold her in his ebony arms and tell her she would always help anyone if they needed it, but now Sera wasn't so sure after everything that had happened. She didn't know who she was anymore. Now, she was just trying to survive and find her siblings.

"How long have you been alone, Sera?" Jim broke the silence, smiling at her.

Sera fidgeted, looking down at her hands before meeting his gaze. "I've always been alone. When the sludge broke out and invaded, it killed my husband, and I barely got away." She inhaled a deep breath. "I went back to our house, or what was left of it, grabbed everything I could, and left. I honestly don't even know how long it's been since everything happened." She trembled as she let the words spew out of her. She was doing what Eric always told her she could do. Open up. Let them in. Let them see her.

Sera looked over at Jim. "What about you?"

"When I got to my car, there was a hole in the ground where it was supposed to be. The sludge started filling the hole, so I ran back to my apartment and locked the door. Then I heard a knock and opened my door to see John and Brandon."

"So the three of you have been together since the beginning?"

"Yes," John said.

"What did you do before everything happened?" Sera asked, looking at both men.

Jim chuckled. "I was a teacher. I taught high school English. I was headed to class early because I had some kids' tutoring before school."

"What about you, Sera?"

She hesitated, fidgeting with her bag. Eric's face came into her mind from the day they'd opened their shop. His muscular, ebony arms wrapped around her as they both stared up at their new sign reading *Martial Arts and Self Defense*. He kissed her on top of the head and met her gaze, smiling. *"We did it, Sera. We did it."*

Blinking, Sera looked up, meeting Jim's gaze. "I was a Self Defense Martial Arts instructor with my husband. We owned a business working with kids and adults who wanted to learn karate and self-defense." Sera looked down and spoke just above a whisper. "I actually really loved it. I loved working with people. I was never good at talking to people, but my husband was . . . he was good with kids. They loved him." A slight smile crept up on the right side of her mouth. She looked up and met John's gaze. Staring, she nodded her head at him. "What about you, John?"

"I was in college. Biochemistry major. I was headed to work at the library when everything happened. I tried to help Brandon's mom but couldn't, so I picked up Brandon, and we went to my apartment." He exhaled loudly and said, "I lost my keys amid everything happening and walked across the hall to Jim's apartment." John nodded and looked over at Jim and then at Brandon. He smiled at Brandon, and Jim nodded.

Sera secured her bag closed and sat, staring at the floor with her thoughts. She finally looked up and met John's eyes.

He was staring at her, but it was as if he was looking right through her. He blinked and focused his gaze as he shifted his weight. Inhaling a deep breath, he adjusted himself, facing Sera, and said, "I've been thinking about what you said." He paused and waited for Sera to say something, but she just nodded. "We know that the sludge is a living organism that's mutated to adapt to its environment to feed. But what I can't wrap my head around is that if water harmed it, why does it victimize humans? The human body consists of sixty percent water, so technically, we would harm the sludge. Right?"

Sera looked up, shaking her head. "I don't know. It's just a theory, because the sludge river doesn't go close to the ocean. As I traveled here, I walked along swamps and marshes, and honestly, I can't remember seeing it near any bodies of water, yet it consumes humans. So I don't know."

"I just can't help but think this is too big of a risk to take without more facts. We don't know for sure that water affects the sludge. Right now, it's just a theory. Your theory." John shifted his weight and exhaled. "What if you're wrong, Sera? What if we all get killed or, worse, turned into one of those things trying to run along the ocean?"

Sera's mouth dropped open, and she shook her head. "I know that before all this happened, you were on your way to becoming a know-it-all scientist, but here in the real world, life is based on risk. If we don't take the risk, we'll die up here. One way or another, those things will find a way in here. Those men will find a way in here, and when they do, it's all over for us. No matter how many facts you think you have, they won't add up to shit if you become one of them waiting."

Sera stood up and faced the door, panting. She didn't know what else to say. *Maybe Sybil was wrong. Maybe he wasn't supposed to be the one helping me.*

She turned around and faced John. "And no one's forcing you to go. I just . . . I don't want to sit here and wait for those things to break in and take over our bodies. I especially don't want to sit here and wait for those men downstairs to break in and kill us." The anger dissipated as she spoke the last words. She couldn't fight with him anymore. *If he doesn't want to go, then there's the door.*

John's forehead furrowed as he glared back at Sera. She shook her head at him and dropped her shoulders. She was done and had said what she needed to say.

"Do what you want, John. Tonight, I'll go down that tunnel and try to find a way out of here. Then I'm going to run over to my sister's house. If you want to sit here and wait for them to come, go right ahead." She stood up, walked over to her bunk bed, and sat down.

"Come on, Furry." Sera's voice cracked when she whispered Furry's name. As she lay down, her body drew into itself. Her chest heaved, and she felt a lump form in her throat. She knew it was an incredible risk to go out into the dark and try to find a way out, but that was all she had. She wanted to find her sister and a way to survive, even if that meant leaving them behind.

John stood up and faced the door, shifting his weight back and forth between his feet. He rubbed his face aggressively and then sighed.

"John?" Brandon whispered.

"Yeah, buddy. What is it?"

"I think we should go with Sera. I don't want to die."

"Okay. Get up on the top bunk so we can rest for a little bit. Okay?"

"Okay."

Sera turned over on her side, facing the wall, and hugged

Furry. "John."

"Yeah."

"I would like for you to go down into that tunnel with me tonight." She didn't look back at him, but she could feel his eyes on her. "I think we should go check it out, and then you can decide what you want to do." She waited for him to respond, but the room went silent.

After a few minutes, she heard John lie down on the floor next to her. "Okay, Sera."

Sera. John's voice hummed, lingering in her heart. She knew that she needed to try to get along with him. Sybil sent her to find him for a reason, and her sister had never led her astray in the past. And even though John was a total pain in the ass, she didn't want to leave him or the little boy to die in this house. Inhaling a deep breath, she pulled the pillow out from under her head and turned over.

"John. Here." She handed John the pillow and met his gaze. His whiskey eyes softened as he stared at her. Sera nodded, flipped off the light, and lay back on the bed.

"Thank you."

Chapter Twenty-Five: Hide and Seek

Sera

A loud rumble against the floor rattled Sera, startling her upright in bed. A hand grabbed her forearm, pulling her back as a breath of heat brushed the nape of her neck. John's voice whispered in the darkness, "Shh, there's—"

Another loud thump smashed against the floor, and then a knocking sound followed.

"What is that?" Sera whispered.

"I don't know. I think maybe . . . someone's banging against the ceiling with a broom or something." John's body shifted, scooting closer to Sera. She slightly turned, facing his body, and felt his fingers slide down her forearm and interlock with her digits.

A gust of loud, muffled voices argued right under Sera's feet. She broke free from John's grip and fumbled along her belt, looking for her light. The beam glowed in front of her, aiming at the door. Furry's cold nose pushed under her free hand, whimpering. Another hard jolt thumped underneath, and then a loud crash followed. Furry jumped up onto the mattress, shivering next to Sera.

"I think they're tearing apart the room below us," Sera whispered.

The vibration against their bodies increased as if they were running along the ceiling, searching for something.

Sera dropped down, pulled her boots on, and headed out the door. She trudged up the incline and pressed her ear against the door. John touched her shoulder, meeting her gaze as he leaned in to listen beside her. She nodded and slowly opened the door.

The attic door was still open, and voices were yelling from inside the house. She clicked off the light and gently closed the door behind them.

As they walked into the attic, another round of loud thumps sounded right underneath their feet. Sera walked over to the bathroom bucket and brought it out. She turned and whispered, "Let's do our business quickly and then go back to the room."

Once everyone finished, John walked everyone back to the room, and Sera stayed back and squatted next to the hidden attic door.

"Rick! Rick! I'm not finding anything!" A man's voice echoed as he walked up the attic stairs.

Sera slowly eased the door closed, and a hand squeezed her shoulder. She jumped and felt another hand on her forearm.

"Shh, it's me."

Sera flicked her light on and met John's gaze. She motioned towards the door, putting a finger over her lips to shush John before turning back to the attic door.

"There's something here. I know it," a man's voice grumbled in front of the door.

Sera's mouth dropped open, and she looked back at John. He scooted up next to her, breathing deeply. His shoulder brushed against hers as he repositioned himself closer to the door. The vibrations underneath them stopped, and a blood-curdling scream rose from downstairs.

"Keep them quiet!"

Sera jerked her head back, meeting John's gaze again. She bit her bottom lip and held her breath. Then, gripping John's forearm, she listened to footsteps creep closer to their hidden door.

"Rain's coming. It'll be here by tomorrow . . . I know it, I know it, I know it," the man chanted over and over again.

A loud hit against the door startled Sera backward, almost knocking her on her rump. John caught her, easing her back over with his hands on her hips.

"It'll be tomorrow. They'll come for us, and we won't have anywhere to hide. We need to find the door. I know it's here somewhere." The man's voice was shaky as he chattered. He sounded as if he was right on the other side of the door, burning a hole in the wood with his eyes. "Keep looking!"

Sera and John jumped as his voice rose to a fierce shout. Sera lunged forward and slightly bumped against the door. She turned back to John, shaking her head vigorously.

"Sir, I don't think there's a hidden room. We've looked everywhere. I think you're—"

"What! I'm what?" he yelled.

"It's the only way we can hide from those . . . those things. They're getting stronger, and it's just a matter of time before they drag us all into their river!" The man's voice started to drift away from the door, and then the stairs rattled as he left the room.

A man's voice spoke close to the door. "I really think Rick's losing it."

Another man said, "We should sneak out and go on our own. No one will ever know if we go now."

Boxes were being moved around near their door and pushed into the wall.

"Ugh, it smells like piss over here, man," one guy said.

The staircase rattled after ten minutes of the two men chatting back and forth. Panting, Sera looked back at John and nodded towards the door. He nodded and pushed the door open, leading the way in. The entrance to the attic was still open, and the sounds of people banging downstairs had stopped. The room was messy, with boxes and items scattered along the floor. Sera sat in front of the attic door and watched as John walked around the room. Sera crawled over to the window and peeked down into the yard.

"I think we should go down now," Sera whispered.

John shook his head.

Sera ignored him, crawled over to the stairs, lay on her belly, and looked down at the second floor. The bottom floor was empty, and the front door was open. Lightning struck across some dark clouds off in the distance, and a deep growl rumbled.

"It's about to storm, and from the looks of it, it'll be a big one. We should go now before the rain comes. More of those beings will come when it does."

"It's not dark yet. You said that—"

"I know what I said, but I have a bad feeling. We need to go now."

John looked back at the attic door, scanning the room slowly before he met Sera's gaze. "Okay, let's go."

Sera walked over to the hidden door to their room and met Jim's gaze. "Close the door behind us and be very quiet until we get back."

Brandon walked over to Sera, looking up at her. She looked down and smiled, turning to go out the door. Brandon walked up behind her and wrapped his arms around her waist. Shivering, she felt a warm surge ping in her heart. Sera hadn't let anyone in since Eric, and when Brandon hugged her, it hit home. She knew no matter what happened, she had to find a way out, not only for herself but for him.

He let go of her and looked up. "Please come back."

Sera felt her eyes moisten as she nodded quickly. "I will."

Brandon walked over to John and wrapped his arms around him.

Sera pulled out her bag and dug around until she found a flashlight. She handed it to Brandon, saying, "Here, buddy, now you don't have to sit in the dark."

"Stay here, Furry. Take care of Brandon." Sera kissed Furry's head. "Okay, let's go." They walked out into the hall, and she looked back and nodded at Brandon as John closed the door.

Sera walked past the closet door and over to the long tunnel leading to the kitchen. She and John both heaved the door up and nodded at each other. Sera first dropped her feet into the dark tunnel and stopped momentarily, gazing into John's eyes. He blinked and slowly nodded once. She looked down and continued into the unknown. She knew this was a dangerous mission, but something told her the tunnel would lead them to freedom.

Chapter Twenty-Six: The Way Out

Sera

Sera's fingers ached as she moved her body down into the darkness of the tunnel. Looking up, she watched John easing the door down gently over their heads. Heavy breathing bounced off the walls, and the familiar stench of a salty musk tickled her nose. She eased her feet down one step at a time until she finally touched the bottom. Squatting, she pulled up the hidden door and looked out of the pantry to see the room was dark, with a whistling wind blowing through the kitchen. Confused, she cocked her head and looked up at John. He stepped down just as she stood up, coming face to face with him.

The tunnel was tight, and she had no room to move away. She gazed up into his eyes and felt deeply attracted to him. His body pressed against hers, forcing her loins into overdrive. His manhood had risen and was pressing stiffly into her abdomen, alerting her that he felt the same. Squeezing her eyes shut, she inhaled a deep breath. *Pull it together, Sera. This is not the time or place.*

Sera cleared her throat and swallowed deeply. "There's a breeze going through the kitchen. It's like one of the windows is busted out. I can't see where it's coming from. Do you think I should crawl through and see where the wind's coming from?"

He looked down at the door and then back up at Sera. "Let me go." John pulled open the hidden door, crawling through it. Sera stepped up onto the stairs to give him room to crawl out. Stepping down, she nervously fidgeted as she waited for his return.

I shouldn't have let him go. He isn't experienced with combat like I am. Sera leaned down, pulled up the door, and peered out. Shaking her head, she stood back. *Where is he? What's taking so long?* A few minutes passed, and the door lifted. "Finally, what did you see?" She climbed up the wall and watched him climb in.

"You were right. One of the windows was busted out, but it looked like someone had boarded them up with a couple of pieces of wood. It actually seemed like the house had been abandoned. I didn't see or hear anyone, so I can't be sure without going out and looking."

"No, we have to stick to the plan."

"Or going down there could lead us to the sludge," John snapped.

"John, we have to try."

John stepped down. "Go up, and I'll pull the door up."

As the door folded over, a cloud of dust particles filled the air. The smells of stale, musky ocean and heavy humidity made it hard for Sera to breathe deeply. A cough threatened, and Sera quickly cupped her mouth, swallowing the air and trying to escape.

Exhaling, she held her beam down into the dark hole and nodded at John. "It's just like the tunnel we just crawled down."

Sera looked down into the hole and back up at John. "Ready?"

John nodded and started down into the tunnel first.

"Wait, John, no, I—"

"It's fine. I should go first. Just in case."

Sera shook her head, and John stopped, looking up at her. "Well, come on."

Blindly, Sera's fingers gripped the indentions as she slowly climbed down into the unknown. John reached the bottom first, and Sera's feet finally touched the ground. Panting, she grabbed her flashlight and held it up as she looked around.

The room was a small, walled-off hidden space attached to the basement. John walked up behind Sera, pressing his body against her back, and put his hand over her mouth. "Shh." Chills ran up her spine as she put her hand over his. John reached down, flipping off the light. He walked her over to the wall and said, "Look."

A glowing light gleamed through the tiny hole in the wall. John pulled his hand away from her lips and pointed to the spot. She cautiously looked in, putting her eye up to it.

There was a river of sludge in the basement's floor. It was glowing a red hue in the darkness. The pungent smell of death and sickness rose, stinging the hairs of her nose as she inhaled a deep breath. Sera shifted her weight, rolling a pebble under her foot. The sludge twitched, and giant black bubbles popped, reacting to the noise she made. Holding her breath, she froze and waited to see what the sludge would do.

She exhaled and saw a long, slender sludge arm rise out of the basement floor. It waved back and forth in the air as though it was searching for something. The sludge slowly started moving towards where she was watching through the hole and stopped. The sludge oozed on the ground and slowly transformed into the size of a person. A woman's body appeared inside the sludge, crouching down on the floor. The arm retracted into the river, and ooze began absorbing into the woman's body. A woman with blonde hair stood up and began opening her eyes. A vibrant blood red glowed from her irises as she slowly blinked her lids open.

Sera pulled back, shaking her head. She looked over at John, pointing for John to look in. He slowly stepped over to the spot and peered in. Shaking his head, he pulled back and looked at Sera. She looked in the hole again, and there was nothing there. The person had disappeared, and the sludge was flowing normally. She pulled back, looking at John. Shaking her head, she looked in one last time, and a glowing red eye met her stare. She jumped back, pushing against John. He opened his mouth, and Sera hastily shook her head, pressing her fingers against his lips. Cautiously, she walked over, peeked in again, and saw the sludge being gone.

Exhaling, she dropped to her knees and shook her head. John held out his hands, motioning, *"What is going on?"*

We have to get the hell out of here. Shaking her head, Sera stood up quickly, waving her arms as she mouthed the words, *it's nothing.* She turned around and walked to the wall, where they entered the hidden room. She flipped on her light and started running the beam along the walls.

It's got to be here somewhere. This house has several doors. I just have to find it, and then we'll have a way out of this death trap. Sera's fingers trembled as she followed the beam up and down the walls, looking for anything unusual. The river was knocking at their back door now, and she knew it was just a matter of time.

She ran her fingers along the walls, searching for anything that could be a part of a door. Turning to John, she pulled him down and put her lips to his ear. "I know there has to be another passageway somewhere. Look for anything out of the place. Or anything that seems weaker than other parts of the wall. I don't know how to describe it better than that."

The walls were made of cold concrete and steel beams. John nodded and went down the wall, running his fingers up and down the panel. Sera followed and squatted down as she fingered the cracks where the floor met the wall. She knew she needed to look for some kind of opening or irregularity. She stopped at the end where the border turned to go back towards the sludge river enclosure when she noticed something off.

A part of the wall had a piece missing and had been

replaced with bricks and pieces of wood. She pushed hard against the slight difference, but it didn't budge. She pulled out her knife, pushed it between the wood and the concrete, and pulled. The door spewed steamy seawater in her face as the surface broke loose. She wiped away the residue, pulling the door open entirely. The flashlight shined through a layer of foggy dust down another tunnel. John walked up behind her with his mouth gaping open.

Nodding, Sera smiled up at him and whispered, "I knew we would find something. This house is full of surprises."

They both stepped into the tunnel, looking around. The hallway creaked as the lining of wooden planks squealed overhead and below their feet. It was as if they were entering a man-made escape tunnel, starting in the basement and going underground to somewhere unknown.

Salty sand seeped through the planks and drizzled over their heads as they walked in. Dropping down, Sera ran her fingers over the flooring and felt moist clumps of sand. She looked over at John and back in front of them. She held up the flashlight, looking down their path. The hallway looked as though it stretched for miles upon miles with no end in sight.

Standing up, she turned to shut the door behind them and nodded to John. He nodded back, and they both began walking into the darkness.

An hour went by, and John cleared his throat. Sera met his gaze, and a slight smile crossed his face.

Sera's right brow twitched as she returned a smile and said, "What?"

"I, um . . . I haven't told you how much I appreciate you helping us out of the basement. We would've died down there. Brandon would have died . . . so, thank you."

"Don't thank me yet. We haven't found a way out."

She looked ahead, and John stopped, grabbed her hand,

and pulled her back. "Hey, I'm sorry I haven't been . . . well, I've been an ass, and I just want you to know I appreciate you helping us."

Sera stopped, pulled her hand out of his, and glared at him. "Well, don't be. I'm . . . I'm not a good person." Sera looked ahead and continued walking.

"Oh, well, I wouldn't have been kidnapped if it wasn't for—" His gaze shot in front of him again, and he thrust his fingers through his mane aggressively as if he were trying to swipe what he'd just said away. He kicked the ground and then started walking again. "Let's just get going," John grumbled under his breath.

"Wait! What?" Sera spat, trudging behind him.

"It's nothing. Let's just go."

Sera grabbed his hand and yanked back. "No, what were you going to say, John?" Sera's voice echoed down the tunnel, singing into the darkness. Sera turned, peering into the tunnel, and lowered her voice to a whisper as her gaze trailed back to John. "What were you going to say?" He turned to walk away, and she grabbed his hand again. "What aren't you telling me? Please."

"It's nothing. I'm tired, and I want to get this over with."

Sera shoved John as hard as she could, throwing him against the side of the tunnel. The wood crackled, and he left an outline of his body on the wall as he dropped to the ground. He looked up at her with fear in his eyes. Sera walked over to him, panting, and glared down at his body, seething with anger.

"I'm sorry. I . . . what aren't you telling me? I know you're hiding something. And frankly, I don't give a shit if you don't want to tell me. You owe me that much. I risked my life going down into that basement to save you, and all you've done is be a total dick to me since the minute I helped you."

John eased up onto his feet and glared down at Sera. "I

don't . . . I don't know how to . . ." He paused and looked over Sera's head, searching the wall for answers. His gaze returned to hers, and he said, "Someone told me to . . . to come to this house and . . . to find you."

Sera cocked her head to the side and took a step back. "What?"

"A woman . . . she told me to get captured and guided me to you."

"A woman? Where is she now? Did the men take her hostage?" Sera spun around and stared in the direction they'd just walked from. She shook her head and exhaled a long breath.

John's hand gently grabbed hers. "Sera." His fingers laced through hers, and he whispered softly, "She spoke to me through my . . . mind. I, um, I didn't know how to tell you because I thought you'd think I was crazy, but I realize now that you and your sister are . . . well . . . alike." His gaze strolled over to the wall with the outline of his body, and then he looked back at Sera.

Sera squeezed John's fingers slightly before throwing down his hand. "Is she still talking to you?" A single tear rolled down Sera's cheek before she swiped it away. She felt her bottom lip quiver, so she bit down. The strong taste of blood filled her mouth.

John shook his head. He opened his mouth and licked his lips before answering, "She hasn't spoken to me since the first or second night being in the hidden room with you. She, uh . . . she told me her name was Sybil, and when you said your sister's name was Sybil, I didn't know how to tell you. I . . . I'm sorry."

Sera stepped further away from John and wrapped her hands around herself, hugging her upper body. Shaking her head, she tried to bury the burning in her eyes. She swiped her face aggressively and stomped past John. "We have to keep moving."

John picked up the pace and met Sera's rate next to her. She felt him looking over at her several times, but she kept her eyes ahead. Sera's heart was aching. She didn't know how to react. *She spoke to him. She led him to me. She led me to him. Why? Why, Sybil? Please? Please talk to me now. I need you. I can't . . . feel you anymore. Please?*

A few hours blew past like it was minutes, but they kept moving. A peculiar noise echoed off the walls in the distance. Sera stopped and listened for a moment before looking back at John. Shaking her head, she began running. Huffing, John ran up beside her, and they held a steady jog together.

Sera stopped and held up her hand, pointing. "Do you hear it?"

John shook his head, panting.

"Water. It's the ocean. We're . . ." She looked up at the ceiling and then back in front of her. "We are in some kind of tunnel along the ocean." Sera broke into a full run, leaving John behind. She finally came to the end of the tunnel and stopped in front of what seemed to be a door a few feet away. Dim light shined through a wooden frame. She walked up to it, pushed the door, and looked out to see sand and the moon's reflection over the water. The tide was rolling in, echoing along the tunnel walls, swishing salty, cool water through the air.

Sand remnants dumped over the doorway like a waterfall and spewed into Sera's face. Panting, John walked up beside her. "I can't believe it. We're right next to the water."

Sera dropped onto her knees, crawling out to look over the top of the sand tunnel. It appeared to be free of the sludge river and beings for now. The sun was barely peeking over the horizon, shining a glimmer of light down the tunnel. Smiling, Sera crouched down and admired the view. It had been a long time since she could just sit and enjoy the beauty of anything.

John crouched down beside her and forced a slight smile. Sera nodded, but her heart was still breaking. Silence rang a loud bell as Sybil remained unresponsive to her pleas. *He said he talked to her. She led him here . . . to me. Sybil?*

A tear rolled down Sera's cheek. She swiped it away and stared out over the water. *Sybil, if you're still out there, please. Please answer me. I'm almost out of this prison and coming to look for you. Please hang on. I'm almost there.*

"Sera."

She looked over, meeting John's gaze.

"You were right."

Sera nodded, but being right no longer mattered. She nodded and exhaled a deep breath before standing up. She peeked over the dune and looked for the house. It was miles away. John grabbed Sera's waist and pulled her down with a hard jerk.

"A man's walking around over there. He could be a being."

Startled, she dropped down and gazed back into John's eyes. He stared at her with a twinge of sorrow. He nodded and said, "Sera, I'm—"

"Don't. I'm the one who's sorry. I'm sorry I hurt you, and we should . . ." She looked away and then back at John and said, "We should get going."

Sybil, I'm coming to look for you. Hang on. Hang on, please.

Chapter Twenty-Seven: Coming To-gether

John

Sera led the way back into the tunnel, and John followed closely behind. He randomly looked behind them to ensure they weren't being followed.

She called me out on my shit, and I just stood there and . . . told her. I told her about Sybil. I think I'm losing it. I can't stop thinking about her. Maybe that's why her sister directed me to find her. To find the solution to this hell that we're all trapped in. To find her.

John and Sera ran back quietly with their thoughts. Once John and Sera saw the door to go inside the house, they slowed down and stopped. Panting, Sera looked up, meeting John's gaze. Her brows softened, and a gentle smile crossed her face. A glint of light twinkled in her ocean blues briefly before she tightened her lips together, returning to being the mysterious stoic woman he'd come to admire.

"You ready?" Sera whispered.

"Yeah."

The door pushed open quickly, and Sera flicked the light on, following the beam to the stairs.

"You can go first, and I'll be right behind you," John whispered.

"Okay." Sera nodded, crawled through the hidden door, and waited for John to join her.

Nodding, John pointed for Sera to step back while he closed the door in the floor.

"Okay, let's get Brandon and Jim and pack everything. Then, hopefully, we can get the hell out of here."

Nodding, John gazed down into Sera's eyes. He couldn't help but smile at her. She was beautiful, and it was a step in the right direction. They had possibly found a way to freedom, and Sera's theory could be right. John wanted to reach out and touch her, hold her, and pull her into him, but he stopped himself and looked up at the tunnel stairs.

"I guess I'll go first."

Sera nodded and stepped back. John reached up and started to climb when he felt a tug on his shirt. He looked back and met Sera's eyes as they glowed in the darkness. He slowly stepped down and faced her.

"What's wrong?"

Sera's head shook vigorously, and she turned, putting her back to him. Her body began vibrating, and she raised her hands to cup her face. John slowly put his hand on her shoulder and turned her around.

"What is it? Are you okay?"

But she wasn't. Her body shivered as the tears rolled down her cheeks. John pulled her into his chest and wrapped his arms around her back, squeezing her tight. She eased her hands from her face and wrapped them around John's abdomen, snuggling her cheek into John's chest. Her body vibrated against John until she finally relaxed. She pulled back and met John's gaze again.

"You, okay?"

"I'm sorry. I'm so sorry about everything. I don't know why I'm mean. I just . . . I didn't use to be like this. I used to be nice and . . . happy. We were so . . ." Sera shook her head and gazed into John's eyes.

John brushed back Sera's fiery hair and searched her face. His fingers ran down her cheek, tracing along her jaw, and stopped on her lips. His heartbeat pounded, thrumming against Sera's face. She stood up on her tiptoes, leaning in slowly towards John's mouth, and stopped just before contact. John's hand pressed against the small of Sera's back, pulling her into him with a swift jolt as he pressed his mouth against hers. Panting, John gasped for breath as their lips collided. His hands rushed down to her rump, and he lifted her into the air, holding her body up.

Sera pulled back and gazed into John's eyes briefly before pushing her lips against his again. He walked her back, pushing her against the wall. His erection screamed against his tight pants as he pressed against her sweet spot. She ran her fingers down and pulled his shirt over his head. She looked down at his chest and saw his tattoos across his chest. She leaned in and kissed his bare skin and then looked up at him as she pulled her shirt over her head. Her erect nubs peeked from the center of her small succulent breasts. John leaned in and suckled them, pulling back as he gently nibbled. Sera's head dropped back, and she opened her mouth, breathing deeply.

John stepped back and set Sera down gently. She looked up, meeting his gaze, and he saw the deep hunger glaze over her glistening blues. Trembling, Sera took a step forward and fumbled over his jeans as she unzipped and released his manhood. His long member emerged readily and pressed into her abdomen. John's hands moved quickly, and he ripped down Sera's pants. He stared down at Sera's pale, rose-tented skin.

Sera took a step towards John, and he grabbed her with one swift movement and had her back against the wall. Sera's breath caught, and she met John's gaze as he slowly rubbed the tip of his penis over her clitoris. Sera's mouth gaped open as he eased himself inside her lips.

John's jaw clenched, and he slowly pressed himself against her tiny body, holding his hard manhood inside her. Trembling, John's breathing was ragged as he picked up his pace, pulling himself out slowly and thrusting back in. Sera's hands gripped his back, squeezing with each entry. Her hot breath blew against his ear.

When John met Sera's eyes, his heart ached. She stared at him, and he felt as if she were looking into his soul—into his heart. An intense feeling of love overcame him, and he stopped. He'd never felt that way before. He felt like she was truly seeing him for who he really was, and it scared him. He put one hand up on the wall and looked away.

Sera's hands cupped his cheek, and she whispered, "Are you okay?"

"Um, yeah . . . I, uh . . . I don't know if I, um . . . I can do this . . . I'm—"

Sera began to move her hips up and down John's shaft. She turned his gaze to hers and pressed her lips against his. He felt his member get rock hard as she rode him. He felt his climax climbing. He wrapped his arms around her waist and pounded against her. She tried to pull back, moaning into his mouth, but he faced her, gazing into her eyes.

"Oh, baby. Come with me. Oh, baby." That was all John could say. He wanted to tell her that he loved her. That he'd been looking for her his whole life, but instead, he felt his erection explode as he filled her up. She shivered under his grip, squeezing her legs as she quivered. He continued to thrust inside her until he had nothing left. Until he felt his manhood finally go flaccid.

Panting, John finally pulled himself out of her and lowered her to the ground.

"Are you okay?" Sera whispered.

John nodded. "You?"

She nodded, and he pressed his lips against her gently, savoring her touch. He pulled back and gazed into her eyes. *I love you.* The words weighed over his lips, begging to be spoken. *I love you, and I can never actually tell you.* He shook his head and stood up, pulling up his pants. Sera handed him his shirt, and they both continued to finish getting dressed.

"We should get going."

Sera nodded.

Chapter Twenty-Eight: The Attic

Sera

John led the way up the narrow stairs and pushed up on the door to the hidden hallway. He grunted loudly and exhaled before trying again. Panting, he looked back at Sera and said, "It won't budge. It's as if something's sitting on top of it."

Sera inched up, carefully standing in front of John, and pushed. She took another step up, used her forearm, braced it against the door, and pushed with everything she had. Her body began trembling with her exertion, but nothing moved.

"I don't understand," Sera whispered. She looked back, meeting John's eyes. "Maybe something's wrong." She turned back to the door, pushing up again. Shaking her head, she whispered, "Let's go back down."

Sera squeezed past John and climbed down, facing the hidden entryway to the kitchen. She pulled up the door and peered into the room. The kitchen seemed empty, so she pushed through and stepped out. The minute she stood up, a bone-chilling scream hollered from underneath the floor. The basement door was ajar, and a glowing white light shined from inside, coming up the stairs.

Shit. Shit. Shit.

"Sera," John's voice whispered on the other side of the hidden door.

"Shh. Wait." Sera stepped back into the pantry, closed the door, and sat against the hidden entrance. A being emerged from the basement, dragging its feet across the floor and leaving a sludge trail behind it. The being stopped and screamed a shrill sound of horror that pierced through Sera. She cupped her ears, bracing herself against the hidden door. The being closed its mouth and trudged to the back door. Sera crept up to the pantry door and watched as the being's body melted to the floor and turned into a liquid ooze. The door began to rattle, and the sludge seeped under the frame, exiting the kitchen. Screams and gunfire rumbled outside the house, and a loud crash slammed against the wall next to the kitchen door.

Sera pushed through the door, tripped, and hit the floor. She shot up and ran out of the kitchen into the dining room to peek around the corner and check the rest of the bottom floor. The house appeared abandoned, so she hustled back to the hidden room and pushed through where John was.

"Where the hell did you go!"

"Come on. We don't have much time!"

"What happened? Damnit, Sera!"

Sera slipped out quietly and tip-toed over to the back door. She peered through a slit in the wood barricading the back door and saw sludge beings walking toward all the guards, surrounding them outside the house.

"John." That was all she could say. John looked in the crack and turned, meeting her eyes. His face paled as his mouth dropped open. Whipping around, Sera grabbed his hand. "This way." They walked through the kitchen and into the dining area.

The stairs creaked as someone was walking down them. Sera's head spun back and forth, looking for somewhere to hide.

"Shit. Shit. Shit," Sera whispered.

She dragged John under the dining room table, and they sat in the middle, watching as two more men ran into the kitchen with rifles and opened the back door. A tall man stumbled out of the family room and stared into the dining room. His hair was sticking up, and he had dark bags under his eyes. His cheeks were sunken in, and his lips were pale and covered in sores. He walked to the window next to the front door and looked out as he rubbed his hands together, chanting something under his breath.

Then he swung around and faced the dining table, screaming as if he was alerting the world. "They're coming! I told you all they would come for us! I told you! They would come!" He laughed hysterically and clapped his hands together.

His body collapsed back onto his rear and sank to the floor. He crawled towards the kitchen and looked up.

"I see you! I see you! I see you!" The man yelled. "I knew it. I knew it. I knew. I was right. I was right. I was right."

Sera scooted back and crawled out from under the table. John followed, and they stood up together, side by side. She pulled the knife out of her pocket and held it up, shifting her weight back and forth between her feet.

The man stood up and wobbled over, almost falling. Smiling, he rolled his head around in a circle. "I told them. I told everyone that you were up there hiding. They didn't believe me. I knew you were. I knew I would find you." The man waved his hands up, yelling.

Sera took a step in and realized his eyes were blood red, and he had black sludge covering his chest and hands. She looked up at John, but he kept his focus on the man.

"I can feel them. Inside." He patted his head with one hand, whispering, "They are in here." He patted his arms and touched where his veins were. He spun his head back and forth, looking around him, and turned to Sera and said, "I know what they want now. I can feel them. I can feel them. I can feel them."

Black, bloody sludge oozed out of his mouth and dripped

down the front of his shirt. As he walked closer, Sera saw something crawling through his arm's veins. She cringed at the sight and drew up her arms, holding the knife erect.

"Let me show you. It doesn't hurt. Let me show you . . . you can feel . . . their power."

"No! That's far enough!" Sera yelled.

The man jumped, and his face changed into something demonic. He opened his mouth, and sludge oozed through his teeth. The evil sound of what shrieked from the beings unleashed from his lips. He took a giant step forward and started coming for them. Sera stepped backward, holding the knife in the air. John stepped in front of her and waved his knife at him. The man took long strides towards them and was right on top of John. The man opened his mouth again and unleashed another round of piercing screams. Sludge seeped out of his mouth, dripping onto John's shirt. He pushed him up against the dining room table, trapping him.

"No, no, no!" Sera spun around him and slashed the man's throat open.

The man's mouth dropped open wider than an average human's, and he bellowed piercing screams that echoed through the house. Sera pulled John by the arm, and the man fell forward, hanging his head over the table. Black, bloody sludge oozed out of his neck and puddled on the table in front of him.

The front door slammed open, and a man with a rifle burst in. He gazed at Sera and John and then looked over at the man's slumped-over body.

"What the hell's going on?" He looked over at Sera again and realized she had a knife. He aimed his rifle up, taking steps towards them. "Where the hell did you come from?"

The man from the table turned around and faced the other man. Strings of black sludge oozed from his neck and mouth as he started hobbling towards him.

"Oh, shit, Rick!"

Rick collided with the man, bulldozing him into the wall next to the front door. Sera grabbed John's hand and bolted past them. Screams of several sludge beings echoed from the kitchen area as they sprinted up the stairs. The man in the dining room screamed, begging for his life as they reached the attic. Gunfire from an automatic weapon fired, blowing bullet holes through the walls and ceiling. The attic stairs rattled as they hurriedly pulled them up. Gasping, Sera ran over to the hidden door, pulled it open, and stopped when she heard someone cough from the corner of the room. Slowly, she turned to see two men sitting in the darkness.

"So, I guess Rick wasn't crazy after all," a man said.

"Nope, and we found the perfect place to hide and have a little fun," another man replied.

From the corner of her eye, Sera saw John charge. Then a loud blast fired, and Sera mouthed the words, but her lips were silent. Time slowed down, and her ears rang a high-pitched squeal as she dropped to her knees, crawling over to him. A blast of pain smashed the side of her face, knocking her off her feet. Blinking, she saw double as she rolled over onto her back. The floor was hard, and the side of her face throbbed with pain.

Coughing, Sera mouthed his name again. "John."

Her heartbeat pounded in her ears as the sound slowly came back in. She licked her lips and tasted a musky metallic liquid in her mouth. A muffled, deep voice echoed above her, and then her body was pulled by her arm.

"Yeah, put her over there. She won't be getting up anytime soon. Just leave her there." A man's laughter echoed as his face looked down into hers, smiling. He nodded and walked away from her. "Yeah, we can have a little fun with this one once the house clears out."

"Hey, look, he's trying to get up. Go finish him off."

"I only have one bullet left."

"Then use your fists, stupid. Go!"

Sera blinked, and her vision doubled, zoning in and out. The floor vibrated with the man's footsteps as he walked away from her. She turned over and inhaled a deep breath before pushing herself up onto her feet. She leaned against the wall of the attic and held up her fists.

"Hey! Asshole!"

"Oh, you want some more?" One of the men laughed, throwing his head back.

Sera closed her eyes and started laughing uncontrollably before stopping and saying, "Yeah, come and get it, pussy!"

She pushed off the wall and planted her feet, standing in a fight stance. Her hand glided down into her pocket, pulled out her pocketknife, and concealed it in her palm. She spat the blood pooling in her mouth and grinned, showing her blood-stained teeth as she waved the man to come to her. She wasn't going down without a fight. And she wasn't going to lose John. She was going to fight or go down trying.

The guy closest to her strolled towards her. "I'm coming for you, baby."

He stood before her, and she smiled up at him, nodding. He reached out to touch her, and she waited for him to get closer. Her smile grew, and she batted her eyes innocently. She slid the knife slowly down between her fingers and waited. The man grabbed a wad of Sera's hair, pulling her to him.

"Oh, yeah, I like it ruff, baby."

The man smiled and eased his hand, loosening his grip. Grinning, she reared back and stabbed him in the jugular with one swift thrust. The man stared at her with wide eyes for a second before blood started squirting out and gushed down his neck. He clamped down on her shoulder, trying to hold himself up. Sera pulled the knife out and slashed across his throat, opening him up. He dropped to the floor and kicked his legs briefly before the gargling stopped.

The second guy stomped towards her, and as soon as he was close enough, Sera uppercut his nose, knocking him back on his rump. Blood spewed from his nose as he looked up at her.

"Oh, you're going to pay for that, bitch!"

He stood up and swung at her. She dipped down, punching him in the gut over and over again. He stumbled backward, holding his stomach. She stomped towards him and punched him in the nose. A loud crackle echoed in the attic, and streams of blood drained down his face. He cupped his nose and started yelling. Sera calmly walked up to him and plunged her knife into his gut. He dropped his hands, and she slid her blade across his throat. He wobbled back and forth for a moment before collapsing to the floor. Sera ran over to John, dropping down next to him.

"John. John."

He opened his eyes and said, "Yeah, you're right. I can't fight very well." He shivered as he cracked a slight smile.

Tears streamed down Sera's face as she gazed into his eyes. "Can you walk?"

"Yeah." He turned, put weight on his shoulder, and cried out in pain. "Oh, fuck that hurts!"

Sera lifted his shirt and revealed a bullet wound in his shoulder. She lifted him up, looked behind him, and saw that the bullet had gone straight through. She lowered him back down, and the hole dripped blood down his chest and stomach. Black sludge stained the front, so she ripped it open, pulled it off his body, and threw it away.

John coughed and chuckled at the same time. "If you want to get me naked, you just had to ask."

Sera pressed her lips against his and whispered, "I can help you, but I need my bag." She stood up and helped pull him to his feet.

Chapter Twenty-Nine: Wounded

John

John grunted, gritting his teeth as a tear rolled down his cheek. Sera opened the door and helped him enter the dark hallway. She pushed open the hidden room door and saw Brandon sitting on the floor with Jim and Furry. Brandon ran over and hugged John around the waist. John grunted and patted him on the head.

"Ugh. Be careful, buddy."

"What the hell happened?" Jim said.

Sera walked John over to the floor next to the bed. He rested his back against the frame and watched Sera grab water and her bag.

"We couldn't go through the hallway door, so we had to go through the attic, and two men were there. They shot John, and I—"

John's head dropped back, and his eyes fluttered closed.

John felt a slap against his cheek and looked up to see Sera. "John! John. You have to wake up. Drink this!" She slapped his other cheek. "Drink this. Come on. Wake up and drink."

She held the bottle up to John's mouth and tilted it up. Water ran over his lips and covered his bare chest. The water mixed with his bloody wound and trailed down his six-pack abs to his jeans.

John pulled away, choking and spewing acid on the floor

next to him.

"Shit, I'm sorry. I'm sorry," he whispered.

"Shh, it's okay. Just relax. Everything's going to be okay."

A burning sensation rolled up his throat and threatened a relapse of sickness, but John swallowed hard and hung his head over his lap.

The zipper to Sera's bag sounded, and John looked over to see piles of her things lying all over the floor. She held up a *Zippo* lighter and a large bowie knife. She flicked it on and waved the flame over the blade several times. John's eyes fluttered open and closed as his head bounced backward, desperate to sleep.

"John, wake up! Please." Sera's voice cracked. Sera lifted John's head up and cupped her hands over his cheeks. He met her glazed eyes and realized her bottom lip was quivering.

John reached out and put his hands over hers. "Shh, don't cry. I'll be okay. I'm just very, very tired."

Sera shook her head and turned back to what she was doing. John closed his eyes briefly before she was slapping his face again.

"Ow! Woman. That hurts! I know that we just had sex, but I'm not into that kinky stuff. I like it—"

"John! Shut up! Drink this!"

John forced his eyes open and saw a bottle of *Jack Daniels* shoved into his hands.

"Well, yes, ma'am."

He turned the bottle up, and the liquid burned all the way down. He handed the bottle back to Sera, and she shook her head and pushed it back towards his chest. "Drink one more."

John took another swig and realized that she was prepping a knife. "Oh, shit. Sera, are you about to stab me with that knife to get the bullet out? I have to tell you that I've never had any surgeries, and I don't think that I'm allergic to anything." John hiccupped with the last word and dropped his head back.

"John, sit up straight. No, the bullet went straight through, thank goodness. I'm preparing a knife to cauterize the wound. But you need to stay awake. I mean it. At least for a little bit longer. Okay?"

Shit, she thinks I'm dying. Well, I'll assure her she's not getting rid of me that easily. Assholes live forever. Weak asses always die first, and it's too late. I'm in love with her. She's stuck with me now.

John watched her as she looked away and dove into her bag again. She pulled out a ball of a piece of cloth and another part of clothing. A *Ziplock* bag full of gauze and medical supplies. A towel and a wooden spoon.

John turned the bottle of booze up one more time and handed it back to Sera. Sera pressed the bottle against the cloth, poured some over the rag, and exhaled a deep breath. Then she turned the bottle up, gulping a long drink, and put the lid back on.

"John, I need to clean your wound first, and it's going to hurt really bad."

"It's okay. I'm feeling pretty fuzzy now," he said with a little giggle.

Sera nodded and swiped her hand down John's cheek. He met her hand and held it for a moment before she nodded again. John returned the nod, and she took the rag with the alcohol on it and began to clean his wound. John gritted his teeth, grunting as she wiped away the blood. She held the cloth up to his chest and poured a little bit of whiskey over the opened wound.

"Oh, fuck me!"

Sera cocked her head to the side and gave John a remorseful look. She grabbed the bowie knife again and ran the flame over it one more time.

"Okay, bear down on this piece of wood." Sera held up the piece of wood for John to bite down on and met his gaze, staring into his eyes.

"Oh, now you give me the wood to bite down on."

Sera's irises began to glow a crystal blue as she held up the knife. John slightly nodded and closed his eyes.

Sera's lips grazed his cheek as she whispered into his ear, "I'm so sorry."

John reached over and placed his hand on Sera's thigh. He squeezed his eyes shut and inhaled deeply when she pulled back from his cheek. The knife touched his chest, shooting a burning sensation into the hole and inside his body. A sharp pain pricked, and John squirmed as Sera was moving the tip of the knife around inside the hole.

She pulled back, and the lighter flicked open again. John relaxed and panted, inhaling deep breaths to calm the pain. Sera leaned in, and the knife was scalding hot as it pressed against his skin again. The smell of burning flesh wafted up into John's nose, making his stomach do flips. He turned his head to the side and ground down on the wood.

Sera finally pulled back and whispered, "Okay. Now I have to do your back."

John opened his eyes and spit out the wood, letting it roll away on the floor. Brandon ran over and picked it up. His eyes were wide as saucers as he stared at John.

"I'm okay, buddy. Promise."

John leaned forward, shivering as his fingers reached for the alcohol. Sera handed it to him, and he turned the bottle up, gulping a long, deep drink.

Nodding, John whispered, "Finish, Sera. Brandon, hand me the wooden spoon."

Once Sera finally finished, she leaned in and pressed her lips to his. He savored her sweet mouth and cupped his hand over her cheekbone. She pulled back and dug through her bag again. She pulled out a t-shirt and held it up. It was white with a picture of an ocean wave and an orange surfboard painted on it.

John let Sera help him pull the shirt over his head and ease his arms into the sleeves. She helped John up and made him lie down on the bottom bunk. His eyes blinked as he slowly drifted in and out. He could hear movement in the room as Sera was cleaning up everything. Then the mattress to the bed moved, and she was lying next to him.

Sera exhaled loudly before saying, "We found a way out. Only now I don't think we can go that way because John was shot."

"Yes, we can," John whispered.

"The way we found is a long dark tunnel going straight down a flight of stairs carved out in the wall. Then a second door opened, leading down to the basement, where we found an exit to the ocean. It's almost too good to be true." Sera yawned deeply and leaned against John. "Don't leave the room. I will rest for a little while with him, and then we'll figure out what to do next."

John reached over and pulled Sera into him. She was a perfect fit against his body. He just wanted to feel her breathing before he let the sleep come.

Chapter Thirty: The Guard

Sera

Sera opened her eyes to John's heavy breathing. She shifted her weight and stretched her bare toes out. A cold, wet, slimy substance began to move up her leg. She shifted and tried to pull away from the wetness when she felt it lock down over her lower extremities. Her heart pounded in her ears, drumming against her chest as she gasped his name through gritted teeth. "John." A burning sensation ran over her fingers and traveled up her arm, absorbing into her skin. She started to choke as the thick, milky substance filled her from the outside in, drowning her. Her body began to convulse, and she was paralyzed.

"Sera! Sera! Wake up. You're having a bad dream." John gently pushed on Sera's shoulder.

Sera's eyes flew open, and she shot up in bed. She leaned over and felt around on the floor for her belt. Her fingers pushed into it, and she pulled out her light, flipping it on. She looked up, and Brandon was standing next to the bed.

"Shit, Brandon. You scared the crap out of me." She put her feet on the floor, panting and holding her hand to her chest. "What's wrong, buddy? Did I wake you? I'm sorry—"

"Jim went into the attic right after you said not to."

Sera looked back, meeting John's eyes before she turned back to Brandon.

"Why did he go up there?" John asked.

Brandon shrugged his shoulders and sat down in front of

Sera. "How long ago did he go out?" Sera asked.

"Right after you fell asleep."

"How long have we been asleep, Brandon?"

"A really long time," he replied.

Thunder rolled off the house's roof and skirted across the ground outside, vibrating the walls.

"Oh, no, is it raining?" Sera asked.

"Yes, it's been pouring outside," Brandon replied.

Sera looked back at John again. *Fuck!* They stared at each other for a moment before she broke the silence. "Should we go out and look for him?"

John slowly shook his head and whispered, "No."

"Brandon, did you hear anything outside of the door?" John asked.

Brandon shook his head and looked back and forth between John and Sera.

Thunder struck again, rattling against the house with a monstrous growl. Brandon lunged forward and wrapped his arms around Sera's neck. As Sera wrapped her arms around Brandon, the door to their room started rattling. Sera jumped up, lunging towards the door. She held it shut with both hands and looked back at John, who was trying to crawl out of bed with his wounded arm. The door began to shake ferociously in the frame, and then a hard shove threw Sera back onto her rump. She knocked into John, and he slammed into the bunk bed. John stepped over Sera, pushing against the door, and Sera ran up beside him. Brandon wrapped his arms around Furry and sobbed on the bed.

The door shoved forward again, opening a small crack to their room. Panting, Sera met John's gaze. His eyes were glazed over with dark bags, and he gritted his teeth, moaning slightly as he shifted his feet. Nodding, Sera slammed into the door, pushing it back into its frame. She didn't know what was behind the door, but she wasn't about to let whoever or whatever it was in without a fight.

After all this time, I finally found a way out, mother fucker, and I'm not about to let you come in here and kill the only family I have.

Gritting her teeth, she slammed into the door again, and it closed fully.

Furry jumped off the bed and stood behind Sera with her hair standing on end. She bared her teeth, and a low grumble rolled up from her chest.

"Shh, Furry. Shh." Sera said.

"Do you think it's Jim?" Brandon whispered.

"No." Sera shook her head. She watched Furry and knew it wasn't Jim. Or the person they knew before the beings got to him. "It's not Jim, buddy. I promise."

"How do you know, Sera?" Brandon whispered.

"Because Furry told me," Sera said.

The door vibrated in the frame with a steady rumble. John and Sera's bodies shook as whatever was on the other side of that door refused to give up. Brandon's eyes glazed with fresh tears rolling down his cheeks as he stared at Sera.

She nodded and whispered, "Take Furry and sit under the covers on my bed. Okay?"

He nodded and walked Furry back over to the bed.

The door slowly stopped vibrating, and silence filled the room. A loud whistle squealed through the cracks of the house's walls, and then a powerful tremor rocked the foundation as the thunder followed. Heavy gusts of wind pushed, screaming against the roof as rain pummeled the house.

Hissing, John cradled his injured arm across his abdomen. He bared his teeth and inhaled deeply when he changed positions against the door. Smiling, he leaned over and kissed Sera's forehead.

"I think whatever it was is gone now." He nodded and turned around, sliding down the door with his back.

Nodding, Sera followed suit and looked over at Brandon. He was lying on the bottom bunk with his eyes closed. Furry was on the bed, curled up at his feet.

"Brandon," John whispered.

Brandon opened his eyes.

"You okay, buddy?"

Brandon nodded and closed his eyes.

"Do you think maybe it's okay to get up, Sera," John whispered.

Sera breathed deeply and shook her head slowly. "I don't know."

Nodding, he pushed himself up slowly from the floor, and as soon as he took a step from the frame, the door vibrated again, knocking him forward.

He fell hard on his knees and groaned, scrambling to regain his balance. Sera stood up and pressed her hands against the door. A demonic screech echoed from the other side as the frame trembled. Sera braced herself and looked up, meeting John's eyes.

Another shrill howl followed, but this time, a man was screaming on the other side of the door. "It burns! It burns!"

Brandon stood up with his hands over his ears, balling. Furry nudged his leg, and he just stood there with tears streaming down his face. He closed his eyes and shook his head. "No, no, no, no, no, no, no! It's Jim, John. It's Jim!"

"Brandon, shh. Be quiet," John said, snapping, shaking his head.

The familiar sound of the evil sang again, and then the door quaked beneath their hands. John and Sera bounced against the door with each brutal hit. The door slowly started to open, and none of them could stop it.

"No!" Sera screamed. She used everything she had and slammed into the door, shutting it again.

Panting, Sera gasped for air as her body ached from holding the door. All she could hear was her heart pounding in her ears. Her fingers ached and were slowly losing against whatever was behind the door. She looked up, meeting John's gaze, just before her body lost momentum and was knocked to the floor. Two men burst into the room and fell in the doorway. Panting, the two men lay on their stomachs, inhaling deep breaths. One of the men sat up, holding up a rifle. He shot up and looked out in the hallway.

"They're coming! Shut the door! Shut the door!"

"Brett! Brett, honey, you have to get up and move. Please, Brett." The man holding the rifle cried as tears rolled down his cheeks. He slowly shoved his friend over enough to shut the door, and then he dropped down on his rump in front of it. Sera and John stood up, staring down at their new visitors. Furry ran up to the men and sniffed the one sitting up first. She snorted and then walked over to the man lying on the floor. She jolted backward and snarled with her hair fluffed up.

The guy sitting against the door kicked at Furry. Sera stepped forward and pulled Furry back by the collar. "Hey, what the hell is wrong with you?"

"Keep your dog away from my boyfriend."

"Is your boyfriend still alive? Is he infected? She wouldn't act like that if he wasn't a threat."

Panting, the guy rubbed his face and slowly crawled over to his boyfriend. "Brett, honey. Wake up, please? Come on." The guy gently shook him.

"Where did you come from?" Sera asked.

"We were running from those things coming out of the sludge. We were guarding the back door when the rain started pouring down. I ran into the house, and they were freaking everywhere. The windows were all broken out, and those things were—" He stopped and looked over at his boyfriend on the floor. "Brett," the guy said, just above a whisper. His bottom lip began quivering as he repeated his name over and over.

"Are they in the attic?" Sera asked.

Sera watched the guy mourn his lover, but she had to ask questions. She knew how hard it was to lose someone you loved. To watch them—

"No, we pulled the stairs up. They can't get in."

"So the attic door was opened?" Sera said.

"Yeah, the stairs were down, but I pulled them back up." The guy's eyes never left his lover. He pleaded for him to wake up as he repeated his name.

"What?" Brett finally answered.

"Oh, thank god, baby." He rubbed his back. "I thought you were dead."

"Is there anyone left downstairs?" Sera asked.

"Look, lady, the only people left downstairs are those things. The attic stairs were down, so we climbed up. I saw an opened door in the wall, so I ran through it, and here we are."

Nodding, Sera dropped her head into her hand and rubbed her face.

"Where's Jim?" Brandon whispered.

"I don't know, buddy," John answered.

Sera looked back at Brandon and then at the man. "Our friend, he . . . he went out, and we don't know what happened to him. That's why we keep asking you if you saw anyone."

"There was no one left but us. The house is being overrun by those things. We're essentially trapped in here."

"Did you shut the hidden door to the attic?" Sera asked.

"No, I'm sorry. We just . . . we ran into that hallway and shoved on the walls until we found one that moved."

Brett's body began shivering on the floor. The other man scooted back on his rump and sat against the door. "No! No, Brett! Please, no." He sobbed. Steam billowed from Brett's body as his legs began convulsing against the floor. "No, not you, too!"

Brett slowly rolled, revealing that his face was covered in blood. His eye was missing, and the muscles glitched with the movement of his body.

"Brett?" the man whispered.

Brett's body slowly raised as if he were a puppet being controlled. His head cocked to the side, and he opened his mouth, spilling black sludge over his teeth. A high-pitched scream rang as he reached his arms out towards his boyfriend.

The man jumped up and ran towards John and Sera, cocking his gun. "Brett . . . I love you so much." His hands shivered as he cried. "I can't. I can't. I can't." He dropped down onto his rump, collapsing into himself. Before Sera knew what was happening, John swiped the gun from the guy's fingers and shot.

A bullet went right between Brett's eyes. Brett fell backward and lay on his back with steam rising from the hole. The guy screamed as his boyfriend dropped to the floor. He hung over, sobbing into his hands. Black sludge oozed from his lover's head and started covering the floor around him.

Sera ran over, grabbed her bag, and pulled out each drawer, grabbing what supplies she could before throwing the sack over her shoulder.

"It's time to go." She looked at everyone directly, in turn. Nodding, she grabbed Brandon's hand and touched the hunched over, sobbing man. "Come with us."

Shivering, he nodded and followed behind. After everyone exited the room, Sera turned and closed the door behind them. She knew the being was only stunned and would be back on the hunt soon.

Sera led everyone up to the attic and stopped to listen at the door. The only sound was a steady rain against the roof. She looked back and turned to push open the door. Flickering lights greeted them as they walked inside. Lightning ran across the angry clouds minutes before a monstrous boom followed. The two men Sera had killed were missing from the dark corner. Slowly, she walked over to the window and looked out. Beings stood right under the window, glaring at the house as if waiting for them to come out.

"Those things surrounded the house, just standing in the rain," Sera whispered. John walked over and peeked down.

"Look behind them. The sludge river has descended into the earth." She looked back at John, meeting his gaze, and then back out the window. John nodded and turned around.

"We'll have to wait for the rain to stop if we want a chance to run out of here without those things chasing us."

"We aren't getting out of here. We're surrounded. They took my . . . my Brett. He's gone." The man plopped down on his rump with a loud thud. Tears rolled down his cheeks as he stared ahead with glossy eyes.

"Sir? Excuse me. What's your name?" Sera whispered.

"Chris."

"Does the sludge river go all the way around the house?"

"Not yet, but you know it's just a matter of time before it traps us and sends its soldiers in to kill us all."

Sera nodded and walked over to the hole in the floor. She dropped down onto her stomach and looked in. The room was too dark to see. She waited for the lightning to flash to get a better look. Thunder rumbled, and a bright light glistened across the room, exposing rows of people standing there. Just waiting. Sera jumped and knocked on the floor with her hand. One of the beings looked up at the hole and stared. Its eyes glowed red in the darkness, and sludge seeped out of the cracks of its mouth.

Sera sat up and pulled back from the hole. She wrapped her arms around her legs and peered around the room, shaking her head.

John walked over to her. "What is it?"

Sera shook her head. "They're everywhere. He's . . . he's

right." She looked out the window and saw the rain rolling down the glass.

Brandon and Furry walked over to Sera and sat with her.

Chris crawled over and put his back against the hidden door. He started to massage his knee in a small circular motion.

"Are you okay?" Sera asked.

"Yeah."

"What's wrong with your leg?" Sera asked.

"Football injury. It's funny. I had a scholarship to play ball, but then everything happened. So I had nothing going for me, and then I found him." His bottom lip began to quiver, and he breathed deeply before whispering. "And now I have nothing again." He looked away from Sera, shaking his head.

Sera nodded and looked out the window, staring at the rain and thinking about how everything had changed. How it had all changed — their lives, their families, loved ones lost, and loved ones found. And now, what was left was them, fighting to live another day.

She looked down at Brandon, sleeping with his head in her lap. Furry snuggled up against him, and John sat next to her. She missed Eric so much that it hurt, but she also felt lucky to have found them. Even though she didn't want to admit it, she needed them.

All this time, she'd been searching for Sybil, for her brother. What she'd found was a possibility — a possible way to kill the sludge and sludge beings. She knew she had to be missing something. Sybil had sent John to help her find the answers.

I know what harms it, but I'm missing something. I'm not seeing what it is that's crucial to fighting back.

Sera's mother's voice rang in her head, *"You're the one who saves us all. Saves us all."*

Her gaze focused on the man, and she whispered, "My name is Sera. This is John, Brandon, and Furry." She pointed to everyone. "I'm so sorry about Brett."

Chris nodded.

"We should all try to get some rest."

Chris stared out the window. John nodded, and Sera lay beside Brandon, snuggling up to him and Furry. She ran her fingers through Furry's scruff until sleep took her.

Chapter Thirty-One: Surrounded

John

John shook Sera awake and then Brandon. He hadn't slept much due to the pain throbbing in his shoulder. He rubbed his face with his good hand and peered out the window. Sunlight filled the room, and the clouds had disappeared a few hours earlier. Sera sat up, and her hair was slicked across her cheek. She still looked beautiful even though she was half awake. Brandon shook John's leg and pointed to the bucket. Nodding, John walked him over and pulled the lid off. The smell hit him first, then Brandon. Gagging, Brandon turned away, shaking his head.

"I know, buddy, but it's all we have right now. Just get it over with, okay." Brandon nodded, and John turned around and faced Chris and Sera.

Chris limped over and said, "Well, I guess it's better than nothing."

"You okay, man?"

"Yeah. Yeah, I'll be fine."

John walked over to the window and looked down to see that the beings standing guard were gone and the place seemed abandoned. Nodding, he peered out over the water, and a sea of white caps rolled out into the horizon. It was as if the storm had never existed, leaving the day full of promise.

"Well, we should get going."

Sera nodded and said, "We can take the attic stairs, since the house is abandoned."

Chris stepped up and said, "That's not a good idea. Those things are everywhere. They'll hear the stairs and come running." He looked behind him and pointed. "Can we not go back through that hidden way and find a better path?"

"We can, but I don't think John can climb down with his arm. There are a lot of stairs that are carved into the wall. It's . . . it's too much for him. He needs both arms to go down. He'll fall, and it's a long tunnel down. The fall will kill him if he slips. Also, we have Brandon and Furry. I just . . . I'm not sure what to do." Sera put her hands on her hips, shaking her head.

Chris nodded and shifted his weight. "I can help."

"What about your boyfriend? We left him in the hidden room. What if he pushed through the door and is out in the hallway? If we go in and he's there . . ." John met Sera's gaze and shook his head. He didn't want to finish his sentence.

"There's another way." Sera piped in. She walked over to the hole in the floor and looked in. After a few minutes, she looked back up and nodded. "The room's empty, and the door is opened. It seems like the house really has been abandoned, but we won't know until we go down." Biting her lip, she looked around the room, and her eyes landed on John.

"If the hallway is clear and we can go through the hidden closet, we can check out the house before Brandon and Furry come down with us . . ." She stopped, looked at Brandon, and met John's gaze again.

"We can find a way to get out of here. We just have to sneak out and not alert the beings while we're at it."

John nodded and looked over at Brandon. Brandon was shaking his head and walked over to John.

"Don't leave me here," Brandon said. "I'm scared. What if they come up here and you're gone?"

John dropped to his knee and shook his head. "They won't. You can wait by the hidden door, and as soon as we check everything out, we will come back for you."

Brandon nodded and gripped John's hand. John stood up and walked over to the door next to Sera.

Sera turned to Brandon and squatted down. "Brandon, listen closely. This is very important."

Brandon met Sera's gaze and nodded.

"Once we come back to get you and go out into the house, you must stay close to John and me. You have to be very, very quiet. Do not scream or cry. Do you understand? If one of those things hears you, they will run and kill us. Okay?"

Brandon nodded with glossy eyes. John knew Sera was being harsh, but she was right. One wrong move or sound, and they could all be killed. Sera looked up and briefly met John's eyes before opening the hidden attic door.

"Brandon, stay here, and we'll be back as soon as we check everything out."

Brandon nodded and wrapped his arms around John's waist first and then Sera's. Sera turned and put her finger to her mouth as she opened the door. She slowly walked into the hallway, following John. The hidden door to the room that contained Brett was still closed. Sera stopped in front of it and listened. After a minute, she nodded and continued toward the hidden closet door.

She slithered through the entryway and held the door for John and Chris to follow. John stepped out of the closet behind Sera, and his mouth dropped. A gust of wind blew through the broken windows, wafting in the pungent smell of rotten flesh and decay.

The floor was covered in a layer of black sludge and dried blood. John met Sera's gaze as they stood over the malicious black ooze that had claimed so many people's lives. Shaking his head, he hurried Sera towards the door and stopped at the frame. The door was ajar, so he stepped through first and peered into the hallway. The front door was open, and glass covered the floor from the windows in the family room. Sera met John's eyes and nodded. He led the way out into the hallway and slowly climbed the stairs.

John's feet crunched over shards of glass and a sandy residue that blanketed the floor. As they drew closer to the front door, the smell of decay heightened, causing John's gag reflex to peak. His shoulder jerked, and a cough threatened to escape, so he cupped his mouth and breathed deeply.

John peered out the front door and then looked back at Sera. She nodded, and they all exited the house, standing on the front porch. A deep sense of dread sent a sharp pain through his gut. Off in the distance, the familiar cries of one of the beings echoed through the dunes. John met Sera's gaze, and they all froze.

"The sludge river . . . it's gone," Chris whispered.

"What do you mean? Sera and I were here a few days ago, and the river wasn't upfront. It—"

"I'm telling you the sludge had broken ground along the front of the house. I saw it yesterday before the outbreak of the beings." He walked out into the front yard and pointed. "There. That's where it was yesterday."

John met Sera's gaze, and they both followed Chris into the front yard. A long rectangular hole had opened a hundred feet from the house. John peered over, leaning forward on his tiptoes to see it was empty. The smell of the river lingered in the air, but the river had receded into the earth and left the hole abandoned.

"Why would it come up for one day and then go back down into the earth? It doesn't make any sense," John said.

Chris met John's gaze and shook his head. John looked back at the house, and a pair of red eyes met his gaze. Before John could react, the being opened its mouth and screamed the same shrill sound they'd all become familiar with. The sound that they needed to run and fast.

John pointed up and yelled, "Run!"

As soon as the being screamed, other beings joined in, and the sounds of them running towards the house echoed off the dunes.

"Go! Go! Go!"

John looked back as they entered the house and saw their heads peeking over the hill. He threw the door shut and followed Sera and Chris up the stairs.

There was a loud crash against the front door, and the house walls seemed to rattle as the beings collided with the structure.

"Oh, fuck!" John whispered.

Sera ran to the closet and opened it, meeting Brandon and Furry.

Chapter Thirty-Two: Escape

Sera

"Come on, Brandon! It's time to go!" Sera grabbed her bag and led Brandon and Furry out of the closet. She stopped them in the closet entryway and shook her head. "Wait!" The floor was covered in sludge.

"Chris, can you carry Brandon, and I'll get Furry."

Nodding, Chris ran over and scooped up Brandon, hoisting him over his back. Sera put her backpack over her back and grabbed Furry from her front to back legs.

John led the way to the door and listened. He looked back at Sera, shaking his head.

"Open the door quietly," Sera whispered.

John nodded and peeked out. The front door was still shut, and the bottom floor was empty. He waved his hand, and they all tip-toed out of the room. As soon as they left the bedroom, Sera sat Furry down, and Chris sat Brandon down.

Run. Sera mouthed.

The stairs creaked as they all rushed down the steps. John led the way to the kitchen, and as soon as they turned the corner, a being was standing in front of the back door. He slowly turned around, facing them.

"Jim." Brandon's voice squeaked.

Chris walked over, picked up a rifle lying on the floor, and pointed it at the being. He pulled the trigger, and . . . nothing. *Empty.*

The being opened his mouth, and a high-pitched scream

bellowed from its ooze-covered lips. He slowly started inching towards them and held his hand up, cocking his head to the side. Brandon started to cry, whimpering as Jim got closer and closer to them.

Chris turned the gun around and gripped it like a baseball bat. "Go! I'll take care of him."

He stood with his feet locked in and waved the gun back and forth, scooting the being backward.

"Chris, the door is right there," Sera whispers, pointing to the pantry door.

Chris turned to the door and nodded. Sera and John stood in front of Brandon and Furry and watched as Jim hobbled towards them again. Chris stepped towards him and swung, slamming the being across the head. The being's head hung over to the side, and black ooze spewed from its mouth, splattering on the floor as his body folded over into itself. His skin flailed about, and the sludge that filled his skin began to bubble over his injured head and neck.

"Chris, come on!" Sera yelled as she shoved everyone into the hidden pantry door.

When she closed the doors behind her, John grabbed her hand and had her walk up the steps slowly so he could fold the door open.

"Shit, John, how are you—"

"Don't worry about me. Just grab Furry."

Chris leaned over and put Furry over his shoulders. "I've got her."

Sera nodded and pulled Brandon up the steps with her. "Come on, buddy."

Brandon shivered tears streaming down his face.

John looked up and met Sera's gaze, nodding.

"Okay, Brandon. You have to be very brave now. These stairs are narrow, and you must hang on and move as fast as you can. Okay?"

He nodded and wiped his face with his forearm.

"Okay, John. How are you going to climb down?"

"I can do it, Sera," John grunted as he stepped down into the hole, using both arms. "Let's just get this over with."

"Okay, Brandon. I'll go first, and then you go."

"Chris, are you okay?"

"Yeah, I got Furry."

The tunnel seemed to go down forever before Sera's feet finally touched the bottom. She licked her parched lips and tasted a salty mildew lingering in the air. She flipped on her flashlight, and John was bent over, panting, and holding his shoulder.

Sera could see John's blood soaking through his t-shirt and trailing down his back.

"Shit, John, we need to get you—"

"Just leave it, Sera. It can wait. We have to get out of this damn house." John said, shrugging her off.

Sera went over to the hidden door and pushed it open. A breeze blew through the door, smelling of the ocean and fresh rain. Chris, Brandon, and Furry walked over and met Sera's gaze, their mouths gaping open.

"This tunnel leads to the ocean."

Chapter Thirty-Three: The Tunnel

John

John followed Sera as she led the way into the tunnel. The wood whined overhead, and a loud gust of wind whistled outside, dumping handfuls of damp sand through the cracks of the ceiling. Brandon squeezed John's hand and looked up, meeting his gaze with a ghostly stare.

"It's okay, buddy. It's just an old safe tunnel, I guess . . ." John peered around and said, "I really don't know what it is. I just know that it leads to the ocean."

Brandon nodded and looked straight ahead.

"Whatever it is, it's really old. Maybe a hundred years old," Chris said.

"Well, I'm glad we found it, because now we have a way out," Sera said.

Furry ran past everyone, stopped, sniffed the ground here and there, and then trotted ahead.

"Not too far, Furry," Sera said.

The tunnel felt like it stretched for miles. Sera's beam reached a few feet in front of them, leading the way. She looked back, periodically meeting John's gaze. Even though she didn't say anything, John could see the worry in her eyes as they continued forward.

Brandon's arm jerked, and he stumbled to his knees. He looked up at John, and a single tear rolled down his cheek.

"You, okay, buddy?"

"Yeah, something sharp stabbed me in the hand."

Brandon held up his hand, and his palm had a small cut. Sera walked over, shinning her beam over the floor. A loud gasp echoed down the tunnel, and Sera squatted a few feet from where Brandon fell.

"What is it? What's wrong?"

Sera's beam walked along the ground and went against the wall, meeting the floor. She leaned over and picked something up, examining it under her light. Another wisp of air blew from her lips as she jolted to her feet, dropping what she was holding. She backed away slowly as she ran her light along the ground again.

"What?"

"It's—"

"Bones," Chris said, finishing Sera's sentence. Chris walked over and stood next to Sera, gazing at the floor.

Sera's beam slowly followed along the floor until it came to a pile of something.

"Oh, Shit!" John said, looking around the tunnel.

John walked over to the bones and looked down at what she'd dropped next to the pile. It looked like a human's pelvic bone. John met Sera's gaze, and they both locked eyes on the bank of bones. John quickly pulled Brandon away from the newly found graveyard and stood on the other side of the tunnel. He paced back and forth and then stopped, looking around him.

"What the fuck?" John realized the tunnel walls were lined with human and animal remains on both sides.

"The sludge beings—"

"No, this isn't the beings. This is from crocks." Chris went over and stood next to John. "Those are from crocodiles. They're migrating to the ocean in search of food. We saw them coming into this tunnel when I was, you know, still with them." Chris pointed towards the house. "It just hit me, and I realized I knew where we were."

207

"I thought alligators and crocodiles only lived in swamps, hunted in freshwater, and liked eating fish and small sea life creatures," Sera said.

A small laugh rumbled in Chris's chest as he shook his head. "You're not from around here, are you?"

Sera shook her head, looking down at the bones. "No, we lived more inland when I was growing up, and then I moved away."

"Alligators and crocodiles rarely hunt humans, but their food source has dwindled like ours." Chris squatted down next to the pile of bones. He picked up a piece of someone's leg and flung it against the wall.

John walked back over to the bones and kicked the pile. He exhaled loudly and shook his head before grabbing Brandon's hand. "We have to get the hell out of here."

A few hours had passed, and the tunnel still stretched on. The bones still lined the wall, meeting the floor as they trudged forward.

Brandon began stumbling and dragging his feet, so John stopped and knelt down so that he could climb up on his back. Within minutes, Brandon's breathing grew heavy, and his legs dangled from his sides.

Sera looked back and waited for John to meet her pace. "Do you want me to take him?"

"Nah, I got him." John forced a smile and nodded.

"I don't remember it taking so long last time," Sera whispered.

"We jogged almost the entire way to the end, remember?"

"Yeah."

"We're probably almost there now." John winced when he pointed up with his injured shoulder.

Sera patted John's forearm and nodded before leading the way with the light. John yawned, his body vibrating as he inhaled a deep breath. He squeezed his eyes shut briefly, and when he opened them, he saw something moving. He froze, squinting, and realized it was the door. The wooden door that led to the ocean had finally appeared and was flapping in the wind. John picked up the pace, and the sound of the wood hitting the frame rattled down the tunnel.

John reached for Sera's hand and laced his fingers with hers. She met John's gaze, nodding, and walked with him, hand in hand, towards the exit.

Furry took off, running towards the door, then stopped suddenly. Her feet slid across the floor, and the fur on her back stood up. A growl rolled up from her chest and exploded out her snout as she released a series of barks.

"Furry?" Sera whispered and sprinted towards the dog.

"Sera, no!" John said as he saw an outline of something giant standing in front of the dog.

Sera stopped just behind Furry and reached out for her. "Furry, come," she said, her voice slightly louder than a whisper.

A deep grumble, similar to a lion's, echoed near the tunnel's entrance, followed by a hissing sound. John's heart dropped into his stomach as he quickly walked towards Sera. When he approached, Sera grabbed Furry by the scruff and pulled her back. He slowly set Brandon on the floor and put his finger to his mouth. Brandon walked backward, trembling. Chris walked around from behind him and nodded.

Sera backed up slowly, not turning away from the beast, and whispered, "What do we do? That thing is over twelve feet long. It will come for us in a minute, and I don't know how to kill it."

"They hiss when they feel threatened," Chris said.

"Oh, you think," John replied.

The beast opened its mouth, and a growl rumbled, sending chills down John's spine.

"Chris, how the hell do we kill it?" John whispered.

"Aim for the eyes or center of the head."

"Aim with what? We don't have any weapons."

"I have a bowie knife," Sera said, holding it up. She peered around them and nodded towards the wall. "There are broken bones everywhere, too."

The ground rattled underneath them, and sand from the roof began dumping over their heads.

"The beast is so big that it's bumping into the walls. He's going to make this damn thing collapse," John yelled.

"Go!"

"Where?"

"Just go!" Chris said.

Chris ran over to the pile of bones and grabbed a couple of long bones. He ran ahead of John and Brandon and waited.

"Come on you, fucker!"

Sera ran up next to him, and John pulled Sera back. "What the hell are you doing?"

"Stop it!" Sera snapped.

The combination of the beast running towards them and the doors flapping in the wind blurred out what happened next. John grabbed Sera's hand and pulled her back just before the beast approached them.

Chris lunged forward, covering the beast's snout, and yelled, "Now, Sera! Now!"

Sera pulled from John's grip and plunged her knife into the gator's eye. Its giant body whipped back and forth, knocking Sera into the wall of bones. Its tail collided with Sera, knocking her body into the structure again and again. She lay on the ground motionless as the beast beat her like a rag doll.

John jumped over the gator, pulling Sera away from it. He helped her to her feet, and she stumbled forward as he tried to ease her upright. She wrapped her arms around his neck, trembling.

"Shh, I've got you. You need to take Brandon and Furry and go to the door. Chris and I will take care of the croc."

"No, John. No, your—"

"Go, now!"

Sera released John's hand and grabbed Brandon's. She stumbled towards the exit, following the wall with her hand. John looked back at the beast and exhaled deeply.

"Well, fuck." He met Chris's eyes and nodded. They walked up to the beast, and John spotted the bowie knife poking out of its eye. The beast was still thrashing back and forth, whipping its tail into the wall.

John pointed to the gator and said, "Are you ready?" Chris nodded, and John lunged, jumping over the crock's mouth. He held the animal's snout shut and yelled, "Now!"

Chris pulled the knife out of the crock's eye and plunged it in again and again until its body finally stopped moving.

Panting, Chris slowly stood up from the monster and stepped away from it. "I think it's finally dying," he said, reaching his hand out to help John climb off the beast.

John looked towards the door and saw Sera, Brandon, and Furry waiting for them. She nodded, and a slight smile arched her brows. The moonlight shined against her fiery hair, and John saw stars reflecting against the ocean's waves for the first time in a long time.

CHAPTER THIRY-FOUR: FINDING SYBIL

Sera

Sera released the door and let the wind slam it against the frame. She turned, meeting John's gaze. This was it. This was what they'd been striving for. *Freedom.* Freedom from the shackles of the house and being surrounded by the sludge river and its soldiers as they slowly closed in around them. Now, Sera had to do what she said she was going to do all along. *Find Sybil.*

Sybil? Sybil, we made it out of the house and headed your way. I know you can hear me. Please, please, answer me. A lump formed in Sera's throat and her eyes burned as tears threatened. She swallowed hard and pushed down the sorrow. Deep down, she knew she didn't feel her sister anymore. She hadn't felt her sister since she opened the basement door to rescue John. But she was so close now. She had to know the truth, even if it meant she was gone.

She looked back, meeting John's gaze. His eyes glazed over before he turned to look out over the ocean.

"I need to go find Sybil now. I have to know if she's . . . okay."

The waves glistened under the moonlight as they thrashed in the deep sea. Sera looked down and watched as the water rolled up the beach and trickled over her boots, sending chills up her spine.

John looked back, facing Sera. "Sera, I—"

She felt what he was about to say, and she couldn't bear it.

No.

Sera's voice lowered to a whisper as she said the last words. "No, John. I'm going over there, and there's nothing you can say that will change that. I have to know." *I have to know.* The words rang in her head. *I have to know.*

Sera took another step back, looked down, watching the water rush over her shoes, and said, "I'll understand if this is where we part. I—"

John's hand touched Sera's chin, raising it. She met his gaze, and he rubbed his thumb gently over her bottom lip. His hand dropped, and he cupped his hand over hers, squeezing.

"Which way is Sybil's house?"

Sera nodded towards the houses and said, "That way."

"Well, then, that's the way we'll go. When was the last time you saw her?"

"In person when my mother died. But we always spoke . . ." Sera inhaled a deep breath and met John's eyes. She'd never told anyone the truth about them. Not even Eric. *Eric.*

Sera looked down and met Brandon's eyes. Chris took a step forward and waited for her to finish what she was about to say.

"We're . . . our family . . . it's well . . . it's different. I don't know how to say it any easier than just . . . say it. We're special. My mother was a Lycan and a Witch, with other abilities that I don't even know where they're from. We weren't . . . close. So she never told me anything. She never told any of us anything, honestly. And my father . . ." Sera grinned slightly. His smiling face came to mind, and she looked away, biting her bottom lip to keep from tearing up. "My father was normal . . . human. He didn't have any magic. He never knew what we were. My mother made it very clear to never-ever tell anyone. So . . . I didn't."

Sera stopped, meeting everyone's gazes. Their mouths dropped and their eyes flew wide.

"I know this is a lot to take in, but it's true. We were all different, and the way that we communicated most of the time was in our minds."

John slightly shook his head and closed his mouth briefly to swallow. His Adam's apple bobbed up and down as he gulped a deep breath.

"I just don't know what to say—"

"That's awesome, lady," Chris said, slightly raising his voice. He slapped Sera on the back and then clapped.

Sera forced a grin and nodded. "But what I was trying to say was that . . ." A lump formed in Sera's throat as she tried to speak. "I haven't heard from her since before I found John. She . . . she stopped talking to me."

"Oh," was all John whispered. "Me, too."

"You're magical, too?" Chris said.

John shook his head. "No, I stopped hearing her voice."

"Holy shit. Both of you heard her talking?"

John glared at Chris and then met Sera's gaze. His eyes softened before he spoke. "She led me to you, and after you brought us to your room, she stopped talking to me, too."

Sera nodded. "I have to go to her now." She looked at Chris and slightly nodded. "I'll understand if you don't want to go. It's something that I need—"

"Sera, I don't have anywhere else to go. I, uh . . ." Chris's eyes looked past Sera, gazing up at the houses over the dunes. He shrugged his shoulders when he looked back over at her.

Sera nodded. She understood and knew it was time to go.

"Wait, Sera. Before we go, I want to test your theory." John pulled Sera's bag from her shoulder and opened it. He pulled out her thermos and water jugs and walked over to the water. He filled them up and handed one to Chris. "Here."

Nodding, Sera watched John. He took the thermos and walked back. "If Sera's theory is right, then the water will at least slow down the sludge beings."

Chris's brow creased, and he cocked his head to the side. "Water?"

John answered, "Water."

"Okay, then."

"We're crazy for doing this. You know that, right?"

"Yeah."

Sera nodded and reached out for Brandon's hand. John took Brandon's other hand and walked towards her sister's house.

The night was dark, but the moon helped guide her back to Sybil. Even though the house was only a few hundred feet from the water, it felt like a mirage as she stared at it. It hovered over a cloud of sand, floating up and down over the surface. The closer she approached, the harder her heart pounded in her ears.

Sera and John led the way, tip-toeing through the sand until they finally stopped in front of the two-story house. A little white picket fence surrounded it with a white gate that had the letter J on the frame of it. When Sera pulled up the hook that held the gate closed and pushed, seashells jingled together, sounding her arrival. She pulled the string of shells from the door and threw them in the sand.

Once everyone was on the wraparound porch, Sera stopped, frozen in front of the door. She couldn't move. Her heart drummed against her chest, and her lungs felt like they were closing. Air barely seeped through her mouth, and she slumped over, holding her knees with her hands. John's reassuring hand rubbed her back, and his lips touched her cheek.

"We don't have to do this if you don't want to. I don't think she's here. I think—"

"She's here. I know she is. I feel her now. She's . . . I have to do this." Sera could feel her sister was there, but she was silent. *Silent. Sybil? Sybil, I feel you. Sybil, please.*

She stood up, reached for the door, and pushed it open.

The house was pitch-dark inside. She couldn't see anything anywhere but knew where to walk from experience. She stepped inside and pulled out her light, turning it on. The room was dusty and bare, as if nothing had been inside for a while. Sera led the way to the stairs and looked up the banister. Sybil's master bedroom door was ajar. She slowly took one step at a time, and before she realized it, she was standing in front of her sister's door. Furry whimpered at the top of the stairs, standing beside Brandon, pawing the air towards Sera. Sera nodded back at them and entered the room.

Sera's beam cut through a lingering haze as she searched for her sister. She slowly guided her light towards the wall her sister's bed was on and stopped. It was her. *Sybil.* She was lying on her back, on her bed, with a white sheet covering her body. Sera walked closer, stopped right next to her sister, dropped to her knees, and reached for her hand. Tears flowed down her cheeks as her body vibrated. Her sister's golden blonde hair had turned to white tendrils flowing down her body. Her cheeks were sunken in with a gray hue, taking the color of her glowing skin. Her tiny body had drifted away into nothing, shrinking down to a skeleton protruding from her flesh. Sera grabbed her sister's hand, squeezing her iced fingers.

"I'm so sorry, Sybil. I tried. I tried to get to you sooner. I—"

Sybil's eyes opened, and a ghostly white stare gazed into Sera's eyes. She squeezed Sera's hand back, and her mouth opened, releasing her breath.

Close your eyes, sister. Sera's lids slowly drifted closed, and visions of her, John, Brandon, Sammy, and so many other people she'd never met flashed through her mind. A storm whirled through the air with blazing red skies and black flashes of lightning. Flooding of red sludge from the river flowed over everything, killing everyone. Sera's hand started burning, and the feeling of her whole body being taken over froze her to the core. She couldn't move. She couldn't scream for help. She just sat there while she was being taken over.

You. Have. To. Find. The. Answer. Find. The. Answer. I. Love. You. Sera. Good. Bye.

Sybil released Sera's hand, and she dropped to the floor. Her body convulsed against the ground, smashing her face into the wood. John ran over and pulled her up into his lap on the floor, holding her against his chest as she trembled. Sera's body finally relaxed, and she hung from his grip, panting. Shaking her head, Sera pushed herself to her feet and watched Sybil's body crumble slowly into the mattress of the bed. Tears drizzled down her cheeks as she reached out to stop her sister from leaving her.

Sybil, please wait. Wait for me. I don't want to do any of this without you. I love you. Please.

Sera.

Sybil? Sera looked up, and her sister was hovering over the bed. Her long golden locks had returned, flowing down her voluptuous, tiny body. She wore a long white gown, and her crystal blues glowed through the darkness of the room.

You can do this, sister. You were always the strong one. When I went back to see Mom in the hospital, I held her hand, and I saw how much she loved you and how proud she was of you. She just didn't know how to show it. She had a vision that you and you alone saved us all. You're the one who stops this and saves what's left of mankind, but you have to believe. Believe in yourself.

I don't know if I can. I —

Yes, you can, and you will. I'll always be with you, no matter what happens. I love you, sister.

Sybil, wait. Please. Don't go yet.

Sybil's spirit form began to drift into the air and joined the dust particles floating around.

I love you, too, Sybil.

John's hand cupped Sera's shoulder, and he turned her

around to face him. She buried her face into his chest and let the sobs come. After a few minutes, she looked around the room and saw Brandon, Furry, and Chris standing in the doorway.

She looked up, meeting John's gaze, and nodded. She had found Sybil, and now she had to move on.

Sera opened the front door and peered around the house. The night was quiet, with distant sounds of the ocean rolling in. She was leading the way back to the water when an odd sound erupted behind them. She turned to look back and felt a gust of wind pushing her body away from the house. Her body rolled and finally came to a stop face down in a mound of sand. She looked back to see Brandon and Furry lying motionless a few feet away. A bright white light exploded in the distance, and a loud siren screeched.

"Sera! Sera! Sera!"

Sera sat up, wobbling back and forth on her rump, searching for John. She could hear his voice, but it was muffled as if it wasn't real.

"John." She mouthed his name, but her parched lips ground together. "John."

Searching, she peered around her and spotted shadows of people off in the distance. She whispered his name again, "John? Is that you?"

A loud explosion trembled under Sera's feet, and a giant fire blasted from the direction of Sybil's house.

Sera wobbled upright and took a step, falling back onto her rear. The sand was thick, and she struggled to walk straight.

"Sera."

Furry barked and ran over to her, then ran around her and barked again before returning to where she'd started. Sera trudged towards her and saw Brandon's hand up in the air.

He was lying in the sand, calling for her. "Sera."

"Come on, buddy. Let's go." Sera pulled him to his feet, looked over, and saw John and Chris walking up behind her.

"It was an explosion at the house. There are military men over there bombing the houses."

Sera looked back at the house and saw dozens of beings running towards them.

"Oh shit! Run!"

Sera whipped around and dragged Brandon behind her as she jogged towards the water.

"Furry, come on!"

When she looked back, the beings were gaining on them. She swung Brandon around to her back and pounded her feet into the sand. Her legs burned as she pushed, and just as she thought the beings were going to reach out for them, the water appeared. She tripped and rolled down the dune, falling into the tide. The beings stopped and stood on top of the dune, glaring down at them.

Sera huddled down in the water as the tide rolled over her body. Panting, she saw John and Chris hunched over with their hands on their knees.

"You were right . . ." He inhaled another deep breath and stood straight up with his hands on his hips. "The beings are staying away from the water."

Sera pulled herself up and walked over to John, nodding.

"Yeah, now we have to figure out where the hell to go now," Sera said.

Chapter Thirty-Five: Test Your Theory

John

A round of gunshots fired just over the sand dunes. Bright lights from heavy artillery fluttered in the sky like fireworks. Sludge beings turned and ran towards the heavy artillery, screaming as they galloped away. A few beings were left behind to stand guard, peering down at them with glaring, blood-set eyes.

John looked at Sera and said, "We should get going before the sun comes up."

"What do you think is happening up there?" Sera whispered.

"I don't know. It looks like someone's bombing the sludge river."

"Which way should we go?" Sera said.

Chris pointed one way and said, "There's a boat marina down that way, and the other way is more beach."

"Boats?" Brandon's voice squeaked.

"Yeah, buddy. Do you like boats?" John nodded.

"I don't know. I've never been on one before."

"Well, we should definitely go then," John replied.

A smile warmed Brandon's eyes as he looked up at John. A sharp pain pinged John's heart as he met his gaze. He wanted Brandon to be a little boy and have a normal life. He wanted him to be able to rest and wake up in the morning without fear of being killed. A lump formed in John's throat as he squeezed Brandon's hand. He nodded and directed Brandon to keep walking.

The beach went on for over an hour before the sun started peeking over the horizon. As the light appeared, the view of more beings guarding the water came into view. They were lined along the dunes, facing the water in pairs. They stood there like expressionless shells, waiting. John knew if one of them stepped too far from the safety of the water, the being would swoop in and kill them.

As the sun was rising, its rays beat down on their backs, heating them up immediately. Sweat ran down John's back and beaded over his brow, blinding his vision. He swiped his forehead with the back of his arm and continued on.

Brandon kicked the sand and shuffled his feet as he walked beside John. Sera walked up next to him and met his gaze, forcing a slight smile. She leaned over, nodded at Brandon, and stopped. Brandon's face was beet red, with sweat pooling over his brow. She took his hand and walked him over to the ocean water. They got down on their knees and threw water over their faces before returning to John. Sera handed Brandon her hat, letting her short red locks drop into her eyes.

She looked up, meeting John's gaze with her twinkling crystal blues. John wanted to pull her into him, kiss her lips gently, and tell her how beautiful she was, but he knew that it wasn't the right time. *It may never be the right time. We may never have ... time together.*

He walked over to her and reached his hand out to hold hers. She took a step towards him and —

"Sera! Look, it's a bridge. A humungous bridge!" Brandon yelled.

A long white bridge floated over the sea like a mirage in a dream. John looked, following the beach, and realized that once they reached the bridge, they would no longer have the safety of the water, leaving them completely exposed. *Shit.* John looked over, staring at the beings. They stared ahead like birds of prey, perched and waiting for them to be vulnerable.

Shaking his head, he looked down at the jug and then over at Sera. *I need to test Sera's theory before we even attempt to walk to the bridge. It has to be now or never.* He looked down at the thermos and then up at the beings. He slowly walked towards one of the beings as he spun the thermos lid open—

"Sera, I'm hungry," Brandon whispered. John looked down at him, and he was wobbling back and forth.

"Okay." Sera dropped her bag and sat on the sand in front of the tide coming in. Brandon sat next to her, cross-legged, and Furry sat next to him with her tongue hanging out the side.

"Can I have some water, Sera?" Brandon whispered. His sunken, glossy eyes hid under the oversized cap, gazing up at her. John watched as Sera pushed the bill of her hat back from his face. A sweet smile creased her lips, showing her matching dimples on each side of her face as she gently petted Brandon's cheek. She looked back and met John's gaze, slightly nodding. John could see that she was afraid. Worried that they weren't going to make it.

John looked towards the bridge and stared. *We have to make it.*

Sera reached into her bag and pulled out the last two water bottles and the last two cans of food. She propped the can opener on the top of the can and began to open it. She pulled out a bowl for Furry, and they all ate and drank quietly.

John met Sera's eyes, then trailed his focus over to Brandon and Chris. *If this doesn't work, I'll find a way to distract the beings so that Sera and Brandon can make a run for it.* John knew that he had to weigh out all his options. He couldn't bear the thought of them making it this far for nothing.

Sera looked up, meeting John's gaze, and said, "I think we should try to find a boat. It may be the only way to escape those things."

Nodding, John searched her face and looked up at the beings standing guard. "We have a problem. Once we get to the bridge, we won't have any coverage anymore. Meaning, no more ocean water to run into when they come for us."

Sera's brows creased. "I know."

"So that means we have to test your theory."

Sera chewed on her bottom lip and slightly shook her head. "How are we—"

John started walking towards the beings, twisting the cap on the thermos again. He knew if he hesitated, Sera would try to stop him.

Sera shot to her feet. "John, wait—"

"No, I have to do this," John whispered as he approached the beings. He met one of the being's gazes and stopped, staring into its empty eyes. Its red irises bore into him as he stepped closer and closer to the figure. It began to open its mouth slightly, and a loud, shrill scream began to bellow from its jowls. John held up the water and shook it, splashing water into the being's face.

The being instantly dropped to the ground, convulsing as smoke billowed out of its orifices. Sludge bubbled and popped on its face as if it were boiling from the inside out. John slowly took steps back and watched as the being's insides seeped into the sand. The surrounding beings turned and watched as one of their own sizzled down into nothing.

"Well, now we know," John whispered. "You were right."

She looked up, meeting John's gaze with a smirk across her face.

Nodding, John walked back over to the water and refilled his thermos.

"Holy shit, dude," Chris said as he threw his arms up into the air, cheering.

"Don't cheer yet. We still have to make it over the bridge."

"Hey, it's a start, man."

Nodding, John secured the jug and led the way towards the bridge.

A white light flicked off the water and shot into John's face. He turned and caught another flash of light, blinding him. "What the—"

He cocked his head to the side and realized it was a mast with a shimmering white sail reflecting off the water.

"Well, there's your boat, Sera."

Brandon started jumping up and down, pointing. "It's a boat, Sera. It's a boat!"

"It looks like it's right next to the bridge. We could jump off the bridge to get to it," Sera said.

"Yeah, if we wanted to die. That bridge is hundreds of feet in the air, and the boat is probably a lot further away from the bridge than you can see. The fall alone would kill us."

Sera shook her head and turned to him. "What else do you suggest, John? We have nowhere else to go!"

"I'm just saying we'll have to figure it out when we get closer."

Nodding, Sera inhaled deeply. "Let's just keep moving."

Chris approached John and asked, "Do you really think this can work?"

"I don't know," John said, shaking his head. "We have to try. You saw what it did to the one sludge being. I think this will keep them at bay long enough to get to that boat."

John took a deep breath and exhaled. Reaching his hand out, he waved for Brandon to come. Furry ran over with Brandon, and they walked away from the water and were approaching the bridge.

John looked back and saw the beings still standing guard on the sand dunes. They hadn't moved or even acknowledged that they were away from the water now.

"Why aren't they following us?" Sera whispered to John.
John shook his head. "Let's not wait to find out."

Chapter Thirty-Six: The People

Sera

The bridge was only a few hundred feet away now. Sera stopped and covered her brow with her hand to get a better look. "People are walking near the bridge."

"I don't think they're sludge beings. They look . . . different."

"How can you be sure?" John whispered.

"Well, I'm not. I just . . . they seem different in the way that they're carrying themselves."

"Sera." Brandon stopped, holding something up. "Look. It's a huge seashell. My mom . . . here." Brandon's shoulders dropped, and he looked at the ground. He was holding a beautiful white shell with a pink swirl along the center.

Nodding, Sera put her arm around Brandon's shoulders and squeezed. "Thank you, Brandon, it's beautiful."

Her heart swelled when she held the little boy. She'd never had any children of her own, but she knew that Brandon had come into her life for a reason. Even though she didn't want to admit it, she needed him more than he needed her. She looked over at John, swallowed hard as a lump hung in her throat, and realized she needed them both.

"Sera, look," John said, pointing at the bridge. More people were walking, moving onto the bridge, pointing in their direction.

Fuck.

Chris turned towards Sera. "Well, they noticed us."

It's our only way off this beach. We need to be able to cross that bridge. Fuck. Fuck. Fuck.

"Yeah." Sera nodded. "Come on, let's keep moving."

John led them to the road, and they all stopped and stared. The roads were littered with abandoned cars and people's belongings. Newspapers and trash twirled in the wind, skipping down the deserted highway. The people who'd just been walking along the road disappeared, and all that was left was silence.

Sera looked up at John, shaking her head. "It's quiet. Too quiet. Where do you think the people went?"

John slowly shook his head. "I don't know. Something doesn't . . . feel right."

Sera looked over her shoulder back in the direction they had just walked. What the fuck! "Where did the sludge beings go?"

Brandon pointed ahead, and Sera looked up to see Chris had already started walking on the bridge. He was bent down, looking through the window of one of the cars.

Familiar screams of sludge beings echoed off in the distance. Sera spun around and searched, whipping her head back and forth, panicking. "I can't tell where it's coming from."

"I don't know," John whispered. "Let's keep moving."

"I don't like this, John. I—"

Gunshots fired, and the ground vibrated underneath their feet. Sera stumbled and held Brandon as the cement tremored.

"What the hell is going on?" Sera looked over at John. He waved for her to keep moving.

Sera stopped, peering down a path of cars jumbled together. The congestion was so thick that they would soon be forced to walk along the tops of abandoned vehicles. *Fuck. Fuck. Fuck.* Sera climbed up on one of the cars, watching John as he walked ahead and wedged his body through the wreckage until he came to a block in the road. A long diesel truck was parked sideways, blocking the entire street.

"Where the hell is Chris? I don't see him. Do you see him?"

John looked back, shaking his head, and put his finger up to his lips, shushing Sera. Brandon tugged on Sera's hand with a ghostly stare. Nodding, she squatted down on the car's hood to get down when she saw something move in her peripheral vision. She slowly looked up to see a man glaring down at her from the top of a car only a few feet from her. His jagged teeth oozed black sludge, dripping down his chin and neck.

Cautiously, Sera stepped down off the car when something moved on the other side of her. She turned her head to see another man to her left. His face was bloody with sludge-covered fangs, staring back at her. He opened his mouth and started cackling uncontrollably. A burst of repetitive laughter echoed out of his chest, and then he abruptly stopped as if he had never started laughing. Sera twitched, jumping back as he stepped towards her.

"Where are you off to, girl?"

Sera looked for the other man standing on the car, but he'd vanished. She glanced quickly around her and then locked eyes with the man talking to her. He licked his lips with his rotten black tongue and smiled. He squeezed his eyes shut, and when he opened them again, a red flash of light pulsed through his eyes. She knew this was something different. It was as if the sludge was evolving. The man was more alert than a sludge being but was somehow infected.

Sera glanced over at John and saw that he was hiding Brandon behind him, and Furry was next to him. She looked for the missing man, but he was still gone.

She turned to face the man to her left. She knew she had to do something. "We don't want any trouble. We're just passing through."

A loud, boisterous laugh rumbled out of the man, and then

he stopped. "No one passes through here. I'm hungry, girl, and we need to eat!"

Sera shook her head, gently put her bag on the ground, unzipping it, and pulled out a pocketknife and the canteen. The man smiled and started walking towards her. Sera twisted the lid open and shook the canteen. A small stream of water shot out, hitting the man. The man lunged forward, knocking the can from her hand, and pushed her back. She jumped up and plunged her knife into his belly. He wobbled back and forth with his mouth open and let out a scream of shrill horror that echoed down the bridge, piercing her ears with agonizing pain. She raised her hands, cupping over her drums until the sounds stopped.

The man dropped to his knees, convulsing as black sludge oozed out of his stomach and onto the ground. The sludge bubbled, pooling in front of him. His body stopped seizing, and he dropped face-first into the cement. Panting, Sera rose and looked back to see John and Brandon on the ground, holding their ears.

The man on the ground slowly stilled and relaxed into the cement. His breath labored and then stopped abruptly. Sera looked down to see the sludge spreading and moving toward her, John, and Brandon. She ran over to the boys, pulled them up, and pushed them towards the trucks.

"We have to go before the other one comes back."

A large semi sat blocking the road and enabling them to cross. Sera climbed up the truck and opened the door. "Come on. Hurry," Sera whispered.

A hissing noise sounded behind them, and Sera looked back to see the man on the ground, with steam rising from his body. She waved her arms at John. "Go, John. Go. Now, you have—"

"No, not without you."

"Go. I'll be right behind you. I promise." A sinking feeling shot through Sera's heart. She knew that she might not make it. John's eyes locked with hers, and he slowly shook his head.

He inhaled deeply and whispered, "Not without you, Sera."

Sera walked over to John and pressed her lips against his. She felt her heart pounding against his chest as she slowly pulled back. "I'll be right behind you. I promise."

John searched her face and gently touched her hair before picking up Brandon.

Nodding, Sera heard John grunting as he hastily pushed Brandon into the truck cab. He looked back, meeting Sera's gaze one more time. Sera looked back and remembered the canteen. She ran over to it and felt it had a little water remaining. She carried it back over to John. "Take it."

He nodded and disappeared in the cab.

"Sera, we're on the other side. Now, come on." John's voice called from the other side of the truck.

"Okay. Okay. I'm coming."

She turned to Furry and saw the man still lying on the ground, sludge oozing out of him. Sizzling crackled, and a gush of steam billowed from his body, wafting into the air.

Furry started barking, ran to one of the cars, and stepped onto the hood with her front paws.

"What is it, girl?"

Furry cocked her head from side to side as if she was hearing something Sera couldn't. Sera slowly walked towards her, and the minute she reached the car, she felt the ground vibrate under her.

"What the—"

The vibrations grew stronger and stronger, and a peculiar sound echoed off in the distance. A cloud of black smoke filled the sky, painting the clouds. Sera slowly crawled onto the car and saw fires burning along the sand dunes they had just walked. Hooding her eyes from the sun, she watched the smoke.

"Hey!" A voice right behind her yelled.

She whipped around, and a brutal hit blasted against her temple. Her body flew through the air and landed hard on the edge of another car. She gasped, the wind knocked out of her. She rolled over, trying to swallow as sharp pains shot through her cheeks. She tried to sit up and felt another blow hit her stomach. Rolling over, Sera coughed and hugged her belly. Warm vomit spewed out of her, burning her throat. Blinking, she saw a puddle of bright red liquid dripping down the car.

The man glared down at her, standing only a few feet away from her face. He reached out, grabbed her arm, and dragged her down the car next to the man she'd killed. Sera rolled her head back and forth, looking up at the truck. The door was closed.

The man walked a complete circle around her before stopping. Pacing, he walked towards the semi-truck and looked up into the sky. Sera waited for his back to turn, ran her fingers down her pocket, and felt for her knife. Nothing. Sera dropped her other hand down, pushed it into her other pocket, and felt nothing. *Fuck. Fuck. Fuck.* She rolled her head back and forth, looking for her bag.

A loud hiss billowed from the man lying on the ground, followed by a popping sound. Sera turned and saw the sludge on the ground slowly moving towards her. She continued to search for her bag and spotted it next to the car. Slowly scooting over to her bag, she kept her focus on the man.

The dead body next to her started convulsing, and a hole burst open on the being's back, releasing a cloud of steam. Sludge gushed out of the hole and raced towards her. Sera jolted up to her feet and sprinted to her bag. She pulled it open, and the man grabbed her arm and threw her back onto her rump. Her body slid against the cement, burning her arms as she grasped the ground, trying to stop.

The man stomped toward her with a demonic look on his face. "You shouldn't have done that!"

Stumbling, Sera rose to her feet with her fists up. "Come on, you mother fucker! Come on!"

The man lunged at her. Sera dipped down and dropped to her knees, dodging him. He stomped towards her, and she weaved to the right just before he grabbed her. He turned, stepping towards her, and she reared back and uppercut his chin. His head was knocked back, and black sludge spewed out of his mouth. Wobbling, he regained his balance and came for her again.

She waited for him to get close before spin-kicking him in the chest. He fell on his back, and before she could step away, he was back up on his feet. Panting, Sera punched him in the chest, spun around, and jump-kicked him in the jaw. He stumbled back and folded into the ground.

Gasping, Sera stumbled forward and ran to her bag to pull out a water jug. She pulled off the lid and waited. The man's body vibrated on the ground as he screeched short screams. He jolted back and forth, trying to stand. Sera took a step forward when she felt vibrating under her feet. Looking down, she saw little rocks rumbling over the cement.

"What the—"

The cars next to her began trembling, and the windows vibrated. Sera looked over at the man, whose eyes were glowing red. Black sludge oozed out of his mouth and ran down the front of his face and neck. Furry ran out from under a car and barked anxiously, throwing her head back and forth toward the direction where they entered the bridge. Sera knew something was seriously wrong. The ground vibrated more and more under her feet, shuffling her body back and forth along the cement.

She walked over to the man and poured her water jug over him. He looked up at her, and his eyes went black as steam billowed from his mouth.

A rumbling roar echoed from the entrance of the bridge. Sera looked up to see heads of sludge beings bobbing as they ran towards her at full speed.

"Oh, shit, Furry! Come on!"

Sera slammed the lid back on the jug and grabbed her bag. She crawled up to the truck, threw her bag in the cab, and dropped back down for Furry. Furry paced back and forth in front of the semi. She pulled her over to the truck and lifted her enough to push her inside the cab. Sera looked back to see beings were just a few feet away. She crawled in, locking the door behind her. The door on the opposite side was propped open. She slowly crawled to the other side and looked down to see Furry sniffing someone lying on the ground.

Oh, no, please don't be John. Please, don't be John.

As she climbed out, she hopped over the body and saw it was Chris. He had blood dripping from his bottom lip.

"Chris!"

Chris moved his body around, moaning. Sera pushed him over, shaking him. "You have to stand up. I can't carry you." Chris turned his head, and his face was covered in blood, with one of his eyes missing.

Sera took a step away from Chris and shook her head. *Oh, no. He's one of them.*

"Sera," Chris whispered.

"Chris, are you ... are you okay?" She took a small step towards him and felt the ground vibrate under her feet again.

Looking up, she shook her head. *They're coming. They're coming.* Her heart pounded against her chest. She didn't know what to do. *Should I help him or just run?*

"Sera, please, don't leave me. Please," Chris pleaded.

Nodding, Sera stared down at him like a doe in headlights before going into action. She squatted down and put his arm across her shoulders. Chris met her gaze with his good eye and gasped as she pulled him to his feet.

"Come on, Chris. You have to run now."

"I . . . I don't know if I can."

Sera pulled him along, forcing his legs to move. Panting, he picked up the pace and kept up with her.

"I'm going to let you go now. Stay behind me."

"I don't know if I can."

"You can do this."

Sera looked back, and he was slowly jogging behind her. She whispered, "Faster, Chris." She looked past Chris and scanned along the semi-trucks. There was no sign of beings, but she knew it was just a matter of time before they figured out a way through.

Sera looked ahead of her and noticed Furry was much further ahead of them.

"Furry, wait! Furry!" Furry took off running and didn't look back.

Fuck. Furry's gone, and Chris's a hobbling mess.

Shaking her head, Sera kept going.

Chapter Thirty-Seven: The Bridge

Sera

Sera and Chris jogged along the bridge, weaving in and out of rows of abandoned cars. Peering behind them, she stopped, panting. The bridge was still clear, but she knew she had to keep moving.

Coughing, Chris swaggered towards her and fell against one of the cars. His mouth dropped open, and slobber drooled down his face as he panted heavily.

"Are you okay, Chris?" Sera held her hand out to help him. He shook her off and glared at her with his good eye.

"I wish . . . I wish that thing had just killed me. I can't see out of my eye. I'm pretty sure I'm blind in one eye." He reached to touch his missing eye and stopped just a few inches short of it. "When he sliced my face, I thought, this is it. I thought he would kill me and take me back to the sludge. But . . ." Chris stumbled over to the bridge wall and peered down at the waves thrashing against it. "He didn't. Why? Why leave me to suffer?"

"I'm sorry," Sera whispered. "I don't know why —"

"Just don't, Sera! I don't need your fucking sympathy. Just —"

"We have to keep moving, Chris." Sera shook her head and shifted her weight from one foot to the other before adding. "And . . . I saw those things running onto the bridge." She looked back at the entrance. "I don't know what to expect." Sweat pooled over her brow as she cupped her hand to shield her eyes to see. Breathing deeply, she met Chris's gaze and said, "Come on."

A sinking feeling ached in Sera's stomach when she glanced back towards the truck. *What if this is it? After all this time of running, we make it this far to be overrun by a mob of beings on the bridge. I thought I was doing the right thing. But I just don't know anymore. I don't know what I'm doing.*

Sera's mom's voice rose from deep inside her and said, *"You save us all."*

Sera rubbed her face until her eyes burned.

She looked ahead and peered through the abandoned cars. *John, Brandon, and Furry are gone. And Chris . . . Sera looked over at him, meeting his good eye. I don't know how much longer I have with him before he —*

"How did John and Brandon die?" Chris asked.

Sera shook her head. "They didn't, or I hope they haven't . . ." Sera glanced back at Chris.

He walked up beside her, shaking his head. "What do you mean? Where are they then?"

"Well, I don't know. They went ahead when I was attacked and didn't come back."

"Are you sure? I didn't see them pass."

"You didn't see me either until I pushed you to wake up."

"Sera! I'm telling you, they didn't pass me!" Chris's forehead furrowed as he gritted his teeth. Inhaling deeply, he glared at Sera.

She stepped back and noticed his eyes flash from ocean blue to deep red as he blinked. She took another slow step backward and looked around her.

"Chris? What happened when you walked down the bridge ahead of us? You just disappeared."

Chris held his head with his hands and began shaking it ferociously. "I don't remember! No, no, no. I can't . . . I can't remember, Sera." He looked up at her, and his good eye was bloodshot. He started walking towards her slowly.

"No! Chris, you stay there. Not one more step!" She searched her pockets for any weapons, but they were empty. *Fuck. Fuck. Fuck!*

Chris continued to take steps closer and closer towards Sera, not breaking eye contact. "I said I didn't see them! I only saw you and him." He grinned maliciously, pointing.

She spun around, and the man she'd attacked on the bridge was standing behind her. She dropped her bag and pulled out the water jug. She took giant steps away from both of them as she opened the lid on the jug.

"Don't be afraid, Sera. It only hurts for a little while, and then he takes care of you. He takes care of all of us." Chris's voice deepened as if something dark had emerged inside him and he was responding. The iris of his eye gleamed a dark, blood-red color, and his body twitched with every step he took.

"No," Sera whispered as she took steps away from the men. "Chris, you don't have to do this. You still have time to do the right thing."

Both men began cackling and then stopped abruptly to stare at Sera. Sera lunged towards the men and splashed water on them. The man from the semi-truck collapsed to the ground and squealed a shrill scream that echoed down the bridge. Chris lunged toward Sera, trying to grab her shoulder. She spun around and threw water into his face. He stumbled forward onto his knees and cupped his hands over his face. Smoke billowed through his fingers as he howled the same high-pitched scream of the beings.

Sera slammed into Chris, knocking him back as she pushed past him with her bag. Her feet pounded into the cement, and her chest heaved, gasping for air. The lid to the water trickled through her fingers as she tried to close the jug in mid-run. She glanced back, trying to catch the lid, and saw Chris standing upright. He met her gaze and started running towards her. His face was smoking, and black ooze seeped through the wounds where the water hit his face.

She could hear his breath wheezing right behind her. She looked back to see his arms extending out, almost reaching her. Panicking, Sera dropped to her knees and tripped him, knocking him on his face in front of her. She jumped up and poured water over Chris's missing eye. Thrashing his limbs, he slapped the jug from her fingers, grabbed her leg, and pulled her down. He climbed on top of her, straddling her body. Flopping back and forth, Sera tried to knock him off, but he held her hands over her head, wrapping his fingers around her wrists.

"Stop fighting it, Sera! We'll win eventually!" Chris yelled. He pulled out a knife and smiled down at it. "Hold still. This will only take a minute." He slowly inched his blade closer and closer to her eyes as black sludge oozed out of his mouth, dripping down his chin. A drop formed, hanging down his chin, and threatened to drop onto Sera's face.

"No!" Sera screamed as she twisted her hands, trying to escape. She pushed against him with everything she had. Her limbs were shaking, and she felt her body weaken. He was inching closer and closer to her face. Trembling, she shook her head, fighting with her last bit of energy. Then, just as she felt her arms giving out, his weight was lifted. Her arms thrust up and were free from Chris's grasp.

Opening her eyes, she looked up to see John standing over her. He was holding a metal bar to his side, panting. Chris's body lay on the ground a few feet from Sera, vibrating as the sludge oozed out of his nose and mouth. John reached down and pulled her to her feet. She wrapped her arms around his waist, burying her face into his chest.

Pulling back, she looked up into his eyes. "You came back."

"After we climbed to the other side, I realized you weren't coming. We waited, and then I heard screaming from those things, so I climbed back up the truck. When I reached the door, I saw a mob of beings running towards us . . . well, towards you and Furry . . . I'm . . . I'm sorry, Sera, I should have . . ." John looked away and then back at her. The sun glistened off his moist brow, revealing dark circles under his eyes. Sera gazed into his eyes and knew he did what he had to do to survive.

She raised her hand, cupping his cheek, and nodded. "It's okay. I understand."

John smiled down at Sera, searching her face. "Then Furry ran up to us and looked back in the direction she just ran from. She was trying to get me to turn around for you, so I did."

A car door opened and shut behind John. Furry's nails clicked as she ran alongside Brandon. Brandon slammed his body into Sera, wrapping his little arms around her waist. He smiled up at her and said, "I'm glad you didn't die, Sera."

"Me, too, buddy. Thank you for coming back for me." A lump formed in Sera's throat as she spoke. Even though she didn't want to admit it out loud, she loved him. She loved them both, and no matter what happened, she would die to protect them.

Furry's snout rooted Sera's hand for a head scratch. As she inhaled a deep breath, a runaway tear rolled down her cheek. John looked down at her and wiped her cheek.

"You okay?"

"Yeah, I'm good. Come on, let's get going."

Chapter Thirty-Eight: Not Alone

John

John followed Sera as they all continued down the bridge. A loud squeal echoed, and then the ground under their feet trembled. John looked back, scanning the way they'd just walked.

"The mob of beings are still back there."

Nodding, John exhaled. "I know. We just need to keep moving. I think we should start jogging to get a better distance ahead."

"Come on, buddy. Can you run?"

Brandon nodded slowly, but John knew he wouldn't last long before they needed to stop and carry him. "It's okay. Let's just walk fast, okay?"

An hour passed, and John stopped, panting, and leaned against the wall of the bridge. He peered down into the water, watching the waves angrily thrash into it.

Brandon sat down with his back against the wall and looked up, meeting John's eyes. His lids were heavy, struggling to stay open. Nodding, John put his hand out for Brandon to stand up.

"Come on, buddy. I've got you." He pulled him onto his back and carried him. Soon after, Brandon's breathing grew loud, and his body went limp.

"You okay, John?"

"Yeah." John nodded, but deep down, he wasn't. His

stomach was a ball of nerves. He peered behind him repeatedly and knew that they were coming. He could feel it in his gut.

As they continued weaving in and out of more abandoned cars, the light quickly dimmed as the sun was setting in the west. John continued to check behind them, peering back at the ominous path they had just walked. *Nothing yet.*

Sera stopped in front of him and climbed up on top of one of the cars. John stopped, lowering Brandon gently to the ground. "Wake up, buddy."

Brandon shivered as he wrapped his arms around John's legs. "I'm so tired, John."

"I know, buddy. I'm sorry. We can't stop yet. We have to find a safe place to go."

"The walkway just gets more congested the further we go. We'll have to climb onto the cars if we want to get across." Sera looked both ways, climbed down, and walked over to John. "I can't see anything, and the sun's almost down now."

Fucking great. More climbing. John climbed up onto a car, looking both ways, before rubbing his face. He knew Sera was right. The only way to keep moving was to climb. He stared ahead amongst the rubble and then looked back at Sera. "I don't see anything either. I haven't heard any screams in a while. I'm scared to know what that means," John said as he dropped down to the ground.

Sera opened her bag and pulled out a flashlight. She handed it to John and said, "Use it sparingly. We don't want to draw attention."

Nodding, John shinned the beam down across the row of congested cars. He held out his hand, helping Brandon up first and then Sera. Metal popping in and out echoed along the bridge as they climbed from car roof to car roof.

The wind picked up, blowing in a pungent smell of fires and burned flesh. A faint squeal echoed behind them, causing

John and Sera to stop. John flashed the beam behind them and saw the path was eerily still. He looked down, gazing into Sera's eyes. She had a ghostly pale stare that pinged his heart. *She's afraid.* And deep down, he was, too.

Shaking his head, he flipped off the light and squeezed Sera's hand in his as he walked forward. Furry whimpered a tiny peep, brushing her paw against his calf. His stomach ached and burned with a deep heaviness, squeezing his insides from the feeling of danger lurking in the darkness. Another gust of wind swooshed, drowning them with an overwhelming smell of smoke. John stopped, peering behind them.

"Somethings . . . somethings not right." John flipped on the light and ran the beam along the path they'd just walked. A flash of light fluttered from over where the semi-truck was parked. Then a bright burst of lights blasted up into the sky.

"Is that a fire?" The lights grew brighter and more prominent as they stood there staring. "I think it's the semi-truck we crossed. I think it's . . . I think it's on fire, Sera."

A loud explosion blasted, trembling a hard jolt under their feet. A bright flash of white light gleamed, and the fire stretched from the semi-truck down along the path of cars behind them. Shadows of sludge beings' heads bobbed up and down as they ran along the bridge. Glowing red eyes glared toward them, and dozens of beings were running their way.

"Oh, fuck! Run!" John yelled. "They broke the barrier and are coming this way!" John picked up Brandon and started skipping over cars. "Come on, Furry!"

A burst of light flashed right behind them and vibrated the bridge, throwing John's body through the air. Buzzing hummed in his ears as his body dropped and slipped between two cars. He looked up to see a flaming ball of fire shoot over his head, drop on the road and set fire to the path right behind him. A shattering growl rattled the cement, trembling the road, and stopped as another blinding white light flashed, fracturing the cars next to him. Pieces of metal exploded, landing on top of him. Blinking his eyes, he tried to roll onto his side, but he was trapped. His heart pounded in his chest, beating like a heavy drum as fear set in.

I can't move — my legs. I can't move them.

John's claustrophobic nightmare throttled the air in his chest. Acid rolled up into his throat and threatened to erupt if he didn't find a way out of this prison. His hands thrashed against the wall of metal, punching against it as hard as he could. An inch of the wall gave a little, and he kicked his foot out, opening a way to escape. He pushed both hands through, like he was jumping off a diving board, and escaped his confinement to see fires surrounding him.

Brandon. Sera. Furry. Where are they?

Inhaling a deep breath, he swallowed the lump in his throat and wobbled a few steps forward. A cloud of smoke greeted him and polluted the air with its stench. John squeezed his eyes shut briefly and then tried to focus his vision. He hovered next to the car, holding on to the roof, and searched for his family. *Family. My family. Oh, please. Where are they?*

Flashes of red and white flames littered the area, engulfing the roofs of rows upon rows of cars. John took small steps forward, and the movement of something out of the corner of his eye caught his attention. *Sera. Oh, Sera.* She was lying on the hood of one of the cars not far from where he was standing.

John hurriedly climbed up onto the cluster of cars, looking around for Brandon as he scooted closer to Sera. *Brandon. Where are you, buddy? I'm so sorry I lost you. I'll find you. I'll find you.*

As he crawled closer to Sera, he noticed Furry on her side, lying on a hood a few feet away from Sera. Panic set in, shivering his digits as he climbed closer to Sera.

She's not moving. Oh, fuck!

John's heart felt like it was trying to burst through his chest. He laid his hands on Sera's chest and felt her breasts move up and down. *Oh, shit. Oh, shit.* John touched her cheek gently before sliding his hand over her shoulder. He gently shook her. "Sera! Sera, wake up. Please, Sera. Wake up!"

Streaks of ash and soot covered Sera's forehead and cheeks. She twitched, and then her eyes fluttered open and closed.

"John." Sera's voice was guttural and raw. She coughed and quickly rolled over, spewing acid over the top of the car.

John looked up and searched for Brandon. *Brandon. Brandon. Where's Brandon?* Brandon was nowhere in sight. *No. No. No. He's here. I just have to find him. He's okay.* John's chest felt like it was going to explode. *My family. Oh, please, where's Brandon? I have to —*

A hard pull tugged at John's arm. He turned to see Brandon standing with a blackened face and blood flowing from his nose.

John wrapped his arms around Brandon's shoulders, squeezing him.

"John, you're hurting me." Brandon squeaked. John didn't care. His shoulders slumped, and he released Brandon and looked him over.

"Are you okay, buddy?" John felt a lump in his throat as he looked him over.

Brandon reached up, touched John's forehead, and pulled back with blood. "You hurt your head."

John touched his head, and a slight sting drew his hands back. "I'll be fine. We have to get Sera and Furry and get out of here."

Brandon nodded.

John nodded and looked past Brandon to see a light flickering over the water. Shaking his head, he pointed to the light, and Brandon turned his head.

Sera was sitting up, holding her head. John turned to her and cupped his hand over her cheek. "Are you okay?"

She nodded and held her stomach as she rolled over to stand up.

John turned and saw the fire spreading quickly. The heat rested at their backs and was drawing in rapidly. The smoke was swallowing up the fresh air, crowding around them.

An explosion tremored the bridge and shook the ground, rattling John's body against Sera. He reached for Sera's arm and grabbed Brandon, bracing himself as the quake thrust their bodies against the hood of the car.

Brandon pulled back and said, "Look! Look, John!"

A giant ship was parked next to the bridge with its lights flashing back and forth along the concrete floor. A light shined on them and moved past, lighting up the sludge beings running from the fires. Dozens of men were yelling from the boat, and a horn sounded.

"I don't think they can see us," John said, pointing. "The light's going back and forth, but it's not stopping at our location. I think we can make a run for it. Brandon, Sera's bag is right there. Do you see it?" Brandon followed John's pointed finger and pulled up her bag from between the two cars.

"Furry, come on, pup. Come on." Furry slowly stood up on the car roof and wobbled towards them. Once Furry approached them, John turned to look back. Sludge beings were fleeing from the flames, running frantically along the edge of the bridge.

"They're everywhere, John," Sera whispered.

"I know. We can't stay here. The fire will be on us any minute, and we'll get trapped if we do." John wrapped Sera's arm around his shoulder and helped her crawl along the car's wheels.

John looked back and saw a thick fog of smoke hovering over all the cars. He couldn't make out anything past a foot in front of him.

Fuck. "Sera, move faster. Come on. Faster. The smoke . . .

it's right behind us."

She peered over her shoulder.

The sound of the sludge beings' screams echoed all around them. Sera met John's gaze with a ghostly stare. Shaking his head, John peered around them, searching for the beings, but the wall of smoke blinded him.

A beam of light from the ship cut through the smoke, drifting back and forth as if someone was searching the bridge.

"Wait," John whispered, holding up his hand. Once the light passed, another loud crash rattled against the bridge, vibrating the floor. John slid between two cars, hitting the ground and landing in a foot of water.

What the fuck! Wetness soaked his feet and ankles as he waited for the quake to stop moving the bridge.

Gunshots unleashed, pummeling into the car's hoods. John pulled Sera and Brandon into his chest, protecting them.

The gunshots sounded like they were right next to him, but the smoke was too thick to see anything. Once the shots stopped, John quickly moved, crawling as fast as she could. "Come on! Come on! Move!" He pulled Sera and Brandon along the cars.

A blood-curdling scream echoed in the distance, and then another round of gunshots sounded. John dropped over Sera and Brandon, waiting for the gunshots to stop flying. Once everything went quiet, John looked up to see that the row of cars had ended and that the bridge wall was only a few feet from them.

"Sera. Brandon. Go. Go. Go." John waved for them to move. Furry followed their lead, and once they were at the bridge wall, they dropped down to their knees. John looked over the railing with Sera and saw a vast ship parked up against the bridge.

"Military. They're on the bridge," John whispered, crouching back down. He turned around with his back against the bridge wall and looked for any men who'd exited the ship. Furry crawled in John's lap, snuggling against him. The visibility was minimal, and the smoke was still thick in the air. He took a deep breath and crawled along the bridge wall.

"Hey!" A man's voice screamed near where he was standing, and then a round of bullets rattled nearby.

Fuck! John froze, crouching down and looking back. He held his arm across Sera and Brandon and scanned the floor. Lights flashed from the ship's direction, and men's screams followed. He turned, waving everyone to follow him along the wall.

John peered into the darkness and saw a white van through the rubble. He looked back, meeting Sera's gaze. He pointed to the vehicle with his eyes and looked back at Sera. Nodding, she looked towards the van again.

John stepped away from the wall and made a run for it. He stopped and pressed his body against the back door. He tried the handle. *Locked.* He walked around to the driver's side and tried the other handle. *Yes. Opened.*

The van's body bobbed up and down as he crawled inside. He crawled past the front seats and peered into the back. *Empty.*

He opened the back door and held out his hand for Brandon. Brandon sat on the floor and watched Sera and Furry crawl in. Sera opened her bag and pulled out blankets, laying one over Brandon and stretching one out over her legs. She briefly looked back, meeting John's gaze before lying on the floor. John cupped his arms around Sera's body, pulling her rump into his abdomen. He closed his eyes and let the sleep come.

CHAPTER THIRTY-NINE: ENEMIES LURKING

Sera

Sera turned over to see the ocean waves angrily hiss, rising into the sky and crashing onto the beach. Steaming pebbles from sandy mounds burrowed under her abdomen and dampened her clothing. She stood up and gazed at the deep gray rows of clouds joining the sky and water as one.

"Sera!" a familiar voice yelled behind her, bellowing through the wall of water crashing over the beach. "Sera!"

She slowly eased her body around to see a figure standing a few hundred feet away. They were trudging along, dragging their feet in the watery mass a few feet from the tide. Sera squinted and held her hand over her eyes to shield the beaming light peeking between the clouds. She stepped forward to get a better look, but the person seemed to move awkwardly, inching along the bank. As she grew closer, she noticed something strange about how the person walked.

"Hello?" Sera yelled.

A familiar pungent smell of burning flesh wafted through the air. Sera's body crumbled forward, clutching her mouth as her stomach ached with uneasiness. Shaking her head, her vision doubled, and she dropped into the muddy sea, hands first. The cool sandy film pushed between her fingers and molded over her hands. She tried to push herself up, but her body felt like a heavy anchor, pulling her back into the angry sea.

Closing her eyes, she squeezed and exhaled a deep breath. Her lungs filled with a fresh breath, and she opened her lids to see the *person trotting towards her. The person looked like a mirage, floating along the beach, drifting closer and closer to her. She rubbed her eyes and tried to focus on who was approaching. Squinting, she cocked her head to the side and gazed up at a tall, slender man with jet-black hair and phantom onyx eyes. His stare tore right through her soul and burned in her gut.*

She felt him ease into her mind and speak, "Hello, Sera. I've been looking for you."

Shaking her head, Sera began pushing back on her rump. Her body sank down into the sand, seeping into the earth with each wash of seawater as it rolled up the beach. Warm water washed over her arms, pulling her deeper into the beach like quicksand. She opened her mouth and tried to scream, but nothing would come out. A hollow rush of air exhaled from her parched lips and drowned her screams with the hissing of the ocean. Trapped.

The man's body flashed through the sand in a quick jump, and he was only a few feet away. His face transformed, and a demonic grin crossed his lips. His eyes began to glow a vibrant red, and his mouth filled with ooze, dripping from the crease of his lips. He took steps toward Sera, his limbs sprawled out like long vines.

Right before he grabbed her, he stopped and stood upright. "No, I think I'll take him first."

Sera drew in a strangled gasp and slowly turned her head and saw her brother, Sam, standing behind her.

Sam. She whispered his name in her head. He looked down at her with his gentle eyes and nodded, speaking to her in his mind.

"It's okay, sister. I love you."

The words stumbled from her quivering lips, "No." But it was too late.

Sam's body was sinking down onto the beach. Black ooze was pooling at his feet and crawling up his body, pulling him down into the sand.

All Sera could hear was Sam's screams, and then it went silent.

"Sera." A soft whisper echoed in the darkness.

Sera opened her eyes, and John was leaning over her. He gazed down at her, stroking her brow. She shot up, gasping for air, and shoved him out of the way. Hot lava burned the back of her throat and threatened to erupt.

"Are you okay?" John asked.

"No," Sera replied, panting. Tears rolled down her cheeks, and the image of her brother being taken by the sludge burned in her mind. "No, I'm not okay, John." The words quivered over her lips as she breathed deeply, trying to push back the sobbing that begged to come out.

She gazed around the van and saw hoses and supplies clanking on small metal shelves built into the walls. Daylight peeked through the window of the back of the vehicle, shining a bright beam of light on a single spot on the floor. Brandon sat across from her, blinking in the shadow of the dark van. Sera crawled over and pulled Brandon into her lap, holding him like a baby against her chest. He wrapped his arms around her back and exhaled loudly.

"I can't breathe, Sera," Brandon whispered.

"Okay." She let go and wiped away a runaway tear from her cheek.

"Do you know if that ship is still parked beside the bridge?" Sera turned and asked John.

John went to the door and crawled out, closing the door behind him. A minute passed, and he returned.

"No, I didn't see it, but I didn't go that far either."

Sera nodded and looked back over at Brandon and John. "Do you think it's safe to go out?"

John shook his head. "I don't know."

"I'm going to go check."

"No, Sera, wait for me."

"I'll be fine."

"No, just wait a minute." John disappeared into the back of the van.

Sera peered through the front windshield, trying to find a safe path. The thick smoke and fires from the night before had gone out, making it easy to see around everything. She pushed down the handle and opened the door slowly. Saltwater and remnants of musky smoke filled the air, forcing the door to open completely. Startled, she jumped back before attempting to exit. Sera poked her head out of the door and stepped onto the concrete. A deep whistle tickled her ears as it echoed along the abandoned streets of the bridge. She gently pushed the door until she heard a click and turned towards the bridge railing.

Muffled voices from several men greeted her as she slowly walked up. *Shit. Shit. Shit.* She stopped abruptly and tried to walk back towards the cars she'd just walked from.

"Hello," a man said.

Sera stopped, exhaling deeply. Looking back, she saw two men running up to either side of her.

No. No. No.

"What are you doing here?" he asked.

Sera shook her head and said, "I'm just passing through."

She lowered her head and turned to walk away from the men.

"Where are you going?" the man said, following closely behind Sera.

She kept her head down and slowly ran her hand down her pocket, feeling for a knife, but it was empty. *Shit.* "I'm just passing through." Sera gritted her teeth. She didn't want to make eye contact with the men. She knew they wouldn't leave her alone, but she could try to draw them away from John and Brandon.

"You're going to need to come with me, miss," the man walking beside her said as he cupped his hand under her elbow.

"No, thank you." She jerked her elbow back, meeting the

man's eyes.

He tilted his head back and cackled a long puff of air before he stopped, pulling her elbow back with a hard tug. "I'm not asking. This area is being quarantined, and you need to come with me."

Sera shook her head and pulled her arm away from the man again. "No. I will not come with you."

"Lady, I can't let you pass. Come with me, or I'll be forced to eliminate you," the man said, stepping in front of her and holding his gun.

Sera turned to face him and looked back and forth to check around her. "Eliminate me? Really?"

She glanced in the van's direction and then gazed into the man's eyes, smiling. "Okay. Fine. Whatever you say." She held her hands up and nodded.

She turned to face the man, and when he looked away at another man, she spun and kicked him in the chest. She dropped onto the ground, rolling her body, and knocked him forward. He dropped hard, slamming his face against the cement, and spewed bright red clumps on the ground. Sera crawled over his body and punched him in the back of the head, pummeling his face against the road.

The second man walked up to Sera, holding his gun erect. "Get off of him and lie on the ground!" He pointed to her and then to the ground with his rifle, screaming commands. She stood up slowly with her hands in the air, and walked towards the man, not stopping. Shaking her head, she dropped her hands and ran towards him.

"Get down!"

The gun fired, exploding a loud pop right next to Sera's ear. She didn't stop and barreled into him with full force, punching his rifle out of his hands. He stumbled backward, and Sera punched him in the face, knocking him onto his back.

The first man got back up, wrapped his arm around her

waist, and jerked her body to the ground. A sharp pain pierced Sera's back as she tried to inhale a deep breath. Coughing, she rolled over slowly, gasping for air. The man walked around her and over to his friend on the ground. She pushed herself up and stumbled towards the gun. The man ran over, kicked the gun out of Sera's reach, and sunk his fist into her face. She dropped onto all fours, coddling her face as blood oozed out of her nose.

Sera forced herself back up and stood with her fists erect. Nodding, she waved him towards her. He came at her, slapping her fist away, wrapped his arms around her, picked her up, and threw her back on the ground. He jumped on top of her, straddling her, and put his hands around her neck. Sera pounded against his forearms and twisted her legs back and forth, trying to knock him off her. He pressed his hands down, pushing her body into the cement.

She grasped at his forearms, tremoring as she tried to pull him away from her. Her body was weakening, and her fingers numbly scratched against his flesh. One arm dropped to her side, and then the other collapsed. Her pinky finger stretched across the ground and touched something metal. She twitched and stretched out her other digits to feel something hard. Her hand reached out and touched the object. *A gun. It's a gun.*

Sera's eyes opened wide, and she turned to see the rifle on the ground. She grabbed the barrel and used everything she had left to slam it into the man's head. The man turned to look at her just as she swung, bashing him right between the eyes. He collapsed next to her, and Sera rolled away from his clutches.

She crawled a few feet away, coughing up blood as she stood. Puddles of blood stained the ground in front of the man as he looked up at her. His forehead was covered in a bright red that dripped down his eye. Sera raised the gun, aimed, and pulled the trigger.

A loud explosion echoed, sending chills down her body. The bullet entered the man's chest, seeping a deep red syrup from around the hole. The man reached his arms out, spewing blood from his lips as his body crumpled back down to the ground.

Exhaling, Sera spun around, and the second man was right behind her. He grabbed the rifle and pulled it towards him to gain power over it. Sera pulled back on the gun with one hard jolt and let go. She jumped back, kicking her leg up as high as possible, and plunged her foot into his face. Blood shot out of his nose, draining down the front of his shirt. He fumbled, dropping the gun right in front of her. Sera leaped forward, grabbed it, and shot.

The man flew backward, falling on his rump. Red stained his right arm and drizzled down to the cement. He pushed himself up and marched towards her. Sera cocked the gun again, aimed high, and pulled the trigger.

The man stopped in mid-step and stared at Sera blankly. His eyes crossed, and he dropped to his knees. A cloud of gray smoke billowed from his forehead, and then a reddish-brown liquid oozed out of his temple. His gaze averted up, locking eyes with Sera. A chill shuddered down her spine and quivered in her heart as she stared back at him. His long black lashes blinked a few times, and then he slowly melted to the road.

She peered down at him, staring at his stone eyes. A rattling noise jarred her out of her daze, and she looked up to see John staring at her. She walked towards him with her arms stretched out. He embraced her, and she felt his heart drumming against her face.

"Are you okay?" John whispered.

She nodded, but a breath caught in her throat. She swallowed hard and forced the tears to stop. Her body shivered as she pulled back and gazed into John's eyes. He wiped away a runaway tear and pressed his lips against her briefly. Nodding, she turned to head back toward the van.

They both jogged away from the attackers and stopped just before entering the van to look back. More men were climbing up and over the railing from the ship. *Great. Shit.*

Brandon and Fury were sitting in the middle of the van.

"Come on, buddy. We have to go now," Sera said, panting.

"Sera, you're bleeding," Brandon said.

Sera looked down and saw blood on her shirt. She lifted it up to see blood where a bullet had grazed her.

"I didn't even know that was there. I'm okay. It doesn't even hurt."

Sera propped the door open to the back of the van and peeked out. The men from the bridge were a few hundred feet away, so she quietly eased out of the van and held up her hands for Brandon and Furry. Furry jumped out, and her nails clicked against the concrete. John stepped out with the backpack and clicked the door to the van shut. Sera turned to Brandon with her finger over her lips, nodding. John led the way out, and she followed through a line of cars, disappearing into the rubble.

After about a mile, Sera stopped, panting. She met John's gaze and nodded. He looked out over the water and then met her eyes with furrowed brows. Sera cocked her head to the side. "What is it?"

John sat down next to her and exhaled deeply. "Why did you go out there without me? I asked you to wait, and you didn't. They could've killed you."

Sera squeezed her eyes shut and shook her head. "I didn't see anyone and thought it would be okay—"

John's voice deepened as he snapped, "Oh, you thought it would be okay. Oh, okay, well. You almost got yourself killed. You knew there were men and sludge beings everywhere and went for a little walk. Okay, that makes perfect sense." John shot up onto his feet. "Come on, Brandon, let's go."

He's mad at me. Really mad. What the fuck? "Hey."

John kept walking.

"Hey, what the hell, John." Sera followed behind him, talking to his back. *"I don't know who you think you are trying to tell me when and where I can go. If I want to go –"*

John spun around and stared down at Sera with glazed eyes. His nostrils flared as he took a step towards her. "Just shut up, Sera."

"Excuse me!"

"You heard me. You're fucking selfish, and you don't think about the consequences of your actions."

"Fuck you, John. You don't know me, and you sure fucking hell can't tell me what to do. I was doing what I thought would help us. And I took care of it. You don't get to tell me what to do." She pointed her finger up at him and glared into his eyes. "You don't even know me. What have we known each other for? A month at best? You can't –"

"Whatever! Do whatever the hell you want. Kill yourself. I don't fucking care anymore. Just do it on your own and leave me and Brandon the hell out of it."

Sera took a step towards John when a noise sounded behind her. John started to turn away from her, and she grabbed his forearm, holding her finger up to her lips. She mouthed the words *shh* and shook her head. She looked behind her, and the eerie feeling of someone watching them sent chills down her spine. A cool breeze drifted across the bridge from the water, smelling of rotten fish and death. *Something's not right.* She pointed for them to start walking again.

After walking about a hundred feet, John stopped them and pointed across the bridge towards the water. Sera looked and saw something peculiar. It was another bridge running parallel to the bridge they were standing on.

"Wait? What the –"

He nodded and said, "It's kind of hard to explain. It is a second bridge."

He pointed at the bridge and said, "There's an island down there. It's a tiny island called *Pigeon Key Island*. It's a historical island where tourists would travel by ferry and learn about marine life and historical buildings built in the early nineteen-hundreds. A hurricane devastated the island, so they built this bridge for highway access."

Sera smiled, looking up at John and then at the island.

"Do you think we should try to go there? Do you think the sludge is there?"

"Honestly, I don't think the sludge could survive there. There's too much water. We would probably benefit from an island, and the resources would be unlimited there. We could fish and make freshwater contraptions to convert salt to fresh. It would be a great place to go." John shook his head, staring at the island briefly before turning to Sera. He exhaled and said, "But the question is, how will we get over there? We would need to jump into the water and risk being eaten by sharks, drowning, or shot at by men on that ship. Not to mention that it's hundreds of miles away from this bridge. So, how, Sera? How would we get over there?"

Sera met John's gaze, and his stare was cold and angry.

Heat struck her and rushed through her veins. She poked her finger in John's face, waving it around. "What! What is it, John? Why are you so mad at me?"

"Hmm, let's see. First, you never listen to me. Ever! You continuously get yourself into danger, and I'm never there to help you because you won't let me help you!"

John walked away and then went back over to Sera and said, "I want to . . . I want us . . . we need to stay together. I can't—" John turned around, stomping away from Sera, and stopped between two cars. He stared up into the sky, and his Adam's apple bobbed when he swallowed. A ping shot through Sera's heart when she realized what he was saying. *He's in love with me.* The words rang through her mind.

Sera exhaled loudly and walked towards him. The second bridge flickered in the sunlight as light peeked through a row of gray clouds in the sky. Sera peered over at the bridge and back at John. Inhaling deeply, she stepped in front of him and gently touched his arm. He stared ahead with glossy eyes and didn't acknowledge her standing there.

"John?"

She dropped her head against his chest and wrapped her arms around his waist. His heart thumped against her face as she swallowed back a lump forming in her throat.

John inhaled a deep breath and exhaled loudly. "We could probably make it over there somehow."

Sera nodded and rubbed her face against his chest, squeezing her fingers around his back.

She looked up at him, and he dropped his head, gazing into her eyes. "John, I'm scared to death that you'll get hurt. I'm trained and know how to defend myself. That's why I go alone. I've already lost—" The words hung in her throat. "I can't lose you, too."

"Sera, I don't want to. Let me help you. From now on, no matter what, we stay together." He pulled her hard against him and kissed her nose. "You're stuck with me." A slight smile creased his forehead. "And I'm stuck with you." John's manhood hardened.

"Okay," Sera said, smiling.

Sera peered over at the island and watched the treetops sway back and forth in the wind. The clouds were gathering in a circular motion, blowing the waves angrily into the air. Sera met John's eyes again, and they looked at Brandon and Furry. Brandon had deep gray sunken circles around his eyes, and his tiny frame was paper thin with pale skin covering his protruding bones. She looked back up at John, and their gazes met. She didn't speak, but John's eyes told her he knew what she was thinking about Brandon. They had to find somewhere to go, and soon. Brandon was wasting away, and he might not make it if they didn't do something soon.

Sera walked over and sat next to Brandon. "We just have to go a little further, buddy, and we can try to go over to that island. What do you think about that?"

Brandon's eyes were glossed over, and his bottom lip hung down. He swallowed and nodded his head. "Okay."

Sera pulled him into her chest and ruffled his hair back. She leaned over and kissed the top of his head, swallowing back a lump in her throat.

She stood up and brushed off her rump. "Okay, let's get moving."

Nodding, John pulled Brandon onto his back and led the way, following the bridge on the same side as the ship. He looked back at Sera. "The ship is far enough down the bridge that they can't see us for now, but we should still be careful."

John slowed his walk and waited for Sera to catch up.

"What is it?" Sera whispered.

"If you really want to do this." John peered over at the island and then back at Sera. "Then we need to try to get as close to it as possible."

"Do you really think we can make it?"

John stopped, stared at the island, and said, "Well, it may be our only choice."

Chapter Forty: Dead End

Sera

Sera slowed behind John as he came to a stop. Panting, she hunched over to catch her breath. John slid Brandon down from his back and sat against the cement.

Sera walked over to the railing and peered out, gazing into the angry sea. The waves were growing in size and pummeling against the side of the bridge. A high wind pressed against Sera, scooting her backward as she tried to stare into the water.

John whipped around and slumped his shoulders forward. He exhaled a loud sigh as he opened his mouth and gazed up at Sera. "There's a storm coming."

Sera nodded and peered out over the water. "If we really did want to jump, this would be the time, wouldn't it?"

"Jump!" Brandon's voice squeaked as he looked up at Sera. He blinked, moisture filled his bulging eyes, and his body shivered slightly as he spoke. "I can't swim, John. I'm scared. I can't swim!" Brandon's voice echoed along the bridge.

Sera shook her head at John and ran over to hold Brandon. Brandon's tiny body shuddered against her chest as the sobs rattled from his fragile frame. *He can't swim. He can't swim.* The words echoed in her head. *What if we're making a mistake?*

She patted his back and waited for him to calm down before she spoke. "It's just something that John and I have been talking about. It's just in case something happens." She looked over at John and then back down at Brandon. "Do you understand?"

Brandon nodded and laid his head back down on Sera's chest. She leaned over and kissed the top of his crown before looking up and meeting John's gaze. John's brows furrowed as he looked down at Brandon. Furry walked over, burrowing her snout under Brandon's chin, and pushed his head up. She licked his tears and nudged his hand to pet her.

"What about Furry?" Brandon asked. "Can she swim?"

"Yes," Sera nodded. "Dogs are natural swimmers. Have you ever seen a dog swim?"

He shrugged his shoulder. "I think."

"Well, you know how dogs paddle their paws." Sera motioned with her hands and legs to show Brandon.

"Yeah."

"That's what you need to do if we have to jump in. You move your hands and feet like a dog." Sera nodded. "Okay?"

"Yes."

"Okay," Sera said, pulling Brandon against her chest and hugging him tightly. "It's going to be okay." Her breath caught in her chest as her heart pounded against Brandon's body. She let go of Brandon and met his gaze. "Come on, buddy, we have to get going." She held out her hand, pulling Brandon to his feet. Sera looked back at John and nodded before they continued walking.

What felt like hours passed, and they continued to walk. Finally, John stopped and looked over the railing. A strong breeze blew his t-shirt snuggly against his body, showing his six-pack abs. The sun was retiring into the water and quickly dimming the light over the bridge. The island appeared to be inching closer and closer. Sera looked up at John, and he looked back at her, nodding.

Sera stared out over the water before turning to John. She opened her mouth to speak, and something out of the corner of her eye caught her attention. She turned and looked behind her to see something moving next to the line of abandoned cars against the other side of the bridge. Squinting, she realized it was men strolling on either side of an abandoned car.

Sera slowly stepped away from the railing, motioning her head to the side for John to see. John slowly nodded and picked up the bag. She reached down, pulled Brandon up onto her back, and started jogging again. She dipped down and headed between the abandoned cars, weaving in and out of open view. The vehicles were narrowing closer together, so she slowed down and felt a prick on her ankle. Sera looked back to see Furry pawing at her. Furry's lips ruffled, and a low yip spewed from her snout.

"What is it, Furry?"

Furry came to a halt and looked back, whining. Sera looked up to see John struggling to fit between two cars with the backpack. She stopped and hunched down, waiting with Brandon dangling from her back. Sera lifted her body slightly so that John could meet her eyes. Raising her hand, she lifted her head higher into the air and saw something move behind John. Two men carrying rifles were running hunched over just a few feet from where John was standing.

No. No. No. John. Sera waved her hands slightly, telling John to hurry. Then she pointed behind him. He slowly glanced over his shoulder. His gaze shot back to Sera wide-eyed. He nodded and hurried through the cluster of cars.

Sera eased Brandon to the ground and turned to face him. "Brandon, do you remember how I said you have to swim like a dog? Doggy paddle. Remember?"

"Yes." Brandon nodded.

"It's time, honey. You need to be brave, hold your breath, and then doggy paddle as fast as you can when you get to the water to make it to the top. Then I want you to swim to the island as fast as you can. Promise me! Promise me you won't give up. You swim and make it to the top and swim to the island. Promise!" Sera felt the tears rolling down her face as the words left her lips.

Brandon nodded at Sera, staring into her eyes. She knew this could be it. This could be the last time she would ever see them again. Shaking her head, Sera swiped the tears away and looked up for John. The men were only a few feet from him now. John looked up, and their gazes met. The little bit of sunlight gleaming through the ocean's growl glistened off his sandy hair. A smirk crept up one of his cheeks, and his eyes told her he knew they were right behind him. He was stalling to give them a head start. He nodded slightly once and batted his lashes with one long blink.

Shaking her head, Sera opened her mouth to speak when a familiar sound echoed across the bridge. The eerie symphony of the monstrous beings they'd tried to outrun had caught up with them, and now they were back to emerge with a vengeance. Frozen, Sera scanned the surrounding area as darkness slowly engulfed the little bit of light on the bridge. She slowly reached out, motioning for John to come to her when the hairs on the back of her neck stood on end. The pungent smell of rotting death wafted in the wind first, and then a crackle of metal echoed to her right. Sera slowly turned and saw a being standing atop a car a few feet from them. Its glowing red eyes glared toward the men walking with guns. It opened its mouth, and a horrific squeal screamed over the bridge.

John walked over to Sera and squatted. "We have to—" John started to say, but his words were cut short.

The concrete below their feet began to tremble, rattling them against the ground. Sera's body shifted forward, and she caught herself in John's grasp.

A barrage of gunshots began firing a few feet from where they were standing. The rooves of the cars they were hiding between quaked as someone fell hard against it, and then the ground began to vibrate again. Sera lifted her head to see flashing lights skipping across the bridge. Three men were huddled together, shooting at a being. The being's body flapped in the air, shuttering as each bullet pummeled into its body. John met Sera's gaze, staring at her with glazed eyes. He slightly nodded and looked towards the bridge wall. Sera's bottom lip quivered as she lifted her hand up to John's cheek. She nodded, and they both stood up. John led the way around the cars and headed for the bridge.

"Halt! Stop right there!"

Sera spun and faced two men holding guns. Nodding, she looked back at John and down at Brandon and Furry. She pushed her rump back, bumping against John and Brandon to continue walking backward towards the bridge.

"Hey! I said stop—"

Another malicious growl echoed, cutting the man off. Sera slowly turned back and saw a being standing right behind them, blocking the railing. Her heart pounded against her chest as she inhaled deeply. She cupped her hands around her family and tried to protect them from the being. Furry's body bounce-barked toward the monster, lunging in its direction. Sera looked up, meeting the being's red eyes. Blood seeped out of the tear ducts, flowing down its face. It cocked its head to the side and slowly walked towards them with its arms extended.

"Move! Get down! Get down!" The men yelled behind her. His voice sounded like it was a hundred miles away even though he was merely a few feet from them.

Sera's head spun back and forth between the man and the sludge being. The being was inches from grabbing her and making her one of them. She looked back at the man and knew it was now or never. She pushed John and Brandon back, knocking them to the ground. She dropped in front of them just before gunfire shot, filling up the being. Shaking her head, Sera looked at John and Brandon and then at the railing. She motioned to John to follow her to the bridge.

Sera peered over the water and watched the waves angrily crash into the bridge's pillars. The sky was dark, with bolts of lightning flashing through the gray storm clouds. The island stood ominously across from the bridge, peeking out of the gigantic waves thrashing against each other.

Sera gazed up into John's haunted eyes. He looked out over the water and then back at her, shaking his head.

Gunfire was exploding feet from where they were standing. Sera reached down, grabbed her bag from John's arm, and threw it over. His hands followed the bag as it went over, and then his limbs went limp. She stepped down and hugged Furry tight.

"It's going to be okay, old girl. I'll be right behind you." She squeezed her arms around her neck and struggled to pick her up.

John stepped down, grabbed her from front to back, and stepped onto the railing. He kissed her head and threw her over. Sera watched Furry go down, leaning over the bar.

"She made it." Sera sighed.

She reached over, wrapping her arms around John's waist, and kissed him.

He squeezed her and whispered in her ear. "I love you, Sera."

She pressed her lips hard against his and pulled away. "I love you." Her throat caught as tears rolled down her cheeks.

She stepped down, walked over, grabbed Brandon's hand, and walked him up the ledge.

John leaned over and wrapped his arms around Brandon. "Swim, buddy. Swim as hard as you can."

Brandon nodded, looking up at Sera.

"Brandon, don't let go of my hand. Whatever you do, don't let go." Sera looked over at John and then down at Brandon.

"Let's all jump together. We can all hold hands."

John and Brandon both nodded.

"Are you—"

"Hey! Get down from there! Get down—"

Sera looked over at John and then at Brandon. They stepped up onto the railing and then stepped off.

Sera felt the air rise from her belly to her throat, stealing her breath. For a moment, she felt free, like a bird sailing on gusts of wind floating through the sky. She opened her eyes to see Brandon's eyes closed and John staring down. Looking down, she could see the water was closing in. She closed her eyes and took a deep breath.

CHAPTER FORTY-ONE: THE OCEAN

Sera

A wall of pain shuttered through Sera's body as she drifted down into the unknown. She blinked to see Brandon's lifeless body sinking just out of her reach. She reached for his hand and activated her arms and legs, pumping them against the wild sea. Brandon's limp body hung from her gripping fingers as she pulled his dead weight upwards.

Just a little bit more. Just a little bit more. Sera's mouth trembled as the last of her air bubbles escaped to freedom. Her chest heaved, begging for relief. She reached out, pushing her fingers through the dark water, hoping to free herself from the pain cutting in her chest. Her head emerged, shooting out of the water like a torpedo, and then Brandon followed behind.

Coughing, she inhaled and exhaled long, deep breaths of sea air. Acid rolled up her throat, burning her insides as dark water expelled in front of her. Her limbs burned, and she shivered as she tried to continue to paddle to keep her body above water. Brandon was floating on his back, his body bobbing up and down into the water. Sera clutched Brandon's shirt, holding him close to her. She leaned over and listened for his breathing. A faint sigh tickled against her ear.

"Oh, thank goodness. Brandon? Brandon? Come on, buddy. You have to wake up. Brandon?" She shook his upper body, rubbing against his chest. She peered down at him lying on top of the water and then around her.

The water was angry, thrashing against each wave with a monstrous hand, twisting and throwing anything in its way out into the abyss. Fear rushed through her, and shivers spiked a sharp pain in her stomach.

"Brandon! Brandon," Sera yelled.

Shaking her head, she started pumping her legs. Panic set in, pummeling a hard drum against her chest. She spun around, searching for something, anything. The sea was open but felt like a box closing in around her.

John. John? Where's John? And Furry. Oh no. Where are they? She spun her head back and forth. A lump filled her throat, choking her as she gasped.

"John! John!" Sera screamed. "Furry!" The words lingered on her lips, trailing into the darkness of the thundering sky approaching. A colossal wave swished upwards, rolling a mound of water under Brandon and Sera. Sera's stomach turned as the tide drew their bodies high into the air and dropped them deep into the unknown. She rode the wave, holding Brandon, and saw rows of giant waves approaching.

Oh no. Sera's mouth dropped open, and she watched as the storm wrapped around them and was now on top of them. She inhaled one last time and squealed his name, hoping he would appear with her dog. "John!"

A bright light shimmering across the sky cut off her voice. It traveled down into the water and was followed by an evil howl that cracked across the water.

"Wait! Wait!" She pleaded but knew her cries would be un-answered. She spun around, swimming in a circle. Lightning flashed again a few hundred feet away and spidered across the sky, lighting up over what looked like a bridge.

The bridge. Oh, yes, the bridge!

Thunder echoed over the water and hummed an angry growl. Sera paddled her feet and stared in the direction of the bridge. She knew the island wasn't far, and if she could just find the general direction, she could swim toward it. *Come on.*

Come on. Come on.

The lightning flittered across the sky, spidering down until she saw the bridge railing peek out in the light. She gripped one hand on Brandon's shirt and the other moving to keep them afloat. Another flash of light flickered over the water, showing the treetops of the island.

"The island! Brandon, it's the island!" She pushed harder, kicking her legs with everything she had. Her calves burned, but she pushed forward, pulling Brandon with every thrust of her arm.

A wave rolled, running towards her and Brandon again. Sera stopped and stared up at it as it approached. It rose over twenty feet in the air. She wrapped her hand around Brandon and took in a deep breath. Water pummeled over their heads, shoving them deep into the dark waters. Sera threw her hand out, pulling against the cold water. Her body vibrated as she pumped her legs against the current.

Sera shot out of the water, spewing salty residue from her lips. Brandon plopped against the top of the water and floated, bumping against her body. Another wave of water rolled towards her. She pumped her legs, trying to outrun the monster chasing her. The water gained on her and dunked them deep into the abyss again. Brandon bounced against Sera's chest, knocking the wind out of her. A gust of bubbles expelled, and she opened her eyes to see the surface over a hundred feet away. She kicked her legs against the water, pushing as hard as she could, fighting against the burning pain shuttering through her chest.

Sera's body emerged from the sea and she inhaled a deep breath. Panting, she blinked and opened her eyes to see a spotlight run over the water. She followed the beam and watched it stretch across the dark water to the island. A loud horn blew two times, and then on the third one, it lasted over a minute.

Sera peered over the waves and saw the ship parked next

to the bridge sailing towards the island. It was headed straight for them.

Oh no. Oh no.

Sera turned and swam, pumping her arms against the angry waves. Brandon bounced against her body like ping pong with each stroke. A loud hum echoed over the water, and then a gust of wind pressed against Sera's face. Lightning flashed, and another wave lifted Sera's body into the air. She felt her limbs being pulled up higher and higher into the air, sucking against her insides as she lifted and then she dropped.

She felt Brandon's body being pulled from her fingers. Her grasp was loosening, and she felt his body pull from her grip. *Brandon. No, Brandon. No. No. No.*

She swiped her fingers through the dark water, blindly searching for him. Just as she thought she couldn't hold her breath any longer, she caught his shirt flapping in the water. She pulled him into her and pumped her legs. Her body exited the water, and she gasped for air. Brandon's limp body floated on top of the water, pressing against her. Panting, she looked around to see that the boat had passed and that she was closer to the island.

Shivering, she looked back to see the waves were a few feet away, so she exhaled a long breath and started kicking her legs again. She aimed for the direction where she last saw the island and didn't stop. Water sprayed into her mouth and face, burning her eyes and nose. She coughed, spitting saltwater, and wiped her eyes. She stopped in mid-stroke and looked around. Warm drops of rain ran down her face and into her mouth. *It's raining. Freshwater.* She opened her mouth and drank the droplets sprinkling over her lips.

"Brandon! Brandon! It's raining, buddy! Oh, please, wake up! Please, Brandon!" She shook his chest and then wiped his hair back from his forehead. "Come on, buddy. Please. Please, wake up." A sharp pain burned in her nose as she inhaled a deep breath. Her heart rattled against her chest. *What if he doesn't wake up?* A heavyweight pulled against her heart when the thought crossed her mind. Shaking her head, she looked towards the island and then back at Brandon.

"Sera."

Brandon's tiny voice whispered, warming Sera's heart. She blinked, releasing the tears pooling in her eyes. Looking down, she saw Brandon's eyes open. He reached his arms out and wrapped them around her neck.

"Brandon! Oh, Brandon! Get a drink, buddy. It's raining. We're in the water. We're going to be okay." Her voice crackled as tears rolled down her cheeks. "It's going to be okay, buddy. It's going to be okay."

Brandon opened his mouth and swallowed drinks of rainwater. After a few minutes, he raised his head, looking around.

"Okay, you need to put your legs into the water and paddle. You need to help me swim now. We still need to make it over to the island."

Brandon nodded and put his hand on her shoulder.

"Ow! Well, that's a good start."

The waves began rolling up and down again into tall peaks. A spidering flash of light scattered above their heads, and the thunder echoed off the waves. Sera gazed into Brandon's eyes before nodding. "Ready?"

Brandon nodded.

"Okay, swim. Swim, Brandon. Go. Go. Go."

Brandon let go of her, and they swam as hard as they could. The storm continued strong, blowing monstrous waves around them. Another flash of lights flickered above Sera, lighting up the sky. She looked up to see the island was so close. *We can make it. We can make it.*

"Brandon, look! Look! We're almost there!"

Sera stopped and watched, waiting for the lightning to flash again. A twinkle of light fluttered over her head and draped across the sky. Squinting, she stared at the island and saw the boat docked beside it.

"No, they're going to the island."

"What is it, Sera?"

Shaking her head, she peered at the island and looked at Brandon. "It's nothing, buddy. Come on. We're almost there."

A loud growl echoed over the water again. Sera looked down and realized they were being raised high into the sky. A giant wave rolled under them and was going to throw them into the darkness. Sera opened her mouth, gasping at the height the wave was standing. She reached out and pulled Brandon against her body. She opened her mouth to speak, but the words screeched as she spoke. "Hold your breath!"

The hit slapped Sera in the face, pulling Brandon hard from her grip. She reached out and wrapped her arms and legs around his tiny frame, holding him until the water stopped pummeling their bodies. Their bodies bounced and swirled deep in the water. Sera felt Brandon's body squirm and kick as he tried to swim back up to the top. She let go of him with one hand and pulled down at the water with the other, trying to swim up. Sera's chest ached as her lungs desperately needed air to breathe. Her fingers reached out of the water first, and then her head finally emerged. Brandon coughed and spewed saltwater and chunks of stomach acid in front of him. Panting, she held Brandon and herself up, paddling her feet until Brandon stopped vomiting. He looked up at her and nodded, exhaling deep breaths.

Sera relaxed, leaning her head back, and felt something tap her on the back. She lunged forward and turned around to see darkness. She pulled Brandon back and stared, waiting for the lightning to flash again. A flash of light trickled across the sky and illuminated a mass in front of them. Sera reached out and felt thick rock protruding out. She peered around and realized it was the island.

I can't believe it. We made it to the island.

Another flash of light fluttered over the island, showing palm trees violently swaying in the wind.

"It's rocks. We made it to the island, Brandon. The wave must have thrown us the rest of the way."

Sera swam cautiously to the rock and tried to grab somewhere to pull herself up.

"Brandon, Brandon. Come here."

Brandon swam in front of her, reaching out to grab some of the rock. It was too high up, so he tried climbing up. He slid back down and looked back at Sera.

"I'm going to hoist you up. Wait for me, and I'll be right behind you."

She dipped into the water, put her hands around Brandon's waist, and pushed him onto the rocks. She bobbed back out of the water and held onto the side of the stone to catch her breath. Panting, she planted her feet on the rock and pulled herself up. Once up, she flopped onto her side.

Brandon put his hands on Sera's forehead and leaned down into her face. "Sera, are you okay?"

"Yes, buddy." She huffed deep breaths. "We made it." She rolled over onto her back, panting.

Once Sera caught her breath, she stood up and gazed at the rock. The island seemed dark and gloomy, with giant trees wafting angrily in the wind. Lightning spidered across the sky, showing bits of the island. Sera peered around and saw an opening in the rock in front of them. *A cave.* She reached out, grabbed Brandon's hand, and walked towards the cave.

Chapter Forty-Two: The Island

Sera

Sera and Brandon walked blindly into a cave hidden in the rock. The cave was a narrow tunnel with only enough room for her and Brandon to walk side by side. She stopped just a few feet inside the entrance and sat down on the ground. The rain picked up outside and poured down against the floor of the entryway. Lightning fluttered across the sky, and a monstrous growl illuminated the viscous waves they left behind. Sera peered into the cave and saw a dark tunnel disappearing deep inside the rock. She dropped her head back against the wall, closing her eyes.

"Sera?"

"Yes."

"Where are we?"

Sera looked out over the water, and another blast of light fluttered across the clouds. Brandon jumped and gripped Sera's arm, hiding his face in her shoulder. She wrapped her arms around him, pulling him close. Yawning, she stretched out her legs in front of her and relaxed.

"I don't know, buddy. Let's close our eyes and try to get some rest. Okay?"

Brandon looked back into the darkness of the cave and shivered in Sera's arms.

"Sera? Are there monsters in there?"

"No, buddy. We left the monsters back on the bridge. We're just in an old cave." Sera's voice echoed off the walls, trickling down into the cave's darkness. "Now, close your eyes and try to sleep. Okay."

"Okay." Brandon yawned a deep moan and shivered against Sera.

"Do you think John and Furry are on the island, too?"

Sera felt a heavy lump form in her throat as she tried to reply to Brandon. Swallowing, she squeezed her eyes shut and felt a singe of pain shoot through her nose and into her eyes. A warm tear escaped, running down her cheek.

"I . . . I don't know, buddy. I hope so."

"Sera?"

"Yes."

"Did you have any kids before?"

Sera shook her head, "No, I, um . . . I didn't have time to."

"Did you want kids?"

Sera nodded her head, "Yes. Very much so."

Brandon turned his head and gazed out over the water. "I'm glad you found us."

"Me, too."

She squeezed Brandon tight and kissed his head.

"I love you, buddy. Now go to sleep."

"I love you, too."

He nuzzled his head against Sera's shoulder and quickly went to sleep.

Sera gazed out the cave door and waited for the storm to pass before finally closing her eyes.

The next morning, Sera woke up to feet standing in front of her face. She shot up quickly to see Brandon standing there.

"It stopped raining, and the sun's out, and it's really nice here. I went outside to see the island, and we're on the side where there are big rocks," Brandon said excitedly.

Sera rubbed her eyes and looked around the cave. The sun was smiling bright, lighting up the day. A cool, salty breeze blew through the entrance, whispering down the tunnel. Sera looked behind her to see that the tunnel wasn't as dark and gloomy as it had appeared the night before. A glimmer of sunlight peeked through a hole in the rock ceiling, lighting up the path.

The ocean was only a few feet from where they slept. Giant waves rocked back and forth in the sea, calmly thrashing against the rocks they'd climbed up the night before. Sera stood up slowly and took steps toward the door. Sharp pains shot through her feet from the cave's floor, and her legs felt like heavy weights with each step she took. She looked down to see her limbs and arms were covered in bruises.

"Ugh!" Sera grunted.

She peeked out the cave door, and her breath caught. A ship was anchored next to the island. It appeared to be the same boat as the one parked next to the bridge the night before. She dropped back against the cave wall and looked at Brandon.

"Brandon, did you go outside already?"

"Yes! I walked back there, too!"

"Why didn't you wake me?"

"I tried, but you were snoring really loud, so I let you sleep." He walked past Sera and headed for the cave door.

Sera reached out, grabbed his shirt, and pulled him back.

"Ow, that hurt!" Brandon jerked away from Sera.

"Get away from the door, Brandon! Didn't you see the ship? Did anyone see you?"

"Yes, I saw the ship, and it's humongous! I don't think anyone saw me. I didn't see anyone out there. Do you want me to go look for people? Hang on, I'll go see!"

"No! Brandon, no. We don't want people to know we're here. Remember how I said we can't trust anyone? We have to be very careful. Remember?"

Brandon nodded.

She peered around the cave door again. The ship was banked right up against the island. A long rope hung down from one side, flapping in the wind.

The island appeared to be a lot larger than she'd expected. The rocks they'd climbed up the night before only went for a couple hundred feet one way before it turned into a grassland filled with trees. She tried to see if there were any people visible on the island, but the trees concealed everything.

Sera stepped back and stared down at Brandon. An image of John's face and Furry pup flashed in her mind. Shaking her head, she looked back into the cave.

"Sera? Are you mad at me?"

She exhaled and looked down at Brandon. "No. We just . . . we have to be careful, buddy. We can't trust anyone, ever. Okay? Do you understand?"

She looked back into the cave and peered down at the end. A beam of light was flowing in from a hole in the top of the tunnel.

"What is that, Brandon? Did you walk back there, buddy?"

Brandon nodded and said, "There's water down there."

"Really? It could be fresh water. Let's go see."

The further Sera and Brandon walked, the narrower the tunnel became until it stopped at a dead end. She could hear the water running down into the rock. She dipped her hands into a crystal-clear pool and cupped it over her lips. The cool, refreshing water tasted fresh and clean. She gulped down long drinks and stopped to wave Brandon over. He did the same, and they sat down on their rumps, smiling at each other.

Sera cupped handfuls and washed off her face, arms, and hands. She helped Brandon wash off and exhaled a long breath. "Well, we need to go into the forest and find John and Furry."

She looked back at the ceiling and tried to size it up. The

hole looked big enough for her and Brandon to squeeze through. A cool breeze blew through the tunnel, ruffling her fiery hair back. She gazed out the cave entrance and saw the clouds skating across the sky. The aquamarine blue met the sky, and she couldn't tell where the sky ended and the water began.

"Look, Brandon. It's beautiful here."

Brandon nodded and smiled up at her.

"Brandon, can you climb up there and look out of that hole? I'll help you up."

He looked up at the ceiling and then back at her. Nodding, he stood up and walked over to the hole.

"Just peek out, okay?"

She knelt and patted her knee, waiting for him to step on it. Wrapping her hands around his waist, she lifted him up onto her knee.

"Now run your fingers along the rock and find a rock you can grab hold of and pull yourself up with. Okay? It's kind of like climbing a tree. Have you ever climbed a tree?"

"No."

"That's okay. You can do it, okay?"

Brandon pushed Sera's head and ran his fingers along the rock. His body lifted from her grasp, and before she knew it, he was climbing through the hole.

"Slow down, Brandon. Peek out, remember?"

"Okay, Sera."

Sera held her breath and stared up at Brandon's dangling feet. Her heart pounded in her chest. She knew it was risky, but she had to know if they could climb out without being seen by the people on the boat.

"Sera, it's huge up here. There's a big forest with giant trees. Fruit trees!"

"Shh, Brandon. Quiet. Do you see any people? Or anything else?"

"No. No, people. I can't see the ship. The trees are in the way. There are a lot of fruit trees, Sera. Bananas! There are apples! There's—"

"Brandon! Shh! Okay. Okay. Climb up the rest of the way and wait for me. Okay? Wait for me!"

"Okay!"

Sera watched his feet exit the hole and exhaled a loud breath. *Okay, my turn.* She jumped up and grabbed some rocks, pulling herself up. Her fingers vibrated as she lifted her weight up. Once she gripped the top of the hole, it was easier for her to pull herself out. Brandon grabbed her forearm and pulled as she exited the hole. She dropped her body over, panting, and looked up into the sky. Giant trees flapped violently in the wind. Many bright yellow bananas wafted back and forth, threatening to fall from their perch. Brandon was right. There were fruit trees everywhere. An apple tree covered in bright red balls swayed back and forth like earrings hanging from a lobe. Brandon walked over and stood over Sera, smiling from ear to ear.

"See. I told you. Fruit trees."

He looked up, nodding at the trees. It was like a fantasy that had come to life. A sweet smell lingered in the air, wafting a mouth-watering fragrance of fruits and flower nectar.

Brandon spun around with his hands in the air. "I like it here, Sera. Can we live here? Look, Sera! Look!"

Brandon bolted into the forest. Sera jumped up onto her feet. "No, Brandon, wait—"

He held up a handful of bananas, and his long, skinny legs galloped back toward her, panting.

"Bananas!"

She looked down at him, nodding. "That's wonderful, Brandon. You can't just run off like that. Remember, we have to stay together. Okay?" He plopped down onto the ground and had a banana opened and shoved in his mouth before she finished talking.

"Mmm!"

He handed her one, and she pulled the bright yellow layers back, exposing the heavenly fruit inside. She pushed the fruit into her mouth and slowly enjoyed the explosion of sweetness on her tongue.

Brandon crammed another banana into his mouth, packing his cheeks like a chipmunk. He smiled, and chunks of fruit pushed through his teeth. Sera leaned over, ruffled his hair, pushed the rest of the fruit into her mouth, and chewed.

She stood up slowly, looked around, and brushed off her pants. Then she put her hand out for Brandon and pulled him up.

"Brandon, I have to go behind that tree for a minute to use the restroom. Can you come with me and turn around?"

"Ew, I don't want to see you poop!"

"I'm not going to poop. I need to pee, and I don't want you alone. Just turn around. Okay?"

"Okay."

Nodding, Brandon followed her over to the tree and turned around. He kicked the wood and mumbled something under his breath.

Sera finished up and stepped out from behind the tree. "Come on, buddy. We should get going. Stay with me and keep your voice down."

Brandon looked around and wasn't paying attention.

Sera stopped him and grabbed his arm. "Brandon. Are you listening?"

Brandon looked up at her and shook his head. Sera looked away and then back down at him.

"We have to be quiet. We don't know who's here, and we don't know who we can trust. Do you understand? You have to keep very quiet. Okay?"

Brandon nodded and looked up at Sera wide-eyed. Sera

turned around and started walking through the forest.

Chapter Forty-Three: You Are Not Alone

Sera

Sera led the way through the tall grass into the forest. She stopped, holding her hand out so that Brandon could grab it. The grass became higher the further they walked, reaching Sera's knees and Brandon's waist. Stopping periodically, Sera peered through the trees for anything or anyone lurking in the shadows. Even though the forest seemed abandoned, she knew it was always too good to be true.

The sun slowly made its way west, hiding behind a row of oaks. The morning quickly turned into late afternoon, and Sera looked around and only saw more pines surrounding her. *Shit. This place is a lot bigger than I expected.*

She stopped and wiped her brow when a familiar sound — a bark — echoed in the distance. Brandon jerked his head, looking around him.

"It's Furry!"

"Wait, Brandon. We don't know that for sure yet. Just —"

Sera turned around and saw something moving through the trees. She dropped down in the grass, pulling Brandon down with her.

"Sera! It's —"

"Shh!" Sera put her hand over Brandon's mouth and pointed.

A man holding a rifle stepped out of the bushes and

buttoned his pants. He was wearing a black cowboy hat and had a cigarette hanging from his bottom lip.

"Hey, kid! Kid!"

Brandon flinched, and Sera gripped her arm tight around him.

"What the fuck! I told you I was trying to take a shit! What the hell do you want?"

"I think we found something! Hurry!"

"I'm coming. I'm coming!"

Sera slowly lifted her head, looking for the man. He disappeared through some trees, so she repositioned herself and crouched down in the grass.

"Brandon?"

He looked up at her with wide eyes.

"I want to get a better look to see how many there are."

He nodded.

"Stay close behind me. Okay?"

Brandon nodded again and opened his mouth to speak. Sera put her finger up to her mouth and shook her head.

Brandon's shoulders slumped, and he exhaled deeply.

Sera slowly crawled towards the trees the man had disappeared into. As she approached, she saw three more men standing on a dirt path. They were wearing green camo with caps and backpacks. Each one was holding a rifle and had a knife secured to his belt.

"What is that?" a man asked the others.

"I don't know," he replied.

A boisterous horn sounded, echoing through the forest. Brandon dropped into the grass, covering his ears. The men shouted something at each other, but the horn was too loud for Sera to make out what they were saying. They all began jogging towards the siren and disappeared into the woods.

Another alarming horn rattled through the trees and blew for almost a minute.

Sera waited for the sound to stop and stood up. She leaned down and pulled Brandon to his feet. "Stay here. I'll be right back." She nodded, looking down at Brandon.

He nodded, rubbing against his ears.

Sera took cautious steps out into the open and walked over to whatever the men were looking at before the horn sounded. A pungent smell of death slapped Sera in the face, wrinkling her nose as she approached the area. Holding her breath, she scanned the ground, looking for whatever could be the culprit. Then something lying between two trees caught her eye. It looked like a person. A dead person. As Sera got closer, she realized it was a dead little girl lying on her side. *Oh fuck! No, please don't be what I think it is. Please. We came all this way.*

She slowly walked around to the side her face was on and gazed down at her. Sunlight beamed down between the trees, accentuating her skin. Her flesh had turned a sickly gray, and her limbs were bruised. She looked like she was decaying and had been lying there for at least a couple of days. Sera turned to walk away when something else caught her attention. The girl's body was deteriorating, but her face seemed untouched. She cocked her head to the side and tried to see her eyes more clearly but couldn't. She looked behind her and scanned the area. A long stick was lying on the ground, so she jogged over, picked it up, and jogged back. Sera held the wood with both hands and pushed on the girl's body. The body felt like it had hardened and was incredibly heavy. She braced her feet and went to give it a hard shove when something touched her arm.

"Sera."

Sera jumped back, dropping her stick, and spun around with her fists erect. Brandon stood there with bulging eyes. Panting, she exhaled loudly and dropped her fists.

"I told you to wait for me, Brandon."

"What are you doing?" Brandon asked. "She's dead and

smells really bad." Brandon held his hands to his face, covering his nose and mouth.

"I know. I'm just . . . nothing . . . it's nothing. Let's go," Sera said, shaking her head.

She dropped the stick, checked around them, and returned to the high grass.

She looked up, and the sunlight peeking through the trees was gone, leaving them with little daylight to find John and Furry.

The tall grass started to thin out, and clusters of trees took its place. A thicket of blackberry bushes resided among the trees, making it impossible to get through. *Shit.*

"Ow!" Brandon fussed to her right.

"Come on, we'll have to find a way around these bushes. We should grab a couple of handfuls to eat along the way."

"What are they?"

"Blackberries. Do you like blackberries?"

"I don't know."

"Well, try them."

He popped one in his mouth, his cheeks twerked first, and then his lips squeezed together. He looked over at Sera with a look of horror. Sera had to bite her lip to keep from smiling.

"I don't like it."

"Yeah, I gathered that." Sera chuckled.

As she made her way around the bushes, she looked down to see the ground was rockier with less dirt and grass. She looked up at the trees and tried to find one she could climb. Brandon slowly followed behind her, kicking his feet.

"Brandon, get up here with me. Stop messing around."

Brandon ran and then stopped, holding himself.

"I have to go, Sera." He bounced back and forth.

Sera nodded. "Okay, I'm coming."

"No! I can't go if you're watching me."

"Brandon, I'm not going to watch. I'll turn around and look

the other way."

"No. I won't go far, I promise. It's just right over there. Okay?" Brandon said, bouncing.

"Okay, fine. I'll wait here." Sera said, nodding.

Brandon nodded, running behind a tree. Sera walked over, stood on the other side of the tree, and waited. The wind picked up and blew Sera's body back against the wood. She looked up into the sky, watching the limbs slap against the base of the oak. She peered down at her dirt-covered feet and then at her filthy hands. Inhaling a deep breath, she looked to her right and left.

"Brandon, how's it going, buddy?"

Sera kicked her feet and waited for him to respond.

"Brandon?" Sera asked again, but a little louder this time.

"Brandon?" Sera said and walked around the tree. She saw his poop sitting in a pile on the ground, but there was no Brandon.

Sera gasped as all the air left her chest. A lump formed in her throat, choking her as she tried to swallow. She spun around in a circle, dizzily feeling like the trees were closing around her. She stopped and squeezed her eyes shut to try and ground herself. *Brandon. Brandon. Brandon.*

"Brandon!" She tried not to yell his name, but fear vibrated in her chest. She turned and walked over to where Brandon had been standing to look around. She peered through the trees, trying to see if anything caught her attention. Her eyes scanned across the tree line and then back again, going from left to right, from right to left again. *Brandon, Brandon, where are you?*

Gone. He's . . . gone. Sera pushed her feet forward and started walking. *He couldn't have gone too far.* The forest thickened with trees and spikey bushes, stabbing and cutting into her forearms as she tried to push through them. The sunlight was dimming quickly, and a chilly breeze whistled through the trees, blowing leaves into her face. Sera swiped them away and spun around to dodge the falling foliage.

The hair on the back of her neck stood up, and she felt like she was being watched. She turned to look and saw hundreds of trees staring back at her. All the trees and bushes began mirroring each other. She spun around and around, dropping to her knees, and covered her face with trembling hands. Tears flooded her face as she swallowed back her sobs.

How could I lose him? He's just a little boy. I can't believe I let him out of my sight.

Once the sobs ended, Sera opened her eyes and wiped her face with her hands. *No, everything's okay. I'll find him. Get up, Sera. Stop being a crybaby.* She stood up and inhaled a deep breath. Nodding, she started walking again. The wind pushed her body back and whined as she entered its current. A strong smell of seawater wafted through the air, and then she heard ocean waves crashing over a beach. She stopped, dropping her mouth open. *The beach. John. Furry.*

Sera picked up the pace and felt her feet sink as she tried to move faster. Looking down, she saw the rocks and grass change into mounds of sand.

"Sand. It's sand." *Yes, yes, yes.* The minute she whispered the words, she heard a round of barking. It was so close — maybe a hundred yards away. Another violent brush of wind blew against Sera, pushing her body away from the direction she wanted to go.

The trees broke ahead of her, and a glimmer of sunlight and water twinkled. She pushed her feet against the white, slumping through the thickness of the sand as quickly as possible.

Another round of barking echoed. *Oh, please be Furry. Please be Furry!* It was so close she could almost see it.

Sera stopped before the trees and peeked through to see Brandon and Furry. They were running along the beach, laughing and smiling in the sunshine. A tear rolled down Sera's cheek and dove into her lips. She smiled and shivered as her body relaxed and let the sobs come. She wiped her eyes and stepped out onto the beach. *John. Where are you?*

Furry ran alongside Brandon down the beach. Brandon rushed out into the ocean tides and then ran to Furry. Furry jumped in the air and hopped in front of Brandon. Sera stood there smiling until she spotted a ship sailing around the corner of the island. She stepped out into the open on the beach and whistled for Furry. Furry stopped hopping and looked in Sera's direction. Sera waved her arms for them to come and whistled again. Furry took off at full speed, running towards her. Brandon followed behind.

Then she saw John step out into view. He raised his hand up in the air and waved. Sera waved, jumping up and down. Her heart swelled. Tears rolled down her cheeks again, dampening the front of her shirt. She waved, smiling, and then remembered the boat. She stopped and pointed to the ship and then waved for everyone to hurry to her.

Brandon and Fury quickly ran over to her, but John slowly limped. It looked like he was dragging one of his legs in the sand. Shaking her head, she watched him slowly walk to her.

"Hi."

"Hi." Sera wrapped her arms around him and squeezed.

John's lips found hers, and he held her tight in his arms for several moments before letting her go.

"I didn't know if you made it," he whispered.

"Barely." She chuckled and shook her head with a half-smile. "I'm so glad you did."

She reached down, scratched Furry's head, and pulled Brandon into her abdomen, squeezing him.

"You left me back there, Brandon. What did I say about staying together?"

"I heard Furry, and I knew you wouldn't listen, so I came to find her and John. We were going to come back to find you."

"From now on, we stay together. No matter what! You could have been killed or worse. Do you understand?"

Brandon nodded his head and wrapped his body around John's leg.

"Ow, be careful, buddy."

John winced, pushing Brandon away from his leg.

"What happened?"

"Nothing. It's nothing. I'm just a little sore."

"But you were limping. I saw you limping, John."

"I'm fine. It's just a little bruise."

"Let me see it then." Sera unbuckled his belt, unzipped his pants, and pushed them down.

She looked up and met his gaze. Shaking his head, he winked at her. "I would rather you pull them down for something else."

A smile brightened Sera's face, and she shook her head.

A huge bruise covered John's upper thigh. "Oh, John. What happened?"

"Last night, the water, or I guess the storm, threw us against the cliffs. I was able to push Furry onto the rock, but the wave slammed me into it, and, well, as you see, today I'm all bruised up."

"Yeah, it's bad." Sera nodded and pulled his pants back up gently.

"But I've got the bag, so that's good, right?"

"Yeah. Let me carry it for a while. We need to go into town and see if we can find any supplies. Brandon and I found so many fruit trees near the caves on the other side of the island. Oh, and fresh water, too."

"Fresh water?"

"Yes. Inside the cave we spent the night in," Sera replied. "We can go back and fill up the thermoses with water so you guys can get a drink and have water for later."

John nodded. "Okay."

Sera reached out and grabbed her bag. She opened it and pulled out her flashlight. The bag was waterproof, and luckily, the ocean hadn't damaged anything in it. She flipped on the light and handed it to John. "Hold this."

Sera shined the light into her pack as she dug for her shoes. The ocean had taken off her last pair, and she had to wear her backup to protect her feet.

She looked down at John's feet and saw he still had his on.

Nodding, he said, "Boots. Nothing's pulling these off. They're military grade."

"Well, that's good." She smiled.

"Okay. Let's get going."

CHAPTER FORTY-FOUR: MONSTERS

John

John followed Sera back to the cave where she and Brandon had stayed the previous night.

"If we need to, we can sleep in the cave tonight. It's not the most comfortable, but out of sight."

A brief wisp of cool air whistled through the trees, sending chills down John's spine. He peered through the pines and scanned the tall grass as he followed Sera. An eerie feeling struck as if they had eyes on them. He spun around, searching the grounds, but saw nothing but woods.

"What is it?" Sera whispered.

Shaking his head, he scanned the grass again before looking at her. "I don't know. I feel like someone or something's watching us, but I don't see anything."

John stepped, and his foot got tangled, knocking him over. He reached out and felt a long piece of wood with a cracked side next to his calf.

Sera walked over and put her hand out. "You, okay?"

John reached out for her, and a pungent smell wafted towards him. He jerked his head back and forth, trying to see where it was coming from. Sera stopped, and her head spun around, looking through the trees.

"Do you smell that," John asked.

"Yes." She pulled John to his feet, meeting his gaze. "We passed a dead girl earlier. Her body was over here somewhere. She was decaying as if she'd been there for a while."

"Wait. What?"

"Yeah." Sera nodded and met John's gaze. He slightly shook his head as he breathed deeply. They both knew what it could mean. "Some men were here earlier looking down at the body, and then the ship's horn sounded off. I guess it was calling them in. I don't know."

"Was it the same ship from earlier on the bridge?"

"I think so." Sera nodded, scanning the grass. "I think the body's over there somewhere."

Sera took small, calculated steps toward the center of the woods.

"There." Sera pointed. A dark mass covered some of the tall grass. John slowly walked over and stopped in front of the body.

The person's mouth was opened, and black ooze stained the cracks of the crease of their lips.

John's chest tightened, and a deep burning sensation plunged into his stomach. He knew what this meant. The beings, the monsters, had found a way to come here, and now, after everything, they still weren't safe. *Is this ever going to be over?*

"Oh, shit." Sera gasped.

"What?"

"It's not the same girl, and she's—"

Brandon pulled Sera's hand and pointed. "Look."

John turned around, and dead bodies were lying everywhere.

"One, two, three . . . ten, eleven, twelve . . . nineteen, twenty, twenty-one. They're . . . everywhere."

Sera gazed up at John and said, "This wasn't here earlier. We saw a dead girl. One. But . . . "

John peered through the trees, gazing at all the dead bodies lined up. It was like a graveyard of incubating sludge beings awaiting their time to be awakened. Blinking, John shook his head and saw something moving out of his peripheral vision.

He dropped down in the tall grass and pulled Brandon and Sera down, too. John reached for Furry and held his finger over his mouth for everyone to see. His heart pounded against Furry's back as he held his breath. He raised his head slowly, peering through the trees. There was no one there. Exhaling, he rose and looked around.

"What did you see?" Sera asked.

John shook his head and said, "Something was moving out of the corner of my eye. We have to get out of here."

He looked around, scanning the area.

"Come on," John whispered and waved his hand.

Sera led the way, and John held his hand out for Brandon to take. They stayed amid the trees, trying to keep out of sight. John looked up and saw a clearing open up between the oaks. The ground began to get rockier, and he looked back at Sera, meeting her gaze.

Sera nodded. "We're almost there."

Brandon smiled, looking up and pointed. John followed Brandon's finger and saw fruit trees swaying next to the oaks. Nodding, John raised his finger up, reminding him to keep quiet. A heavy wind picked up and blew through the pines, blowing in another rotten smell. John stopped, holding his hand up for everyone to stop. The pungent smell grew stronger and stronger the further they walked. Then, just as they were about to step out of the safety of the pines, four men holding rifles walked out from the clearing.

Fuck.

The men marched down the path, staring straight ahead. Peering around Sera, he felt something was off.

There's no way those men are here out of coincidence. *Fuck. Fuck. Fuck.*

John looked around, searching the area. He knew there was something more to the graveyard of sludge beings.

Why are those men marching toward the dead people?

John met Sera's gaze and dropped down onto his belly. He crawled back and stopped next to Brandon and Furry. Sera stayed ahead and peered through the high grass.

John turned his head, scanning the area, when something caught his eye. One of the dead girls was standing at the end of the walkway. She cocked her head to the side and opened her mouth. The familiar blood-curdling scream they'd all learned to be cautious of sounded only a few feet from where they were hiding.

The men marching down the path turned around, saw the girl, and opened fire. The girl sprinted at full speed towards the men, jumping on the closest one and pushing him to the ground. She put her arms around his neck, opened her mouth, and screamed. The man pressed the end of his rifle against her chest and pulled the trigger. The girl bounced off his gun and stayed there as he filled her with bullets. She opened her mouth, oozing black sludge down her lips and dripping onto the man shooting her. The sludge dripped over his body and flowed into his mouth like a river going home. The man's eyes rolled into the back of his head, and he started convulsing, dropping the gun on the ground, still holding the trigger. Bullets struck the trees and hit one of the men he was marching with. The man that was shot fell to the ground, holding his chest, while blood pumped out of him and littered the grass.

The man finally released the trigger, dropped his arm onto the ground, and lay motionless. The girl crawled off him and wiped her mouth. She walked towards the next man standing, opened her mouth, and screamed her eerie cries.

One of the last men turned around and started running away. He looked back and saw the girl standing there with her head cocked to one side, watching him run. The last man standing opened fire and started shooting the girl. She bounced with each hit, dropping to the ground. She rolled over onto her belly and started twitching. The man ceased fire, stood there, and stared.

He looked in the direction the man had run to and then back at her. Shaking his head, he slowly approached her and stopped before reaching her body. He reached out with the barrel of his gun, pushing on her back with the tip of the rifle. He leaned forward and stared closely into her face. Her eyes popped open, and he jumped back.

She was up like a flash of lightning, pulling him down, and was on top of him before he could react. He raised his rifle, and she ripped it from his fingers and threw it away. She opened her mouth and sank her teeth into his neck. His screams echoed through the trees for a split second before his voice was muffled by gargling. Her body began to vibrate as black sludge oozed from the corners of her mouth. The man fought against the girl briefly before his arms dropped to the ground, letting the sludge invade his body.

The girl stood up and wiped her mouth.

The being walked past the dead soldiers on the ground and walked deeper into the forest when something caught her attention. Stopping, she turned around and scanned the woods. Her gaze stopped on where they were hiding, and she cocked her head to the side and started walking towards them.

John squeezed Brandon's little body, holding his breath. He knew this was it. They didn't have anywhere to run now.

Fuck. Fuck. Fuck. John closed his eyes, breathing deeply.

He knew that he was going to have to get up and fight. Fight for Sera, Brandon, and Furry. After all these years of not caring about anyone, he finally realized that he'd fallen in love with her. He'd fallen in love with his family, and he would rather die than watch them be killed.

He looked over, meeting Sera's gaze. He stared into her crystal blues and nodded. She shook her head and mouthed the words, *No*, but John had made up his mind. He slowly nodded and started to push himself up when a loud horn screamed through the forest. John and Sera's heads spun to look. The girl had stopped and was looking in the ship's direction. She turned on her heel and jogged in the direction of the noise. John dropped his head into the grass, panting. His heart was pounding like a heavy drum in his ears.

John stood up, walked over to Sera, and grabbed her arm, pulling her up. He pressed his lips against hers as he wrapped his arms around her. He reached out, not breaking his lips from hers, and pulled Brandon into a hug, too.

Nodding, he pulled back, and Sera's eyes glossed over. He searched her face, memorizing her beauty.

He looked back to where the being was and said, "Let's go."

"This way. It's this way, John." Sera's voice croaked.

"The ship might be near the cave. I don't know."

"The cave is just past that clearing."

"Yeah, that's where the fruit trees are, too!" Brandon said.

John looked over at her and nodded. "We have to try."

Sera nodded, and they began jogging until Sera stopped, holding up her hand. She pointed to the ground, and John saw the rock covering the ground. Nodding, she pointed towards an opening in the trees.

Sera walked up to it and stopped. "They anchored the ship right in front of the cave. We can't stay there tonight. I'm going to try and sneak in to get some water." She looked back at Brandon and said, "Brandon, do you see any bananas on the ground? Don't go far and find a couple for John to eat."

"Okay!"

Sera opened her bag and pulled out a canteen and an empty jug to fill with water.

"I'll go with you," John said.

"The hole to squeeze in the ceiling of the cave is tiny. I barely fit through climbing out. You won't fit. I have to be the one to go," Sera whispered, looking at John.

"Be careful, Sera," John whispered.

She gazed up at John, nodding.

The sun was trickling down into the water, leaving a tiny bit of light to see with. John watched Sera walk over to a spot on the ground and drop to her knees. She put her feet in first, and then the rest of her body dropped into the unknown.

Brandon handed John several bananas and sat to peel one for himself. John shoved half into his mouth, chewing with two big clumps in each cheek.

Sera's hand popped out of the hole, and a water jug dropped onto the ground. She climbed out and carried two water jugs, one in each hand.

Panting, she sat on the ground and grabbed a banana from John's pile. John grabbed the water and chugged it loudly. Sera pulled out a bowl for Furry and gave her a drink, too.

John met Sera's gaze and nodded once he finished.

"Well, we can't stay here tonight," John whispered.

Sera looked back toward the cave and then met John's gaze. "No."

"To town then?"

Nodding, Sera said, "Yes. Let's go to town. John?"

"Yeah."

"I'm sorry I drug us here, thinking it was a good—"

"It's okay. You didn't know. I didn't know. I don't think it's safe anywhere anymore."

Sera nodded. "Yeah."

CHAPTER FORTY-FIVE: SURROUNDED

Sera

A shadow of darkness cast over their path as they traveled blindly towards what they'd hoped was the town. Stars began filling the sky, twinkling through the treetops.

Brandon smiled and pointed up. "Look, Sera, stars."

"I know, buddy. It's beautiful."

A couple of hours passed, and Sera looked up and saw an opening in the trees. As she approached, she saw a glimpse of asphalt peeking through leaves and brush that covered the road.

She looked over at John, meeting his gaze. Shaking her head, she whispered, "Should we follow it? Maybe we can hide in the trees and follow the road. It should lead us to town, right?"

"I don't know." John looked both ways and then looked back at Sera. "Yeah, honestly, I think it's our only way."

"Okay." Sera nodded.

Sera followed John back into the forest, hiding in the trees that aligned the road. A sense of uneasiness sank in her stomach. She peered around her, checking the path they'd just walked. Something didn't feel right, and she knew that whatever it was could easily sneak up on them in the dark.

She peered behind her and saw Brandon lagging. She reached out for his hand and tried to pull him along, but his head bobbed up and down with exhaustion. John stopped and pulled Brandon onto his back. Sera pulled the strap of her

bag tightly over her shoulder and followed John, peering behind her randomly.

A cold breeze wafted through the air, sending chills down
Sera's spine. She stopped to peer down the road when a peculiar sound rattled a few hundred yards away. She stopped
and tapped on John's shoulder. He looked back at her, and
then his gaze went to the road. Headlights beamed down the
street, racing along the narrow clearing. An old truck sped
past, whirling brown leaves into the air. Sera dropped down
and peeked out the shrubbery as the truck's taillights disappeared around a sharp curve.

John met Sera's gaze. "We should follow that truck."

John nodded and sat Brandon down on the ground. "I need
you to walk, buddy."

Nodding, Brandon rubbed his eyes and grabbed John's
hand.

Sera led the way through the trees toward where the truck
had driven until she approached a sharp corner. The road was
guarded by a mass of trees, blocking the view. She cautiously
crossed the barrier of trees and saw a clearing open up a few
hundred feet ahead. A bright light flickered in the sky, and
then the smell of smoke wafted through the air. Sera stopped
and stepped out of the tree line for a better look.

"What is that—"

A person screaming echoed through the air. Sera ran back
into the trees, shaking her head. Another set of lights flickered, and then the flames of a large fire peeked over what
looked like a large building.

"I think it's a—"

A loud explosion rumbled, and then a great flame rippled
across the top of the building.

"What the—"

"I don't think it's safe here. I think we should keep going."

"But, what if—"

"Somethings not right," John whispered.

Nodding, Sera went further back into the tree line and stood next to John and Brandon. They continued to walk until they came to a large structure. A twenty-foot-high stone wall stretched around what appeared to be a housing community.

Sera headed for the wall and stood in front of it.

"Sera, Wait!" John whispered. She waved her hand at him and shook her head.

The wall was faded off-white, with green ivy climbing up the side. A shrill scream bellowed from inside the structure, and several voices echoed as if someone was fighting. Sera cautiously walked up to it and tried to find a hole to look in.

"Sera," John whispered again, gritting his teeth.

A loud crash from the other side of the wall shook the stone, and it rumbled under Sera's feet. Startled, she jumped and returned to the forest when a smokey barbeque smell drifted through the air. She turned and glanced over her shoulder again and saw a hole peeking out from under a clump of overgrown grass along the wall.

She looked back, meeting John's gaze. He waved his hands for her to return, but she shook her head and slowly walked back to the wall.

I have to know. A deep sense of needing answers pulled her back over. Pointing, she whispered, "Drain holes. I can look in. I . . . I need to know, John."

John stomped out from the safety of the trees and stopped next to her. "Damnit, woman. Something's not right about this place, Sera. I can feel it."

"I want to look in."

"Then fucking hurry!" he snapped.

"Don't talk to me like that, you dick!"

He stared down at her, shaking his head. "Hurry!"

Sera dropped down to her knees and peeked through the hole.

A group of people were gathered around a big bonfire. Its flames reached over ten feet high, swirling over what looked like a stack of logs on one side and a spit on the other being turned by two men.

An uneasiness burned in Sera's stomach once she realized what she was looking at. A large piece of meat was strapped to the spit with a wire rope. As the men turned the rod, the meat turned to reveal a person's face sizzling in the flame with their mouth gaping open.

A person stepped in front of the hole, covering it with their calf. Sera fell back on her rump and looked up at John.

"We have to get off this island tonight."

"What did you see?"

"I saw —"

The gate began to open, rising into the air. Sera scrambled to her feet and ran into the trees with John.

The same old truck exited the walled-in area and flashed a spotlight into the trees. The wall dropped back down behind the vehicle. Sera lifted her head and watched the vehicle. An idea struck, and she knew it might be her only chance of getting away from the building.

"Get down! Are you trying to get us caught?" John snapped.

The truck stopped, and a spotlight shone in their direction. Sera stepped up and started walking into the light with her hands up.

"Stay here!" Sera whispered.

"Well, well, well, honey. Where did you come from?" an older man yelled from his truck. He was sitting in the passenger seat with a rifle strapped across his chest. A young boy was behind the wheel, holding the spotlight.

Sera slowly approached the truck, dropping her face into her hands, pretending to cry.

The older man jumped out of the truck, put his arm around

her shoulders, and patted her back. "There. There. You come with me now, young lady."

Sera slowly walked with him until she was only a few steps from the truck, then grabbed the man's gun from his chest. She pointed the barrel at his chest. "Get on the ground! Now!"

The man tried to grab the gun, and she slammed the butt of the rifle into his nose. Blood gushed down his face, staining his shirt.

"You broke my nose, you stupid bitch!"

He started walking towards her, and Sera cocked the gun. "Don't make me shoot you in front of your boy!"

The man slowly crouched down and dropped to his belly. The boy stepped out of the truck with his hands up.

Sera gazed into the boy's eyes. "I'm sorry, I have to do this."

The boy nodded and slowly lay down in the dirt.

Sera waved for John and Brandon to come. Furry ran over, sniffed the boy's neck, and started licking his ear. The boy giggled and petted her fur.

"Come on, Furry!" Sera said as she patted the inside of the truck.

John entered the driver's side, and Brandon and Furry were in the middle. Sera nodded at the boy and closed the door. John drove away, and the old man hopped up, waving his arm back and forth.

For a few miles the road was laced with trees, but then it finally opened to a row of houses. A suburban housing district came into view, with Cape Cod homes that looked abandoned with broken-out windows and opened doors.

John slowed down, idling down the road. He looked back and forth, scanning the houses. Suddenly, he slammed on his brakes and stared at a home at the end of the street. Nodding, he turned the corner and went behind the houses into the alley.

"There," John said.

He pulled behind the house, jumped out of the truck, ran to the garage, and opened the door. The garage was empty. John jumped back into the vehicle, turned the lights off, and rolled forward into the garage.

Lights from the end of the street flashed down the road seconds after he pulled into the garage. He turned off the truck, jumped out, ran to the garage door, and pulled it shut.

Sera sat quietly in the truck and listened. The squealing tires screeched down the street, revving past the house and turning down the next road.

John nodded and said, "Come on, let's go in."

Slowly, Sera stepped out and led Furry and Brandon into the house.

"It's dark, Sera," Brandon whispered.

"I know, buddy. We have to leave the flashlights off for now."

"Come on," John whispered.

He grabbed Sera's hand, and Sera held Brandon's hand. They pushed the door open and slowly walked into the house. The floor creaked with each step, reeking of musky seawater and mildew. Sera stopped in front of the garage door and stared out the ajar front door.

John walked ahead of them, checking the rooms. Yawing, Sera strolled into the hallway and waited, hugging Brandon.

"I think everything's okay," John said. "Let's try to get some rest, and then we'll figure out something tomorrow."

Sera nodded and followed John into the master bedroom. John locked the door behind them and walked Brandon over to the bed. The bed covers were pulled up and made nicely. He pulled them down and tucked Brandon in. Sera leaned over and kissed Brandon before pulling the covers up to his neck. Furry jumped up onto the bed and circled around three times before she laid down in a ball at his feet. Sera petted

Furry's head and kissed her, too.

She turned around, walked into the bathroom, and shut the door. The room was pitch black, so she felt around for the sink and tried the faucet. No water. She turned, following the wall to the toilet, and took the lid off. She reached her hands into the tank and dipped them into the water, splashing her face and washing her hands.

John walked up behind her and slid his hands around her waist. He turned her around, kissing and hugging her tightly. He ran his fingers under the back of her shirt, reached around, and fondled her breasts. Her nipples rose, and goosebumps flowed down her body. Sera pulled back, panting. "John, we need to . . . we should go—"

John cupped his mouth over hers, pushing her body against the wall. He pulled back, ran his lips down her neck, and dove into her nipples.

Sera held his head and pushed it back. "We can't do this. John? John?"

John stood up and put his lips to hers, gently caressing her tongue with his. No matter how much her head said no, her body screamed yes. Sera knew this could be the last time she could make love to him. It could be the last time that they could be together.

He pulled back and hovered his lips over hers. Sera felt his warm breath kiss her mouth.

"I want you, Sera. I can't stop thinking that we'll die tomorrow . . . and . . . I want to . . . I want you to know that . . . even though you really piss me off and drive me crazy. That I . . . I love you."

Sera put her hands up to his cheeks, staring into his eyes.

"I love you, too, John."

She gazed into John's eyes and blinked tears. Moisture flowed down her cheeks, stinging her nose as she inhaled deeply. John wiped her tears away, nodding. She reached her trembling hands under his shirt and slowly pulled it over his head. He ran his fingers under Sera's shirt and pushed it over her head. She pushed down his pants, and his hungry member exited erect and ready.

John pulled down Sera's pants and helped her kick them off. He held her hand and pulled her over him as he lay down on the floor. Shivering, she straddled his body and gazed into his eyes as she gently grabbed his manhood and eased it inside her.

John's eyes glazed over as he stared at her with a hunger she'd never seen before. His lips quivered, and he squeezed her hips as she slowly swallowed his sex deep inside her.

Quivering, her body filled with heat and ached in her groin as her climax climbed. Sera bit her bottom lip, holding in her cries of ecstasy. Her womanhood spasmed, and she felt herself vibrating all over.

John sat up, wrapped his arms around her waist, and held her body against his. His mouth cupped hers as he slowly made love to her.

Sera pulled away from his and picked up her speed, ramming his sex deep inside her. He gripped his fingers around her hips and squeezed as his manhood hardened and filled her insides. Sera's mouth dropped open, and she gasped as he held her down over his pulsating groin.

Panting, Sera wrapped her arms around John. He embraced her, and they breathed as one. She knew she needed to let go of him, but something inside her craved to hold him a little longer. She wanted to cherish this moment with him, for he might be right—it may be their last time together. She pulled back and pressed her lips against his. Her fingers ran through his hair and down his back into another hug.

Sera pulled back and whispered, "Are you okay?"

"Yeah." John barely replied before his mouth pressed against hers again. He wrapped his arms around her waist, squeezing her tightly against him. She didn't want him to stop. She savored his lips, gently swiping her tongue against his. Finally, he pulled back and gazed into her eyes, searching her face before he ran his thumb over her bottom lip. He forced a smile and nodded. Sera replied with a nod, and they both stood up and got dressed. John's fingers laced with Sera's, and they entered the bedroom where Brandon was sleeping.

Furry lifted her head and dropped it back down. Sera crawled into the bed beside Brandon and pushed herself under the covers. John slowly peeked out the window, turned, and crawled into bed. He laid behind Sera, wrapped his arms around her waist, and put his hand on Brandon.

They all fell asleep.

CHAPTER FORTY-SIX: THE BOAT

Sera

Sera woke up first and looked around the room, not recognizing where they were. Sunshine beamed through a crack in the window, warming the bedroom. She rubbed her eyes and sat up. John twitched behind her, and Brandon was snuggled up against Furry.

Sera slowly crawled out of bed, walked to the bathroom, and sat on the toilet. As she did her business, her eyes scanned the room. It had been dark the night before, so the room appeared different in the daylight. The bathroom had a long rectangular window next to a double sink. The blinds were crinkled along the side as if a dog or cat had damaged it looking out.

She finished up and walked over to peer out. The road was empty, with some trash rolling down the street. The wind squealed, pressing against the glass as if it were trying to break in. Sera turned to walk back into the bedroom when something caught her eye. She looked back and saw a luminous white sail winking at her as it reflected in the morning light.

"A sailboat," she whispered.

She hurried into the bedroom and shook John. John flew up in bed, wide-eyed with his hands out in front of him, almost knocking Sera to the floor.

Sera grabbed his arm. "I'm sorry I woke you. I want to show you something."

He rubbed the sleep out of his eyes, crawling out of bed.

"Look." Sera pointed between the broken blinds.

A gleaming white sailboat was floating on the end of the island.

"Do you think it's close enough to the island for us to get to it?" Sera whispered.

"I don't know," John said, shaking his head.

He stared out the window for a long moment and then walked to the toilet to relieve himself. He finished up, went into the room, and checked the window. Peering out, he inhaled a deep breath and exhaled slowly. John looked back at Sera and then back outside.

"I can see the boat's sail peeking over the houses." He shifted his weight and then looked back at Sera. "Do you really think we can go there without being caught?"

"I think we should try. It's probably our only chance."

Nodding, John walked over to Brandon and shook him slightly. "Come on, buddy. Time to get up."

"I'm hungry, Sera."

Sera looked back at him and nodded. "I know, buddy. Me, too. I have some bananas in my bag. Will you grab them for all of us?"

Nodding, Brandon jumped out of bed.

John opened the bedroom door, looking out first. He held his hand up for Sera and Brandon to wait as he walked down the hallway. John disappeared out the door and returned after a few minutes.

Brandon handed John a banana, and they all ate what little food they had in silence.

"Okay, we should get going," John whispered as he shoved the last bit of banana into his mouth.

Sera followed John down the hall and stepped into the family room. Her shoes crunched down on something littering the floor. Glass and several bricks covered the area. John touched Sera's hand and nodded. She followed him into the kitchen and opened all of the cupboards. *Bare.* The kitchen had been picked clean, and the refrigerator door was propped open with a layer of green film covering the base.

"There's nothing here. We should get—"

A loud horn rang outside as if it were right out front of the house. Sera dropped down, pulling Brandon and Furry with her. John met her gaze and crawled to the family room to look out the window.

He crawled back, shaking his head. "I don't see anything."

"It sounded like the ship," Sera replied.

John nodded, and Sera crawled past him towards the bedroom they slept in. She grabbed her bag and started for the door when a round of gunshots fired outside. Sera stopped, gazing up at John. John ran back over to the window, peering out.

"It's men. They're running in rows down the road." He breathed deeply and said, "There are at least thirty of them. Come on, let's go back to the truck," John whispered.

"They're coming, Sera," Brandon whispered, pulling his hand from Sera's grip. He pointed through the garage door and out the front door. Sera turned and saw men marching down the street, stopping to look toward their house. One man held his hand up and pointed in their direction.

"Shit!" Sera pulled Brandon into the garage, locking the door behind them.

"They're coming, John!" Sera ran over, picked up Brandon, and put him inside the truck floor with Furry. She pulled out a blanket and covered their bodies with it.

"Stay here. No matter what happens, don't let anyone know that you're here. Okay?"

"Okay," Brandon squeaked. Sera leaned over and kissed the blanket where his head was.

She looked up to see the garage window was completely

open—there were no blinds or curtains to block out the sunlight or peering eyes.

"John, I—"

A loud bang ruptured in the family room, and footsteps thumped through the house. Sera gazed up at John and shook her head. Then, the garage door handle twitched from inside the house.

"This door's locked!" A man's voice yelled from inside the house.

"Well, kick it in!"

Sera's heart pounded in her chest. She knew it wasn't long before someone was going to break in. They were surrounded, and she didn't know what to do. She gazed into John's eyes, shaking her head.

The back door bounced against the house's frame, threatening to cave in at any minute. Sera's eyes glided over to the door, waiting for them to break through.

"This damn door must be made of—"

A shrill scream echoed outside the house, drifting through the garage walls like an evil haunting. Sera met John's glossed-over eyes and spoke just above a whisper. "It's them. They're here." They had followed them to the island and were now standing outside the house, trapping them in.

"Ahh! Watch out!" A man's voice squealed outside the door.

A round of semi-automatic gunshots fired right outside the garage door. Bullets pummeled through the walls, leaving tiny peepholes. John and Sera dropped down to their stomachs and covered their heads.

Sludge beings howled outside the garage door, and a loud crash rattled the house's wall.

Screaming echoed right outside of the garage and stopped abruptly. The gunshots followed suit, and silence filled the house.

Sera lifted her head, meeting John's eyes. His Adam's apple bobbed up and down as he gulped, staring at her with a haunted gaze. Nodding, he whispered, "Go get into the truck."

She crawled over and started to climb in when she looked up to see a being peering inside the window. Freezing, she slowly dropped down and raised her finger to her lips. John crawled over to her and lay on his stomach.

The being's shadow cast across the wall behind her, moving back and forth. She waited for the shadow to disappear before she looked up to see if it was gone.

Nodding, she looked over at John. He nodded and slowly rose to his feet. He walked over to the window, peeking out. He looked right and then left before turning back to Sera. Nodding, he motioned for her to get into the truck.

John slipped into the driver's seat and quietly closed the door. "They're exiting the forest, walking towards the main road, and surrounding the men. A cloud of black smoke is covering the sky from an explosion or something."

He looked towards the window and then back at Sera with a furrowed brow. "We're being surrounded. We may not . . ." He stopped mid-sentence.

Sera knew what he was about to say but shook her head. "We have to try, John." Nodding, she looked out the window and then back at him. "We'll make it. We just have to get to that boat."

John turned over the engine and threw it in reverse. He exhaled deeply and punched the gas, bursting through the doors. Pieces of wood and metal flew, landing on the truck's hood.

Gunshots and screaming echoed as they sat briefly in the alley at the back of the house. John looked over, meeting Sera's gaze. His face softened, and he gripped the steering wheel. He slammed the ignition down into drive and nodded.

Sera reached her hand out, bracing herself on the seat of the truck. She mouthed the word *Go.*

Sera knew that it was a death sentence, and once they pulled around to the front of the house, they would be right in the middle of the chaos.

John punched the gas, flew around the alley, and drove up onto the main road. The truck bounced up and down over a curb and went right out into the middle of the war. Bullets were being fired from soldiers on one side of the alley near the street, and sludge beings were standing over dead men on the other.

John gripped the steering wheel, plowing over beings and dodging soldiers.

"Hold on!" John yelled. He cut the wheel, doing a complete circle, trying to dodge groups of men fighting against beings. Sera braced herself, gripping the handle hanging from the truck's frame.

"Which way! I don't know where to go!" John yelled.

"That way! Go that way!" Sera pointed towards the sailboat.

"Fuck!" John slowed to turn the truck around, and a being looked over at him. It turned and sprinted towards them.

"No! John! Go. Go. Go!"

John looked over at her, and a loud crash slammed against the driver's door. The being collided with John's side, breaking through the window.

Sera's voice was hushed. She swallowed hard and tried to mouth the words, but all she could do was watch. A ringing hummed in her ears, and she felt like her head was swimming against a strong tide. *John. John.* She mouthed his name, but nothing came out. Peering over at him, she watched him fight against the being. It was reaching into the truck and trying to pull him out.

Something clicked inside her, and she opened her mouth.

"No!"

Sera lunged across the truck and pulled John's arm. John punched the gas and tried to throw the being off, but it wasn't budging. The wheels screeched, and it hit a curb, bouncing into the grass. Wood shavings flew into the air, and a mailbox slapped against the windshield, reading *The Johnsons*. John slammed on the brakes and turned to the being.

A loud gunshot exploded. Sera looked to see smoke bellowing out of a double-barrel shotgun. The man holding it dropped the nose of the gun down and nodded. Panting, John relaxed into Sera and nodded back.

The being was slinking up and down next to John's door, trying to regain its posture. Its face had a hole blown in its side, with black oozing from its injury.

"Go, John. Go!"

John backed up and turned back onto the road. He gunned it and drove past the rest of the people at war.

Brandon peeked out from under the blanket. "Are ya'll okay?"

"Yes, get back under the blanket, buddy."

Further down the road, men convulsed on the ground as black sludge took over their bodies. John looked over at Sera and pressed harder on the fuel. The truck roared as it sped past the watching beings.

"I think we're almost there," Sera whispered.

John slowed down and drove up to a gate. He threw the truck in park and left the engine running. Looking around, Sera walked out and peered through the fence to see if she could spot the sailboat.

"I don't know if it's in there," she said.

"It doesn't matter. We came this far. We can try to find a different boat if we have to."

"Okay." She nodded, grabbed her bag, shoved the blanket in, and helped Brandon out.

John walked up to the gate and stared inside. "The gate goes all the way around." He looked up at the top of the twelve-foot fence and then at Sera. "We're going to have to jump it."

Nodding, Sera threw her bag over first, and then she helped Brandon to the top.

"Can you help me get Furry over, John," Sera asked.

The beings' screams echoed from behind them. John gazed into Sera's eyes. *We're so close to escaping. Just a little further now, and we can be free. Finally free. Free.* The words lingered in her head. She'd been a prisoner to the sludge for so long that it felt like freedom was an impossible thing to have. *Freedom.*

Sera wanted it. She looked at Brandon, waiting on the other side, and felt her heart sink. If she couldn't be free, she at least wanted it for him. She wanted him not to be afraid anymore — to have a normal life.

Nodding, she looked back toward the screams of horror lingering nearby. "Come on. We can make it."

John picked up Furry, draping her across his shoulder, and began climbing the fence. Once he reached the top, he balanced himself and helped Furry jump down. Sera followed and turned around to crawl down the other side when she saw them. Sludge beings were running toward them. Hundreds of them. Breath caught in her throat as she blankly stared down at them in a daze.

Shaking her head, she crawled down and dropped to the ground. "Go! Run! Run! Run!"

John looked back at her and picked up his speed. He reached down, grabbed Brandon's arm, and pulled him. Sera grabbed her backpack and followed behind until they came to the first boat.

"It's sailed away, Sera! We'll have to swim over to get in," Brandon said.

Sera's eyes scanned along the dock for anything she could

use to swim out on. A little shed was sitting at the end of the pier. She ran over to it and tried to open it, but it was locked. She reached into her bag and pulled out her thermos, slamming it against the lock. The lock finally dropped to the ground, and she flung the door open and saw keys hanging inside the door. She grabbed them and put them in her pocket. A rope, two fishing poles, a tackle box, a net, and a box with yellow lettering that read *raft*.

"Yes! John, a raft!"

Sera grabbed it, ripped the box open, and pulled the little cord on the side. The box inflated into a full-size raft that held four people.

"Yes!" Sera dropped the raft into the water and walked Brandon over first and then Furry. She threw her bag in and draped the rope connecting the raft to the dock so it wouldn't float away.

The screams of the beings were getting closer and closer. Sera could see their movement out of the corner of her eye, but she didn't want to look. She ran over to the shed, grabbed all the supplies, and threw them into the raft.

"We can load everything in the raft and float over," Sera said.

"Sera, they're coming!" Brandon screamed.

Sera tripped as she dragged the last of the supplies to the raft, and the boat sunk into the water as she dropped it all in.

"John, get in."

John sat down on the raft and turned, holding his hands out. The boat sunk into the water, almost pushing it under. Sera unwrapped the rope, keeping the raft from floating away, and threw it into the boat. She reached in and grabbed the weight, tied a rope around it, and handed it to John.

"Use this to throw into the boat so you can climb in."

"Wait, what! I'm not leaving you here, Sera! No way!" John yelled.

Sera dropped to her knees, pushing the raft away from the dock.

The sludge beings were coming up behind her. She could hear their feet jogging down the dock. She grabbed her thermos, filling it with water.

"I'll catch up! I can swim. There isn't enough room, and the boat will sink if I try to get in now."

"No! Damn it, Sera!"

Sera screamed, "Paddle!"

Sera mouthed the words *I love you* to John. She knew that this was it. She had to give them a chance to get away, a chance for freedom.

John shook his head, screaming her name.

Sera slowly turned around, and the beings were already on top of her — hundreds of them — surrounding her. She raised her thermos to pour water on them. Their screams echoed through her mind, screeching down her spine. She shook the thermos, and streams of water soaked one or two of them, dropping them to the floor. Steam rose from their convulsing bodies as black oozed from their bubbling skin.

Sera stepped backward as other beings pushed past the beings on the ground and began attacking her. She turned to run and jump into the water, but it was too late. One of them grabbed her arm with its mouth open and released its evil squeal. Sludge oozed from its orifices and slithered down its arm to her.

Sera's arm felt like lava was crawling up her limb and absorbing into her body. She opened her mouth to scream, but her throat locked up and closed off the air going into her body.

"Sera! Sera!" Sera could hear John's voice drifting through the wind. She looked around her, only able to move her eyes, and felt the sludge absorb into her veins and take over her body. She was paralyzed. Her body was being invaded, and she was — *dying*.

"Jump, Sera! Jump!"

Sera twitched and looked into the blazing red eyes standing across from her.

John's voice echoed from a distance. "Jump into the water!"

Sera looked around and saw the water right next to her. All she had to do was step over. *Just take a step, Sera. Take a step.* She looked back into the sludge being's eyes, opened her mouth, and said, "No." The words burned her throat as they screamed over her frozen lips.

She closed her eyes, squeezing them shut. She tried to move her leg over, but nothing happened.

Gritting her teeth, she screamed.

Her eyes flew open, and she stepped over, collapsing into the water. The cool water absorbed into her burning body, soothing the pain that was taking over. She couldn't move her limbs. She just dropped into the water, sinking into the darkness.

Bubbles expelled from her nose and mouth, fluttering up towards the top of the water. The burning in her body began to subside, and she started to feel like she was regaining control over her body again. Blinking, she felt the sludge extracting itself from her limbs and fizzling into the water in front of her. She cocked her head to the side to see the sludge boil as if it was being cooked in the water. Then a loud explosion thundered, and Sera's body was thrown with a giant wave. She slammed against something metal underwater and drifted deeper into the sea.

Sera opened her eyes again, and it was dark. She was several feet deep into the abyss. Looking up, she could see the daylight reflecting off the surface. A sense of urgency hit Sera. She knew she needed to swim. She needed air. Her arms pumped upwards first, and then her legs followed suit. Her chest thrust out, begging for a breath of air. The sunlight glistened closer and closer to her face before she burst through the surface, gasping for air. Coughing, she spewed a gallon of salt water in front of her.

Once Sera caught her breath, she searched for John and Brandon.

"John!" Her voice cracked as she tried to mouth his name. The back of her throat was on fire, and she felt the pain rush down her chest. Licking her lips, she tried to yell again.

"John!"

She started swimming and looked back and forth, searching for them.

Boats swished in the water like sitting ducks up against the dock.

"John!" she screamed again.

Silence. She climbed up some stairs attached to one of the docks. She pulled herself up and looked for them.

A dog barking sounded. Three barks and then silence. Sera started walking quickly towards the barking. Her body felt like it had been hit by a truck as she tried to move faster. Her arms and legs burned, and she felt sharp pains in her chest. She slowly snuck to the walkway, clutching the railing as she looked around.

A dog barking echoed again, and this time, it sounded closer.

Sera walked along the walkway towards the barking when she saw their boat. It was slowly sailing out to sea. She saw the beings standing on the dock, watching them sail away.

Sera ran down to the end of the pier and waved. "John! John!"

John turned around and looked back. Sera waved her arms up in the air.

Furry's feet propped up onto the side of the boat and sounded off. The beings turned their gazes toward her and started running. Sera went up the walkway and stopped because she knew she couldn't outrun them, so she turned and jumped back into the water. She pumped her arms and legs until she finally reached the raft floating next to the boat. She climbed up into the raft, falling over.

"Sera! Sera, are you okay? We thought . . . we saw . . . Sera?"

Sera rolled over onto her knees, pulling herself up, and looked up at John. John left and returned with a rope, lowering it down for Sera to pull herself up.

She tied the rope around her waist and let John pull her into the boat. She climbed over the side and dropped into the deck. Brandon laid over her chest, hugging her neck. Furry licked her face and ran back and forth, all frisky.

Sera rolled over onto her knees and stood up slowly. She was standing right in front of the cabin window, staring at her reflection. She gazed at herself and saw her eyes flicker red. Jumping back, she looked down at her body and checked for any marks.

She looked over at John and then back behind her. The beings were standing on the boat dock, watching them float away.

John walked over to Sera and put his arm around her. "Are you okay?"

Sera nodded. "Yes."

Chapter Forty-Seven: The Crash

Sera

The boat rocked back and forth, slamming Sera into the wall behind her. They sat around the table, staring at each other, as a growl rumbled over the ocean. A flash of lightning trickled shadows down the sailboat's walls, revealing the fear that struck everyone's faces.

Brandon hugged Furry, and a small squeak slipped from him as another rumble sounded outside.

"Let's go lie down," Sera said.

"Do you really think it's safe?"

Nodding, Sera stood up and walked down the little hallway to the bed. "Come on, we should all sleep together tonight."

Brandon crawled in first, and Sera and John followed with Furry at their feet.

The next morning, sunlight beamed through the little window in the hallway. Sera sat up in bed and yawned, stretching her arms up in the air. Brandon, John, and Furry had already arisen and left her in bed. She stood up, walked down the hall, and climbed the stairs to the ship's deck.

As soon as she was up top, she saw green palm trees swaying in the wind. John was standing near the front of the boat with Brandon and Furry.

"Hey, we wrecked."

John nodded, but his eyes were glazed with a ghostly stare.

She knew he feared history would repeat itself and that they would be stranded on another island with crazy people or more beings.

"I don't see anyone yet."

John nodded and looked back at the golden beach their boat hovered over.

Brandon started climbing over the sailboat and dropped into the water.

"Brandon, no. Wait!"

John reached down, but Brandon had already escaped. Furry looked back, whining, and jumped out of the boat, running towards her boy.

Sera ran up to John and jumped out of the boat, too. John followed, and as soon as their feet touched the beach, people started gathering near the trees.

"Sera, look!"

A group of people stood under the swaying palms, staring. Sera.

Sera's breath caught in her throat. She stopped in mid-run and looked up to see him.

Sammy.

The End.

ABOUT THE AUTHOR

I believe that every story we write contains a piece of our soul, living on through the characters we create. We should always write with integrity and be proud, regardless of the ending. Let our minds flow so our hearts will be grateful.
—Jennifer D Torseth

www.ingramcontent.com/pod-product-compliance
Lightning Source LLC
Chambersburg PA
CBHW062037170626
46813CB00001B/356